Simon's Sanctuary

Ernie Macatuno

To those who crossed the seas, plains and mountains
for the good life in America.

About the Author

Ernie Macatuno is a journalist who shifted to music and literature with works like *The Son of God—Jesus Christ in the eyes of his disciples,* an account on the life and teaching of Jesus Christ, based on the Gospels of Matthew, Mark, Luke and John, and the novels *Ardor Left, Leandro's Odyssey, Simon's Sanctuary* and *Gabriel's Legacy.* A self-taught pianist and composer, he has written and composed *Fisherman's Wharf,* a musical about San Francisco's popular tourist spot.

He is known in Filipino journalism circles for his sparkling and incisive style of writing. He was an associate editor of *Sunday Times Magazine* and political writer of *The Philippines Free Press.* He taught journalism in University of Santo Tomas, his alma mater, and literature in De LaSalle University. He was editor of a number of community publications in California, where his editorials and feature articles were read avidly for their depth and range.

Txu 978-787 U.S. Copyright Office, Library of Congress
ISBN: 1974552276
$10.50 per copy
This book is available in Amazon and Amazon Kindle.

Chapter One

Simon Matin looked around the moment he left his car with his friend Phil. Vermont Avenue and its handsome brownstone buildings were washed by the sunlight of a lovely Sunday afternoon in Los Angeles. He was charmed. He walked on toward the sidewalk with Phil, who was railing at the King trial, just as he did back in his car.

They were going to Shannon's Bookshop. Its silvery sign splashed with sunlight hurt his eyes, and he lowered his gaze to the sidewalk. The headline in the newspaper vending machine there reported about the "Violence Feared In King Trial."

"The press," he said, "is sowing fear and panic over the trial."

"Does that surprise you?"

"Not really."

He was following the progress of the trial. Concern was general in Los Angeles over its black residents' likely violent reaction to an acquittal of four white police officers accused of beating up a black motorist named Rodney King.

"A year of it without letup," Phil said, frowning. "I'm sick and tired of it! Look at what it is doing to L.A. Crime is on the rise because the cops are so distracted from their work by the trial. I just want it ended so they can do their job."

"It may not end the way you want it to end if the police officers are acquitted."

"Have you got anything against that?"

"No. I've got nothing against anyone, not the cops, not the blacks, not the whites, not anyone."

"It is their problem, not ours."

"It is, indeed, but like everyone else in the city, we'll most likely be affected by its outcome. I can only hope it turns out well."

He smiled, amused, as they resumed walking, at Phil's long shadow advancing on the pavement. Phil looked tall there. While he was neither tall nor short at five feet and seven inches, Phil was short. He stood only up to his chin. This was Phil, an old man with gray hair dyed black and a goat-like beard, walking beside him, a short stage player from Project 4 in Manila.

They were passing by the sidewalk café adjacent to the bookshop when the smell of brewed coffee wafted invitingly toward them. He glanced at the cafe patrons seated at the small round tables there. They were conversing quietly, drinking coffee. Some were reading books and magazines.

From a table near him, he could hear two young men, apparently philosophy and history students, arguing on who between the French writers Camus and Sartre had exerted a greater influence on contemporary European thought. French existentialism was alive and well, there at the sidewalk cafe, the closest thing Los Feliz District had to a literary salon.

They walked on toward the glass display window of Shannon's Bookshop and feasted their eyes on the books displayed there.

"We have some new arrivals here," Phil said.

"Some new arrivals," Simon said, frowning at a book with the title of *The Mystery of the Aztec Death Rituals*.

He looked away, his attention drawn to another book with its mind-blowing title of *Black Holes: Windows to Another Universe*. He looked on, wide-eyed, at the book's artwork of moons and planets being sucked into the bowels of an imploded star. Its blurb claimed that its gravitational pull was so strong, nothing, not even light, could escape from it, and that beyond the dead star was another universe.

He shook his head in disbelief at what the book claimed. There was, as far as he was concerned, only one universe. It was above him where he stood, there on the sidewalk in Vermont Avenue in Los Angeles. Its source and spiritual essence lay in God in heaven, where he and his loved ones hoped to be taken at the end of their days on earth. The book was a lot more speculative than the Big Bang Theory of an expanding universe, an assertion which he viewed also with skepticism.

"We have here," he said to Phil, "another example of finite, but vain human minds trying to define and measure the limits, the beginning and the end of infinity."

"What are you talking about?"

"This book in front of me. Take a look at what it says about a parallel universe."

Phil peered at the book and said, "If that is what their telescopes showed them, then, that is what it must be out there—another universe."

Suddenly his eyes turned wide from shock, and he said, "Another universe? I've never heard of anything as wild and fantastic as that!"

"It is, indeed, a wild fantastic notion."

"Those scientists' brains must have been muddled from watching, night after night, the stars and the planets in the dark universe."

He saw Phil's interest lay in other subjects when he said about a book in front of him, "Now, here is one book I would love to read in bed."

His curiosity piqued, he glanced, frowning once again at the book's title of *Sex Between Doctors and Their Patients*. Its arresting cover showed a young beautiful female doctor examining a seated male patient, the stethoscope in her hand pressed to the man's hairy chest.

"What's the matter with William Keith?" he said about the bookshop owner. "Black holes, the ancient Aztec death rituals, and now this! Has he run out of plain wholesome books to display here?"

"It's variety time in Shannon's Bookshop, led by doctors having sex with their patients."

"There you go again. If it is not the trial, it is sex that you are always talking about."

His eyes kept to the book, Phil ignored him and said, "Look at that bumper. It's top of the line, a limousine with teats in the middle!"

His only friend in Los Angeles besides Jonathan, Phil was fun, but what he said was not funny at all. It was gross, its metaphor mixed.

He looked away, displeased with Phil, and caught instead a reflection of his face in the bookshop's glass display window. He had a plain face, his lips thick, his nose short and his dark wavy hair with flecks of gray parted slightly to the left in the old-fashioned way he combed his hair. There was nothing remarkable about his looks, but he had keen eyes now staring owlishly at the interior of the bookshop.

A bespectacled middle-aged man, no doubt a college professor, his bald head shiny in reflection of the light above him, was bent over an open book in his hands. A young man walked by in the aisle. He was in a sweatshirt with the letters USC printed at the shirt front. The young man paused before a bookshelf and scanned it with his finger pointed to a row of books.

He watched them, feeling a certain affinity with the professor and the student. Sunday afternoon for Shannon's clientele, made up mostly of professionals, teachers and students, was a time for browsing its bookshelves for a dose of the written word.

Like him, they were there to explore its bookshelves, or to look for a particular book. They may also have their own libraries at home. Reading in his apartment in Avery Avenue was a pleasurable and addictive exercise of the mind, although his small bookshelf there held no surprises for him. He had read every volume there while seated snug on his easy chair. It gave him this good feeling of being at home, just as the bed he shared with his wife Clara gave him this warm feeling of intimacy with her.

Walt Whitman's *Leaves of Grass* caught his eye, reminding him that he was there to buy a copy of Pablo Neruda's book of poems. He liked the Chilean poet's verses he had read in Phil's copy a few days ago, while they were having a couple of drinks with Jonathan at the Keg Room.

He had decided since then on getting his own copy, not only for Neruda's poetry, but also for the kinship he shared with him. They were both exiles. The poet from Chile, as he had seen in a movie, was banished to Italy for his socialist politics, while he fled his homeland out of fear for his life.

Phil asked him, "Did you find anything here interesting?"

He shook his head.

"Very well, let's go in."

They turned toward the bookshop's glass door and went in to the tinkling of the doorbell. They exchanged greetings with William Keith, who was as usual at his checkout near the door. They walked toward an aisle, accompanied by the *Summer* in Vivaldi's *The Four Seasons* piped in from the ceiling.

Shannon's Bookshop was a writer's bookshop, a cultured person's own kind of place. The smell in the bookshop of old and newly printed books and magazines added to the pleasure Simon felt in simply being there. The bookshop had an air about it of keen intellectual pursuit. He was in a place where what he put inside his head counted far more than the money he parted with when buying a book there. Indeed his own kind of place.

"Let us look for the Neruda book," Phil said.

They walked on toward an intersection of aisles and turned toward a bookshelf set against a wall in the bookshop's farthest aisle. He watched Phil as he inspected a row of books in front of them.

"We are in luck," he said. "There is one copy left."

He pulled out the slim volume, gazed briefly at its cover, and gave it to him. The book cover was smooth to his touch. He turned its pages and stopped at the page on the *Southern Sea,* and read:

> *It's a lonely place;*
> *I've spoken before*
> *of this place that's so very lonely,*
> *where the earth is full of ocean.*

"A rhythmic cry of solitude in this month of April," Phil said grandly.

He nodded. What Phil said came together with an image he had then formed in his mind's eye of Neruda, perched on a rock, as he gazed at the seashore lapped by the waves of the blue Pacific Ocean.

"Neruda, like T.S. Eliot, has a smooth style of writing. Enjoy the poet while I look around," Phil said as he walked away.

He read the book, but blinked his eyes after a while from the dim light in the aisle. The tall bookshelves along the aisle obstructed much of the light in the ceiling. He skimmed the pages of the book.

A man walking by in the aisle distracted him further, and he closed the book. He will read it later on, snug on his easy chair in his apartment.

A stool stood in the aisle, and he sat down there, grateful for this amenity in the bookshop. His feet were beginning to hurt from all the walking he had done with Phil, earlier in Santa Monica.

He watched Phil, who was reading a book farther down the aisle. He looked lonely in this solitary activity. They shared this feeling from the life they led of self-imposed exile in America. Phil's gray hair, dyed black, was shiny from the light in the ceiling. It told of his futile attempt to deny the many years that had passed since he left Manila. Phil was a stage player in love with literature.

They first met in his college symposium in Laguna where Phil was a guest. They became friends and had often met since then in bookstores, in college symposiums, in Phil's stage performances and in the bars in Ermita, which Phil frequented. Then, just like that, Phil disappeared.

He was pleasantly surprised to see him again, years later, in MacArthur Park in Los Angeles, at the celebration there of a Philippine-style town fiesta. Phil told him then why he left the country. He was a marked man for ad-libbing in his stage performances against the dictatorship Ferdinand Marcos had then imposed in the Philippines.

So, as fate would have it, here they were thrown once again into each other's company. Their haunts in Shannon's Bookshop, in Los Angeles' Central Library and in the Keg Room, and the long walks they took gave him a welcome break from his menial job of busboy, dishwasher and janitor in L&S Restaurant.

Phil himself was hardly better off. To survive in America, he held a string of dull jobs, the latest of which was in assembling cassette tapes. He made several attempts at acting jobs in Hollywood, where the farthest he got were two walk-in parts. The odds were against him. Oriental roles in Hollywood, which fit him, came few and far between, and these were mostly of the martial arts type in which Phil, who was old and short, was ill-suited.

He could get a lot of acting jobs in the Philippines, and he could go back there, now that the dictator Marcos had been toppled from power. But, despite the unsatisfactory kind of life he led here in America, it was unlikely of him to leave the country. He could not bear the stigma of going back to the Philippines having failed to make it in America. He had staked a future for his family, no longer in the Philippines, but here in America. To secure his future, what he needed was a lifetime career job, like Jonathan's position of administrative officer of Asia Pacific University.

He sighed. Someday, with a better job, he hoped to live with his family in a place as nice as the house in Atwater Village where Jonathan, a bachelor, lived alone. Phil introduced them to each other at the Keg Room.

Like him, Phil was an apartment dweller. He was reminded of Manila's working-class district of Tondo every time he visited Phil in his apartment in Sunshine Park. Many of the apartments there were at all hours of the day filled with loud music and smelling faintly of fried fish and garlic. An immigrant community, a babel of tongues was spoken there—Spanish, Tagalog, Mandarin, Vietnamese, Thai, Hindi, and English now and then.

Jonathan had told Phil to move out of there. It was unlikely, though, for Phil to do that. He was too old and set in his ways to make a big move like changing his residence.

He watched Phil as he proceeded toward the magazine section. He picked up a magazine from the magazine rack there and, after flipping through its pages, he began to read. This was Phil without the theater mask: a comedian whose heart was aching for some members of his family separated from him by the Pacific Ocean. After several attempts that spanned nearly twenty years, Phil had finally succeeded in bringing over to the United States, six of his ten children.

Phil called it "the first wave" of his family's "invasion" of America. Job and marriage had scattered them, though, throughout the country. A married daughter was in Florida. A son was in New York. Another daughter was in Hawaii. A married son was in Texas, unable to sponsor his own family for immigration, for he had passed himself off as an unmarried person for its shorter wait for an immigrant visa. Phil's two youngest boys were living with him.

His wife and their four older children were left behind in the Philippines. He divorced his wife and could not sponsor her for immigration. As a single person under his brother's sponsorship, he got his immigrant visa soon enough for him to sponsor for immigration, his six younger children. Phil's four older children faced a longer wait for their immigrant visas, while his wife was waiting for one of their daughters' sponsorship to become current, so she could also come to America.

He sighed in sympathy with Phil for those moves he made to bring his entire family to America. It was a sad tale common among Filipino immigrants. He was sorry for Phil and others like him, but at the same time could not help but take great satisfaction at his luck and ability to bring his entire family with him to America.

The Neruda book in his hand, he joined Phil at the magazine rack and looked over Phil's shoulder, at a travel advertisement in the magazine he was reading.

"Paris, city of light and romance," Phil said. "I love it almost as much as I love Ireland. How I wish I could visit it someday."

"Everyone loves Paris, but why the Emerald Isle?"

"For the way James Joyce so beautifully described Ireland, Dublin especially, in his writings."

He nodded. He won't disagree with Phil's admiring view of James Joyce's writings about Ireland. He himself was an admirer of the great Irish writer, but then, Phil was confusing reality with literary creation.

"You will be disappointed," he said to Phil, "if you will visit Dublin purposely to see it as James Joyce described it in 1904 in *Ulysses* and in *The Dead.*"

"Why?" Phil asked as he returned the magazine to the magazine rack.

"Dublin in 1904 no longer exists except in the pages of James Joyce's books. Think about it. That was almost ninety years ago. They no longer have horse-drawn cabs like the one described in *The Dead* as what Gabriel Conroy and his wife Gretta took in going back to their hotel. The house in Usher's Island, where Gabriel's aunts lived, and where they held that memorable annual dance, may no longer exist; so too with the brothel where Leopold Bloom and Stephen Dedalus romped around with the whores there. Even if the brothel and the whores are still there, can you imagine yourself carousing with those harlots more than a century old by now?"

"The mere thought gives me the gooseflesh," Phil said, but then he looked doubtfully at Simon and said, "You are pulling my leg."

"I am not. Are you not after Dublin in 1904? Then, don't leave out the characters of that time as James Joyce described them."

"But you said they no longer exist."

"Exactly. Unless they are blessed with exceedingly long lives, like James Joyce, they will be long dead by now."

"So?"

"The point I'm driving at is this: it is best to leave the Dublin and the Ireland of James Joyce where they belong—in the pages of his books. If you want to visit Dublin and the rest of Ireland, do it for their present sights and in the company of living people, and not with the ghosts, no matter how engaging, of great literary creations."

"Amen to that."

It was almost six o'clock, Simon's wristwatch showed him. It was time for them to leave. It was Sunday and Shannon's Bookshop was closing early. Clara, with their daughter Lorna helping her, must be preparing dinner by now. Sonny, their son, must be doing his homework, or watching TV.

He walked with Phil toward William Keith's checkout and paid for the book.

"Would you like me to put your book in a bag?" William Keith asked him.

"No, thank you. I like the feel of a new book in my hands."

They said good day to William Keith and stepped out of Shannon's Bookshop

The tables outside the café were still occupied by patrons, but inside was a vacant table.

He asked Phil, "How about a cup of coffee?"

"Coffee at this time of the day? It is Happy Hour at the Keg Room! We should have instead a round of beer there."

"Not now. Clara is expecting me home soon."

"I see. So your wife wants you to be home early."

"What are you driving at?" he said, annoyed by what Phil had insinuated. He was not a henpecked husband.

"Nothing," Phil replied. "C'mon, a round of beer in Keg Room won't take us long. Besides, we might find Jonathan there. Were you not planning to talk to him about the teaching job you are eyeing in Asia Pacific?"

"All right, we'll go there, but let me call Clara first."

They walked toward a phone booth. He called Clara, while Phil, as he waited outside the phone booth, hummed softly a German beer hall song.

"Don't wait for me; go ahead with your dinner," he said to Clara. "Phil and I are going to look for Jonathan at the Keg Room."

He paused and listened. Then he said, "Of course, I've not forgotten our appointment with our lawyer tomorrow morning. Don't worry, I won't be home late. "

Chapter Two

His face pressed to the pillow, Saul Levy felt for his wife Agnes' soft warm body. His hand found nothing but the cold bedsheet. He turned on his back and saw the bedroom bright with the morning sun. Across the bedroom, his wife was seated at the dresser. She was brushing before the mirror there, her hair black and shiny from the washing. He sighed. He had only been dreaming about their previous night of lovemaking.

He looked on at her. Her beautiful oval-shaped face showed in the mirror her big brown eyes looking on brightly, her lips parted in a smile. She had nothing on her, but a slip that showed her bare light-brown back and slim arms. The sight of her, fresh from the shower like spring flowers, sent the blood in his arteries rushing up to his head. He was about to leave the bed and walk up to her and hug her, but stopped himself in the same instant. That would be a crude thing to do. He must first see from her a sign of ardor. Just then, he saw her looking at him in the mirror.

"Time you woke up, you sleepyhead. Up you go! The world waits for you to conquer," she said, smiling at the stock expression she said in prodding him out of bed.

She stopped brushing her hair and looked at his reflection in the mirror. A sign of ardor! He savored the sight of her, looking at him. She was waiting for him to come to her. A fresh urgent wave of desire to take her came over him. It was her, not the world, whom she wanted him to conquer!

He swept the bedsheet aside. He was about to move out of the bed and go to her, but then she had resumed brushing her hair. She was now looking instead at her face as reflected in the mirror.

He stayed seated on the bed, sore with himself for having been so slow and tentative.

"Why did you not wake me up?" he said.

"I did, but you were sleeping like a log."

He left the bed. He was going to her. He just could not help it. She watched him in the mirror as he came to her.

He paused when he saw a reflection of himself in the mirror. He looked awful and predatory with his bleary eyes, his disorderly black curly hair, and his chin and upper lip dark with a night's growth of beard and facial hair. But nothing could stop him. He walked on and laid his hands on her shoulder.

"You look so lovely and desirable this morning," he said to her. "We can have another one. Just a quick one."

"Again? After a night of it? You can never have enough of it, can't you?"

"No."

"I would like to, but I have already taken a shower, and I don't want to be late for work."

"It won't take long."

She made no reply.

He took it for her consent, and he caressed her soft lustrous hair, her shoulder and her arms.

She did not yield, as he hoped she would. She brought instead her face close to the mirror and began applying makeup on it.

He gazed at her in the mirror, his lips pursed in disappointment at having been rebuffed by her.

"I thought you might want it, too," he said in a lame effort to save face.

He retreated to the bathroom, switched the light on and shut the door. He swore at himself, his narrowed eyes looking back sullenly at him in the bathroom mirror. She had tactfully avoided telling him to his face that he looked awful. He could never arouse her with him looking like that. He sighed. He was not himself then. He did not even look like that.

He opened the faucet, bent down on the sink and splashed cold water on his face. It had an immediate bracing effect on him. He wiped his face with a towel and brushed his hair with his palm. He looked at himself again in the mirror and was pleased by the remarkable change in his face. His eyes now gazing brightly at him and his hair no longer so disorderly, he looked much better now, the self-reproach he felt then, now gone.

This was the real Saul Levy looking at him in the mirror. His eyes were gray and deep-set, his brow wide and furrowed by an active mind, his nose pointed down sharply to his thin mouth and his jaw, strong and firm to his touch.

Middle age maybe creeping on him, but he still had the looks, the charm, not counting the intelligence, that made him attractive to women, not that he still indulged in that sort of thing. Agnes was the only woman in his life ever since they were married, but he kept out of nursed conceit this opinion of himself as a closet Lothario. At times, like last night and this morning, he felt like he was a twenty-year-old sexual athlete.

He took a quick shower and was back in the bedroom, rubbing himself with a towel, as Agnes, who was already dressed up, was moving toward the bedroom door. She walked back to him, kissed him lightly on the cheek and brushed his hair with her palm.

"Don't take too long in dressing up," she said, "or your breakfast will get cold."

She had walked out of the bedroom before he could kiss her back. He looked on, pleased by her unexpected affectionate gesture, at the same time wondering about her lack of ardor a while ago. He remained mystified in the twelve years they had been married by such changes in her moods.

Suddenly he remembered her warning not to tarry. He went to the closet and dressed up in a gray flannel suit and tie. He joined her in the kitchen and sat down at the worktable where they usually took their breakfast. The smell of food whetted his appetite.

"Have coffee first. Breakfast will be ready in a minute," she said as she gave him a cup of steaming hot coffee on a saucer.

"What are we having for breakfast this morning?"

"Something you like."

He smiled and drank his coffee. It coursed down his throat, hot and pleasant, like the bright sunny morning he could see through the French window overlooking the garden at the back of the house. It promised to be another pleasant working day. He watched, pleased and with keen anticipation, the food she was putting on the table.

At age forty, Saul Levy was getting stout from too much of the rich tasty food that Agnes cooked for him, and his sedentary job as an immigration lawyer. He was reminded about this by the tightness of his pants at his waistline.

He wavered for a moment between concern over his growing potbelly and the inviting food on the table. Besides fried eggs, there was a Filipino dish called *Adobo,* a pork-and-chicken stew marinated in vinegar and soy sauce she cooked the day before, now warmed over in the microwave oven. He yielded to the inviting sight and smell of the food and filled his plate with fried rice, which he topped with a fried egg and several spoonfuls of Adobo.

"This is very good," he said after he had eaten a spoonful of the food. "C'mon, dear, sit down and join me."

"I hope I have put enough soy sauce and vinegar in my Adobo," she said as she sat down at the table and watched him take another bite.

"It is delicious," he said as he looked appreciatively at her for the trouble she took in preparing their breakfast every morning.

He was a lucky man. Some married men he knew had nothing but coffee for breakfast. Their wives either did not know how to cook, or would not take the trouble of preparing breakfast for their husbands.

He continued eating, not even glancing at her when she made the sign of the cross and said grace. Afterwards, a smile on her face, she put food on her plate and began to eat.

"I guess you will be having another busy day today," she said after a while.

"Monday is always a busy day for me."

It was all a part of their ritual at breakfast, where they began their workweek. She liked to pry into his job. While this suggested domestic intrusion, he liked to think of it also as a show of her interest in his job. It pleased him.

They went on eating their breakfast. Only a small piece of the Adobo was left on the plate. She refilled it from the bowl of Adobo and returned the plate to the table.

He asked, as she resumed eating, "By the way, what is today?"

"It's April four. Why do you ask?"

"Your friends Simon and Clara Matin will be coming to the office this morning."

"They are not exactly my friends. I've already told you that. The man called on the phone. He said he learned about us through a mutual friend, and that his wife and I are provincemates. You know how it is with us. We depend on personal references, but I don't know them at all. Anyway, can you help them?"

"I'll know that only after I have talked to them."

He drank his coffee, his thoughts on the Matins, his prospective clients, who learned about him through their community grapevine. They preferred to be represented by an authority on immigration law like him, and one whose wife was also a Filipino.

"Simon Matin sounded desperate when he called," she said.

"Most of them are."

She watched him empty his coffee cup. The coffee maker was right behind her. She stood up and refilled there his coffee cup.

"Thank you," he said as he took it and put there a spoonful of sugar and stirred it.

"I can't blame the Matins for coming to America," she said as she sat down on her chair. "They also want the good life here—a nice home, a car, fun and shopping, as in the coming fair."

"Come now, you don't have to bring it up again."

"I still think it's a mistake for you to get a booth there."

He kept silent. He would rather not discuss the booth. It was a sore point between them. It was his fault, though. He should have told her beforehand that he was taking a booth for his law firm at the Fil-Asian Fair to be held in two weeks' time in Los Angeles.

He was invited as a guest along with Agnes and an awardee at the fair. What the award was for, he was told vaguely was for his outstanding services to the Filipino community. Although he saw it as nothing but a selling tactic, still he felt obliged to return the favor by taking a booth at the fair. It concerned Agnes' people, though, and she resented not having been told beforehand about it. He could see her resentment in her face.

"You'll only be wasting your time and money there," she said. "What is the point in getting a booth there where no one will come? I know them. No one will ever be caught going there and be identified as a TNT."

He did not reply, for she had a point there. No one going to his booth would want to be identified as a TNT, short for *"tago ng tago."* It was a Tagalog euphemism for an illegal immigrant or an overstaying tourist hiding from the immigration authorities.

"We are offering free consultation," he argued back. "A lot of people cannot resist that."

"The Matins are people in need of help. Will they consult with you there?"

"Why not? They are after legal help, not other people's opinion about them."

"They can always see you in your office."

Score another one for her, he thought in appreciation of her repartee, but then he argued back, "As I have said, the booth is for those who want free legal advice."

"I still think you are making a mistake in getting a booth there."

He did not reply. Their argument will lead nowhere. Let any further talk about the booth be buried in silence. He turned his attention back to the food on his plate and ate with undiminished zest. His stomach was full and heavy by the time the grandfather clock in the dining room had chimed the hour, reminding them it was time for them to leave for work.

"That was good," he said as he patted his stomach appreciatively.

He saw how what he said had so pleased her that she smiled and leaned forward, and he in response likewise leaned forward and met her light kiss on his cheek.

"I like it when you enjoy eating what I cook for you," she said.

The booth in the fair had been forgotten.

They cleared the table and, after putting the used plates and other utensils inside the dishwasher and the remaining Adobo inside the refrigerator, they went back to their bedroom. He made one final visit to the bathroom while she made last-minute touch-up work on her face before the dresser mirror. Then she took her turn at the bathroom while he checked the rest of the house, the doors, the lights, the kitchen appliances and picked up his briefcase in his study. They met in the living room and walked toward the main door.

He was about to open it when suddenly he dropped his briefcase on the floor and took her in his arms. He had to get over his disappointment early that morning.

She yielded and was warm and soft in his embrace. He held her tight as on her lips he tasted roses.

They lingered at the door, locked in an embrace, until he felt her gently push him away. He was about to open the door when suddenly she held him on the shoulder and looked at him closely. She was going to kiss him.

She took instead a hankie from her purse and, as she wiped away with her hankie, a mark her lipstick had made on his lips, she said, "Let me remove the evidence of the crime you have just committed. "

"What sort of crime have I committed?"

"The crime is stealing a kiss."

"Your Honor, I plead guilty as charged."

"I will give you a suspended sentence, provided you will promise never to do it again."

"I would rather go to jail than make such a promise."

He was smiling as he then picked up his briefcase, opened the door and, after they had passed out, closed it. They walked on, holding hands, toward the carport, their faces wreathed still with smiles at their happy married life.

They parted as they were approaching her car, a late-model Mercedes Benz, parked beside his car, a gray Jaguar. She was driving and she walked toward the driver's side of her car, while he opened the driveway gate.

He was waiting for her to drive through the gate, but was surprised instead to see her coming to him.

He said, "Did you forget something?"

"My lunch box. I must have left it in the kitchen."

He nodded. Her lunch box was that important to her because she will have nothing of the food served in the cafeteria of the computer company where she did promotional work.

"Here is the car key," she said. "You might want to start the car and warm the engine while I'm getting my lunch box."

She walked back to the house while he stepped inside her car. He put his briefcase on the car floor on the passenger side and turned on the ignition. The engine roared to life and then settled down into a steady hum.

He was waiting for her when he saw the garden hose lying on the grass. She called him from the house while he was watering the lawn the day before and forgot to go back for it. He left the car on idling and picked up the garden hose and coiled it around its iron holder nailed to the wall of the house. In so doing, his hands collected dirt from the garden hose. He turned the faucet on, the nozzle turned away from him, and washed his hands with the water streaming out of it. Then he turned the faucet off.

"That is better," he said to himself as he rubbed his hands dry.

From where he stood, there in the lawn, he had a nice view of their home and, beyond the picket fence, their neighborhood in Pinewood Street. The trees that lined the street were, in springtime in Los Angeles, taking a new leaf, the grass in the lawns there turned a verdant green. A couple of cars were coming out of the carport and the garage of the handsome homes. It confirmed the impression, fixed in his mind, of its pleasant atmosphere. Santa Monica was a fine satellite city of Los Angeles.

Their home, unlike his neighbors with their American style homes, was in the light and airy style of a French Mediterranean home. Agnes' taste in housekeeping was stamped in the living and dining sets of rattan, the antique chest and the old grandfather clock. Her taste in art was French Impressionist: a Monet reproduction in the living room, a Toulouse-Lautrec copy in their bedroom, another Toulouse-Lautrec copy in the dining room. She could also be eclectic. A small version of Rodin's *The Thinker* brooded in his book-lined study. A copy of a Modigliani was the sole painting in the hallway to the kitchen. Here and there, also hanging on the walls, were a number of originals by Filipino masters. There was music too in the stereo system and the Steinway piano that stood in a corner in the living room, near the French window with lace curtains. Homes like it spoke of achievement of the kind of life people seek in America— secure, comfortable, tasteful, its affluence understated.

He felt good, the feeling arising from the wonderful view, a full stomach and the bit of romance he and Agnes had by the door.

Her purse and her lunch box in her hand, she walked briskly toward her car. He closed the gate after she had driven out of the driveway and joined her in her car. It was a short ride to the bus stop at the corner of Wilshire Boulevard and Lincoln Avenue. He gave her a casual peck on the cheek as he was about to leave her car. He told her to drive safely as he shut the car door. From the bus stop, he watched her drive away.

There were times like today when he preferred to take the bus in going to work. He could use the thirty minutes or so it took the bus to get to downtown Los Angeles to go over his workload for the day, or just as good, to be alone in his thoughts. The bus was half-full and quiet. He liked that, his thoughts turned to Agnes.

He saw her for the first time while on a mission in City Hall.

It was love at first sight. She was then working there as a clerk, while he was a young immigration lawyer a few years after finishing law in Xavier Law School. He saw her a few times after that, the woman of his dreams, but did not dare to approach her then. A misstep might ruin everything for him. From discreet inquiries he made about her, he learned quite happily that she fit the woman of his youthful fantasies. From his readings of Conrad, Maugham and Michener, from the movies he had seen and the magazine articles he had read, he had formed the image of his ideal woman as someone from the south seas—sensuous, affectionate and devoted. She was beautiful, although not of pure south seas stock. She was Eurasian, a Filipino with Spanish blood in her veins. Her hair was black; her skin light brown, like a permanent tan. She had the easy charm natural to her people, as attested to by a smile often on her face.

They came to know each other only after he had persuaded a mutual friend to introduce them to each other. He found her mildly curious about him, and that was all he needed to get going on her. He made up every conceivable excuse to call her on the phone, give her gifts and write her notes, funny and suggestive. He took her to shows and concerts. They often ate out, and when she had become truly fond of him, she cooked for him in her apartment in North Hollywood, or in his house in Santa Monica. They did not have sex until they were married. She would not have it until then. Like the conservative women of her race and religion, she did not take sex casually. She considered it a procreative act done only within the bounds of marriage. For that, he loved and respected her even more.

He was Jewish, while she was a Catholic, but religion never came between them. She attended Mass every Sunday while he went to a synagogue on the Sabbath. He was not as devoted, though, as she was in the practice of religion. It arose, not from lack of exposure to his faith, but rather oddly from his own view of it. He often wondered if his people had been waiting for thousands of years now for the Messiah, who may have long come and gone. Jesus may have been the Messiah. They may have failed to recognize and accept him as the Messiah because of their preconceived notion of their Savior as someone who will free Israel from bondage and make it a great earthly power. In other words, a political or military leader like his namesake King Saul. The Israel they had in mind did not jibe with what Jesus proclaimed of his kingdom as not in this world, but in heaven, and that his mission was not to conquer the world, but to save the world from sin.

The thought that Agnes will be pleasantly surprised were she to learn that her Jewish husband had been entertaining such thoughts, made him smile. She was a devout Catholic and she will pursue the matter and work on his conversion to her Christian faith. But he will not go that far.

He had read somewhere that the end of the world will come once the Jews had started believing in Jesus as the Messiah. Assuming this to be true, he will not be among those who will hasten the end of the world by subscribing to this Christian belief. He was satisfied with the way things were between him and Agnes, where neither of them had crossed over to the other's faith. They were married one year after they first met and, as in a storybook romance, lived happily ever after. They remained childless in their twelve years of marriage, but they could not have everything. They had each other, and that was enough.

As the bus moved on, he saw three male Latinos, who looked like farm workers who had just recently crossed the southern border of the United States, peering at a store's display window in Beverly Hills. It struck him as odd that they were window-shopping there. They were not the type who would do that there. He looked on as the bus passed them. They were all over California. He had provided legal representation for some of them. At that, he remembered his briefcase lying on his lap. He set it upright and, after flipping its lock open, he thumbed through the folders inside and pulled out the folder on Juan Sindromas. He began reading the report written by his young associate, Steve Claremont. In the introduction, Steve wrote that Sindromas claimed to be an agriculturist employed by a vineyard in Fresno, seeking a green card.

He was engrossed in reading Steve's report he hardly noticed the man seated beside him had stood up and left. A teenage girl took the seating space he left. The smell of cheap perfume rose about her as she sat down beside him, assailing his nose. To avoid reacting in a way that might offend her, he held his breath, releasing it until he was used to the strong fragrance. He glanced at her from the corner of his eye, relieved to see her looking ahead. He turned his attention back to Steve's report. After a while, the girl glanced curiously at the folder in his hands and asked, "What are you reading?"

The question, asked in such an abrupt manner by a complete stranger, took him by surprise, but he replied, "I am reading a legal report."

"Are you a lawyer?"

"Yes, I am a lawyer," he replied, his interest waning when he noticed her chewing gum.

That and her heady perfume told him their grade of culture differed.

"What kind of a lawyer are you?" the girl asked.

"I am an immigration lawyer," he replied in a dry tone of voice.

The girl looked ahead and said nothing more.

A legal report may not be as interesting to read as a romantic novel the kind of book, he presumed, the girl read. While she was young and pretty, he found her abrupt manners, the gum she was now chewing like a goat, and her heady perfume too much for him. They had nothing in common. He gave a sign that he wanted to be left alone by giving Steve's report the full attention it did not deserve.

The bus pulled to a stop on Fairfax Avenue. The girl got off from the bus without saying a parting word to him. He watched her from the corner of his eye as she stood at the street corner. She was looking around as if she was not sure where she was going. The bus moved on. He sat back, having gained nothing from the fleeting connection he had made with her. It began with a trite question from her that led nowhere. That was all there was to it. He stopped thinking about her the moment she disappeared from his sight, his thoughts by then having turned elsewhere.

While he was devoted to Agnes, that did not make him turn a blind eye to beautiful women. Taking the bus not only was a time for remembering and thinking things over, but also for admiring beautiful women. He returned the folder to his briefcase and snapped it shut. He put on his smoke glass so he could look around unnoticed by the other passengers.

A pretty blonde woman at the other side of the aisle looked like Diane. They had a great time together. He was then in his first year in law school. He had not seen her since they broke up. A week earlier, also in a bus, he thought he saw Marlene. They went steady on his graduation year in Xavier. Then she went to Sorbonne on a scholarship. She met there a Frenchman and promptly forgot him.

He crossed his arms as he thought again of Diane. He could have married her, but did not. The differences between them were far greater than the foremost thing they had in common. It was sex. He could not build a happy and successful marriage on that alone, no matter how much they enjoyed doing it. Eventually Diane felt him turn cold and distant. She was heartbroken when they went their separate ways. Parting with Marlene was nearly as painful. He pressed his lips at those depressing thoughts and listened as a paramedic truck, its siren blaring, came from behind the bus. The bus driver pulled over and let the paramedic truck pass.

His thoughts had turned elsewhere. There was Ruth. She came to his life after he had passed the bar. She was also Jewish. Her family fled to Holland only days before Hitler assumed full control over Germany. They were among those who had the foresight, or were just lucky, to escape from the clutches of the Nazis. He and Ruth had talked about the past, finding comfort in sharing their thoughts and experiences. He could have married her and was really fond of her. They had so much in common, but in the end, they parted ironically because Ruth was also Jewish. By then, he realized he could not share his life with someone from his own race and religion. To do so was to face a dreary future chained to a dreadful past. He wanted in a woman, an escape from that past, which haunted him, and he found it only in Agnes.

Thinking about the terrible things the Nazis did to his family and his people would so upset him it would sometimes send his head throbbing with pain. He was surprised with himself this morning at the absence of any aches and pains as he recalled his family's past.

If his family did not flee Germany when Hitler and his Nazis began persecuting the Jews, things would have turned out differently for him. There would not have been a Saul Levy. With the help of their German friends, they fled to Amsterdam and there reestablished their family's jewelry business. Unlike his father's siblings, his father continued on to California, where he met and married his mother. Of his family members who stayed in Amsterdam, only one survived the Holocaust, an uncle who later died demented by his ordeal. He learned all of those as a young boy. The family's past haunted him ever since. It clung to him, a permanent presence in his life, like his own shadow.

"C'mon, honey, we're getting off here," a man seated across

the aisle said to the woman beside him, as the bus was pulling to a stop at the corner of Wilshire and Normandie. They stood up and joined the other passengers getting off from the bus. They were headed for the handsome buildings on Wilshire Boulevard. Two women, both in blazers, caught his eye. They were pretty. He saw them as he was boarding the bus in Santa Monica. They seemed like the kind of people who landed in the pages of fashion magazines and appeared on TV shows, they who enjoyed the good life in Los Angeles. He will never see them again, but it was enough: he had his fill of a visual feast and memories, sad and happy. The time he spent in the bus was worth it.

He got off from the bus on Seventh Street in downtown Los Angeles. From there, he walked toward a tall building on Flower Street. His office was in the ninth floor. Four men and two women, all of them prospective clients, were in the receiving room, waiting to be called.

A short dark-complexioned man was seated on a chair. He showed his eagerness to please him when he stood up, smiled and nodded at him. He was not pleased with the man's fawning gesture, and he acknowledged it with a nod, dismissing it at the same time with his free hand tamping the air.

The man sat down as directed. To put him at ease, he smiled too and greeted him a good morning. The man kept on smiling. He turned to the others and said good morning to them as well, the man's fawning gesture reminding him of the power he held to determine these prospective clients' future in America.

He stepped inside his office and glanced at Therese. His secretary-receptionist was already at work. She was going over some papers in her desk. She looked up at him and greeted him a good morning. An engaging smile was on her beautiful sensuous face crowned with golden hair. He was charmed and he smiled and said good morning to her, too. It set the mood for another busy, but pleasant day in his law office.

"How was your weekend?" he asked her.

"Fine. You can see it in my tan."

She turned up her chin , the better for him to see her face, and stretched out her slim arm. Her face and arm were tanned a salmon pink from her natural complexion of very light pink.

Her beauty had so attracted him, he leaned toward her desk

for a closer look at her. He nodded, pleased, at her smooth rosy cheeks. Then he drummed his fingers playfully on her outstretched arm, the thought coming to him about the admiring looks she must have drawn as she worked on her tan. Here was a *Venus de Milo* lying on the sand, cast not in marble, but in flesh and blood.

He asked, as he withdrew his fingers from her arm, "Is that the fruit of a day you spent on the beach in Santa Monica or Redondo?"

"Neither," she replied, smiling. "I had my tan in Laguna Beach. I've got a friend who lives near the beach there."

"You drove all the way there for a tan?"

"As you can see, it's worth it," she replied, smiling still.

A smile was on his face too when he left her desk and proceeded to his room. He waved, before opening the door, at Nola and Susan, his two other employees, who responded with knowing smiles.

He stepped inside his room and went to his desk. He laid his briefcase there, flipped its locks open, pulled out the folders there and laid them on his desk. The briefcase was lighter now when he put it inside the cabinet behind his swivel chair. It tilted slightly when he sat down there, ready to start work. He turned to musing instead.

Why women like Therese went to a great trouble to get a tan had always puzzled and amused him. She looked fine in her light pink complexion. It maybe a little on the pale side, but then, there was nothing wrong with that either. There was also Agnes, who spent a great deal of time and money in beauty salons to make her complexion a shade lighter. Women were seldom satisfied with their looks. They were always trying to improve on what God gave them. Vanity made them do it. So did he as a lawyer.

Like everybody else, he was showing something of himself before the world, and he had something to show, right there in his office. It was tastefully decorated. The furniture, like his mahogany desk, was in the Italian Renaissance style. Hanging on a wall of green felt wallpaper in gilded frames were excellent copies of a da Vinci sketch and a Cézanne still life painting, which Agnes gave him on his birthday five years ago. A computer with a printer, a fax machine and the telephone on his desk were his communication tools to the outside world. A wall was lined with legal books. The wide glass window behind the cabinet looked out into another office building across

Flower Street. To his left was another wide glass window with a million-dollar view of Los Angeles that extended as far south to the hills of Rancho Palos Verdes and beyond that, to the Pacific Ocean.

He turned his gaze to the door Therese had opened, their clients' case folders nestled in the crook of her arm.

"Who is first on the list?" he asked as she was putting the folders on his desk.

"Your wife's provincemates—Simon Matin and his wife Clara. Do you want me to call them now, or would you rather have your coffee first?"

"I will have my coffee first, and give me a few minutes to review my caseload. If Steve has arrived, tell him to see me. You can show the Matins in after I have talked to him. You can also take these with you," he said as he gave Therese the folders from his briefcase.

She left but came back in a short while with a cup of coffee on a saucer. There was nothing like it to pep him up before working.

He was taking the cup and saucer from her when his palm slid like a caress on her smooth warm hand. She seemed startled, but not offended, for she was smiling as she then left the room, nearly colliding with Steve Claremont at the door. The feel of her soft warm hand lingered in his palm, and he nodded absentmindedly at Steve, who said, "Good morning, chief," as he sat down on a chair with his elbow planted on his desk.

He looked on at his young associate, who was tall and broad-shouldered. A knee injury closed for him a career in professional football, and he turned to law. His close-cropped, brown hair crowning a strong-jawed, clean-shaven face suggested a Western upbringing: an All-American young man from Idaho.

"Did you go to Solvang, chief, as you planned to do last week?" Steve asked him about the Dutch village, a popular tourist spot north of Los Angeles.

"We did not. Agnes and I stayed home. How about you? Did you go out of town?"

"We did. We camped in Big Bear Mountain, a beautiful place, away from the smog in Los Angeles for a change, but even there, we heard nothing but the King trial. Would you like to bet on the verdict? It will be out soon."

Like Steve, he had been following the progress of the trial. If the beating by four white police officers of a black motorist named

Rodney King had not been caught on the video camera by an amateur photographer and shown on television all over the United States and the rest of the world, it would not have generated such a great interest and concern in Los Angeles.

He was worried at the outrage among the city's black residents over the beating incident. The videotape showed King being kicked to the ground and struck with nightsticks by several police officers, while other police officers looked on. It was the first week of April 1992, and the trial, held in Simi Valley, north of Los Angeles, was coming to its end.

"How do you size it up?" he asked Steve.

"The cops will go free."

"Despite what the videotape showed?"

"What it showed may not be convincing enough to the jury. The man, while down on the ground, may have said something that provoked the cops, or he may have been resisting arrest."

"Come now, could he resist arrest while down on the ground and with blows from the cops' nightsticks raining down on him?"

"I'm not sure if the videotape has definitely established that."

"And while you won't accept what the videotape showed, you will rely on the presumption that King had said or done something that so provoked the police officers into beating him up."

"More or less."

"You know very well that policemen are not justified in using excessive force, even when they are provoked."

He watched Steve shift his weight on the chair. Steve was in an untenable position, but he came back at him.

"The people I have talked to are convinced that the cops will go free," Steve said.

"Are you saying that as a lawyer, or as someone like those people with their own preconceived notions about the case?"

"I don't think we can divorce one from the other."

"A good lawyer can and should."

"Anyway, it is too close to call. Whatever will be the verdict, once it is handed down, that will be the end of it. We may hear some noise if the cops are acquitted; that is all."

"An acquittal will do more than make some noise."

Images then flashed in Saul's mind of the residents in the black community of Watts in South Central in Los Angeles fighting the police and National Guardsmen in five days of riots. It started as a simple case of a black motorist arrested for drunk driving that grew out of control. It resulted in scores of lives lost, homes and buildings damaged, looted and burned to the ground.

He asked Steve, "Do you remember the Watts riots here in 1965?"

"Vaguely. Los Angeles is far from Idaho, and I was only a small boy when it happened."

"It can happen again. All they need, which the trial might provide, is a little provocation and they might break out into another riot."

"You seem to keep track of what is going on here."

"I was born and raised here, and I have always made it a personal concern of mine to know what is going on here."

Steve nodded.

"By the way," he said. "It is not too early for me to tell you that it is Vicky's birthday on the twenty-ninth of this month. I hope you and Agnes can attend a little celebration we'll be having at home."

"Agnes and I will be glad to attend it."

"Therese said there is something you want to take up with me."

"It's about your report on this agriculturist, Juan Sindromas."

"What about him?"

"Have you checked the fruit farm he said he is working for?"

"I'm expecting a reply soon from Fresno to the inquiry I made about Sindromas. I noticed, though, when I interviewed him that he said things that don't agree with each other."

"Let us be careful with people like him. They make up stories and manufacture documents to support their immigrant applications."

"I can't agree with you more. I was also intrigued by what this alien told me about others like him our office could represent. They seem to be like locusts swarming all over California."

Saul gazed, surprised and disapproving, at his associate. While there was some truth to what he said, it was not for him, an immigration lawyer, to be prejudiced against immigrants.

"We are immigration lawyers; we should not keep opinions like that," he said. "We won't take Sindromas as a client unless we are sure he is on the level. Give his case top priority."

"Right, chief," Steve said as he rose from his chair. He stood up and gave Saul a fake salute.

His lips pursed in disappointment, he watched Steve leave the room. He could attribute to lack of exposure, Steve's negative views on immigrants. Steve was new in the office and only a few years from law school. Idaho, where he was born and raised, was altogether a different world from Los Angeles. Steve must accept the reality of a melting pot that was the world of Los Angeles. He must shed his prejudice against immigrants, especially those of color.

He frowned at the comparison Steve made between locusts and immigrants. He also called them aliens, a word that may officially designate immigrants, but which he himself found offensive. It conveyed an image of people who were strange, hostile, dangerous and inferior. But his associate was intelligent and eager to learn. He will just have to guide him along.

Therese came back with Simon and Clara Matin as he was taking one last sip of his coffee. He stood up and shook hands with them as Therese was introducing them to him, after which she stepped out of the room. He sat down on his swivel chair as the couple were seating down facing each other across his desk.

"My wife Agnes told me you are also from Zambales," he said, smiling at the couple to put them at ease.

"Yes, we are, or my wife is," Simon said

"I have been there once, for a couple of days," he said. "It's a nice place, the weather there a bit like Los Angeles during summer."

His eyes darted from Simon to Clara as he asked himself what it was that she found attractive about her husband. Simon looked so plain, almost ugly, while Clara, even now, maybe at forty- something, had retained much of her youthful good looks. She seemed to have an easy charm like Agnes. It showed in her face despite the worry and discomfort she must feel to be in his office.

"So," he asked them, "what can I do for you?"

"We would like to be legal permanent residents before our tourist visas will expire," Simon replied.

"How long have you been living here in the United States?"

"About five months," Simon replied.

"Why did you not seek legal help earlier?"

"We asked around, but hesitated until now about seeing a lawyer," Simon replied.

"We might be reported to the authorities if we are seen going to a law office," Clara said.

"Lawyers don't do that," he said.

Clara's cheeks flushed in embarrassment. Simon glanced at her and then said to him, "My wife was not referring to lawyers, but to those in our community who squeal on their own countrymen."

He nodded in acceptance of Simon's defense of his wife.

"So, you just left things as they are," he said.

"We are also waiting for this new immigration amnesty," Clara said. "We heard there is one coming. That is the talk in our community."

The answers he was getting from Simon and Clara Matin were beginning to annoy him, and he said to them, "Why, then, did you come here? You could have just waited for this amnesty, which, I must tell you, is not coming, at least not in the immediate future, if ever it will come."

"I'm sorry if we have been complacent," Simon said. "We should have sought your help earlier. It has become an urgent matter for us from what happened to our neighbor. His father died in the Philippines, but he could not leave to attend his father's burial. He knows he will not be readmitted because he has overstayed here. We want to avoid that from happening to us."

He relented and said, "Let me see what I can do for you," as he picked up the folder on the Matins and took out the information sheet they had filled out earlier.

"Let us see about your options," he said, as he read their information sheet. "So, you don't have immediate relatives like parents, siblings, or adult children who could be your sponsor."

Simon shook his head and said, "We have none of those."

"Are you working?" he asked Simon.

"Yes. I'm a busboy, dishwasher and janitor in a restaurant."

"Without a green card, my husband could not get a job fit for his experience and education," Clara said. "I work for a jewelry importer, 'under the table,' like my husband."

Saul raised his eyebrows at the odd phrase used by Clara in describing the manner they worked and how hard it must have been for them to work "under the table."

"By that," he said, "you mean you are working without a government work permit."

Simon and Clara nodded.

"Did your employers ask for your green cards or work permits?"

"They did not," Simon replied. "They guessed as much when we did not show them any of those documents. They pay us in cash, so there is no record we are working for them. It's a common practice here, I think."

"You know, of course, you are not supposed to work without the work permits. You might find yourselves in big trouble if you are found to be working without them."

Clara and Simon gazed at each other, a worried expression appearing in their faces.

He said quickly, "I said that, not to scare you."

"I know, but we have no choice," Simon said. "We have to earn a living."

He nodded. He could get nothing from this line of questioning with Simon.

"How about you, Missis Matin?" he asked Clara. "What kind of work do you do for the jewelry importer? If you are a gemologist or something like that, you are doing technical work. That will set you fine for a working visa as a skilled worker."

"I do clerical work like typing and filing. I also do the invoices. Is that technical enough?"

"I'm sorry, but it is not."

"So, our employers cannot sponsor us even if they should decide to," Simon said.

"They can, but your job as a busboy, dishwasher and janitor is unskilled work."

He raised his hand and said, "Please, don't get me wrong. It is good honest work, but it will take years before the category for unskilled workers will become current. The same thing with you, Missis Matin. You're doing semiskilled work. It will also take years before that category will become current. They are not much to go by. What you need immediately are work permits and an extension of your stay here, pending your application for legal permanent residence, that is, assuming I can work out something for you."

He gazed in sympathy at Simon and Clara, who looked dejected. The years he had been in law practice had not made him callous to a sight like this of the Matins, who were frustrated in their goal of getting legal permanent residence in the United States.

The room was so quiet he could hear a car horn blown in the street, nine stories below them. He looked on at them as he searched in his mind for a way by which he could pursue their case.

"Tell me," he asked them, "Why did you come here to the United States?"

Simon seemed to hesitate, but then he replied in a grave tone of voice, "We came here out of fear for our lives in our own country."

He gazed, surprised and uncomprehending, at Simon.

"Will you explain that to me, please," he said.

"We were targets both of Marcos' military agents and the Communist rebels," Simon said. "We had to flee our country."

It was just a few years after the Filipino people had toppled from power in a bloodless four-day revolution the dictator Ferdinand Marcos.

Clara said, her voice raised in fear and anger, "They were gunning after us! They have already killed my father! We are next!"

Simon leaned forward and tapped Clara's arm. It calmed her down.

"I'm sorry to hear that," Saul said, "but you have nothing to fear, now that you are here in America."

He showed nothing of the excitement he felt from what he heard from Simon and Clara. They were persecuted, their lives in danger in their own country. They deserved political asylum. That was the very thing he needed to pursue their case. A pall of gloom seemed to have been lifted from the room.

"Tell me everything, from the beginning," he said to them.

Simon drew a deep breath and said in a calm voice, "Our troubles began early in 1978. By then, five years had passed since Marcos imposed martial law in our country. I was teaching history and literature in a small college in Laguna, a province near Manila. I could not accept the evil dictatorship Marcos had imposed on us, and I taught my students to fight in every way they could for the return of freedom and democracy Marcos stole from us."

"I can imagine how the authorities there reacted to that."

"As expected, they did not like what I was doing."

"Our friends and relatives warned Simon to stop speaking against Marcos."

"Did you?"

"No. I felt so strongly against the tyrant, I could not stop fighting him."

"My husband is a man of high moral principles. He sticks to what he believes in, even at the risk of going to jail, and that is exactly what happened. He was arrested and jailed. Oh, the terrible things they did to him there!"

She broke down in tears. Simon took out a handkerchief from his pocket and, nodding solicitously at her, he gave it to her, who wiped with it the tears in her eyes.

They gazed at each other, and Saul, in watching them, could almost feel the soothing effect Simon's eyes had on Clara. They seemed like windows to a keen mind that understood perfectly his wife's feelings. Here he was, a witness to them sympathizing with each other, implying by it their deep abiding love for each other. He felt he was intruding on them, and he turned his gaze to the window with a grand view of Los Angeles.

Clara blew her nose on the handkerchief and, after wiping it, she said, "I don't want us to go through all of that again! I don't want to go back to our country!"

"Those terrible days are over for you," Saul said to her. "As for your continued stay here, I'll see what I can do."

He asked Simon, "How long were you kept in jail?"

"I was in jail for ten months. After I was released, I tried going back to my old teaching job, but it was filled while I was in jail. Other schools turned me down. I realized then that I had been blacklisted and I could not get a teaching job in our country. We moved to Zambales, to Clara's widower father's house. He had a small farm and a ranch there. We helped him till the land and raise poultry and livestock."

"At least you had something to live on. It must have been nice to live in peace in the countryside."

"Country life is nice. We love it," Simon said. "But with the NPA there, we also did not find peace in Zambales."

"What does this NPA mean?"

"It is short for the New People's Army, the Communist rebels' armed force," Simon replied. "By then, and until we left, they were all over Zambales and in other provinces in the country."

"So, you had your troubles with both the Communist rebels and Marcos' military agents."

"That is correct," Simon said.

"You must have gained the notoriety, both Marcos' military and the Communists kept an eye on you."

The flippant remark he made, although uncalled for, masked an admiration he was beginning to feel toward Simon and his wife.

Simon shrugged it off and said, "We did not like them and they did not like us. That is all there is to it. We just wanted to be left alone. We moved to Zambales where we hoped to live in peace. The farm and the ranch were not doing very well when we first came there. It took us several years of hard work before we could get them going, but in so doing, we also got ourselves noticed by the NPA. We became a target for extortion.

"One day, we received a note from the local NPA demanding a portion of our farm income. To say no was to court big trouble. So, we gave them what they wanted. They took a fifth of our rice harvest, a big bite from our income, which was just enough for our needs. They also took many of our poultry and livestock. They issued receipts for what they took from us, which they called 'revolutionary taxes.' They were so sure of themselves they already had a shadow government they thought would one day wrest power from Marcos. I kept the note and the receipts, for even then, I was thinking of writing a book about those two evils in our country: the Marcos dictatorship and the Communist insurgency."

"Have you started writing it?"

"I have the basic structure in my head, but I have yet to start writing it."

"At least they left you alone."

"But not for long. One night, several NPA guerrillas came to our house. They had learned that I was once a teacher. They wanted me to do intelligence and propaganda work for them. They also wanted to recruit Sonny, our son, as a courier."

"What did you tell them?"

"This time I told them no."

"You did the right, but risky thing."

"Yes, a risky thing it was. They took my refusal as a proof that I was in the pay of the military, or at least its sympathizer. I was a marked man. One night, several weeks later, they attacked the town's police and military stations and some of the houses, including our house. My father-in-law was killed. I was wounded in the leg.

Ten people were killed in that NPA attack."

"You are lucky to survive it. Was this reported by the newspapers?"

"Yes, by the Manila papers later that week."

"Did you keep copies of the newspaper reports?"

"I did."

"What did you do then?"

"We fled to Manila. We left everything behind except those we could carry in our hands. We left the ranch and the farm under the care of our tenant. We got out just on time. Several nights after we fled, the NPA raided the town again. The Communist rebels were after us, while the military kept us under watch."

"Was it not obvious to them that the Communists were gunning after you and your family?"

"The military took us for Communist sympathizers when they learned we were giving the rebels aid. We were indeed doing that, but they did not know it was extorted from us in the form of those so-called 'revolutionary taxes.' The military in Zambales also learned that I had been jailed before in Laguna for opposing Marcos. I was therefore considered an enemy of the Marcos dictatorship. We were getting it both from the Marcos military and the Communist rebels."

"What happened in Manila?"

"For a while we did well enough there. A friend gave me a job in his printing shop, while Clara, to augment our income, went around in our neighborhood, selling home-cooked snacks and pastries. For quite a time, we lived anonymously among its millions of residents. But they eventually found us. One day, we saw strangers hanging around in our neighborhood, asking about us. We did not want to take any chances, and we moved quietly out of our apartment."

"Did you get to know who those people were?"

"No. They could have been Communist rebels or Marcos' military agents. To make matters really bad for us, Ninoy Aquino, the chief political opponent of Marcos, whom Marcos jailed for seven years on trumped-up charges, our rallying point for the return of freedom and democracy in our country, was murdered at the airport tarmac as he was returning from exile here in the United States.

"Marcos and his henchmen claimed a lone Communist gunman named Rolando Galman killed Ninoy with the tall tale that

Galman had managed to get through a cordon of three thousand soldiers surrounding the airplane and shoot Ninoy.

"This is what actually happened. Ninoy was praying, his fingers on his rosary, when two soldiers took him out of the airplane full of journalists. He was going down the airplane's rear staircase, the two soldiers a step or two behind him when one of them shot and killed him. Ninoy was shot from an angle. The bullet entered the upper part at the back of his head and came out below his lower lip.

"A journalist's tape recorder placed at the airplane window recorded one of the soldiers shouting, '*pusila, pusila,*' a Visayan word for 'shoot, shoot,' before the shot rang out that killed Ninoy.

"The entire country believed Ninoy was murdered on orders from Marcos and his wife Imelda. Marcos at that time was seriously ill. They were so afraid Ninoy might take advantage of Marcos' illness and, in returning from exile here in the United States, lead an uprising against their dictatorial rule.

"If the Marcoses could do that to Ninoy, how much more to a small fry like me? People then took to the streets almost every day in massive protest demonstrations against the tyrant Marcos and his wife Imelda. Manila was in turmoil, while the Communists were now in control of much of the countryside and would soon be besieging Manila itself. The situation was so bad, we had to flee our country."

Saul had seen on TV and read in the papers about that particularly bad time in the Philippines, and he asked Simon, "What took you so long to fight for the ouster of Marcos?"

"I have asked myself the same question as to why our countrymen had for so long allowed themselves to be fooled and later intimidated by Marcos. It is partly due to image building. Marcos was a bluffer, not the brave war hero the image of which he had long foisted on the Filipino people with his war medals. He got some of them, not in the battlefield, but in an exchange of political favors in Congress, while the rest were fake medals. This came to be known only after he had been toppled from power.

"Marcos, when he was a young man, was convicted and given the death sentence for murdering the man who defeated his father in a local election. He was then a law student. He was in jail when he took and topped the bar exams while appealing his conviction. The Supreme Court disregarded the legal and moral standards in his case and overturned Marcos' conviction with the cynical outrageous reasoning that it would be such a waste for this brilliant young man to be given the death sentence while completely disregarding the crime he committed of murdering a man.

"Marcos was a criminal, a murderer who should have never gained any elective public office. But the crime he committed was ignored by those who voted him a congressman, then a senator, then the president. They deserve Marcos and the dictatorship he imposed on them. Unfortunately for the rest of the country, it suffered as well from the terrible consequences of his evil rule."

"But don't you have a mechanism that could have prevented Marcos from using martial law as a means of imposing dictatorship in your country?"

"We have the Philippine constitution itself. Martial law is supposed to be a temporary limited measure to fight foreign invasion or local insurrection, and not to change our system of government, as what Marcos did. Martial law was not even declared to resist the Japanese invasion in 1941 and the Communist-supported Huk insurgency in the forties and fifties.

"Marcos used as an excuse for imposing martial law, the student protest rallies that often turned violent. They alienated the people. It was only later, after Marcos had been kicked out of the country, that the truth about those violent student demonstrations was finally revealed. Marcos secretly planted agents, including young boys, who then sowed the violence in those student protest rallies. He used them as an excuse for imposing martial law in our country.

"He imposed martial law in 1972 to avoid stepping down from the presidency at the end of his term of office the following year. The Supreme Court, which could have imposed the limits of the martial law Marcos had imposed, made itself, by its cowardly silence, an accomplice of Marcos' dictatorship.

"Marcos then closed down Congress and the free press, killed or imprisoned those who opposed his one-man rule. He and his wife Imelda and their minions then plundered the country and made it like a vast prison camp and their personal estate. They turned our country from a democracy to a kleptocracy."

"What you are saying here is a conjugal dictatorship of Marcos and his wife Imelda."

"She is no different from Marcos. They are two sides of the same coin. I'll give you an example of the kind of person she is. One time, she ordered the construction of a theater for her film festival. Several workers died in an accident there. Its construction might be delayed if they will take the time to remove the bodies, so she ordered them cemented over instead of having them dug out and given a proper church burial. Her film festival flopped. The participants snubbed it when they learned what she had ordered done to those poor workers. Their ghosts have haunted that theater ever since.

"Marcos had the Filipino people under his thumb until Ninoy Aquino's assassination in 1984. It so angered them, they finally summoned the courage to fight Marcos in unrelenting street protest rallies. To show to the world that he had popular support, Marcos called for a snap election in 1986, assured of winning it by cheating his opponent, Ninoy's widow, Cory. The whole world found him out when the computer operators who counted the votes fled to a church and there revealed they were ordered to falsify the election results. As a result, Marcos, in the eyes of the world, had lost the legitimacy of his rule on the country. His grip on power began to slip away when some of his top lieutenants broke ranks with him. The people, led by Cardinal Jaime Sin, supported their mutiny. It led to the People Power Revolution in February, 1986 that finally toppled the Marcos conjugal dictatorship from power.

"I was with a huge crowd outside Malacanang Palace, the official residence of Philippine presidents, voicing out their anger at Marcos and his wife when shots were fired at the palace grounds. Moments later, helicopters took off from Malacanang Park across the river. The word spread around quickly that the Marcoses had fled. I was swept along by the crowd that then surged toward the palace.

"I had barely entered the palace when I was greeted there by an offensive smell. I looked around and found the source. It was his waste matter Marcos had left scattered on the palace floor. 'The brave war hero' was so terrified by the shouting and the shooting in the palace grounds, his bowels broke loose on his disposable diapers, pants and boots. Marcos and his wife Imelda plundered the country, destroyed democracy and ruined so many lives. They left the Philippines in such a terrible mess, but none of that was as revolting as Marcos' own stinking mess he left on the palace floor as he and his family then fled to Hawaii, the only president to be kicked out of our country. It was a well-deserved end to the Marcoses' tyrannical rule."

"So, with Marcos gone, you could now breathe easier."

"I'm not sure about that. We might get that kind of rule again. We, Filipinos, don't learn from our mistakes."

"At least, with Marcos gone, things must now be better in your country."

"Not much until now. The Marcoses stole five to ten billion dollars that left our poor country bankrupt. The Communist rebels were by then in control of much of the countryside. It was only a matter of time before they would besiege Manila itself. Many in the military remained loyal to Marcos. The situation remained desperate and dangerous for us. We had to flee our country."

"And you fled here."

"Yes, first chance we got, after a number of tries, when we finally got our visas from the U.S. Embassy."

Saul had seen people like the Matins lining up at the U.S. Embassy in Manila, one time he visited it with Agnes. He learned from the embassy staff that many of the applicants were at the embassy gate as early as four o'clock in the morning. Many of them were repeatedly denied their visa applications. The Matins were among the lucky ones who passed.

"Your perseverance has paid off," he said.

"We were lucky in our last try. The consul who interviewed us was kind and understanding. We had to convince him, though, that we were returning home after our visit here. The title to the Zambales farm and ranch now in Clara's name was a proof that we had something to go back to in our country. But we may have won the consul over with what we told him was our main purpose in visiting America."

"And what was that?"

"We told the consul we always wanted to see Disneyland. The consul smiled and, as he stamped the visas on our passports, he told us to enjoy our visit to Disneyland."

"A little humor, well delivered, can sometimes do wonders," Saul said. He paused and then said, "Have you tried living in places other than Los Angeles?"

"We saw no need to," Simon replied. "We were hounded and persecuted in our own country. We have found here in Los Angeles, our sanctuary. It is, to us, like a city of God."

Saul raised his eyebrows in surprise at Simon's reverent regard for Los Angeles. He himself never saw his home city as anything like it. The crime, the smog, the deterioration of the city's core, the racial tension—there was nothing godly in any of those.

He asked Simon, "Why do you call Los Angeles a city of God?"

"Won't you call Los Angeles that if you are in our place? It is, to us, like a city of God, for we have found here, freedom from want and fear."

"I was born here and have lived here most of my life, but I don't see Los Angeles that way. I guess it depends on how you feel about it."

"As I have said, that is how we feel about Los Angeles. We want to stay here, if we will be allowed to. Which brings us to this question: What are our chances of getting green cards?"

Saul pondered over Simon's question. They had reached the crucial point in their interview. He must now tell the Matins if they were qualified for green cards that would allow them to live and work in the United States legally and permanently. He had no doubt they deserved to be helped. They had been persecuted like his own people. Had it not been for other people's help, his entire family may have perished in the Holocaust. He would not have been born then. He could pay back in a small way what they owed those unknown German friends who helped his family flee Hitler and his Nazi goons by helping the Matins in turn. He gazed at Simon and Clara, who had leaned forward in anticipation of what he would now tell them.

"As I see it," he said, " political asylum is the only way you can get your green cards. It will be a long shot, though, with Marcos out and democracy now restored in your country. It won't work for you, unless we can show that your lives will be in danger if you are made to return to the Philippines."

"It will be suicidal for us to go back there," Simon said. "The situation there remains unstable and dangerous for us. Renegade soldiers loyal to Marcos are attempting one coup after another. The Communists' death squads called Sparrow Units are killing people right there in Metro Manila, and in broad daylight. No one is safe, least of all people like us. I don't want us to end up dead like Ninoy."

"Very well," he said to Simon. "We will anchor your case to what you just said. It is factual and persuasive."

"I'm glad to hear that. Thank you."

He gazed, satisfied, at Simon and Clara, who were now

smiling at each other. They now have something to look forward to.

"You have not told us about your fee," Simon said.

"Don't worry about that, it won't cost you a fortune."

He mentioned the amount and said, "You can pay on installment. You can give the first installment to Therese, my secretary-receptionist. She will help you with some forms you will have to fill out. I'm confident that your application for political asylum will pass. You will receive temporary work permits while your application is being processed. They are good for one year, renewable every year until your case comes up for adjudication. Besides your son, do you have other children, and their ages?"

"Our son is sixteen years old," Clara replied. "We have a daughter, who is seventeen years old."

"They are old enough to take at least summer jobs."

"When," Simon asked, "can we get our temporary work permits, so they can work, too?"

"It usually takes a few weeks, sometimes shorter, depending on the volume of work at the INS."

Simon and Clara looked even more pleased.

Simon asked, "Is there anything we should do from here on?"

"For now, all you'll have to do is wait. I'll keep you posted. You can also send me copies of the news reports, the NPA note and the 'revolutionary tax' receipts."

He stood up. The interview was over. He led Simon and Clara out of the room, to Therese's desk. He nodded in a signal to her, and she picked up from her desk the forms she will help Simon and Clara fill out at the conference table near her desk.

Simon said, as he and Clara were shaking hands with him, "We cannot thank you enough for what you are doing for us. We will always be grateful to you."

"Nothing to it, nothing to it, at all," he replied. "It is just a part of our day's work."

He was at the door to his room when he looked back at Therese, Simon and Clara, who were now seated at the conference table. He was happy for his law practice, through which people like the Matins could be legal permanent residents and later citizens of the United States.

He opened the door, smiling at how his interview with them will just about make his day.

Chapter 3

They will soon have their work permits and, after that, their green cards. The thought established itself pleasantly in Simon's mind as he and Clara filled out and signed the form for political asylum. Then he gave the first installment of the legal fee to Therese, who was seated across them at the conference table. They were now officially on their way to becoming legal permanent residents in the United States.

He was so pleased with himself, he could have raised his arms in triumph! But he was restrained from any excessive show of gladness, for that would be improper in the formal businesslike atmosphere in the Levy law office. Even Clara will disapprove it. He thanked Therese, that was all, for her help with the documents.

They all stood up, their work there done. He and Clara shook hands with Therese, as they then left the Levy law office, happy and content.

He kept this feeling of joy repressed as well in the elevator he and Clara took, restrained as he was by its cramped space and the presence there of other passengers. He savored the feeling, that was all, and watched quietly the elevator's floor counter move to one when it reached the ground floor.

They walked through the lobby on their way out of the building and pulled the glass door open for Clara, his eyes squinting at Flower Street drenched with sunlight.

He finally let go of himself once they were out on the sidewalk, as he then raised his arms in triumph and walked with jaunty steps, the soles of his shoes slapping the pavement.

Her eyes wide from shock, Clara said to him,"What are you doing?"

A broad smile on his face, he ignored her and kept on walking with jaunty steps, his hands now thrust deep inside his pockets and his shoulder swinging from side to side.

"Stop it," she said. "You look silly, walking like that!"

"Really? Like what?"

"Like a clown in a circus!"

He halted and said, "I don't care what I look like."

A woman walking toward him halted. Her mouth wide open from shock, she detoured quickly to the other side of the street.

Only then did he realize the weird spectacle he had made of himself. He had even annoyed Clara.

He resumed walking, this time in his usual relaxed manner, his footsteps now light on the pavement.

"Why," she asked him, "did you do that?"

"I'm happy; that is why."

"So am I, but I did not jump up and down the street like what you just did. I never saw you behave like that before."

"I just could not help it, now that the elusive work permits and green cards are within our reach."

"I may jump for joy also, but only when I have mine in my hands."

"You don't have to be so skeptical. We are in good hands, the best among the best. Saul Levy would not have taken our case if he was not convinced about its merit."

"I did not think he would be, at least not at the start of our interview. Did you have such a doubt, too?"

"Only when I felt him groping for the right lead for our case, but as to his inclination, I had no doubt about it. After all, he is married to a Filipino woman like you. I don't think he would want to disappoint his wife, your provincemate, would he?"

"No."

"There is also the fact that he is Jewish. They have been a persecuted people. For ages until the founding of modern-day Israel, they had no homeland of their own. I was therefore not surprised to find Saul Levy sympathetic to us, for we also have our diaspora from our own country."

"How do you know he is Jewish?"

"His looks and his name: they are conclusive. Those black curls and that long nose: they are very Jewish. And his name: it comes straight from the Holy Bible. Saul, of course, is from King Saul, the first king of Israel. Levy, on the other hand, was taken from Levi, the third son of Jacob, from whom was descended one of the twelve tribes of Israel."

Clara smiled at Simon, who was showing off his knowledge of the Holy Bible.

"I can imagine how excited Lorna and Sonny will be once they learn we will soon have our work permits, courtesy of Attorney Saul Levy," she said, her face bright like the morning sun.

"They might also do what I just did."

"We can now make plans. We can now look for better jobs. You don't have to bus and wash dishes and mop the floor anymore in L and S."

"But of course! And I'm moving in that direction. I went with Phil yesterday to the Keg Room to see Jonathan about a teaching post I'm eyeing in Asia Pacific."

"But you told me when you got home last night that you did not find Jonathan there."

"I'll ask him when he drops by in L and S for breakfast. He often does."

"I have always admired you for your drive and foresight. I have no doubt you will be teaching again. We can now seriously consider Sonny and Lorna's college education. We can also start looking around for our own home in a nice neighborhood."

"We will have all of that in due time. But right now, what we should do is celebrate. A lunch with the kids will be perfect if, like what I did, you told your boss you are taking the day off."

"You don't know Rashid, my boss. He won't let me miss even half an hour of work. He frowned when I told him last Friday that I will come in late today."

"Did you tell him why?"

"No."

"Good. Keep it to yourself until we have received our work permits. That will floor your boss."

They walked on toward Seventh Street. Simon looked around, pleased, at the shops and buildings and the people they met on the sidewalk. They were in a swank area of downtown Los Angeles. The buildings' glass windows were gleaming in the sunlight. All around them were chic shops and fancy restaurants. All this confirmed for him his good impression of the United States, formed from his readings, the movies, and what he had heard about it. Like his countrymen, he had looked starry-eyed at the United States.

It seemed less impressive now than what he had imagined it to be, but it was still the good life in the United States, real and palpable. He was right within its midst, feeling for the first time a sense of belonging, now that its own laws will allow him and his family to live and work legally and permanently here, in the United States of America.

They turned at the corner of Flower and Seventh Streets and walked on toward Hope Street. A few cars were running in the street. There were few other people walking on the sidewalk.

At the hotel across the street, the doorman stood beneath its maroon awning. He was waiting for the guests coming in their cars.

It was twenty after ten, a long time yet from lunchtime, when hordes of office workers from the buildings around them will be coming down to the restaurants and fast-food shops in the vicinity.

The thrill he felt at the coming adjustment in their immigrant status began to wane as they were walking on in Seventh Street. He had an analytical mind. The few negative things about America, like racial discrimination, which he had glossed over, now claimed his attention. He himself had been a victim of racial discrimination expressed in a polite, but condescending manner others would not see, nor mind, which he was deeply aware of, this out of his sharp mind and sensitive nature.

He was painfully aware of an invisible barrier that kept him and his race apart from the rest of mainstream American society. He was a Filipino, a brown man from a country of little consequence in the United States and in the rest of the world. But he should not complain. The few negative things he encountered in America were nothing compared to the terrible things he and his family had suffered and endured in their own country.

They crossed Hope Street the instant the traffic light had turned to green. A white couple were walking toward them. As they came near them, he saw how handsome they looked. There was an elegant air about the woman. She was wearing a kind of dress found in the dress shops in Rodeo Drive, where the rich and famous people in Los Angeles shopped. The man walking confidently beside her looked like a model of a men's fashion magazine.

He was not ordinarily impressed by physical appearances, but the man in his well-cut suit and patent leather shoes conveyed wealth and good taste. He was suddenly self-conscious. The coat he was wearing, the only one he had and the best his tailor in Manila could come up with, was drab in comparison to the man's well-cut suit.

He glanced at Clara and saw her looking straight ahead and trying to ignore the woman in elegant dress. His lovely wife could hold up to the woman in natural looks, but her dress, sewn for her by a seamstress relative, while just right in Manila, looked outmoded in

Los Angeles. The clothes they were wearing made them painfully aware of what they were—poor newcomers here. The green cards Saul Levy will obtain for them may change their immigrant status, but not the fact that they were poor political refugees in this country. Aside from green cards, what he and his family needed was time to make something of themselves. By then, he will be as elegantly outfitted as the man in his well-cut suit. As for Clara, blazer will be her outfit when, as he hoped, she will be working in a grand office building on Grand Avenue they were now approaching.

"How would you like to work here?" he asked her.

"What for? To make use of my typing skills?"

"You can do more than secretarial work."

"I can put to use the accounting subjects I took up in college."

"There must be jobs here where we can tie our future."

Any way he looked at it, his job of busing and washing dishes, clearing tables and mopping the floor in L&S Restaurant was not a career job. It was menial work that did not pay enough. Clara had to help out and work, too. She was a clerk for a jewelry importer in a building on Hill Street. Only a few blocks from Saul Levy's law office, it stood at the edge of the shabby part of downtown Los Angeles. He and Clara will welcome a bigger pay and health insurance as well.

What they had was still far better than going jobless, hungry and homeless, like the poor woman they saw there in Olive Street last week. Heaven forbid if they will end up like her.

They saw the woman as they were returning to their car parked in the street. They had just left the anniversary celebration of Clara's hometown association held in a hotel nearby.

The woman was leaning over a garbage bin. The bright lights of a travel agency in front of her showed clearly her pale sallow face and disorderly auburn hair hanging down from her head. She was scavenging the garbage bin. All sticks and rags, she was such a pitiful-looking scarecrow, they felt sorry for her.

They halted, undecided between walking on and making a detour, but their car was parked right there in Olive Street, not far from the woman. They walked on.

As they came near the woman, they saw that she was eating scraps of food she was picking up, piece by piece, from the garbage bin. They walked on, their eyes averted from shock and pity for her.

They had passed the woman and were approaching their car when Clara halted and looked back at her. He was watching Clara, wondering what had come over her, when she took out three one-dollar bills from her purse and walked back to the woman. She gave the woman the money and said she was sorry it was all that she could spare for her.

"Bless my wife for her kind heart," he said to himself as he squeezed her hand.

What he did took her by surprise, she pulled her hand away and said, "What did you do that for?"

"It's for the good thing that you did last week. Do you remember the poor woman we saw there across the street last week? You even gave her money."

"Of course, I remember her. One does not forget someone like her. The poor woman! I never expected to see someone like her in this country. Never! Imagine, eating scraps of food in a garbage bin!"

"There are poor hungry people even here in America, although they are not as many as what we have in our own country."

"I have thought before that no one gets hungry here and no one begs here, for as I can see, there are enough food and other things for everyone in this country."

"That is true."

"Then, how come there are still beggars here?"

"There will always be beggars even here in America for as long as there are those who prefer to beg than work."

She said, a puzzled look in her face, "Are they to blame for what has become of them? They could be just out of luck or too ill to work."

"I will grant you that. Some of them are deserving of help, like that poor woman, but I doubt it if you can say that of the panhandler over there, across the street."

A tin can full of coins and paper money laid at his feet, the panhandler was looking about pleadingly in the customary beggar's pose that called on the charity of passersby.

He looked on, frowning in disgust, at the panhandler. He and others like him were examples of the erosion of America's work ethic. It made this country rich and powerful. Its erosion in turn was leading the country into moral decay. Such a decay he saw was now pervasive in the cult of instant gratification in sex and drugs, in sloth, greed and violence, and in the loss of moral and family values. America, he feared, maybe headed the way of ancient Rome. Internal decay and corruption had so weakened it, it could not resist the barbarians who ultimately conquered it.

"Did you notice," he said to Clara, "how big and strong that panhandler is?"

"What are you trying to tell me?"

"Don't you see how ridiculous he looks? A big healthy man like him begging for alms? He can work anytime if only he has the mind for it. Have you seen men like him begging in the streets of Manila?"

"Never. Only the elderly, the young children and the infirm beg in Manila. What kept our men from begging there?"

"Simple. They are too proud to be seen begging in the street. They would rather steal than beg."

"Why, then, does that panhandler beg?"

"Unlike the poor men in Manila, he is not proud enough to keep himself from begging."

"You also said he is healthy and strong enough to work."

"He is, but you cannot expect him to work when he finds it easier to live on the charity of kindhearted people, and there are many such people in this country. Americans are by nature a friendly kindhearted people, generous to a fault."

"Can the beggars here live on what they get from those kindhearted people?"

"They will stop begging only when they don't get enough from it. You will be surprised by how much they are getting. I have read somewhere that a beggar's average daily take here in Los Angeles is eighty dollars. Can you imagine that? Eighty dollars! That is much more than what you and I can earn in a day's work!"

"Still, a beggar won't amount to anything—not in Manila and not here in Los Angeles. They must be helped get back on their feet."

"There is nothing anyone can do for those who have given up on themselves."

"I'm sorry for them. They are missing out on the many opportunities in this country."

"They are, but not us; we won't."

The glint in Clara's eyes, her hand on his arm as they walked on, sent surging in Simon's heart, pride and determination. They will do well, here in America. Nothing in the world could stop them from achieving that.

They were now approaching Hill Street. At the back of the street was marked in Simon's eyes the boundary between the elegant area they had just left and the decaying core of downtown Los Angeles they were now approaching.

Having by then forgotten the woman food scavenger and the panhandler, Simon looked around cheerfully. A beautiful brown leather attaché case at the base of a white pedestal was on display in the glass window of an office supply store.

"It sure is a nice attaché case," Clara said.

He nodded as he gazed at the attaché case, impressed with its trim design, glossy soft leather cover and gold-plated lock. He looked down at its price tag and, upon reading its price of one hundred twenty dollars, he said, "It is expensive, too."

"But you will be distinguished-looking, holding it in your hand."

"Perish the thought. I have no need for that," he said as he turned his gaze to a pair of fountain pen and ballpoint pen in a blue felt case at the top of the pedestal. "While it will go well with those handsome articles there, I have no need for any of them in my work as a busboy, dishwasher and janitor in L and S."

"You will not always be mopping the floor and busing and washing dishes. You will need the attaché case when you land a teaching job."

"I may buy it only if and when the time for that has come."

Simon's face assumed a grave look as he and Clara resumed walking toward Hill Street. The buildings there and in Broadway, Spring and Main Streets farther ahead were mostly old and unkempt. Poor struggling immigrants like them belonged properly to that part of downtown Los Angeles. Clara worked there. The area they had just left of chic shops and fancy restaurants, of five-star hotels and modern office buildings was for the likes of Saul Levy.

The contrast was sharper farther away, from Main Street to Alameda. This was one depressed area in Los Angeles. He and Clara had shopped a few times in the garment district, which lay in the area.

What a fright Clara had on their last visit there, and he could only blame himself for it. They had made their last stop in a garment store and he was driving leisurely down the street, his attention turned to Clara, who was talking enthusiastically about the bargain she got in the store. Distracted, he made a wrong turn and he found himself driving in an unfamiliar street.

He drove on, increasingly worried by what he saw there. Litter was everywhere in the street. Some of the buildings there were abandoned, their glass windows smashed or boarded up with plywood, their grimy walls sprayed with graffiti. He saw desperate-looking men outside a bar, between a delicatessen and a flophouse. Not far from there, a drunk was keeping beat to his falsetto singing with a liquor bottle in a brown bag held up in his hand.

They had entered by accident the dark recesses of Los Angeles. He made a turn in another street until, fearful that he might only be driving in circles, he drove on in the street until he saw, much to his relief, a sign to an eastbound ramp of Santa Monica Freeway. He entered it without a moment's hesitation and felt, right on picking up speed on the freeway, as if he and Clara had escaped with their lives from some danger lurking, back there.

"Here we are," she said at the building of her employer, a jewelry importer.

"Take care now," he said, as he squeezed then released her hand as the glass door opened for her.

She smiled in appreciation of his parting gesture and walked on in the lobby. Suddenly she halted and walked back to him. Puzzled, he met her near the open door.

"I almost forgot," she said. "Will you buy me a tray of dozen eggs and a box of flour at Tom's? I'll need them for the cake I'll bake when I get home. If you have enough money, you might as well buy the groceries and food items we need for the rest of the week. Lorna knows them."

He nodded in acknowledgement of her orders and watched her as she entered the elevator. He proceeded to the bus stop at the corner of Broadway and Eighth Street and took the Line 14 bus. It was almost empty of passengers. He took a seat by a window and, as the bus moved on, watched the stores in Broadway. Many of them carried Spanish names. The people walking on the sidewalk or peering at the stores' display windows were mostly Latinos. Many of the men there were wearing hats, loud long-sleeved shirts and fancy boots, their faces sporting mustaches. It was a sight that no longer puzzled him as it did when he was newly arrived in Los Angeles.

A city in Mexico may look just like that.

If he could typecast them, it would be by the way they were dressed and swaggered on Broadway, as if they owned the place, just as they did, once upon a time. California was then a neglected part of the Spanish American empire passed on to Mexico when it became independent in 1821. But, as he knew too, the Californios, as the Hispanic settlers and the American pioneers were called, resisted the few years the territory was under Mexico's marginal rule to the extent of establishing California's short-lived republic. Mexico ceded California to the United States in 1848. Whatever notions those fellows on the sidewalk may have on California's past, like him, they could now aim for the big time in Los Angeles.

The plastic bus window was not thick enough to keep out the noise made by the people on the sidewalk and the lively, but repetitive Hispanic songs blaring out from the stores. He learned within a short time of his arrival in Los Angeles that Latinos dominated Broadway by sheer numbers. The public buses made it a convenient shopping destination for them, most of whom had no cars.

Some of the pedestrians were gaping at the shops, the buildings and everything else around them, a sign that they were newly arrived in Los Angeles and undergoing some kind of a culture shock.

He watched them, smiling in amusement, for he himself had gone through the same experience. In due time, like him, they will get used to the place. Unlike him, though, most of them came illegally and will stay illegal. Getting a lawyer to help them legalize their status was, for them, a bothersome and avoidable expense.

His case was altogether different. He was not undocumented. He had never been in illegal status. Saul Levy was only essentially changing his status and that of his family from tourists to legal permanent residents by way of political asylum. He had something to preserve and protect. Too bad if those people on the sidewalk were caught and deported, but they could always try to cross again from Mexico, as they had been doing.

He, on the other hand, did not have the luxury of a second chance in this country. If he blew it, that will be the end for him and his family in America. They cannot swim across the Pacific Ocean, as the Latinos could cross the United States' porous southern border.

The bus, by his count, had made five stops by the time it had passed by the premises of the *Los Angeles Times*. By then, the bus was full and passengers filled its seats and crowded its aisle.

The bus moved on and turned left on First Street as he tried to ignore the noise, the faint smell of sweat, and the four or five teenagers who, while talking in Spanish and slang English, were engaged in horseplay in the crowded aisle a few feet away from him.

He won't get himself worked up over the teenagers' loathsome behavior, and he ignored them by looking outside. He ignored as well the young children who added to the irksome noise with their own demands, complaints and lusty persistent crying, and he had thought that, on leaving Manila, wrongly it turned out now, he was past those city bus rides that were just as noisy and cramped as this one. At least this bus, like all the other buses in Los Angeles, had air-conditioning. It held in check body heat and odor from fouling up the air inside the bus. Without this cool air, it would have been intolerable inside the bus.

The child in the arms of a woman seated beside him began to stir. The woman brushed with her palm the child's back, sending him back to sleep. They looked like native Indians, their skin dark brown from long exposure to the sun. The woman's gnarled hands and her deeply lined sunburned face and hollow cheeks told him this was a peasant woman who had eked out a living from the sun-baked soil of Mexico or in any of the Central and South American countries. He had read on those countries and was struck by their similarity with his own country, like the violence, the corruption and the widespread poverty. The chief victims were the native Indians like this woman seated beside him. If she had stayed in her country, she and her child would have faced nothing but a life of hardship, poverty and misery.

He looked outside, pity and sympathy welling in his heart for the woman and her sleeping child. He could only imagine what she went through to get to the United States. Perhaps she braved a crossing at night of the Rio Grande to Texas, past border guards, and then moved on to Los Angeles. She may have crawled with her child strapped to her back in the rumored tunnel from Tijuana to San Diego. Just as likely, she may have made a risky run with her child across the border to Arizona. She made it with her child, never mind if in the process she had forked over her life savings to the human smugglers who brought her and her child across the border to the United States. He had seen on TV such illegal border crossings.

Compared to them, he and his family had an easy time in coming to the United States. All they did was talk the consul, who faced them across the glass window in the air-conditioned U.S. consular office in Manila, into stamping U.S. visas on their passports. Their airplane ride from Manila to Los Angeles was just as pleasant.

The bus moved on. He had by then slipped into a benign indifference and was used to the noise inside the bus. He even glanced tolerantly at the unruly teenagers. Their behavior had annoyed him because it did not conform to the deportment he expected of young people like them. He had compared them with his own children, who behaved properly. But he and Clara had brought up Lorna and Sonny differently from those rowdy young people. He should give them allowance for that. He should be more tolerant. After all, whatever were their cultural and behavioral differences, they shared one thing: they were newcomers making a try at the good life in America.

A friendly gesture was in order, and he could express it best to the woman seated beside him.

"Su hijo es muy bonito," he said to the woman with the little Spanish that he knew.

The woman, her eyes wide in surprise, murmured shyly, *"Muchas gracias, senor."*

A smile on his face, he nodded, pleased with himself for having let out his feelings with the peasant woman. He was satisfied with himself, and he settled himself comfortably on his seat to enjoy the view outside.

A short while later, he said to the woman, *"Adios, senora y buenos dias."*

He made his way through the crowded aisle to the exit moments before the bus stopped on Spencer Street. He got off there and crossed it at the turn of the traffic light to green. Fairfield High School was at the other side of the street. He was more than halfway across the street when he heard shouts and cheers coming from the school's playing field.

His watch showed him the time: ten minutes past eleven o'clock. The trial run for the school's track team was still going on. He hurried on. Sonny was there, competing for a slot in the school's track team. Lorna was there too, cheering for her brother. She tagged along purposely for the track tryouts. School was out in Fairfield

High for the spring break. He was glad for that. It left many vacant slots in the school parking lot. He parked his car there to save on the exorbitant parking fees in downtown Los Angeles. He and Clara took the bus in going to Saul Levy's law office.

He saw, the moment he entered a corner of the playing field, a serpentine line of some fifteen to twenty runners who were making a turn in the oval toward the finish line. He recognized Sonny among the runners in his yellow jersey with black side stripes. Sonny was figuring in a close finish with the two leading runners. He was right behind the boy running second and a few paces behind the leading runner.

Suddenly Sonny spurted forward and passed the runner ahead of him. He sprinted after the leading runner, but then the leading runner picked up speed too and crossed the finish line a stride ahead of Sonny.

The crowd in the bleachers, made up of the school's students, roared in approval, which they accompanied with the clapping of their hands.

His face was beaming as he too applauded Sonny's wonderful run. He was tempted to tell the man beside him that the runner-up was his son. But he restrained himself, for he was averse to bragging. It was enough that his son had done well.

He watched Sonny as he and the other runners then joined the crowd in the bleachers. The school's football players watching from the sidelines took their turn at the playing field. The crowd cheered when the public address system then announced the runners who had made it to the finals. He smiled and nodded, pleased and satisfied, to the announcement of Sonny's name.

The shadow on the grass of a bird in flight then led him to the bleachers. He looked up and saw it was a hawk, a lone bird flying in the sky. Like the hawk, his son had soared and higher still he will soar, in athletics and in academics in Fairfield High. He had A-1 children. Lorna and Sonny were straight-A students. All in one morning his family had done exceedingly well. His children will be pleased to learn about the result of the interview with Saul Levy.

Just then, a boy and a girl stood up and began to dance, to the delight of the crowd in the bleachers. They swung their arms and hips to the beat of rock music from a portable radio and the enthusiastic clapping of the crowd.

He watched the dancers, touched by the spontaneity of their dance and the crowd's hearty response to it. He was seeing there an expression of young people's natural exuberance and the easy connection they made with each other. His children were in the crowd. They were a part of it. They belonged there. They had formed deep enduring friendship from shared learning experiences with their schoolmates. His children were happily adjusted to their new school and their new country.

A smile broke out of his face when he saw Sonny and Lorna waving at him. They peeled off from the crowd and stepped down from the bleachers. He met them at the playing field's main exit.

"Did you see Sonny run, Dad?" Lorna asked him.

"Yes, right to the finish."

He turned to Sonny and said, "That was some race you ran, son."

"I could have won it," Sonny said regretfully.

"It was only the trial run," Lorna said to Sonny. "You will make Smith eat dust at the finals."

"Thanks for the vote of confidence," Sonny said to his sister.

Sonny's face, a cross between his face and Clara's, and better looking, glinted with perspiration. He wiped it with the towel slung over his neck and shoulder.

He laid an arm on Sonny's shoulder as they walked on toward the parking lot. Flanked by his children, they looked like a remarkable trio. Sonny to his right was a few inches taller. He was the quiet type. Lorna to his left was Clara's bubbly young version of herself. She reached up to his ear.

"As I have told you often enough," he said to them, "you cannot always win. The important thing is to give your best always to whatever you do. You ran a good race, Sonny. It is not to flatter you when I say that a few more yards and you could have overtaken the leading runner."

"Next time, Dad, at the finals, I'll do exactly that. I'll beat Smith when we run again."

"Good, that will be showing them—you, beating all the other runners. Not only did you do well in the race, you learned from it. It's another lesson for both of you. You will succeed in whatever you aim for if you try hard enough. Don't ever forget that."

"I know it, I know it," Lorna said. "You are leading up to

something, Dad. I know it is good news. Our lawyer can get us our green cards, right, Dad?"

He looked back and, finding they were by themselves, he said, "Our lawyer will apply us for political asylum, a step in getting our green cards."

"It sounds heavy and complicated," Lorna said, the tone of her voice turned low and somber.

"It is to us, but not to our lawyer. He knows what to do."

"How long do we have to wait for our green cards, Dad?" Sonny asked.

"I don't know. But we can have temporary work permits in just a short time."

"How do you like that? I can work now," Sonny said. "I can help even more with our expenses."

"Me, too," Lorna said with renewed enthusiasm. "Once I get a job, I'll buy us a new car."

"Another car? We already have our car," Sonny said.

"How about a trip to San Francisco?" Lorna said.

They looked back when they heard someone calling out to Sonny. Rod and Andrew, Sonny's friends and classmates, were walking briskly toward them.

He knew them quite well. They often came to their apartment to do their homework with Sonny. A typical-looking pair of young high school students, Rod was of medium height and had dark curly hair. He was originally from Argentina. Tall and skinny Andrew had a brown hair, a true Anglo.

"Good morning, sir," they said to him.

He returned their greeting and saw in the way Rod and Andrew, Sonny and Lorna were looking at each other, their need to be by themselves. He must leave them so they could talk freely.

"I'll wait for you in the car," he said to Sonny and Lorna as he walked away.

Every sound in the parking lot beneath the bleachers was amplified, and he could hear the conversation between Lorna and Sonny, Rod and Andrew.

"Betting is going on for the final race. Do you want to bet on yourself?" Rod asked Sonny.

"No. I don't gamble," Sonny replied. "You place a bet if you want. I'll run the race for you."

"Very well if that is what you want," Andrew said. "But you might want to know the odds are even between you and Smith."

"Make it eight to two in favor of Sonny," Lorna said. "My brother can easily outrun Smith."

Simon never gambled, and he taught his children not to gamble. He was confident, though, as he was approaching their car, that a bet placed on his son will be a sure winner.

Chapter 4

Sonny was turning their car toward Avery Avenue when Simon saw boys playing soccer football in the street.

"Slow down," he said to Sonny, his hand tamping the air to stress his order.

He watched the boys closely. One never knew what they might suddenly do. They might sprint across the path of their car in a test of Sonny's reflexes and of how fast they could run.

"Why do those boys appropriate the street for their game?" Lorna said from the backseat. "Where do they think they are—in Mexico? This is a street, not a playing field."

Simon kept quiet so as not to add to Lorna's annoyance with the boys. They will just have to be more tolerant of them. They were only taking after their elders, who did as they pleased, there in Avery Avenue.

Sonny drove past a car parked in the street. Someone underneath its raised hood was working on its engine, in violation of a local ordinance which prohibited car repairs done in the street. It was typical of how their neighbors flaunted the law. Their kind of breeding was also evident in the loud Hispanic music blaring out from an apartment there.

The boys stopped their game and watched sullenly as Sonny drove their car past them. He drove on and passed a palm tree on the sidewalk. A discarded mattress was leaning on it, the ground around it littered with trash.

He turned their car right, toward the carport, which sloped down to the sidewalk, and stopped it at its parking space in the carport's right corner.

They had arrived home, the first unit in the ground floor near the tall iron gate of the two-floor apartment building.

Simon frowned the moment he left the car. The carport's right wall had been defaced again with graffiti. The vulgar taunting scrawl was not there early in the morning. The wall had been whitewashed only the other day. It took him and Clara weeks of nagging before Gonzaga, the apartment owner, had an earlier graffiti on the wall whitewashed. Now this. It will take another round of nagging before Gonzaga will have it whitewashed again. Gonzaga will take his time since he did not live there and did not have to put up with that unsightly and provocative graffiti.

Sonny and Lorna had also seen the defaced wall.

"The gangsters are at it again," Lorna said.

"You know who did it," Sonny said as he watched the boys playing soccer football in the street.

Simon watched the boys, wondering if they were the guilty party. They were playing on and seemed innocent of the deed. The teenage gang infesting their neighborhood could have done it. It made its presence known with the graffiti its gang members sprayed on walls and street signs. There were gangs too in his home country, but they seldom indulged in vandalism like that.

"We should move out of this place, Dad," Sonny said.

"You know how I've long wanted us to move to Glendale, but we won't pass the credit check there."

"I like Glendale, too," Lorna said, "but, Dad, there maybe other nice places in Los Angeles that don't require a credit check."

"I know, I know," he said, as he dismissed Lorna's suggestion with an impatient wave of his hand. His heart was set on Glendale. He liked it from the very first time he visited it and walked down on its clean and quiet tree-lined streets. Glendale could wait, though, until he had established a good credit record, a requirement in renting an apartment there.

"Get the groceries," he said to Lorna and Sonny.

They took out from the rear seat of the car the bags of groceries they bought on their way home in Tom's Supermarket, two blocks away on Third Street.

They were approaching the gate when someone in the apartment above the carport said to them, "What are you two doing here at this time of the day? Are you not supposed to be in school?"

The friendly voice was Mama Berta's. The old woman was at the window of her apartment overlooking the street.

"We have no classes today; it's the spring break," Sonny said to Mama Berta.

"Would you like us to help you baby-sit the children?" Lorna said to Mama Berta.

"Of course, you know how much I like that," Mama Berta replied. She earned a living baby-sitting six young children.

"We'll go there after lunch," Lorna said.

"Very well, I'll wait for you," Mama Berta said.

Simon listened to the friendly talk between Mama Berta and his children. They earned a little money by helping the old woman baby-sit the young children. He watched them, pleased with them, as they passed through the gate Lorna had opened with her key.

A frown replaced the pleased look in his face when he saw the storage cabinet in front of their car, unsightly with rags hanging down from its sagging partly open door. It had been ransacked again, although it contained only rags and soiled clothes worth nothing. It was forced open in a burglary attempt long ago. Gonzaga never bothered to have its lock fixed, for it will only be forced open again.

He walked toward the cabinet, opened it, threw the rags inside and closed it. Then he washed his hands from the faucet in the carport.

As he next checked the car doors, the thought went through in his mind that he could not be too careful with the kind of neighborhood he had. The ransacked cabinet, the graffiti on the wall, the discarded mattress leaning on the palm tree, the ground around it littered with trash, the boys playing in the street, a man doing repair work on his car in the street, the loud music blaring from an apartment—all of those confirmed his children's low opinion of it

Their neighborhood was actually much worse than that. Starting late in the afternoon until late at night, the men in the other apartment buildings will then be out in the street and on the sidewalk, plying the illicit drug trade. A month ago, two young hoods mugged a neighbor living upstairs as he was leaving his car in the carport. Another time, he was jolted from his lunch by a gunshot. He looked out from the kitchen window and saw someone slumped dead on the steering wheel of a car parked in the street. He learned later on that the man was killed for cheating on a drug deal.

He would not have taken the apartment had he known the kind of neighborhood he would have. But they were then in a hurry to leave the house of Clara's cousin in West Covina. They proceeded there on their arrival in the United States and lived in the garage converted into living quarters. The wife of Clara's cousin's did not like them, why he never knew. They were not freeloaders; they paid rent. She forced them out on the pretext that she was converting their living quarters into a game room.

Through Phil, who knew Gonzaga, they got the apartment in the ground floor of the apartment building. It was one of three units in the ground floor, the rest, five of them, were in the second floor. The apartment was shabby, but Gonzaga promised to repaint the walls and change the carpet. That was almost five months ago, and he was still waiting for Gonzaga to keep his promise. At least Gonzaga did not require a credit check. Being new in the country, they had no credit record yet. The rent was low and he took it right away. He was glad the unit they had chanced upon was in the ground floor near the gate. They did not have to climb the stairs in the apartment building.

He waved a friendly greeting as he looked up at Mama Berta. She smiled and waved back at him. She was at the window of her apartment, the self-appointed sentry of their apartment building. It was their own compact community of Filipinos kept off by the tall iron gate from the rest of the neighborhood.

He glanced, out of habit, at a house at the left side of the apartment building. The old man, as usual, was seated on his rocking chair beside his wife at the porch of their rented home, vintage 1920s. A gaunt tree turning a new leaf marked the boundary between the old man's house and the apartment building.

"Buenos dias, senor y senora. Esta muy buen dia," he said to the old man and his wife.

They smiled and returned his greeting, also in Spanish. The old man then pointed at his lawn and commented at how the rains the week before had made the grass there a verdant green again, although crab grass had also appeared there.

He shook his head in faked sympathy. The old man was complaining about crab grass to him who did not have even a single blade of grass outside his apartment. The only vegetation there was in the few potted plants on the ground, below the plate glass picture window in the living room.

The old man then switched to talking about the crops he used to raise as a young man in Sonora. He nodded as he listened to the old man, whom he considered as a friend, although they never went beyond exchanging friendly greetings every time they saw each other.

It was a routine he established the first time he saw the old man a few days after their arrival in the apartment. He never dropped by the old man's house for a chat. He never even knew the old man's name. The Latinos, though, who dominated their neighborhood, had noticed this friendliness between him and the old man, and it served him well.

They looked up to the old man. He must have been somebody big, back in Mexico. As a result, the teenage gang and the drug peddlers infesting the neighborhood never gave him and his family any trouble except for the graffiti on the wall and the ransacked storage cabinet in the carport.

Two young men walking by on the sidewalk bowed their heads as they said to the old man and his wife, *"Buenos dias, senor y senora. Tenemos buen dia aqui."*

He felt sorry for them as he watched them. They kept their cultural identity intact by speaking solely in Spanish. It had the unfortunate consequence of enclosing them in a kind of linguistic cocoon. Their inability to speak in English kept them apart from the rest of the country and the many opportunities it offered.

The old man returned their greeting and resumed talking about his life as a young man in Sonora.

He said to the old man, *"Tiene tierra rica alli, senor."*

The old man nodded, smiling, in response to the compliment he made to him.

He did not want to be detained any longer, though, and he waved in good-bye as he said to them, *"Hasta la vista! El buen dia es para todos nosotros."*

He walked on toward the gate and opened it with his key. He was closing it when he saw through the vine-topped chain-link fence, Myrtle at work in her garden. She was bent over a flowering plant, aerating its soil with a trowel in her gloved hand.

A woman in her late sixties, her hair the color of hay, she spent a great deal of time gardening. The result of her work, he observed with great admiration, was Myrtle's garden decked out in a riot of colors. There were flowers all over the garden, solitary, in pairs or clustered in beds of verdant green leaves. Trees veiled with leafy branches hovered over her garden. It was like a meadow in their neighborhood of asphalt street, the old couple's bungalow, Myrtle's ranch-type house, and concrete and wooden apartment buildings.

"How are you this morning, Myrtle?" he said to her.

She looked up over her shoulder and said, "Oh, it is you, Simon. I'm fine, just fine."

She stood up, smiling, baring white even teeth, the trowel in her gloved hand caked with mud.

She asked, "How about you? How are you doing?"

"I can't complain, not with this nice weather."

"What a nice weather we are having. It is just right for a day in Griffith Park."

"You already have your own corner of Griffith Park, right there in your garden."

"Thank you," she said, smiling. "It's so nice of you to say that."

Suddenly she turned toward the street and looked up, her mouth hanging open in astonishment. He looked up too and saw the ball the boys were playing with, hurtling toward him and Myrtle. He raised his arm to ward it off, but the ball fell short. It bounced instead against the gate, then on the sidewalk, landing finally on top of the hedge in front of Myrtle's house.

A boy ran toward the hedge, picked up the ball and threw it back to his playmates. He was about to run back to the street when he saw a packet secreted in the hedge. He pried it out with his fingers and removed its plastic wrapping. He yelled in delight when he saw that it contained cocaine. He held it up promptly for his playmates to see.

The other boys came quickly, jostling each other for a close look at the drug. A boy asked for a share of it, which in an instant rose in a unanimous demand from the other boys. The finder said no, and to avoid the drug from being forcibly taken away from him by his playmates, he fled to his home, an apartment at the other side of Myrtle's house.

He was standing by the glass picture window of his apartment the day before when the police in an unmarked prowl car swooped down on the drug peddlers. One of them must have hidden the packet of cocaine in the hedge.

He watched the boys, very much disturbed, as they returned to their game quite unaware of how they had been corrupted so young by this evil presence in their neighborhood.

"Did you see how they went after that drug, like it was a bag of candy?" he said to Myrtle.

"It is terrible. They are only kids. We did not have anything like that here before those people moved in here."

He nodded in sympathy to Myrtle, whose eyes were fixed wistfully to the street. She told him once that Avery Avenue, until fifteen, twenty years ago, was a quiet pleasant street lined with homes like hers. She was the last holdout, the last of the original homeowners in the neighborhood. Her neighbors sold their houses and moved elsewhere.

With their departure, the character of Avery Avenue changed. Except for Myrtle's and the old couple's homes, all the houses there were torn down for the apartment buildings now lining the street. Transients now made up most of its population. Its racial makeup had changed too from predominantly white to Hispanic, with a sprinkling of Filipinos living in their apartment building.

It was not the same quiet peaceful neighborhood Myrtle knew before. It was now a hotbed of the illicit drug trade.

Men dressed in T-shirts and undershirts, naked to the waist on warm days and with tattoos on their arms, backs and chests, sold cocaine and marijuana from late afternoon to late in the evening, there in the street and on the sidewalk. Money and drug changed hands every time a car came and pulled over. The drug transactions were made within view of those very same boys playing soccer football in the street.

The police often raided the street, but for every drug peddler they caught, another one would take his place. They were part of the drug cartels whose tentacles extended from Mexico and Central and South America. They brought to his neighborhood and the rest of the United States, this scourge of drug addiction.

He never knew why Myrtle stayed on in her house. Mama Berta told him once that Myrtle had been trying to sell her house, but could not get the right price for it. The old woman was, however, not a very reliable source of information. More likely, Myrtle stayed on out of pride and stubbornness. It was her home and no amount of drug peddling done right at her doorstep could force her out of it.

They parted wordlessly, Myrtle to her gardening and Simon to his apartment. He glanced at Myrtle before ascending the few flights of steps to his apartment. He was sorry for her. She was stuck there in a good neighborhood turned bad. At least he and his family could leave for a nice place like Glendale. He needed only to establish a good credit record with the secured credit card he was expecting in the mail any day now.

The apartment, as he opened the door, was not as bright now as it was earlier in the morning. The sun was then shining through the wide plate glass picture window and on the couch, its back set against the windowsill. The picture window had a nice view of the vine-topped chain-link fence and Myrtle's house and garden.

He looked around at his apartment. His easy chair stood in a corner with the small bookshelf beside it, near the couch where Sonny slept. The cabinet, with the telephone on top and a radio-cassette recorder in a shelf, stood facing the picture window, its back set against the wall. The TV set faced the door to the apartment.

From the kitchen came the smell of frying onion and garlic. Lorna was preparing their lunch. He could hear from the bathroom, Sonny singing in his off-key voice, the Beatles' *Hard Day's Night*. His son had many talents, but singing was not one of them. Unlike Lorna who sang well, he did not inherit Clara's fine singing voice.

He was filled with a sense of home as he looked around at the apartment. It was small, shabby and old, but it was their home. They slowly acquired things that made a home—the couch, the cabinet, easy chair, small bookshelf and dining set they bought in thrift stores, the television set staring blankly at him, one of two they owned, the other one placed in the master bedroom.

They arrived in the apartment five months ago without a single piece of furniture. For the first few days of their arrival there, they ate on cardboard boxes set upright and watched TV while seated on the carpet, their backs against the wall. It was fun, though.

He went to the closet near the door to the master bedroom and heard more clearly, Sonny singing in the bathroom, its door an arm's length away from him. He took out his slippers from the shoe rack hanging in the closet door and dropped them on the carpet. Then he removed from his right foot his shoe and sock and slid his foot into the right slipper. He followed this procedure with the other foot, after which he put his shoes with the socks inside into the shoe rack.

For the next step in this procedure he usually followed on arriving home, he entered the master bedroom cramped with a double bed and a cabinet with a TV set on top, and changed into his house clothes. Lorna's bedroom near the kitchen was smaller. It had a single bed and a small cabinet.

He returned to the living room, whistling *Some Enchanted Evening,* and sat down on his easy chair. His elbow laid on the armrest, he scanned with his finger, the books in his bookshelf. He looked on at Neruda's book of poems, smiling from the pleasure he got in reading through it last night. He settled, though, for Malamud's beautiful short story, *The Magic Barrel.* It was one of his favorite short stories, and he had not read it for some time. He pulled out the book on great Jewish short stories, where the story was one of the selections, and began to read it.

The minutes passed. He saw Sonny leaving the bathroom and opening the other closet there where he kept his things. He read on with his ears cocked for Lorna's announcement that lunch was ready. The smell of food wafting from the kitchen made him hungry. He closed the book, stood up with the book nestled in his arm, and went to the kitchen.

He asked Lorna, "Is lunch ready yet?"

"A few more minutes, Dad, but I cannot do everything here. Where is Sonny?"

She looked for Sonny in the living room. Sonny was not there, and she went to the master bedroom.

Simon, in the meantime, had lifted the pot cover and gazed at the marinated pork cooking in oil, garlic, onion, soy sauce and vinegar. He could hear, as he looked on at the food, Lorna and Sonny having an argument in the master bedroom.

"But I'm reviewing for the tests after the spring break," Sonny said.

"You have the whole day to do that. Help me with the kitchen chore and set the table."

Lorna returned to the kitchen, followed by a grumbling Sonny.

He watched them, amused at how Lorna dominated her younger brother. That was the pecking order among Filipino siblings.

They went about with their chores in the kitchen, while he returned to his easy chair. He resumed reading the short story where he had left off at the point in the story where the matchmaker had arranged a date for the hero, a young rabbi looking for a wife. He read a few more pages and closed the book and put it back in the bookshelf. He had lost the mood for reading, his attention drawn again to the food. He glanced at the kitchen and the dining table: there was no sign yet that lunch would soon be ready.

He felt, as he then turned his gaze to Myrtle's house and the apartment building behind it, grateful for the things he and his family were enjoying in America. A busboy, dishwasher and janitor like him earning below the minimum wage could afford to buy and eat the same kind of food the President of the United States ate at the White House.

With the thirty dollars they spent in Tom's Supermarket, he and his children went home with several pounds of beef and pork, a bag of chicken leg quarters, a bag of potatoes, fruits, shrimp, two marinated milkfish, vegetables, two trays of eggs, a bag of flour, a small sack of rice and a gallon of milk.

They bought enough food in Tom's Supermarket to last the four of them for an entire week. They could save even more by shopping at the produce market in Stanford Street, or in Central Market in Hill Street. Sometimes, on Saturdays, he and Clara would leave their apartment early in the morning and drive all the way on the Harbor Freeway to the seafood market in San Pedro, where the seafood there was fresh and cost less.

He smiled, pleased to know that good food was always at their dining table at mealtime. Clara and Lorna never missed cooking something filling and delicious—the pork stew for lunch today, maybe steamed fish tonight, or roast beef tomorrow.

The smile on his face disappeared, replaced by a frown, at how far different it was back in his homeland with its meager fare at their dining table there. Food there was expensive and often scarce, an absurd situation considering that it had bountiful lands in which to plant food crops and raise poultry and livestock. It had rich marine resources until pollution, trawl and dynamite fishing had destroyed them. Hoarding by the Chinese merchants, who controlled the country's retail trade, and primitive production methods made it a rice-producing country that imported rice, a sugar-producing country that imported sugar. Its feudal inefficient and corrupt economic system turned for the worse during the Marcos dictatorship. Marcos and his wife Imelda plundered the treasury and the nation's patrimony. They stole his freedom, even the food on his dining table.

Thinking about Marcos and his wife had so upset him, to divert his mind, he turned his gaze outside, to Myrtle's house and garden. He and his family had managed to get out of their homeland. They could now have here in America, a bright future denied them in the Philippines. But it will not be easy. The elation he felt moments after he and Clara left Saul Levy's law office was long gone, replaced by a sober appraisal of this country they now call home.

America maybe a country of immigrants, but he knew racial prejudice had always been a problem here. While things were not as bad now as before, there was a possible backlash by mainstream American society to present-day immigration. Most of the immigrants before came from Europe. Those coming now were mostly from Asia, the Middle East, South and Central America, Mexico and Africa. This made racial division sharp.

He creased his brow at the possibility, though remote, of America returning to some dark periods in its history. Native American tribes and the blacks were not treated well then, along with the general prejudice against Jews, Catholics and Asians.

Thinking about them was getting too much for him, and he turned his gaze to the sky. Storm clouds of racial conflict and prejudice had now and then darkened the sky over America, but he had read enough of American history to know that those events that had passed in his mind constituted but one small critical view of this country. They were deviations from the principles of freedom, justice, equality, fairness and tolerance America was founded on. Efforts were always made to correct those deviations. No price was too great, as in the issue of the blacks' slavery, the Americans abolished to the extent of engaging in a bloody civil war over it.

It was those blacks' misfortune that they lost in the intermittent tribal wars in Africa and sold as slaves by their fellow blacks. It was their good fortune that they ended up in America where, unlike in other times and in other lands, they received a generally benign treatment and were eventually accepted as part of the mainstream American society.

Had the blacks' slavery happened, not in America, but in Nazi Germany, instead of getting their freedom through Abraham Lincoln's Emancipation Proclamation, they would have been exterminated by Adolf Hitler, along with millions of Jews and other people Hitler considered as inferior to his German Master Race.

He turned his gaze to Myrtle's house and garden hemmed in on three sides by apartment buildings. Their residents were mostly immigrants like him. Myrtle and her home symbolized America under siege by the teeming millions from Mexico, Asia, Africa, the Middle East and South and Central America trying to get into the country. On the other hand, in becoming truly multiracial, America was making itself a color-blind country. This will be the real Brave New World and it was beginning to happen in America. It is the kind of world where he and his family belonged.

Despite its ills, vices and shortcomings, America, with its democratic principles, its capacity for tolerance, its deep sense of fairness and its riches and openness, was to him a land of freedom and opportunity. They were qualities that made it his ideal sanctuary from the evil that hounded him in his own country.

Lunch was almost ready. This was announced by the clatter of plates, spoons and forks Sonny was putting on the dining table.

He stood up and followed Sonny to the kitchen for a look at the food. Lorna was done with cooking. A dipper in her hand, she was about to ladle the soup.

"I hope your pork stew tastes as good as it smells," he said to Lorna.

"Try it, Dad," she said as she gave him a fork. "You will like it; it is very tasty."

"Let Dad be the judge of that," Sonny, who stood behind Lorna, said.

Lorna, in reaction to what Sonny said, swung her elbow at his stomach.

Simon frowned in disapproval of what Lorna did to Sonny, a reaction he did not really feel, though, for he knew Lorna was fond of her younger brother. She was simply annoyed and embarrassed that Sonny had questioned her skill in cooking, right in his presence.

He was satisfied to see them regard him respectfully as he then removed the pot cover and looked down at the pot. Steam rose from it, nearly stinging his face had he not drawn back quickly enough. The food looked inviting, though, with steam rising from it, for he liked his food hot. He waited until the steam had dissipated, then he speared a piece of pork with the fork, blew at it until it had cooled a bit and then shoveled it into his mouth. He chewed the meat, savoring its delicious taste.

"It is good," he said to Lorna. "You cook like your mother."

"Mom is a good teacher," Lorna said, smiling.

"Can I also have a taste of it?" Sonny said.

"Sure, get as much as you want," Lorna said as she gave Sonny a fork.

Simon nodded, pleased by Lorna and Sonny having made up with each other.

He went to the dining table and said, "All right, children, time to eat."

His cheeks bloated by the meat he was chewing down with gusto, Sonny took the plates of food from Lorna and put them on the table. He did the same with the bowls of soup Lorna had ladled from the pot. Then they joined Simon at the dining table.

He nodded in a signal for their mealtime prayer. They then bowed their heads, made the sign of the cross and prayed:

"We thank thee, O Lord, for this thy gift which we are about to receive from thy bounty, through thy only begotten son, Jesus Christ, our Lord and Savior. Amen."

They began their lunch with the soup. It was delicious. Simon, who was hungry, finished his soup in no time at all.

"Can I get you more soup, Dad?" Lorna said.

"No. That is it for me with the soup. I'll now try the main course."

He filled his plate with rice and pork stew and ate with uncustomary speed. It was his first meal of the day. He had only a cup of coffee earlier in the morning, which he even shared with Clara. She was then too nervous and excited about their meeting with Saul Levy for her to take the trouble of preparing their breakfast. He had no appetite then. Sonny and Lorna took their breakfast in a fastfood shop near their school with the money Clara gave them. He glanced at Sonny, his mouth crammed with spoonfuls of rice and stew he was eating with gusto.

They were surprised, midway in their lunch, when they heard the apartment door opened and closed. Clara had arrived. She was not expected home until late in the afternoon.

Lorna and Sonny stood up. She took Clara's hand and pressed it to her forehead in the traditional Filipino gesture of respect and greeting to an elder. Sonny did the same.

"What happened?" Simon asked Clara. "Why are you home early?"

"Why not?" she replied. "Are we not celebrating our successful interview with our lawyer?"

He looked on, puzzled, at Clara. They had not planned any celebration.

"Go on with your lunch while I change into my housedress," she said as she proceeded to the master bedroom.

Sonny resumed eating while Lorna set a place for Clara at the other end of the dining table, facing Simon. Clara returned, now clad in her housedress, to a bowl of soup waiting for her. She sat down, made the sign of the cross and said grace.

"It looks like you are having a good lunch," she said when she was finished praying.

"Lorna whipped up a good lunch from what I told her and Sonny about our forthcoming work permits," Simon said, as he proved his point by shoveling a spoonful of rice and pork into his mouth.

"Sonny and I will look for work as soon as we get them," Lorna said.

Clara smiled and nodded but said nothing. She dipped her spoon into her soup.

"I will try both the Tasty Burger and the Captain's Fried Chicken," Lorna continued. "I have some friends working there. They can give me a tip about an opening there for a cook or a cashier."

"That is right down your alley," Simon said to Lorna, his glance then turned to Sonny.

"I don't mind working as a hamburger flipper, if that is the only job I can get," Sonny said. "But I would rather be an auto mechanic. I won't mind the dirty work since it pays more."

"Do you know enough about fixing cars?" Simon asked Sonny.

"Of course, Dad, I've taken it up in school. Besides, I have trained on Mad Max."

Simon smiled. He meant only to challenge Sonny into trying that kind of job. Sonny was a good mechanic; he saw this from what he had done with Mad Max, as they called their car. A classmate gave it to Sonny. He took it away from his classmate's backyard, where it was gathering dust and rust. He put the car in good running condition with what he had learned in auto mechanics in school.

He could now see the same pride and confidence in Sonny's face when he announced, after working for days on the car, that it was ready for a road test. The car ran smoothly. They had been driving it, trouble-free ever since.

"You should have seen Sonny's classmates drool with envy the first time he drove our car to school," Lorna said to Simon.

He watched and listened as his two children then engaged in a talk as if they were by themselves, and he and Clara were not around.

"You know," Lorna said to Sonny, "you can earn bundles of money with your mechanical skills and not only with cars, but with computers, too."

"I'll go into computers, too. You can be sure about it. I want to earn more money so we can have our own home in a nice place like Pasadena."

"So you can just walk to Cal Tech. I know you want to study there."

"You bet I do."

"You are perfect for Cal Tech."

"Pasadena is far from USC. I know you want to study there."

"I can always take the bus."

"You will also have to save a lot for USC, the same way that I'll have to save a lot for Cal Tech."

"Besides flipping hamburgers, I can do more baby-sitting for Mama Berta."

It would be like reaching for the moon, Simon told himself about Sonny's ambition to study in Cal Tech. So will a medical course be for Lorna, who wanted to take it up in the University of Southern California. He and Clara were earning just enough for the rent, their food and other family expenses, but they could find a way. If they could achieve the nearly impossible feat of coming to America, so could they achieve their goal of a college education for Lorna and Sonny.

"By the way," Sonny said to Lorna, "have you returned the Tagalog movie we borrowed from Mama Berta?"

"No, not yet."

"Why not?"

"Mom has not seen it yet. Do you still want to see it, Mom?" Lorna asked Clara.

Clara gazed, startled, at Lorna and said, "Do I want to see what?"

"The movie we borrowed from Mama Berta. Do you still want to see it?"

Simon glanced at Clara, who had lapsed into silence after a show of interest in the talk at the table. She had been picking at her food, too.

"You can return it now to Mama Berta," she replied.

"But it is a great movie," Lorna said.

"Very well. You can ask her if we can keep it for one more day. I will see it later today."

"I'll tell her that. Sonny and I will help her baby-sit the children after we have taken our lunch."

Simon took the last spoonful of the pork stew on his plate and glanced again at Clara. There was something odd about her coming home early, supposedly for a nonexistent celebration, and then this unusual silence. Like him, she should be hungry by now, but she hardly touched her food.

She stood up. She was finished with her lunch.

"You hardly touched your food," he said to her.

"I'm not hungry."

He threw her a puzzled look. Why was she not forthright with him? She owed him an explanation for coming home early. He will ask her about it after the children had left. He watched her clear the table with Lorna and Sonny. He was inclined to help them, but here at home, he was the boss, not the busboy. He was getting in their way, though, and he left them and went to his easy chair. He sat down there and watched the view while waiting for them to finish their chore at the dining table and in the kitchen.

A short while later, Lorna said, as she was leaving with Sonny, "We are going now, Dad."

He nodded and watched them as they stepped out of their apartment. They will do their homework with the books and notebooks in their hands while helping Mama Berta baby-sit the children.

Clara appeared from the kitchen and proceeded to the master bedroom. He followed and found her seated on the edge of the bed.

She seemed to be upset.

He said, as he stood in front of her, "Problem? Will it help if you will tell me about it?"

She made no reply.

He was not discouraged by her lack of response, and he said, "Why did you leave work early?"

"I had to."

Suddenly she burst into tears. He gazed at her, his eyes wide in surprise. Whatever it was that made her cry, though, he must give her aid and comfort. He sat down beside her and put his arm on her shoulder.

"It's all right; it's all right," he said. "Cry on if it will make you feel better."

She wept on. He caressed her hair and her shoulder. It had a calming effect on her, and she stopped crying. He watched her wipe with her palm the tears in her eyes.

"Now," he said, "can you tell me what is troubling you?"

"I quit my job. I had to get away. My boss attacked me."

"What?" he said, his head jerked back from shock.

He was suddenly seized with fear and panic as the image then flashed in his mind of his wife struggling against her boss.

"But I fought back," she said. "I pushed the animal away! I said I will call the police, but he just laughed. 'Try doing that,' he said. 'The authorities will then know you are working here illegally.' He came to me again, but I kicked him in the shin and hit him in the chin with a stapler. He staggered down on the floor. I grabbed my purse and ran to the door. I opened it, looked back and saw the brute, still on the floor, raising his fist at me. The animal!"

She was shaking from anger, and tears were welling out again in her eyes. He caressed her hair and shoulder. It calmed her down.

"You have got nothing to fear," he said to her. "You are now home, safe with me."

He saw her catch her breath, and he said, "Let me get you a glass of water."

"I'm all right now," she said, but he was already at the door.

He went to the kitchen, his mind seething at the thought of the brute who attacked his wife. Back in the bedroom, he stayed calm, betraying nothing of his own anger so as not to upset her any further. Now in the kitchen, as he was picking up a drinking glass there, he finally gave in to his pent-up rage. Had the glass not been thick enough, he could have crushed it in his hand and injured himself. That calmed him down. He filled it with water and went back to the bedroom. He gave her the glass of water and watched her finish drinking it. He took the glass back and put it on top of the cabinet. Then, in a low restrained voice, he said to her, "You know I'm not a violent man. I avoid trouble if I can."

Suddenly he pounded his palm with his balled fist and said through his clenched teeth, "Had you been harmed, I'll know what to do to that animal!"

"Don't do anything, please!" she pleaded as she grasped his hand. "Nothing bad happened to me. Let us leave it at that."

It calmed him down. He must not do anything he might only regret later on, but he must know too everything that happened.

He sat down beside her and said, "Did that animal make any advances before?"

"I caught him a few times leering at me, but I did not give it a thought then."

"Did you notice anything unusual before it happened?"

"Nothing, I saw nothing unusual. I went on working, but at around twelve noon, Rosemary and Beth, my two co-employees, went out for lunch. I was left alone with him. He came to me and showed me a birthstone ring. He told me I could have it. I asked him why he was giving it to me, and he said he wanted to make me happy, but that I should also make him happy. I realized then what he was getting at, and I gave back the ring. Suddenly he pulled my hand and tried to embrace me!"

She paused, her chest heaving, and buried her face in her hands.

"What is this happening to us?" she cried. "Can't we be safe, even here in Los Angeles?"

He was so affected by what his wife said, and he brushed her hair and shoulder to comfort her. What a terrible thing his wife had been through! And all because she did not have a green card or a work permit. Without them, she was prey to her fiendish employer. He heard but doubted then horror stories about employers forcing their female employees working for them illegally to have sex with them. Now, here was his own wife, nearly a victim herself!

"You are unharmed; that is the important thing," he said.

"We will soon have our work permits. We could then work without fear of anything from anyone."

"Oh, what a comfort it is to be close to you," she said as she then turned and clung to him.

He was touched, and he put his arm around her. A man had nearly succeeded in violating and in possessing her. No! She was his alone! He held her tight and he could feel in the softness of her breast the beating of her heart. She was his alone! He gave vent to this desperate feeling with his mouth pressed possessively to her lips. It sent him wanting her, and he laid her down on the bed. Then he stood up, went to the door and locked it.

Chapter 5

Simon watched a couple just finished with their breakfast as he was going with his work cart to the dining area in L&S Restaurant. He pushed it toward their table the moment they left it and headed toward the restaurant's glass door. The couple had left uneaten large portions of fried eggs, a mound of fried rice, and most of a fried milkfish.

He shook his head. If they were not hungry enough, they should have taken only coffee instead of ordering a full breakfast and leaving all that food on the table. It was a waste of food and money.

Back in his home country, putting food on the dining table was a hard daily struggle. Even now, here in America, with its abundance of affordable food, he did not waste any. He finished the full breakfast Clara had cooked for him earlier in the morning.

Whatever the couple did with their food was their own business, though. They paid for it. His job was to clean up the table.

He picked up a plate and removed with a rubber spatula, the food left there and dropped it into a plastic trash bag at the side of his work cart. He put the plate on the top shelf in the cart, picked up another plate, and followed the same procedure. Then he put the cups and saucers in a lower shelf, the forks and spoons in a receptacle.

It was a simple mechanical work he did with characteristic energy. His pay was small, but he was sure of receiving it on the fifteenth day and end of the month. L&S Restaurant was a small family operation, but it had been ten, twelve years in operation now, a laudable exception to his compatriots' business ventures in America.

These were mostly poorly ran marginal operations: here today, gone tomorrow.

His spirit raised by the reassuring thought about the stability of the restaurant, he wiped the table quickly with a damp cloth and then wiped it again with a clean dry cloth until the table was clean and ready for the next occupants. The task done, he took a pause.

It was early morning yet. Except for a man having a leisurely breakfast by himself, the dining tables in L&S Restaurant stood empty.

He looked out through the restaurant's plate glass window at another fine working day in Los Angeles. The sky was blue with but a few puffs of cotton-white clouds in the horizon, and not a sign yet of smog over the city.

Rainbird Avenue was deserted except for a few passing cars. It was only seven-fifty, and the delicatessen at the street corner, the video rental shop, the thrift shop and the beauty parlor across the street were still closed. They won't open until nine or ten in the morning.

Were he not at work in L&S, he would now be taking a walk in the city streets. His fascination with Los Angeles had not waned in the five months he and his family had been living there. But its sheer size discouraged him from seeing its entirety on foot, which to him was the best way to see Los Angeles, or any other place.

So, he confined his long walks, by himself or as often with Phil, to the area from downtown Los Angeles to Hollywood and west to Fairfax. Sometimes they walked along the sea, from the end of Wilshire Boulevard in Santa Monica, to points south as far as their legs could carry them.

Taking those long walks with Phil stimulated his mind and body. They talked about whatever came in their minds. They saw places of interest. His haunts there and the long walks he took were among his few pleasures in living in Los Angeles. Its balmy weather allowed him to walk in the city sidewalks for hours, even in the middle of the day, without drawing beads of perspiration. Perhaps next Sunday, he could take a walk in Hermosa Beach, alone or with Phil.

He turned away from the glass window when he heard Leonard Ky clearing his throat. Leonard was standing behind the food counter, moon-faced and almond-eyed. The owner of L&S had hinted that he had done enough idling. He was not there a tourist admiring the view. Leonard was paying him three dollars and twenty cents an hour to clear the tables, wash the dishes and keep the restaurant clean.

It was back to work for him, and he pushed his work cart toward the kitchen sink at the back of the dining area. He put the plates and the utensils in the kitchen sink and opened the faucet. He let the water run and then tested its temperature by the feel of his hand. The water was still cold. As he waited for the water to turn warm enough for him to do the dishes, he glanced at the kitchen a few feet away from him. It was busy with the women cooking. Antonia was turning over with a basting spoon and a turner, rice frying in a big pan. To her right, Naty was waiting for Josefino, the kitchen helper, who was cutting up into small cubes a slab of pork at a table behind them.

"Is the pork ready?" she asked Josefino.

"In a moment," Josefino replied.

He scooped into a tray a mound of diced pork. He said, as he brought it to Naty, "Here it comes."

She stepped back and looked on as he put the pork on a big frying pan where onion, garlic and other spices were frying in cooking oil. Naty then turned them over repeatedly with a basting spoon, mixing the pork and the spices in the hot cooking oil.

"Put more garlic to improve the taste," Antonia suggested.

"I've put more than enough of it," Naty replied curtly.

Simon had done enough idle viewing of the kitchen, and he put his palm again across the running water. It was now warm enough for him to do the dishes. He preferred doing this chore with his bare hands. With rubber gloves, he could not tell if the dishes were clean enough. Doing this many times a day, five days a week, had made his hands raw and nearly arthritic. The pain could get so bad at times, he had to take a non-prescription painkiller, in addition to the liniment he applied on his hands at night.

He was, in a few minutes, finished washing the dishes. He wiped his hands dry with a towel and returned with a mop to the dining area. More patrons had come in, five in all. They were moving in a line, pushing their trays on the counter toward Leonard.

A nurse was first on the line. He glanced at her as he swept with the mop the floor underneath a table. A regular patron, she worked in a hospital nearby. The other patrons standing behind her were regulars, too. He knew everyone of them by the face. They were all his countrymen who liked to start their workday on a full stomach.

Leonard wrote down the nurse's order in his notebook. Then he peered through the small kitchen window and said, like he was singing a song, "One Daingsilog!"

Two more patrons came in. As the line lengthened, Leonard took their orders quickly. A short while later, he turned again toward the kitchen window, to Antonia, who had announced from the kitchen, "One Daingsilog coming!"

Leonard took the nurse's breakfast—a plate of fried rice topped with fried milkfish and two eggs, fried sunny side up—and put it on the nurse's tray.

At the same time, Leonard's wife Sonia, the cashier, was filling a cup with coffee from the coffee maker behind her. Then she put the free coffee on the nurse's tray.

The food looked and smelled inviting, but the nurse was looking at it doubtfully.

"This fish looks old and pale," she said.

Leonard smiled and said, "You eat it for its taste, not for its looks. It is fried just right. If it is overcooked, it becomes dark brittle and bitter. That is not how you always liked it."

"Well, if you say so," the nurse said, satisfied with Leonard's explanation.

A plate of sliced tomatoes was on the counter. The nurse picked up the fork from her tray and speared with it two slices of tomato and put them into her plate. She took out from her purse three one-dollar bills and gave them to Sonia, who then put the money in the cash register in front of her.

The nurse went to an empty table and sat down there.

Simon paused from his work with the mop and watched approvingly as the nurse drank her coffee and began to eat. She and the other restaurant patrons were enjoying L&S food prepared without frills that was as filling as it was reasonably priced.

The man eating by himself had left, leaving no food on his plate.

Simon nodded approvingly: that is the way to eat.

A car was moving toward the parking lot in L&S. The table the man had left should be cleared fast. He left his mop leaning on a wall and took his work cart from the kitchen.

He put there the cup, the plate and other utensils used by the solitary eater and cleaned up the table quickly. He knew from experience that more of the regular restaurant patrons will soon come in. L&S was a small restaurant and every table there will be occupied by then.

It had five tables for two persons, three set against a wall and the other two against the glass window facing Rainbird Avenue. Some of the restaurant patrons, while waiting for the food they ordered, had taken the five tables for four persons in the middle of the dining area. Two persons were eating at the long table that faced a side street. The rest of the chairs there, six of them, stood empty. But not for long. More of the regulars who took their breakfast there will be arriving soon.

He returned his work cart to the kitchen and resumed mopping the floor. It was worn and cracked in certain spots. It was as old as the paint on the walls of the restaurant. Originally in beige, the walls had taken a grayish hue with age and from the soot in the kitchen. He was finished mopping the floor in a short while. He glanced at the kitchen as he was returning the mop to the utility closet. It was messy. Trays of food, raw and cooked, were on a table. Boxes were piled, one on top of the other. The kitchen floor was clean, though. It was the cooks' work area. He seldom went there unless he was asked to clean it up. Otherwise, he will only be getting in their way.

He was going back to the dining area when he saw Jonathan coming from the parking lot. He was walking with a noticeable limp with his prosthetic right leg. Out in the sun, he looked older than his age of fifty or so years. His hair and mustache were gray, but his disposition was not similarly gray. He smiled at Simon, who had opened the door for him.

"What is up?" Jonathan asked him. "Are you coming tonight?"

"Yes, I am. I've got something important to take up with you. Phil and I went the other Sunday to the Keg Room. We were hoping to find you there."

"I did not feel like going out that day. You yourself don't usually go there on a Sunday. I did not see you either last Wednesday, but Phil was there."

"I had to attend to something at home."

"What do you want to see me about?"

"I'll tell you tonight at the Keg Room."

"Tonight, then."

"Enjoy your breakfast,"

He returned to his post, a stool near the kitchen sink, while Jonathan proceeded toward the food counter. He picked up a tray there and laid there a fork and a spoon. He pushed his tray toward Leonard.

His pencil and notebook in his hands, Leonard asked him, "What will you have this morning, Jonathan?"

He said, as he was looking at the menu posted on the wall, "How about Adobosilog?"

"Good choice. The pork our supplier gave us this morning is on the lean side."

Leonard checked on his notebook, the food Jonathan had ordered.Then he peered through the kitchen window and said, "One Adobosilog for Jonathan."

All the tables were now occupied, and Jonathan waited for his breakfast at the food counter.

"So," he said to Leonard, "how is the restaurant business?"

"Hard. We barely survive."

"Spoken like a true Vietnamese restaurant owner—always talking poor."

" I'm not kidding. Look at our old car there," Leonard said as he pointed at a car in the parking lot. "We have not changed it in years."

"Come now," Jonathan said as he slapped the air in disagreement with Leonard. "I know you own several cars."

"Yes, in my dreams," Leonard said as he turned his attention, back to his notebook.

Jonathan, for lack of anything to do, looked out through the glass window facing the side street. It was deserted, but then a man came to the back door of the delicatessen and opened it.

Just then, Antonia peered from the kitchen window and said, "Here is Jonathan's Adobosilog."

Leonard picked up the plate of food and put it in Jonathan's tray.

Jonathan nodded approvingly at the Adobosilog's inviting smell. The pork dish, marinated in soy sauce and vinegar, had been cooked brown enough, the eggs fried sunny side up, while Sonia put on his tray, a cup of the free coffee.

He paid for the food, took the tray and walked toward a dining table in the middle of the dining area, where a couple were taking their breakfast.

There were two vacant chairs there, and he asked them if he could take one of the chairs there. The man nodded, and Jonathan joined them at the dining table. They ate their breakfast quietly. The couple stood up once they had finished their breakfast. They were about to leave when Jonathan nodded and smiled at them in a show of appreciation for letting him share their dining table. He was also finished with his breakfast in a short while.

He was leaving L&S when he saw Simon, who was coming out of the kitchen with his work cart. He left it near the water dispenser and walked Jonathan to the door.

"I'll see you then tonight at the Keg Room," Jonathan said.

"All right. Have a nice day," Simon said, as he tapped Jonathan on the shoulder.

He watched Jonathan as he was walking away, and felt sorry for him. Jonathan had a good job as the administrative officer of Asia Pacific University and a nice home in Atwater Village, while he was a mere busboy, dishwasher and janitor in L&S Restaurant, renting an apartment in a bad neighborhood. Unlike Jonathan, though, with his prosthetic right leg, he was a whole person, with nothing damaged or missing in his body.

It was a terrible unkind thought passing through his mind, and he dismissed it with a frown and a shake of his head. He went back to his work cart and pushed it to the dining table Jonathan and the couple had occupied and began to clear it.

It was the busiest hour in the morning. All the dining tables were occupied except the one Simon had just cleaned up. The regulars at the long table he called the "Court of Saint James" were now "in session." They were eating breakfast and talking at the same time. A tray of food in his hand, a man in a security guard uniform took a vacant chair in the long table. A man in a parking attendant's uniform asked him, "Where is Pedrito? Is he not coming today?"

"No, he is not," the security guard replied. "He called in sick yesterday."

"Sick? Sick of what?" the parking attendant asked.

"Sick of life, of himself, of everyone," the security guard replied. "He must be looking now for a place to live after his wife drove him out of their apartment the other night."

"Why, what happened?" the postman seated beside the security guard asked.

"He was caught in the act with a girl and in their own bed at that," the security guard replied.

"Take a pee, if you have to, but not in your own backyard," the parking attendant said to laughter at the long table.

Simon pushed his work cart toward the water dispenser, away from the vulgar petty talk at the long table. He looked outside at the parking lot and saw a man he called Mr. Showoff getting off from his brand-new American car with his wife and their two children.

Mr. Showoff gazed at his car admiringly and flicked away a tiny leaf that had landed on the windshield while his wife and their two children went ahead to L&S.

He had often heard Mr. Showoff brag about his distinction as one of the top men and the only Filipino in an American marketing company. He knew, though, that Mr. Showoff's job there was in running errands for his American bosses.

The man looked around imperiously and, satisfied with the impression he had made with himself, he walked with his chin thrust out toward L&S. His wife and their children took the unoccupied dining table while he placed their order at the food counter.

"Give us the best that you have here," Mr. Showoff said to Leonard in a brusque tone of voice.

"Take your pick," Leonard said, as he pointed at the food trays in the food counter.

"I don't want any of those. I want fresh cooked food."

"We have Tapsilog, Adobosilog, Daingsilog and Tosilog. They are all good."

"We'll have one of each of them and be quick about it. We are hungry."

"One each of Adobosilog, Tapsilog, Daingsilog and Tosilog," Leonard then said at the kitchen window, at the same time that Sonia was putting in Mr. Showoff's food tray, the four cups of free coffee.

Mr. Showoff was putting down the food tray on his dining table when he saw something there.

"Hey, you! Come here!" he shouted at Simon.

He came quickly to Mr. Showoff's dining table.

"This table is dirty," Mr. Showoff said, his finger pointed at a wet spot on the dining table.

Bottles of ketchup, vinegar, fish sauce and a sugar dispenser had hidden the dime-size wet spot.

Simon looked on at the wet spot, wondering how he could have missed cleaning it. He mumbled an apology and wiped the offending wet spot clean with a dry piece of cloth, after which he looked on as Mr. Showoff was putting on the dining table the four cups of coffee.

"What are you standing there for?" Mr. Showoff said to him.

Simon was so jolted by the man's rudeness, he retreated quickly to his work cart. He pushed it toward another dining table vacated just then and, his brow still burning in humiliation, he removed the used dishes and wiped the dining table clean—really clean, with absolutely no wet spot left there!

His work on the dining table done, he returned with his work cart to his work station near the water dispenser and gazed in scornful silence at Mr. Showoff. He came to L&S as much to eat as to show off his new car. He had humiliated him, a busboy, to show himself superior to him. In the process, Mr. Showoff had only betrayed his poor breeding and bad manners.

He looked on at Mr. Showoff, who was now eating like a pig. He was not surprised to see the likes of him in L&S. Mr. Showoff was of a type common among his countrymen, friendly to his peers, mean and condescending to those he considered to be socially and economically inferior to him, and slavish to his American bosses.

He will not let this Gunga Din spoil his day. Rudyard Kipling's literary character maybe just as deferential to his British masters, but at least he was not mean and condescending to his fellow Indians, as Mr. Showoff was to his fellow Filipinos.

But enough of that obnoxious character! He frowned as he dismissed from his mind all thought about Mr. Showoff and turned an ear to a familiar refrain from the parking attendant at the long table.

"You should have seen my apartment building in Manila," the parking attendant said. "It has ten doors with a restaurant occupying the corner unit in the ground floor."

"Where is it located?" another man, an insurance agent, asked.

"In Sampaloc, but we sold it last year."

"I know that area quite well," the security guard said. "I got my promotion to police captain while I was assigned there. One time, I'll show you my medals and citations, some of them I received from the mayor himself. I could have been the deputy chief of police had I cozied up to the politicians."

He looked on as the men at the long table listened to the security guard, bored expressions on their faces. It was not the first time the security guard had talked about his days of glory in Manila.

"Great work you were doing then, unlike your present job in the movie studio," the parking attendant said to the security guard.

"Not when I think of its importance to the movie studio," the security guard shot back. "When I'm assigned at the gate, no one, absolutely no one, can pass through without my okay. I also secure the premises when I am on night duty. I cannot take my job for granted, considering the role I play in the movie studio. This is not to mention the fact that I rub elbows with those gorgeous movie stars."

"Come now," the parking attendant said to the security guard, "Do you really rub elbows with them?"

"Not only that. One of these days I just might find myself in bed with a starlet. You know how they go for the dark type like me."

The "Court of St. James" broke out into a raucous laughter.

Simon turned his gaze away from the men at the long table having their usual cynical vainglorious talk. He expected that kind of big talk from them. It was their way of making up for what he could imagine were the resentment and the disappointment that festered inside each one of them. Their work experience and qualifications in their homeland meant nothing here in the United States. They and their country were poorly rated here, so that try as they might, they could not duplicate here in America, their days of power and glory in the Philippines.

The parking attendant was formerly an assistant vice president of a major food company in Manila. The postman was formerly a department head in the postal bureau, while the insurance agent was formerly an assistant manager in a chain of drug stores. The security guard was formerly a hotshot police captain in Manila. They were this and that in their homeland—all of those in the past tense.

He sighed as he watched the restaurant patrons eating breakfast. They were belittled as much for the color of their skin as for their reputation as a people with poor abilities. They were treated like hired help, good only for menial jobs, or jobs that required little or no technical skills and even less executive responsibilities.

A line of patrons had formed in the counter, waiting for their turn at the dining tables. Four patrons had just stood up from their dining table when Simon was already making his way there with his work cart. He worked, his mind still on the men taking their breakfast at the long table. They should not ask for more, here in America. They were getting there, no more, no less than what they deserved.

He shook his head in sympathy for them and the other restaurant patrons, as he went on cleaning the dining table.

How fate had been so unkind to their homeland and its people. They were made up of primitive tribal villages that, left to themselves, might have developed into one nation. They fell instead under the Spanish colonial rule, which then did the job of forming them into a nation. Centuries of harsh Spanish rule had made them servile, fatalistic, cynical, mediocre, selfish and uncaring, lethargic, poor imitators of their Spanish rulers, a culturally and economically emasculated people. Their growth and development as a people were stunted by more than three centuries of oppressive Spanish colonial rule tempered mercifully by the Christian faith the Spaniards themselves had brought to them.

He cleared another table, his mind working without interruption. It did not help them any that they came from a middling country muddling through from the time it became independent in 1946. Their government and their leaders, since their country became independent, but never more so than during the Marcos conjugal dictatorship, were as corrupt as they were incompetent. Their leaders looked at working in the government, not as a means to serve the people, but as a means for their personal gain and advancement.

Millions of Filipinos were now working abroad, mostly as domestic helpers and construction workers—the servants of the world. They were hailed as heroes for their dollar remittances, which kept the national economy afloat. That millions of them were working abroad was in fact an indictment of their government and their leaders. They were abroad for the jobs and opportunities for a better life denied them in their own country. So was he, here in America as an exile from persecution and a seeker of opportunities for a better life denied him and his family in their homeland.

He cleared another table and then disappeared in the kitchen.

He came back a few minutes later and replaced with sparkling clean glasses, the nearly empty glass tray beside the water dispenser. Then he pulled out from his work cart a clean dry cloth and wiped with it the glass in the food counter.

Four women eating at a dining table near the food counter were talking about the Fil-Asian Fair.

He himself had fair tickets for his family and friends.

"We can get here free tickets to the fair; that is what it says there," one of the women said as she pointed at the fair poster taped on the restaurant's glass window.

"Why don't we ask for some tickets?" another woman said.

She approached Leonard and said, "Can you give us some of your fair tickets?"

"Let me see if I have any left," Leonard replied.

He opened a drawer underneath the countertop, looked down and shook his head.

"I'm sorry," he said, "but I have run out of fair tickets."

He asked Sonia, "Do you have any fair tickets there with you?"

"I haven't got any left."

"Sorry about that," he said to the woman, "but I'll keep some for you when we get another batch from the fair organizers. How many do you want?"

The woman looked back at her companions.

"Five tickets for each of us will do," one of the women said.

"Make it twenty," the woman said to Leonard.

The matter with the fair tickets settled, the woman thanked Leonard and went back, satisfied, to her dining table.

It was past nine o'clock and, except for one vacant dining table, the dining area was full of patrons who, while eating, were talking and gossiping amid an occasional clatter at the dining tables.

Simon stayed at his post near the water dispenser, his owlish eyes surveying the restaurant. The thing about L&S was that it was ethnic. Its owners were. Leonard was a Vietnamese while his wife Sonia was a Filipino. Leonard fled to the Philippines when South Vietnam was overran by the Communists. He met Sonia in a refugee camp there. They fell in love, were married and were allowed to immigrate to the United States a few years later. L&S was ethnic, from the food it served to the people who worked and ate there.

A white couple, the man in a coat and the woman in a blazer, came in. White people seldom came to L&S, and they attracted everyone's attention there.

"Who do we have here? A couple of foreigners have just walked in," the parking attendant said to laughter at the long table.

The couple hesitated at the door when they saw everyone in the restaurant staring at them. The woman pulled the man's arm, suggesting by that the mistake they had made in going there, and that they should leave immediately. But then, they saw Mr. Showoff welcoming them with a nod and a broad smile on his face.

Simon winced at Mr. Showoff's toadying attitude, and he murmured, "Bootlicker."

The white couple were encouraged, though, by Mr. Showoff's show of friendliness and they walked boldly toward the food counter, just as Naty was filling a food tray there with a fish dish. They looked disapprovingly at the glassy-eyed milkfish laid on their side in a bed of sauce and fat.

"The foreigners don't seem to like the fish dish," the postman said.

"They won't eat anything whose eyes are staring at them," the parking attendant said to another round of laughter at the long table.

Simon watched and waited for what the white couple would now do. He was not surprised to see them walk stiffly out of the restaurant. Laughter rose again at the long table as they were passing out of the glass door. The other restaurant patrons joined in the laughter except Mr. Showoff, who frowned in disapproval of the other restaurant patrons' boorish behavior toward the white couple.

"Hey, Leonard, next time, see to it the heads are removed before the fish dish is brought out here," the insurance agent said to more laughter in the restaurant.

Leonard kept silent and did not join in the laughter. Simon knew why. Leonard regretted the loss of the two patrons. To a pennywise restaurant owner like him, the two patrons were two patrons; a dollar lost was a dollar lost. Leonard's silence told him, though, that Leonard was realistic enough to accept, though with some regret, the loss of the white couple's money rather than antagonize his regular patrons by any show of disapproval of the way they treated the white couple. The men at the long table ate in L&S every day. They were of far more value to his restaurant than the white couple who had strayed there and will most likely never go there again.

They were once again by themselves and the men at the long table resumed talking about their days of glory in the Philippines.

He watched them, wondering how they, who habitually deferred to white people, had found the temerity to laugh the white couple out of L&S. Perhaps they were getting back at white people in general for the condescending treatment they were getting from them.

With the white couple now gone, L&S had assumed once again the ambience of a typical Filipino restaurant, patronized solely by Filipinos. They were that exclusive.

He saw this from the way they glanced curiously and made snide remarks at the white couple who had strayed there. They considered L&S their own turf, a very small turf, though. It extended only as far as the glass door of the restaurant. Beyond that lay the rest of America—the white couple's own turf. Out there, the jokers at the long table, the other patrons in L&S, and all the rest of their compatriots, himself included, were the foreigners in this country. Too bad, their laughter and the snide remarks they made about the white couple had only made them feel even more isolated. They were left out of mainstream American society by the color of their skin, their national origin, the language they spoke, down to the kind of food they ate. They may make money those they left behind in their homeland could only dream of, such was the material abundance in America. Like Mr. Showoff, they may drive brand-new cars. They may live in nice homes with a TV set and a computer in every bedroom. They may take a cruise in the Caribbean this year and visit the Philippines the following year. The good life in America lay open to them. They enjoyed it, though, only among themselves, in isolation from the rest of American society.

He gazed resentfully at Mr. Showoff and the men at the long table. He would avoid their company if he could, but could not. He fled his own country, fearful for his life, sick of the violence, corruption and the poverty there, only to land here in America a busboy, dishwasher and janitor's job that constantly reminded him of all of those, and much more. He must endure for five days a week the company of these pathetic swellheads with their mean and petty talk, their bad manners, their boorish behavior, and then clean up the mess they leave in their dining tables.

He pushed his work cart toward the dining table Mr. Showoff and his family had just left. Unlike the L&S patrons who talked big, he was averse to bragging. Unlike them who wanted a lot in America, all he wanted there were just a few things, like food on his dining table, peace and security for his family, and a good future for his children. That should not be asking too much, he thought agreeably, as he removed the food left there, the plates and the cups, the forks and the spoons, and with a dry cloth wiped the dining table clean.

Chapter 6

Simon was done with his work in L&S and he was seated at a dining table there, watching idly Leonard and Sonia, who were counting at the cash register, their day's earnings.

He had washed the dishes, the forks and spoons, the glasses and the coffee cups, the pots and pans and the food trays. He had cleared the dining tables and cleaned the bathroom and mopped the floor, everything that was required of him.

Antonia appeared from the kitchen and gave him a bag of food. It was his share of the food, when there was any left in the kitchen and the food trays, which Leonard and Sonia gave away to their employees.

"Thank you and have a nice day," he said to them as he left the restaurant.

"Another day, another dollar," he said to himself as he stepped inside his car and drove home, his thoughts on Clara and their children.

They were now on their third day of job-hunting. They wasted no time in looking for jobs as soon as they received their work permits in the mail last Saturday. They must raise their family income so Lorna and Sonny could go to college and they could have their own home.

He parked his car in the carport with those ambitious thoughts in his mind. He was passing through the gate when he saw Clara, waving at him from the picture window. He waved back at her and walked up to their apartment. The door was suddenly opened and Clara came out and hugged him.

"Guess what?" she said. "I've got a job! I got hired as a cashier!"

He gazed, happy and astonished, at her and said, "Really! Where?"

"At the Super Bargain Store!"

"That is great! This calls for a celebration!"

He saw, as he entered their apartment, Lorna and Sonny doing their school assignments seated on the carpet strewn with books, ballpoint pens and other school paraphernalia.

They stood up, and he gave the bag of food to Lorna, who then took his hand and pressed it to her forehead in a gesture of respect for him. Sonny did the same.

He nodded, pleased and satisfied with his children. He and Clara had brought up in Lorna and Sonny respect for their elders. It was a trait he seldom saw among Filipino children born or raised in America. They even mimicked American children who address their parents and their elders by their first names, sometimes even by their nicknames.

Lorna opened the bag of food and looked down at what it contained.

"Is this," she said, "for the celebration of Mom's new job?"

"Nothing of that sort," Simon replied. "They are leftovers from L and S."

"Yuck!" Lorna said, squirming.

"Hey!" Sonny said to Lorna. "You should appreciate what Dad brings home from L and S. Dad may have cooked them himself."

"If I did," Simon said, "people will now avoid L and S."

Their laughter had barely died down when he asked Clara, "How did you get your new job?"

"You won't believe how I got it," Clara said as she led Simon toward the dining table, at the same time that Lorna was proceeding toward the kitchen with the bag of food while Sonny had resumed doing his homework.

Clara said, as she and Simon had sat down at the dining table, "I spent two fruitless days in Glendale Galleria and Beverly Center, looking for a job, not knowing it was right there, not far from where I used to work."

"Which Super Bargain Store is it?"

"It's the store in Broadway near Seventh Street."

"I'm not so familiar with Broadway. Show me the store's location there."

"Let us say the two streets meet here," she said as she drew with her finger, a cross in the air to show the intersection of the two streets. "It's right there," she said, her finger pointed to the store's imaginary location, "two or three stores from the street corner."

He nodded when he had fixed it in his mind and said, "If I got it right, it is located in a basement. We have been there once, I think."

"Right. It is part of a chain of retail stores in California. Randolph, the store manager who hired me, told me it has a dozen branches in Los Angeles alone."

The store, as he remembered it now, was in the busiest stretch of Broadway in downtown Los Angeles. He passed by it from the Line 14 bus he took after seeing Clara off to her work in the jewelry shop. It seemed to him as not a very nice place to work. Clara was so eager for her new job, she overlooked the odd characters infesting that stretch of Broadway. Will she be happy and feel secure working in a place like that? But, then, it may not be as bad as it appeared to him. Moreover, they could not be so choosy with jobs.

"How," he asked Clara, "did you get the job?"

"I saw the 'help wanted' notice in the storefront window and went in. I filled out an application form in the office. Randolph read it, asked a few questions and told me, right then and there, that he was taking me in."

"When will you start working?"

"On Monday next week."

Lorna joined them at the dining table.

"Mom," she said, "can we have the leftovers for another day? We can eat at Manny's to celebrate your new job."

"Yes, let's do that? We have not eaten there for a long time," Sonny said. He was listening while doing his homework.

Simon watched Clara, who seemed to be considering their children's suggestion.

"No, not tonight," she said. "I have my choir practice. We will do the celebrating on Sunday."

"But are we not going to the fair on Sunday?" Lorna said.

Clara replied, " We can go to Manny's after the fair."

The matter about eating out having been settled, Clara turned her attention to the portable electronic organ on the dining table. It was right in front of her, and she moved it to and fro until she was satisfied it was at the right distance from her.

"Time for my choir practice," she said.

Simon asked, "What are you practicing on?"

"As usual, a Gregorian chant."

"It would be nice if you can sing for a change, Franck's *Panis angelicus* or Schubert's *Mille cherubini in coro*. You have not sung them in the church since we came here."

"I would love to do that, one of these days, if Reilly will let me," she said about her choirmaster.

She put a music sheet on the organ's sheet holder. The lead singer in the choir of St. Stephen Church, she took her choir singing seriously.

She moved her fingers deftly on the keyboard, the sound it gave, low and somber. Then, she began to sing, her voice coming out clear and controlled.

Simon loved music, and he had a wide taste for it. It ranged from Bach, Brahms and Beethoven to the Beatles, from Mozart to the mazurka, but the Gregorian chant Clara was singing and playing on the electronic organ had no melody for him, not even with Clara singing it with her fine mezzo-soprano voice.

"Keep it up, keep it up," he said as he stood up.

Clara smiled, pleased with Simon, whose hands were sweeping the air like an orchestra conductor as he proceeded toward the master bedroom. He appeared to be keeping up with the Gregorian chant she was singing when he was actually moving away from it.

He returned to the living room a few minutes later, now dressed in his house clothes. He yawned the moment he had sat down on his easy chair. It was not that he was drowsy. It was more from shedding the tiredness in his bones and muscles from a hard day's work in L&S.

Here at home, he was not a busboy clearing tables, a dishwasher washing plates, cups, pots and pans, a janitor mopping the floor, a worker following orders, but the head of his own brood in his own turf.

There was Clara in high spirit from her new job, singing a Gregorian chant to her own accompaniment on the electronic organ. There was Sonny, seated on the carpet, doing his homework. There was Lorna in the kitchen, preparing their dinner.

All of those filled him with a sense of home and family. He

was a lucky man, happy and content. He was done with his tasks, another workday was behind him. He was at rest, and it came to him then, a poem from his college days. He shut his eyes as he recited it in his mind:

> *"Let us go, then, you and I,*
> *When the evening is spread out against the sky,*
> *Like a patient etherised upon a table;*
> *Let us go through certain half-deserted streets,*
> *The muttering retreats*
> *Of restless nights in one-night cheap hotels. . . . "*

He stopped abruptly, his eyes blinking in confusion. His memory had suddenly failed him, and he could not recall the rest of T.S. Eliot's poem. He used to recite *The Love Song of J. Alfred Prufrock* in its entirety, like an evening prayer, by himself, or in drinking sessions with his classmates back in his college days. He shut his eyes and rubbed his brow as he tried to recall the rest of the poem. Instead, what came back to him were disconnected words and phrases like sawdust restaurants and strange German words.

Was he getting old? Was this an early sign of Alzheimer's disease? The thought of losing his memory frightened him, and he tried to pass it out of his mind by looking outside the window.

Across the vine-topped chain-link fence, Myrtle was preparing dinner in her kitchen. So was Lorna preparing theirs. After dinner, he will drive Clara to her choir practice in St. Stephen Church. From there he will proceed to the Keg Room for an evening there with his friends. Distracted by what he saw and was planning to do, his worries over his fading memory faded away. It was only a temporary thing.

The bookshelf now claimed his attention. Reading was a link he kept with teaching, which he had been aching to do in the United States. He pulled out a book at random. It was one of his favorites— Father de la Costa's *Readings in Philippine History.* He turned the pages and stopped at the page on the sparkling essay of Diaz Arenas on Philippine cabs and carriages. His eyes focused on the page, he began to read, his concentration undisturbed by the deep tones of the electronic organ and Clara's fine singing voice.

He had finished reading the essay and had turned the pages to the Propaganda Movement when suddenly the sharp sounds of gunfire and the shouting by angry frightened men jarred his eardrums. Sonny had switched on the TV set and was rewarding himself with a war movie for the homework he had done. He read on, ignoring the noise from the TV set.

Just then, he saw Lorna as she sat down on the carpet beside Sonny.

He often wondered why his children and their friends, whenever they came visiting, watched TV seated on the carpet. Sitting on a chair or on the couch was more comfortable. He stopped reading—the noise was too distracting. The book on his lap closed, he watched them.

"Don't you ever get tired of watching those violent war movies?" Lorna said to Sonny.

He ignored Lorna and kept on watching the movie. Suddenly Lorna yanked the TV remote control out of Sonny's hand.

"Give it back to me!" he shouted.

She ignored Sonny as she fiddled with the remote control. The TV set switched channels abruptly, from the war movie to a situation comedy, then to a talk show. She settled for the situation comedy.

Sonny moved to take the remote control from Lorna's hand.

"Oh, no, you don't," Lorna said as she held the remote control away from Sonny's reach.

"Stop it, you two!" Clara shouted at them.

Sonny stood up, upbraided and frustrated, and looked down resentfully at Lorna.

"Rasputina!" he said to her, who was giggling, her eyes glued to the TV set and the remote control wrapped firmly in her hand.

Sonny retreated to the couch and took from there, a cassette tape recorder. He sat down on the carpet, his back against the couch, and tried its control knobs. It gave out nothing but a sharp irregular sound. He looked at it closely and sighed as he put it down on the carpet. No doubt, it was broken. He stood up and walked toward the closet near the bathroom where he kept his repair kit.

He was right behind Lorna when suddenly he stooped down and flicked her ear. She cried out and swung her arm at his legs, but he had by then jumped beyond her reach and with three quick strides had landed in the bathroom closet. He had shown the swiftness of his feet that won for him last week, the final track race against Smith.

"Yah, yah, yah, yah, yah," he croaked, twiddling his fingers at Lorna.

Clara stopped singing and gazed sharply at them. Lorna turned her gaze back to the TV set, while Sonny opened the closet door and took out there his repair kit. He walked back to the couch, grinning at Lorna, who remained frowning.

Simon watched, amused, his wife and their children. Sonny and Lorna were having another petty quarrel. The Gregorian chant Clara was singing and playing on the electronic organ had no melody for him. He saw them, though, as an ordinary entertaining scene of family life in the Matin household.

He watched, curious, as Sonny opened the cassette tape recorder with a screwdriver and inspected it.

"Where did you get it?" he asked Sonny.

"It's Mang Damian's, Dad, our neighbor upstairs. He will pay me ten bucks if I can fix it."

"Can you fix it?"

"I'll find that out soon enough."

He sorted out a bunch of wires and found the culprit—a broken wire. He soldered the wire and made adjustments with the control knobs. Then he switched on the cassette tape recorder. It ran just fine.

He watched, impressed, at how quickly Sonny had repaired the cassette recorder. It seemed easy to do, but finding the broken wire, or whichever caused the problem, was not. It needed someone mechanically skillful like Sonny.

His son had also fixed their car and kept it in good running condition. He earned money fixing things for their friends and neighbors. He kept a small part of his earnings for his own expenses and gave the rest to Clara. Lorna helped out too by baby-sitting Mama Berta's young wards.

It pleased him to see his children giving their share for the family upkeep, at the same time that they were saving for college. He was looking forward to the day when Sonny will be taking up aerospace engineering in Cal Tech, and Lorna taking up medicine at the University of Southern California.

He resumed reading, happy and content with those thoughts. He stopped after having barely read a page when he heard Clara sing, "Amen!" She was finished practicing the Gregorian chant.

"That is it," Clara said as she stood up. "All right, you two," she said to Lorna and Sonny, "set the table and prepare our dinner."

He watched Clara as she proceeded to the master bedroom with the portable electronic organ and the music sheet cradled in her arm. He returned the book to the bookshelf and followed her. He helped her put the organ inside its cloth case.

"This is one property of ours that has long paid for itself," he said as he put the electronic organ, now in its cloth case, and the music sheet inside the cabinet in the bedroom.

"How?" she asked.

"With the beautiful music you make with it."

"Thank you, you flatter me."

She regarded him meaningfully and said, "You are up to something."

"No doubt I am. I want to make beautiful music with you, too."

She smiled.

"Whenever you like."

"Not now. The kids. Tonight, when they are asleep."

He nodded. No point in rushing it. It was not the right time.

She went to the closet and took out there a pair of ladies' denim pants and a loose shirt she will wear for her choir practice.

Denim, he decided, will be fine on him, too. He joined her in the closet and pulled out from a hook there, his old pair of denim pants.

Chapter 7

Simon watched the car ahead until it had stopped at the near end of a row of cars facing the lower wall of St. Stephen Church. Then, with his car's headlights sweeping through the dark church parking lot, he drove it beside the other car. He kept the engine on idling and watched Clara as she opened the door at her side of the car.

"I'm going now, dear," Clara said to him. "Don't be late in picking me up."

She stepped out of the car and walked with Elsa, the driver of the other car, toward the side door of the church.

"Are we taking up any new hymns tonight?" Elsa asked Clara. "I missed last week's practice."

"No, we are not. We will practice the same Gregorian chants. Reilly should let us sing some contemporary hymns for a change. Singing those medieval hymns makes me feel so old."

They were laughing as they entered the church.

Satisfied that they were now safe inside the church, Simon drove out of the church parking lot. He was going to the Keg Room.

Traffic in Vermont Avenue was still heavy at that time of the night, and it took him a bit longer to cover the distance of a few miles from the church to Los Feliz District, where the Keg Room was located. Traffic had slackened, though, by the time he reached the bar.

He gazed sideways at the bar while waiting for the oncoming cars to pass. The bar beckoned. Vines fanned out from a flower box to its light blue facade, the lettering in its name, fanciful. The Keg Room had oddly a feminine touch for its mostly male habitués, who indulged in the mostly male activity of drinking beer, wine and liquor.

He turned his car left to the bar's parking area at the back and entered the bar's poolroom to a game of pocket billiards going on there.

Some male spectators were watching a player making calculations for a difficult shot.

His cue rod trained to the white cue ball, the player was aiming for the number six object ball near the left corner pocket, and the number eight ball near the right corner pocket. Satisfied with his calculations, the player took aim, but then a spectator suddenly handed to him a glass of beer.

"You will make a better shot after a swig of this," the spectator, apparently a friend of the player, said.

The player hesitated, but then he accepted the offer and drank the beer.

Simon knew no one there he could talk to, and he turned his gaze to the bar separated from the poolroom by a wooden wall and a curtain of wooden beads at the entrance.

Over there was his own kind of hangout. He went there, not out of habitual dissipation, but for the company of Phil and Jonathan. He liked it too for its warm and cozy atmosphere. The bar had no windows and was always dark. Light came from a small neon lamp behind the bar counter, between rows of wine and liquor bottles, and a lamp between two tables a few feet away from the bar counter. The poolroom was better lighted with long fluorescent lamps hanging above the billiard table.

The Keg Room's bar, with its cozy atmosphere, reminded him of the bar in the movie *Casablanca,* although there were important differences. The bar patrons in the movie were seeking ways to escape from the clutches of the Nazis in Casablanca, while the bar patrons in the Keg Room were having a good time there with friends in the enjoyment of the good life in America. There were other differences. He was no Humphrey Bogart, while the lady standing behind the bar counter was Suprath, the Thai lady manager, and not Ingrid Bergman. Instead of the black pianist in the movie playing on the piano and singing *As Time Goes By,* the jukebox in the Keg Room was playing softly, *Moon River.*

"Finish it up," the spectator urged the player.

"No, thank you. I've drank enough of it," the player said.

He gave the beer glass back to the spectator and returned to his game. His eyes trained to the cue ball, the player hit it with his cue rod. *Tok!* was the sound the cue ball made on impact with the target number six ball, which then rolled and dropped into the left corner pocket. The cue ball then rolled toward the number eight ball, sending it rolling and dropping also into the other corner pocket.

Loud cheers followed the player's sensational shot.

"That's a tournament-class shot you just made there," the spectator who offered the beer said.

The player responded with a thumbs-up sign. He took another shot, not a good one this time.

Simon had seen enough of the game, and he left the poolroom. He swept aside the curtain of wooden beads and, upon entering the bar, smiled at the familiar faces that met him at the bar counter.

Suprath welcomed him with a smile.

Jonathan, who was seated on a stool, gazed sideways at him and said, "There you are, finally. Your beer is getting warm and stale."

"I had to drive Clara first to her choir practice," he said as he sat down beside Jonathan.

He tapped Jonathan on the shoulder and waved in greeting Lew and Mark.

The two Americans were seated beside each other at the corner of the bar counter. They were drinking beer, their ties loosened up and their white shirtsleeves rolled up to their elbows in keeping up with the bar's casual atmosphere.

Seated on the bar counter's other stools were other male patrons drinking beer, wine and liquor.

"That is a nice dress you are wearing," he said to Suprath.

"Thank you," she said as she gazed admiringly at her dress and brushed it with her palm. It had sleeves and was in lavender. Wound around her waist was a cloth belt, also in lavender. She had a nice figure, as nice-looking as her face kept vibrant and youthful-looking by her sunny disposition.

The sportscaster announced on the television set on a wall, a second foul for a Los Angeles Lakers guard. The Lakers were playing against the Chicago Bulls.

"Who is leading?" he asked Jonathan.

"The Bulls by three points. You can place your bet with Mark, if you want to."

"It is one round of beer for the loser," Mark said.

Simon had no instinct for gambling, especially when the bet was the equivalent of his pay for more than two hours of work in L&S.

"You will have to leave me out of it," he said, "but it will be a Bulls game."

He smiled at the chorus of protests that met his prediction of how the game will end.

"Not this one," a man at the bar counter said. "The Lakers will win."

"And by a wide margin," the man beside him said.

Suprath asked Simon, "The usual?"

"Yes, the usual," he replied.

She took out a bottle of beer from the cooler underneath the countertop. Then she poured on a glass, the beer he ordered until she had filled one-half of it with the beer and placed both the beer bottle and the glass in front of him.

He took out from his wallet two one-dollar bills and said, as he gave them to her, "Keep the change."

He said, as he then raised his glass of beer, "Here is to all of us."

The others in the counter followed suit. One of them said, "Here is to the Lakers, too."

He nodded in acknowledgemen t of the bar patron's tribute to the Lakers. Then he drank his beer and sighed, pleased, as it coursed down his throat, cold and strong.

It will go well with food, and he asked Jonathan, "How is Manang Sepa's? Do they have anything special there?"

It was a restaurant Jonathan also frequented.

"Nothing special," Jonathan replied, "but the food there is always filling. You should join me there for dinner one time before coming here. It will be on me."

"Why not? A free meal is a free meal."

"Will this coming Friday be okay with you?"

"Let us make it on Friday, next week. I have something to do at home this coming Friday."

"Very well. It will be on Friday next week."

He craved company, he thought of Jonathan, while taking a mental note of his friend's daily routine. Jonathan often started the day with a breakfast in L&S, then to work in Asia Pacific University. He usually took his dinner at Manang Sepa's, then off for the next two to three hours at the Keg Room, depending on the company there. He would take a cab when no one in the bar could take him to his house in Atwater Village.

A shadow crossed his face at the thought of the lonely life led by Jonathan. At home in Atwater Village, Jonathan had only beer and TV for company.

"Is Phil coming tonight?" he asked Jonathan.

"Not tonight. He is in Florida for a couple of days for one of his grandsons' christening. I thought you knew that."

"He did not tell me that the last time I was with him when we came here the other week."

Lew heard him and he said, "Did I hear you say Phil is in Florida? He seems to be doing a lot of traveling these days. Only last month he was in Hawaii."

"He has a big family scattered all over the United States," Simon replied. "He makes it a point to visit them as often as he can. Do you know how many children he has? Ten."

"Did I hear you right? Phil has ten children?" Mark said.

"Phil doesn't seem to believe in family planning," Lew said.

"He does," Simon said.

"If he does," Lew said, "how come he has so many children?"

"That is what he and his wife had planned for their family—ten children," Simon said, laughing.

The others laughed too, their laughter becoming louder when Jonathan said, "Phil measures his virility by the number of children he has fathered."

Lew then raised his glass of beer and said, "Here is to Phil and his great fatherhood."

Everyone in the bar counter raised their glasses and drank their beer, wine and liquor.

"I would love to have a job like that," Mark said, smiling.

"Same here," Jonathan said. "And you can watch me do it."

Simon glanced doubtfully at Jonathan. His friend was telling a trivial lie. How could Jonathan, a bachelor, do that? Jonathan had no female company, only drinking friends like him. And how far would he go for a friend? He will find that out soon enough. It was time he took up with him the teaching job he was eyeing in Asia Pacific.

"Can we talk over there?" he said to Jonathan, his eyes turned toward a table beside the lamp.

"All right," Jonathan replied.

"Will you excuse us, please?" he said to Lew and Mark as, their beer glasses in their hands, he and Jonathan went to the table.

Jonathan drank his beer while he looked around, satisfied no one in the bar counter could hear them. He did not want it known in the bar that he was looking for a job.

He leaned forward the instant Jonathan had brought his beer glass down on the table and said quietly to him, "I won't beat around the bush. I'm looking for a job."

"Why? Did they fire you in L and S?"

"No, they did not, but I want to shift to teaching."

"If I remember right, you told me once you used to teach history and literature in the Philippines."

"It is an old love I would like to go back to. Can you help me get a teaching job in Asia Pacific?"

Jonathan rubbed his chin while considering his request.

"We are in the middle of the term," he then said, "and I don't know of any opening right now for a teaching position in our school. We also don't offer subjects on Philippine literature and history."

"I can teach American literature and world history, and I am thinking of the summer session or the fall term."

Jonathan took another swig of his beer and then looked down at the table. He seemed to be considering what to say to Simon. Then he said, "I'll see what I can do. I'll ask around."

Simon nodded, pleased, and said, "I can hardly wait for the day when I will be teaching again, and I can only thank you for that."

"Don't thank me yet, not until I have done you this favor. But you are right, it is time you changed jobs. How long have you been working in L and S?"

"About five months now. I got it within a few days of our arrival here. Look at what my work there has done to my hands," he said as he showed Jonathan his reddish palms. "They are raw from cleaning tables and washing dishes."

"Teaching is not hard on the hands as it is on the brain. Of course, it is preferable to busing and washing dishes. You will have to go on working in L and S, though, until you can get a teaching job."

"I can get it with your help."

"As I have said, I'll see what I can do. Is there anything else you want to take up with me?"

"That is just about it."

They stood up and went back to the bar counter.

The way the game was going, Simon appeared to have made the right prediction. The Lakers were trailing the Bulls by a wide margin. The bar's Lakers fans were not giving up on their team, though. They kept on rooting for it, although all their cheering could not turn the game around for the Lakers. They drank on as they watched the game except Simon, who was nursing his glass of beer. He was driving and limiting himself to just a bottle of beer.

The game went on to the final stretch. Suddenly they shouted when the Bulls' Scottie Pippen threw a long pass to Michael Jordan, who then dribbled the ball toward the goal, a Lakers guard pursuing him.

"C'mon, stop Jordan," Lew said for the Lakers guard to catch up with Jordan.

But Jordan was way ahead of the Lakers guard. He dribbled the ball from the free-throw line and then jumped and dunked it into the ring. The men in the bar counter groaned in disappointment. With only a few seconds left, the game was over for the Lakers.

"I told you it's a Bulls' game," Simon said to Jonathan.

"At least," Jonathan said, "they are going down, fighting."

"Do you want your round of beer now?" Suprath said, smiling, to Mark.

She always came out the winner in any betting of drinks in the bar.

"Please do," Mark said to Suprath.

"You might want to know," Lew said to Simon and Jonathan, "we will soon be showing the three tenors' concert in Rome."

Simon nodded and smiled. The concert, to be shown by the television station where Mark and Lew worked, was something he would want to see. A concert by Domingo, Pavarotti and Careras, three of the world's greatest tenors, will be a very special treat.

"I hope you will show it on a Sunday, so I can watch it at home," he said.

"You can see the concert right here," Suprath said.

"Here?" he said. It seemed out of place in the bar.

"Why not?" Lew said. "We all need, at least now and then, something highbrow here."

"I will be looking forward to that," Jonathan said.

Simon glanced at the wall clock in the bar and stood up. It was eight-thirty, time to pick up Clara from her choir practice. It usually ended at nine o'clock. He would rather be early than late. He did not want Clara waiting all alone in the dark deserted church parking lot.

He said to Jonathan, "Do you want me to drop you off in your house before I pick up Clara?"

Jonathan seemed undecided about his offer.

Mark then said to Jonathan, "We'll take you home."

"Very well. Good night, people," he said as he waved in good-bye to everyone in the bar counter.

Chapter 8

Saul stood frowning as he waited with Agnes for the start of the Fil-Asian Fair in Los Angeles Convention Center. It was springtime in Los Angeles, but the morning was still too cold for him in his thin embroidered shirt called *Barong Tagalog* that Agnes had made him wear for the fair. His shoes were new and tight, and his feet hurt. He glanced at his watch, the second time he did so in the last few minutes. It was eight-thirty, way past the start at eight o'clock of the ribbon-cutting ceremony that will officially open the fair.

He became even more upset when he saw, across the ceremonial red ribbon strung up at the entrance to the convention center, utter confusion there. The fair's staff members, distinguishable by the blue ribbons pinned on their chests, were giving each other unheeded orders and counterorders as they got in each other's way or walked around aimlessly. Farther inside, the booths within his view were being given hurried final touches.

Ramon Dalaran, the fair organizer, was with a girl near the entrance. He could see from the frown in Dalaran's face and hear from the harsh tone of his voice as he was speaking to the girl, that he was scolding her.

"What is going on there?" he asked Agnes, his chin thrust out toward Dalaran and the girl.

"Dalaran is scolding the girl for misplacing the pair of scissors needed for the ribbon-cutting ceremony."

"Is that what is holding us?"

Agnes nodded.

Saul frowned in frustration at how this small detail had held up the opening of the fair. He watched the girl when she escaped the moment Dalaran's attention was turned to a man coming to him. The man said something to Dalaran. He nodded and hurried away.

Saul had seen enough of the confusion inside the convention center, and he turned his gaze to the other guests who were conversing while waiting at the entrance for the start of the ribbon-cutting ceremony. The photographers, cameras in their hands, their leather cords slung over their necks and shoulders, were likewise waiting, ready to take pictures. The Rondalla, a group of musical players, stood near the entrance. They were tuning their string instruments and seemed oblivious to everything else going on around them. At least, he noted, some people knew what they were there for.

His face lit up when the public address system struck up the *Stars and Stripes Forever*. He nodded in approval of it. The confusion inside the convention center and the long wait aside, the band music now gave the fair a festive air.

"That must be the signal for the start of the opening ceremony," he said to Agnes.

"Not just yet. They are still looking for the scissors."

Saul shook his head in dismay.

"A little more patience, dear," Agnes said to him. "This is their first time to hold a fair. We must give them allowance for that."

"I have been doing that for more than half an hour now. I won't mind doing it still, but it is getting too cold for me in this Barong Tagalog you made me wear. My feet are also killing me."

"I'm sorry about that, dear, but it should not take long now."

He nodded, his bad disposition eased up by Agnes' show of sympathy. She had been, in contrast, in buoyant spirit from the time they left their house earlier in the morning. She had finally convinced herself that the fair, which was the Filipino community's day of fun and shopping, was something worth visiting, and that getting a booth there may not be a bad idea at all. The delay in its opening need not dampen his enthusiasm as well.

He glanced at her. She was so charming and beautiful in her dark blue blazer over a yellow blouse. She had toyed with the idea of wearing a native dress, just for the fun of it, but at the last minute decided against it. As she put it, she was every inch a Filipino woman, and that whatever she wore will not change the way she looked.

His disposition now improved, he looked around at the fine spring morning in mid-April in downtown Los Angeles. By noon, it will be warm out there. The tall buildings around the convention center were pointed to the sky. Their glass windows reflected the sunlight, making him feel warm.

He looked down at his embroidered shirt and brushed it with his palm. It looked fine on him. She had it tailored for him on their last visit to the Philippines. She was right: it was perfect for the occasion. He wore it only on special Filipino affairs like today at the fair, where he and Agnes were among the special guests.

The fair's festive atmosphere now made him smile, pleased. It was like the town fiestas he had attended with her. The difference was it was being held in Los Angeles and not in the Philippines. He looked behind him at the parade participants. Some of them were in colorful native attire. The senior citizens' groups and civic and fraternal organizations were identifiable by their placards. Farther back, cordoned off by a yellow restraining ribbon, the crowd, growing by the minute, waited to be let in.

Dalaran came back and apologized for the delay. Then he asked the guests to form themselves in a line in front of the ceremonial ribbon.

So, Saul nodded, they had finally found the missing pair of scissors. He looked on as a young woman in native dress handed it to the man standing in the middle of the line: the guest of honor, the Philippine consul general who will cut the ribbon. The martial music playing in the public address system was switched off. Everyone fell silent.

He and Agnes, along with the other guests, held the ribbon. The instant it was cut, the people around clapped their hands while the photographers, lights flashing from their cameras, took the pictures. The Rondalla then struck up a lilting Filipino folk song.

"Well, we are finally off," Agnes said to him.

They and the other guests, following Dalaran's direction, lined up for the parade inside the convention center. Dalaran then waved his hand forward. Led by the Rondalla playing on the lilting music, they moved forward, behind Dalaran and a priest beside him, who was whisking holy water at the booths along the aisle.

They turned at a corner of the aisle, and Agnes held on to his arm. His heart leaped in pleasure at the softness of her breast, pressed to his arm. She was humming along the song, which she had played a few times on their piano at home, her head swaying to its lively beat. He glanced at her, happy to see her looking so happy.

The goods displayed in the booths along the aisle began to look interesting even to him by the time the parade was halfway in the convention center. But, unlike her, he was not a compulsive shopper. He will opt out of the shopping she will later do. Otherwise, he will only end up carrying her purchases and paying for them as well. He glanced again at her. She seemed to be taking a mental note of the booths they were passing by.

"I can imagine what you are planning to do here later on," he said to her.

"What else can I do here except to shop? And I can see there are a lot to buy here, but I need some shopping money," she said as she thrust her palm to him, like a beggar pleading for alms.

They moved on, smiling.

He nodded in approval when he saw his booth, its sign, "Levy Law Office," staring out proudly at him. The blurb below the sign read, "The immigration law office that opens doors to America." Below the blurb, in large letters, it read, "We provide free initial consultation." Written at the bottom were the office address and telephone number.

Steve and Therese, Nola and Susan were at the entrance to their booth, their teamwork suggested by the red T-shirts they were wearing, with the words "Levy Law Office" printed in the shirt front.

He glanced at the interior of the booth. Near the entrance was a long table for use by Therese, Nola and Susan. Facing each other across the table were a number of chairs. Lying on the table were brochures, his writings on immigration and a pile of magazines. Behind the table, screened by a white sheet, was the cubicle where he and Steve will take turns in providing free legal consultation. A mural done in watercolor ran almost the entire length of the white sheet. It showed people of various races marching through the portals of the Levy law office, to the towns, cities and farms in America. The message was clear to those who want to be permanent residents or citizens of the United States. The booth was simple and functional. Steve set it up with hired help.

"Well done, people, with our booth," he said to Steve and the others.

"Score one for the law firm, chief," Steve said as he shook his clasped hands at the side of his head to show a job he had done well with their booth.

"What do you think?" he asked Agnes after they had passed the booth.

"It has a welcoming air about it; it is not intimidating," she said as they moved on with the other parade participants.

The parade passed through several aisles more, lined with booths. It ended in the entertainment area of the convention center.

Saul and Agnes, along with the other guests, walked up to the stage and formed themselves in a line, facing the audience.

He was about to sit down on the chair behind him to give his feet, which were hurting again, some relief, but then, a petite woman in native dress, the program host, was about to address the audience. He remained standing and watched and listened.

"Good morning! I am Precy Montes," the woman said. "I'm pleased to welcome you to the first Fil-Asian Fair in Los Angeles."

She asked everyone to remain standing. Another woman

joined her. She led in singing the *Star-Spangled Banner*.

Saul sang it along. He was an American, proud to sing his country's national anthem.

The woman next led in singing the Philippine national anthem, and he could hear the audience singing it with great fervor. It was their own national anthem and, in singing it, they were giving expression to their own culture here in America. While they may affect American diction and acquire American traits and habits, at heart they will always be Filipinos. They will never be like him, a pure Anglo. But he was fond of them, for his love for Agnes extended to her people.

He nodded in approval of her, who was singing with fervor, their national anthem. Agnes' attachment to her homeland had not been diminished by years of living in the United States.

His feet continued to hurt. He would have sat down and removed his shoes to relieve the pressure on his feet, but Precy Montes had then called for the priest. He remained standing as the priest, in his invocation, called for God's blessing upon the fair and the people attending it.

The blank expression in the faces of many in the audience showed him that the invocation was a ritual they followed mechanically. It showed, though, how much their Christian faith played a role in their lives. Here they were, starting their fair with a religious invocation. The Filipino calendar in his study at home was full of religious holidays and festivals. The Philippine towns he had visited with Agnes were dominated by massive stone churches. Manila, he had observed, was a city of churches.

He glanced at Agnes, who was listening intently to the priest. A deeply religious person, she prayed upon waking up in the morning, at bedtime and before meals. She never failed to attend Mass on Sunday. He was not much of a praying person himself, but had agreed to the few times she had told him that prayers helped people a lot.

The priest was finished with his invocation, and he was finally able to sit down along with Agnes and the other guests on the chairs behind them. He removed his shoes to ease the pressure on his feet. He watched Dalaran as he took his turn at the microphone in the middle of the stage.

Dalaran cleared his throat and said, "Ladies and gentlemen,

allow me to welcome you to the first Fil-Asian Fair in Los Angeles. This is a happy day for us. This is the result of many months of preparation. . . ."

Dalaran suddenly stopped in his speech.

He saw, in the blank expression that had appeared in Dalaran's face, that Dalaran had lost his nerve, or his memory had failed him and he could not proceed with his speech.

Agonizing moments passed. His feet were still hurting, and he wondered who between him and Dalaran was in greater pain. He looked on at Dalaran, and it seemed to him that Dalaran was torn between making a retreat and going on bravely with his speech. For Dalaran to retreat, though, was to lose face and, to a Filipino like Dalaran, that was unacceptable.

He was not surprised when Dalaran then cleared his throat and went on bravely with his speech. He spoke in halting English, his speech lacking both in verve and with the right verbs. These repeatedly clashed with his subjects. The arbitrary shifts he made with his tenses compounded his problem. Dalaran was unintelligible.

Dalaran's speech left him confused and disappointed. How he wished Dalaran were speaking instead in Tagalog, in his own language. But like his fellow countrymen, Dalaran would rather brave the stormy seas and the treacherous reefs and shoals of the English language, than steer straight and clear in the calm open sea of his native tongue. He learned that much from Agnes. They considered their own language pedestrian, suitable only for casual conversation, and not for an occasion like the Fil-Asian Fair where to speak in English was considered a mark of distinction. He could attribute it to their colonial mentality and its prejudice against anything native to them, including their own language.

He sighed as he recalled a similar problem with other immigrant groups, the Latinos in particular. Many of them came ill-suited for life in America. They lacked the verbal skills, which they hardly bothered to master in their homelands prior to their immigration to America. As they then found out, learning English in America could be a daunting task. Only a few of them could master it. The rest, unable to communicate well, were thus shut out from mainstream American society. Having been shut out, more by lack of communication and other required skills than by racial bigotry, they turned inward to their ethnic enclaves, an example of which was right now before his eyes. He was sad to see the audience made up almost entirely of Filipinos. They were also kept away from mainstream American society.

Dalaran struggled on with his speech, and he could feel a pained silence in the audience. Some of those standing at the edge of the audience had started to move away. He glanced at Agnes. She was watching Dalaran, apparently feeling sorry for him, and he felt the same way.

The audience applauded halfheartedly at the end of Dalaran's speech. The consul general spoke next. He listened, the pressure on his feet eased up, but now, he could feel his stomach grumbling for food at the faint smell of coffee and food coming from the food stalls in the convention center. He and Agnes had taken only coffee before they left the house early in the morning.

Precy Montes took over the microphone after the consul general had finished with his short speech. She said, "We now take pleasure in presenting our honored guests, their plaques of appreciation."

The guests were called one after another. He put on his shoes shortly before his name was called. He walked toward Precy Montes and Dalaran as they handed to him, his plaque of appreciation. The crowd applauded as he accepted it. He walked back to his seat, limping slightly.

"Do your feet still hurt?" Agnes asked him.

"It is not as bad as before," he replied as he sat down and gave the plaque to her.

"Are you sure?"

"Yes, I'm sure," he said, smiling for her solicitude.

The other guests seated nearby had overheard them and they stared ahead, seemingly amused.

Agnes had noticed nothing, though. She was reading the engraved commendation on the plaque when she whispered to him, "I'll be happy if this plaque will entitle you to a discount at the booths."

He stopped himself from laughing and smiled instead. The plaque was a very ordinary thing with him. More than a dozen of them he had received from various organizations were tucked away in a cabinet in his study at home. There should be a lot more out there waiting for the right occasion to be handed out to him, what with the five hundred or so Filipino organizations, Agnes had told him, that were registered in Los Angeles alone. These were hometown and provincial clubs, alumni associations, and fraternal groups, among others. Most of them were in hibernation. They would come to life only at the election and induction of officers, and for anniversaries and during Christmas. But they provided a convenient means of giving chosen individuals like him recognition in their community. Without those organizations and their activities, they would be just one anonymous mass of people in Los Angeles.

The Rondalla took its turn at the stage. As it began to play a Filipino love song, Precy Montes and Dalaran retired to a corner of the stage.

Simon listened, his eyes turned to the audience. Some distinctively tall fair-complexioned Americans stood out there. Two of them had young boys, obviously their children, perched on their shoulders. Like him, love had made them cross the racial divide. A few Americans he had seen in the booths were there for commerce. They were merchants who would go anywhere in the world, not least of all to Los Angeles' own convention center, in a quest of the mighty American dollar. A sprinkling of Americans manned the entrances and patrolled the aisles. They were there because they worked there. Otherwise, the Filipinos had the convention center, all to themselves.

As he watched the audience made up almost entirely of Filipinos, he felt sorry for them. It was not because there was anything sad about their community fair. It was, in fact, a typical festive gathering of Filipinos. But they seemed to be walled in, not by stone and cement, but by an invisible barrier. They seemed to be isolated from the rest of the city. He had seen images like that in a Charlie Chaplin movie, *The Great Dictator,* which showed a similar isolation of the Jews in a Jewish ghetto.

He shook his head in regret of how their isolation from mainstream American society did not make them cohesive. He learned from Agnes about their crab mentality of pulling each other down instead of pushing each other up, about their proverbial lack of unity, and of how mean, envious, jealous and condescending they were to each other. As she had also told him, they had this common notion that one's neighbors, friends, associates and even relatives were not as deserving of the good fortune of having made it to America. And yet he could also see the grand time they were having at the Fil-Asian Fair. They must be that kind of people who envied, disliked and resented each other, but since they had no one else but themselves to turn to here in America, how they then tolerated and even accepted and enjoyed each other's company.

He could hear, as he was watching the audience, an indistinct hum above the voices there and distant music in the booths. More people were coming in. The aisles and the booths were gradually being filled with them. In time perhaps there will be more blending of the races in Los Angeles and in the rest of the country.

He glanced at Agnes. She herself was the result of such a blending. She was lovely as ever, a beautiful living argument for mixed marriage. She would stand out there, lovely and sophisticated with her fine Eurasian features.

The Rondalla had barely finished playing the love song when Precy Montes returned to the microphone. She swept her arms with flourish toward a group of young barefooted dancers waiting at a wing of the stage, and announced, "And now here to perform our famous bamboo dance, the *Tinikling,* are the young dancers of the Santa Ana Cultural Group."

She left the stage as the crowd applauded the young dancers who were coming to the center of the stage. They were in native attire, the two girls in sheer embroidered blouses and red shiny skirts, the six boys in loose embroidered shirts, their red pants rolled up just below the knee. They carried with them four bamboo poles and four blocks of wood.

They smiled at him, Agnes and the other seated guests. Then they turned and bowed before the audience.

It was the first time for Saul to see the Tinikling, and he watched eagerly as the young dancers made ready with their dance.

Each of the two pairs of dancers, a boy and a girl each pair, watched and waited while the two pairs of boys handling the bamboo poles, set apart from each other by a few feet, went down on their knees. Then they made a few practice claps with the bamboo poles in their hands, twice on the blocks of wood they had placed in front of each one of them, and once against each other.

They nodded, and the Rondalla, which had moved to a side of the stage, began to play a lilting song. Each pair of dancers, standing on one side of the bamboo poles, then held each other's hand as they each dipped a foot on the floor, raising them the instant the bamboo poles were clapped against each other, and then crossing quickly to the other side, as the bamboo poles were drawn apart.

Saul had anxious moments as he watched the dancers. A slight misstep and the bamboo poles might hit and hurt the dancers' feet. But as the dance progressed, it became clear to him that the young dancers had timed perfectly the movement of their feet with the clapping together of the bamboo poles.

He watched, entranced: a dip of the foot, then two steps to the other side; a dip of the foot again, then two steps to the other side. He was so captivated by the dance, he kept beat with it, with his hand tamping his knee. The dancers moved about in precise rhythmic fashion to the lilting music provided by the Rondalla and the clapping of the bamboo poles on each other and on the blocks of wood, the sounds they made reverberating throughout the stage: thud, thud, clap; thud, thud, clap; thud, thud, clap. The tempo increased, the dancers moved quicker until, to the trill of the Rondalla's string instruments, they stopped, stood still, and bowed before the applauding audience.

Precy Montes was back before the microphone even before the applause had died down and the dancers had left the stage. She announced the next dance called the *Binasoan* and then left the stage.

Six young women, wearing fine beige native dresses, glided into the stage, lighted votive candles in small round blue glasses perched on their heads and on their palms. Like Dalaran, they may do poorly in English and in other things as well, but not when it came to dancing. It came naturally to them.

He watched, anxiously at times, as the dancers' slim arms and lithe bodies moved and swayed sinuously to the accompaniment of the Rondalla music. They kept their heads high and steady all the while, for a slight tilt would have sent the glasses toppling down, breaking them into pieces and ruining the dance. It went on smoothly and ended to another applause from the audience.

Precy Montes returned to the microphone and said, "May we now request our honored guests to come to the reception area?"

A buffet table laden with finger food was waiting for them.

Saul and Agnes moved along the table. She seemed undecided on which ones to take from among the fried chicken wings, steamed dumplings, egg rolls, sushi and mounds of pyramid-shaped sandwiches laid out there.

She asked Saul, "Would you like to try the ham sandwich?"

He nodded, and she picked up a ham sandwich and put it on his plate laid on top of the plaque in his hand. She likewise put a ham sandwich on her plate.

"Would you like to try the dumplings?" she asked him, who nodded again in agreement.

They took some more finger food as they moved along the buffet table until their plates were nearly full.

Like the other guests, they ate standing up. Agnes had difficulty swallowing down her ham sandwich, and she said, "I need coffee to wash this food down."

"I'll get it for you,' he said as he gave her his plate of food.

She waited while he made coffee. He came back with two cups of coffee and put them on the plates of food in her hands. He took from her the plate of food with the plaque underneath and resumed eating.

They were having a good breakfast. The food was tasty and nicely washed down with hot coffee. They finished eating their food in a short while, after which, he took the used food plates and the coffee cups to the trash can in a corner of the reception area.

He was making his way back to Agnes when he came across the consul general and another guest named Gomez. They were introduced to each other earlier, before the start of the ribbon-cutting ceremony.

"We were just talking about the King trial," the consul general said to him. "You are an authority on the subject. Perhaps you can tell us what will be the jury's likely verdict."

He smiled. By feeding his vanity, the consul general had goaded him into giving an answer, but he was not biting. He won't take sides on such a touchy subject.

"Your guess is as good as mine," he said.

He had his own educated guess on the jury's likely verdict, but he preferred to keep it to himself. The police officers will likely go free. It was just as likely that the black residents in Los Angeles will react violently to such a verdict. Gomez and the consul general will know this soon enough, now that the trial was about to end. The defense and the prosecution were expected to make their closing arguments in a few days. In the meantime, fear and tension had been building up in Los Angeles.

The consul general took his refusal to answer his question as a diplomat would, when he said, "Whatever will be the verdict, justice will be served here. America's judicial system is a model for the rest of the world."

"I cannot but agree with you," he said at the consul general's flattering diplomatic remark.

He was about to move on, he did not want to keep Agnes waiting, but then, Gomez said to him, "You know that better than anyone here. The King case maybe hardly any different from the scores of cases you have handled. I guess the only difference here is its racial dimension."

"I handle only immigration cases, but whatever is the nature of the case, the judicial process is essentially the same."

"I suppose you can say that from experience," Gomez said.

"From dozens of such experiences," Agnes said from behind Saul.

She shot him an annoyed look. He had kept her waiting. Her face brightened, though, when she then said, "You might be interested to know that many of my husband's clients are Filipinos."

The consul general nodded and said to him, "So, you are the man many of our countrymen turn to for help with their immigration problems."

"I'm only doing my job," he replied modestly.

Gomez asked, "Are illegal immigrants all alike in their casual attitude toward their status?"

Saul knitted his brow, puzzled, but too polite to ask Gomez what he was trying to say. Gomez had spoken in an ambiguous roundabout way he knew was common among Filipinos speaking in English.

Gomez saw him looking puzzled, and he said, "Do Filipinos in illegal status take it for granted?"

He replied, "I can say from my own experience that your countrymen who are in that status make every effort to be legalized."

"Can you say that of the other ethnic groups?" Gomez asked.

"It is hard to say. They are in different situations. They see things differently."

Gomez knitted his brow. He did not seem to understand what he said. He was uncomfortable discussing a racially sensitive subject, but felt that what he said needed some explanation.

"Other immigrant groups are not as keen about getting legalized as Filipinos are," he said. "They consider legal services a bothersome and unnecessary expense. They are not as concerned as Filipinos are about getting caught by the immigration authorities and made to return to their home countries, for they can always try coming back without much difficulty."

"Like crossing the Rio Grande or burrowing under your border fence, or by whatever means, fair or foul, just so they can come here," Gomez said.

Saul nodded but said nothing.

"On the other hand," the consul general said, "Filipinos must first obtain visas at the American Embassy in Manila. This is a tremendous obstacle course only a few of them can hurdle. Then, they must incur the expense, a big one for most of them, of flying across the Pacific Ocean. It is certainly worth it for them to be legal."

"That is why many of my clients are Filipinos," he said. "Thanks to my wife, too. She is my contact with your community."

He and Agnes smiled at each other.

"I understand many of the immigrants make it to Los Angeles," the consul general said.

"Yes," he said, "they come here for the jobs, the temperate climate and a culturally diverse population. Los Angeles is a melting pot of various races."

"Or a rainbow of races, as others call it," Gomez said, "but does it not account for a lot of racial tension here, like that brought about by the King trial?"

Saul smiled at the shift in their conversation. The topic had to go back to the King trial. Everyone in Los Angeles seemed to be obsessed with it.

"That is the downside of a multicultural society," he said, "like what we have here in Los Angeles, where people of different races live close to each other. They will just have to be more tolerant and understanding of each other."

Just then, a man approached the consul general and whispered something into his ear. The consul general glanced at his watch.

"You will have to excuse me, I have another engagement," the consul general said. "It is nice talking to you."

He left after shaking hands with Saul, Agnes and Gomez.

"I better get going, too," Gomez said as he too walked away.

Agnes took Saul's arm. It was time to visit their booth.

They saw Therese seated all alone at the reception table in the booth of the Levy law office.

"How nice you look, Therese," Agnes said as she and Saul were coming to her.

"You, too, Agnes," Therese replied. "Saul must be the envy of every man here."

She stood up as she and Agnes hugged each other.

Saul watched them, pleased with the two most important women in his life complimenting each other: his wife who shared his private personal life with no other woman, and his secretary-receptionist who shared more than anyone else his professional life.

"Where are the others?" he asked as he sat down on a chair and laid the plaque on the table.

"They went around for a look at the booths before the clients will come in," Therese replied.

"So, the droves of clients have yet to come in," Agnes said as she too sat down, facing Saul.

"I'll be happy if a dozen clients will come here," he said.

"I'll treat you to a steak dinner if that many will come here," Agnes said.

"You are not kidding?" he said, at the challenge posed on him by Agnes.

"No, I'm not, and you are our witness," she said to Therese.

"Then, be ready to part with your money," he said, smiling.

"Here comes Steve," Therese said as he was coming in from the aisle.

"Hi, Agnes," he said to her. "You certainly brighten, along with Therese here, this corner of the convention center."

He turned to Saul and said with faked seriousness, "We are on war footing here, chief. Three of the competition are also here."

"The more the merrier," Saul said, unconcerned.

Suddenly Steve turned toward the mural and, sweeping forward an imaginary sword in his hand, he called out gravely:

"Once more, unto the breach, my friends, once more;
or close the wall upon with our English dead!"

The appearance of a man at the booth entrance cut short Steve's call for an attack on the enemy fortress he playacted from Shakespeare's *King Henry V*. The man had also been taken aback by Steve's playacting, and he stood hesitantly at the booth entrance. Therese walked quickly toward the man and said to him, "Won't you come in, please?"

The man hesitated, but then he allowed Therese to lead him to Saul, who was waiting for him.

"I'm Saul Levy. What can I do for you?" he said to the man.

"Well . . . Maybe . . . ," the man stammered.

"We'll be more comfortable inside," Saul said, as he led the man to the cubicle.

He looked back at Agnes once the man was inside the cubicle, his forefinger pointed up. One client down.

Therese took hurriedly some forms from the reception table and joined Saul in the cubicle.

It was a different man who walked out confidently from the cubicle, some fifteen minutes later. He nodded at Agnes and Steve, and stepped out toward the aisle where he was soon lost in the crowd there.

"Well?" Agnes asked Saul.

"Well, what?" he replied, smiling, as he sat down on a chair facing Agnes.

"How did it turn out?"

"Good. We'll handle his case. He wants to sponsor his children, one of whom will turn twenty-one in a few months. He even gave a downpayment."

Therese showed the check to Agnes, who smiled as she glanced at it.

"So, you are off to a grand start," she said.

"With a check to boot," Therese said, smiling.

"Eleven more to go," Agnes said as Therese was putting the check in a steel box.

A couple were looking in from the booth entrance.

"Let me take care of them," Steve said.

He approached the couple and said to them, "Can I be of help to you?"

The man said, "Can you help our son bring over here, his fiancée in the Philippines?"

"Of course, step right this way, please," Steve said as he led the couple to the cubicle.

Saul in the meantime was looking around idly. His eyes settled on the pile of magazines lying on the table. He took the magazine on top, gazed at its cover, and said to Agnes, "Enjoy the view, honey, while I do some reading."

"I've got a better idea," she said. "Why don't I sit in while Steve is interviewing the couple? I might learn a thing or two about sponsoring a fiancée."

"Suit yourself," he said.

He was reading a feature article in the magazine in his hands and did not bother to look up when Agnes stood up and walked toward the cubicle.

Simon held Clara firmly on her shoulder. The crowd around them might unintentionally push them apart. He must keep an eye too on Lorna and Sonny, who were walking ahead of them. They were not too far ahead. Satisfied that his children were within his sight, he allowed himself to glance now and then at the booths on both sides of the aisle in the convention center.

The fair was something of a novelty in their community, and he could see how correctly it had been billed as one huge marketplace, as his eyes feasted on its material abundance. There were so many things to buy there, from appliances, to computers, to a car displayed in one of the booths. He could even obtain services there, from legal, to travel, to life insurance and to making one's final arrangements, as what a couple seemed to be doing with the sales representative of a mortuary booth. Those inside the other booths were inspecting or trying out the goods displayed there.

As he walked on with Clara, he became increasingly self-conscious that he might be overdressed in his long-sleeved white shirt. Most of the men in the crowded aisle were dressed casually in jeans and T-shirts, some of them wearing rubber sneakers. A good thing he and Sonny left their coats and ties in their car. Clara and Lorna might also feel overdressed in their long-sleeved dresses. But it was Sunday and they had just come from St. Stephen Church, where Clara had sung with the choir there. They dressed appropriately for the Mass on the reasoning that if they must look good before their fellowmen, so should they look at their best before God.

He walked on with Clara, shrugging in dismissal whatever those in the crowd around them might think of them as overdressed.

They loved to window-shop, as what they will do at the fair. It will be fun and cost them nothing as well. There were things there that they would like to buy, but would rather not. They lived frugally. They spent their money only on the bare necessities, although with Clara's tacit approval, he allowed himself to splurge, if spending a few dollars for a bottle of beer at the Keg Room, or a book in Shannon's Bookshop, could be called that.

He could see at the fair, an example of what Father Finley spoke in his homily in St. Stephen Church about Sunday being a day of blessing in America. It was a day of rest and recreation for him and his family. They always made it a point to go out on Sunday—a picnic in Griffith Park, or lunch of steamed crab and other seafood in San Pedro, followed by a stroll along the tourist shops in the adjoining Ports O' Call, or a visit to Glendale Galleria. Any of those was a fine a way of enjoying the blessings of Sunday in America, as what they were now doing at the fair.

The noise made by the crowd in the aisle and in the booths was so great it nearly drowned out a choral group singing on the stage far behind them. He could catch only snatches of the song, a waltz about the loveliest night of the year. He listened, pleased, to the music, but there will be time enough for the entertainment on the stage. For now, he was thrilled enough to walk on with Clara and bask in the pleasure of simply being a part of the festive fair.

He was walking on with Clara when he saw Sonny and Lorna standing apart from the crowd walking by and watching a booth across the aisle. The moment he and Clara came to them, Sonny pointed at the booth and said, "Is that not our lawyer?"

He nodded when he saw the name of the Levy law office in the booth. Its blurb claiming the power to open doors to America had done precisely that for him and his family.

"Why don't we drop by and say hello to Attorney Levy?" Clara said.

"Good idea," he replied.

Saul put down on the table the magazine he was reading, and he stood up when he saw Simon and Clara coming with what he could guess were their two children.

"So, you have not missed out on your community fair," he said, as he shook hands with them.

"Welcome to our extension office," Therese said to Simon and Clara, who nodded and smiled at her. They also smiled at Nola and Susan who were seated beside Therese at the reception table.

"Therese runs our office here with Nola and Susan," Saul said. "Steve, my associate, is inside the cubicle, attending to some clients."

"It looks like you are having a busy time even here at the fair," Simon said as he glanced at a couple waiting for their turn for consultation.

"We are not too busy for a chat with you," Saul said.

He glanced at Sonny and Lorna and said, "Your children?"

"Yes. Meet Lorna and Sonny," Simon said.

Saul shook hands with them.

Agnes was coming out of the cubicle, and Saul said to her, "Well, dear, you have finally met the Matins, your provincemates from Zambales."

"I'm so glad to meet you," she said, smiling as they shook hands.

Simon introduced Lorna and Sonny to Agnes, and she shook hands with them, too.

He smiled as he watched Clara and Agnes subtly assessing each other. They seemed to like what they saw in each other. From their bearing and the clothes they were wearing, he could see a marked difference in their lifestyles and stations in life. Agnes looked elegant in her well-cut expensive blazer, while his wife, bless her soul, at first glance looked like an innocent lass abroad. But score nine out of ten for their good looks. Clara and Agnes could still turn heads with their charm and beauty.

"How is our lovely province of Zambales?" Agnes asked in a friendly tone of voice.

Before either Clara or Simon could reply, she said, "How I miss it! It's more than five years now since Saul and I visited the country. I miss the quiet country life there, the outings in the beaches and the horseback rides in the ranch. We could stay for only a few days, though."

"How about our famous Zambales mango?" Clara said about the sweet and luscious fruit the province was noted for.

"That, especially," Agnes said, nodding in faked seriousness. "Saul here could never have enough of it, as with one other thing he craves."

Clara did not notice Agnes when, a mischievous smile on her face, she threw Saul a knowing sidelong glance. Saul kept a straight face, though, about their bedtime activity, which she had alluded to.

"But, tell me," Agnes said quickly. "How are things in Zambales and in the rest of the country?"

"It is pretty much the same as when you last visited it," Clara said. "At least that is what I've gathered from our friends and relatives there. Nothing much happens there and in the rest of the country, unlike here where a lot is going on and everyone is busy."

"Busy at work or at play," Agnes said. "Saul told me you already have your work permits."

"Yes, thanks to your husband," Simon said as he smiled and nodded gratefully at Saul. "I'm also happy to tell you that Clara just got a job in a retail chain store."

"That is great!" Saul said to Clara. "Your children too, I suppose, have found jobs?"

"We are still looking, sir, for part-time or summer jobs, so we can continue with our studies," Lorna said.

"We want to work and earn some money, too," Sonny said.

"Everyone works in America," Agnes said.

"Work is all I do," Saul said, "but as for Agnes here, when she is not working, she is out shopping."

"One of my few remaining pleasures in life," Agnes said, smiling. "Which reminds me, what am I doing here? I should be making the rounds now."

She gave Saul a peck on the cheek and said, "I'll have to go. I'll see you later, dear."

Agnes waved in good-bye at Therese, Nola and Susan. She turned to Clara and said, "Would you like to come along?"

"Why not? We were just leaving, were we not?" Clara said to Simon, who nodded in reply.

He shook hands with Saul and waved in good-bye at Therese, Nola and Susan.

He followed Lorna, Sonny, Agnes and Clara as they were entering a booth across the aisle. It sold mainly books and native handicraft. They looked around, but found nothing interesting there.

"Let us try the garden supply booth I saw earlier this morning," Agnes said. "Saul needs a weed killer for the crab grass that has appeared in our lawn and garden."

"Are you not coming?" Clara asked Simon, who was browsing a bookshelf.

"Go ahead," he replied. "I'll catch up with you."

He watched them as they stepped out of the booth. Then he turned his attention back to the bookshelf. He took out a volume of short stories, turned its pages and settled on a short story with a striking opening paragraph. A man had been told he had only a few months to live. He did not want his family put to a lot of financial strain by his death, so he bought a life insurance policy, made the final arrangements with a mortuary, and even ordered flowers in advance. After a day of doing all this, he went home looking forward to a dinner with his wife and their children. Despite all the preparations he had made, the man did not want to die.

An interesting coincidence, he and Clara had bought a family-size plot at the Hillcrest Memorial Park in acceptance of death that will come to all of them.

The stories listed in the book's table of contents showed that he had read most of them. It was not worth buying it. The proprietor looked away in disappointment when he returned it to the bookshelf.

He looked around. There were more books on Philippine history, culture and even cooking. There were maps, flags and pictures of Philippine sceneries. There were also woodcraft, wall decor and bookends, all of them of Filipino motif. He would loved to buy some of them, but found them expensive. He picked up from another bookshelf, a coffee-table book on Manila. He turned its pages, pausing at the pictures of familiar scenes in Manila. Rizal Park in the morning. Roxas Boulevard at dusk. The image of the Black Nazarene borne in a procession from Quiapo Church. He stopped turning the pages when he noticed he had stayed there too long. The proprietor looked away in disappointment when he returned the book to the bookshelf and left the booth.

He joined the crowd in the aisle and looked for Agnes, Clara and the children in the garden supply booth. They were not there. He walked on and found them farther down the aisle in a booth that, with paintings, sculptures and other art objects on display there, could pass off for a tiny impromptu art gallery.

His children were looking around while Clara and Agnes were looking at a painting in front of them.

He saw, as he joined them, why they were so taken by the painting. It was about a village scene, a subject that he loved. Its colors sweet and light, it was an idyllic representation of country life in the Philippines rendered under the influence of the renowned Filipino painter, Fernando Amorsolo.

He looked on, very much interested in the painting. It looked just like a village in his hometown in Laguna. It showed a nipa hut standing near a couple of fruit trees and a bamboo grove overlooking the rice paddies spread out into the horizon. The sky above was blue with bands of cotton-white clouds. It was summertime and the rice paddies lay fallow and drenched with sunlight. It was midafternoon. The trees and the bamboo grove cast shadows on the yard. It was so quiet there but for what the trees suggested was the presence of crickets, trilling on that warm summer day. The dog, the family pet, was curled up at the foot of the wooden stairs.

An old woman, her hair white and gray, was by the bamboo window. She was looking down, indicating she was either at work, knitting or sewing something, or she was engaged in a solitary game of cards. She was smoking the way old women like her in the country smoked native cigarettes, with the lighted end clamped inside her mouth. The rest of the household could be taking a nap in the nipa hut. The children could be playing in the fields, or giving their work animal, the carabao, a bath in the creek.

He smiled. How long ago were those summers of his youth spent like that. He rode with his friends on the carabaos, climbed the fruit trees, flew their kites, and talked about their dreams in life as they lay on the grass and watched the birds flying in the sky.

"A Day in a Village," he decided, would be a good title for the painting. It was a subjective and idyllic representation of country life in the Philippines. It had affected him for what it evoked of his days of youth in his hometown in Laguna. But then, it made him pause at what the painting did not show: the grinding poverty of the villagers, their landlords' abusive treatment, their anger and discontent, their government's indifference. This was the real condition in the country's villages. The painting showed nothing of them.

Clara moved closer to the painting, obstructing partly his view of it. He was distracted, and he realized quite quickly the error he had made of looking for something in the painting that did not have to be there. He was a mere onlooker and yet he had the nerve to impose his political views on the painting, contrary to the painter's right to portray it as a village scene of idyllic charm.

He hastened to correct himself as he looked again at the painting, with all thought suspended, and felt slowly coming back to him, the tug of homesickness for his hometown in Laguna.

Clara and Agnes looked very much interested in the painting.

"What do you think?" Agnes asked Clara.

"It's a very nice painting. I can feel its charm and appeal."

"I feel the same way about it."

"I don't think I know the painter," she said about the painter's signature at the right bottom corner of the painting.

The proprietor, who all the while was watching them, said to Agnes, "His name is Al Genarlo, a young painter making a name in Manila."

He followed it with a bit of a sales talk: "That painting is a very good buy, if you will ask me. It will make your nice home look even nicer."

Agnes nodded and smiled out of courtesy to the compliment made by the proprietor.

"Well, ma'am," the proprietor continued, "you are my first customer, and I want to start the day right with a good sale. I'm giving it to you for only three hundred dollars."

The painting had a price tag of four hundred dollars.

"It is a giveaway at that price," the proprietor pressed on, "and I'm doing this only because you seem to like it so much."

Simon saw a look of doubt had appeared in Agnes' face as she was looking on at the painting. She seemed to be quite undecided now on what she should do about it. A woman's fickle mind was at work. Her mind, made up a while ago, began to waver the moment the discussion turned to the price of the painting. The painting by then had ceased to be a work of art admired for what it portrayed and evoked. It had become instead a mere commercial commodity, something to be haggled over.

"I'll tell you what," she said to the proprietor, "I'll ask my husband to take a look at it. I'll go see him in our booth."

The proprietor raised his eyebrows at this unexpected turn in their transaction, but he agreed with a nod of his head.

"If my husband likes it, we will buy it. I'll even ask him to pay for it. Can you hold on to it while I'm getting my husband?"

"Of course," the proprietor said.

"We must be moving on, too," Clara said to Agnes.

"We will see each other again, won't we?" she said to Clara. "I'll drop by your store one of these days. You have my card and I have your telephone number. Let us call each other."

"Yes, we will do that. We will call each other."

"I'll be expecting also the stuffed broiled chicken you said you will cook for me."

"You can count on it. Have fun now with your shopping."

They left at the same time. Agnes walked back to Saul's booth, while Simon and Clara, Lorna and Sonny went in the opposite direction.

Simon, after a while, looked back at Agnes. She was now far enough from them, and he said to Clara, "I know, you don't have to tell me. I can read your mind. You did not enjoy tagging along with Agnes, when all you could do was watch her buy things like that painting worth half a month of the pay you'll get in your new job."

"I am not a compulsive shopper like her, who has all the money in the world," Clara said. "There are other ways we can enjoy ourselves here, and it is not by spending money we do not have."

He glanced at his wife and nodded. She was right, of course. All they could do there was window-shop. That should be exciting enough, and a good thing neither of them was a compulsive shopper.

"I like her, though," Clara then said. "She seems like a nice person."

"She strikes me as one," he said. "Saul and Agnes Levy make a happy couple."

They visited various booths where Clara went through the motion of examining the goods sold there and asking the sales clerks questions about them. She bought nothing, though.

As for Sonny and Lorna, they had fun filling their bag with giveaways.

"Did you see that?" Lorna said to Sonny at a bank booth taking free pictures.

"Let me take a look," Sonny said as he joined a line of people moving toward the booth counter. He waved at them to join him, but then, a couple had walked behind him.

Simon approached them and, his finger pointed at Sonny, he said to them, "Excuse me, that is my son ahead of you; we are together."

"I'm sorry, but please move ahead," the man said as he and the woman stepped aside for Simon, Clara and Lorna.

He thanked the couple and joined Sonny in the line with Clara and Lorna. Their turn at the booth counter came. Sonny filled out a form for the free picture. Then, following the photographer's instruction, they moved to a spot with a mock-up of a stagecoach, the bank's symbol, behind them, and had their picture taken. The photographer then pulled out the picture from his camera and gave it to Simon. They looked at it. Lorna squealed in delight at how happy and handsome they looked, she especially.

They left the booth after thanking its proprietor and walked along with the crowd in the aisle. At a corner of the aisle was a booth of a movie talent agency. They watched it from a distance.

"Here is your chance to be in the movies," Sonny said to Lorna. "Would you like to give it a try?"

Lorna looked doubtfully at the booth, but then, she said, "Why not?"

She approached a table in the booth where a woman, herself a beauty fit for the movies, was seated. The woman asked her to take a seat and handed to her an application form, which she filled out. She was next ushered to the talent scout's table.

"So, you want to be a movie star," the talent scout said to her.

"Who," she replied, "doesn't want to be one?"

"We will make you one, if you have what it takes to be one. We will know that after you have gone through an interview and a screen test in our Hollywood office. Once you have passed both of them, you will join our roster of talents we represent for roles in the movies and television. The door will then be open for you to the world of celebrities. How do you like that?"

"It sounds exciting. I can already see myself acting in front of the camera."

"We will set you up, then, for the interview and screen test. There will be a small fee, though."

"How much is it?"

She gasped from shock at the amount the talent scout then mentioned. Five hundred bucks!

"I'll have to ask my mom and dad about it. If you will excuse me," she said.

She stood up and walked back to Simon, Clara and Sonny.

"How did you make out?" Sonny asked her.

"They will consider me for an interview and a screen test, but there is a fee for both."

"How much is it?" Sonny asked.

Simon and Clara were likewise stunned by the amount Lorna then mentioned.

"I'm sorry, Lorna," Simon said, "but we don't have that kind of money."

"Our savings will be for your college education and nothing else," Clara said.

"I know you will say that," Lorna said.

"There goes your movie career," Sonny said. "You know, my dear sister, they won't charge you anything if you are the type they are looking for."

"You put me up to it!"

"Now, don't blame me. I did not put you up to it. I just asked you if you would like to give it a try."

"Oh, yes, you did."

"Stop it," Clara said to Lorna. "You did it for the fun of it. You had your fun; that is enough."

Sonny, in a gesture of sympathy to Lorna, laid his hand on her shoulder and said, "Mom is right. You had your fun; that's enough."

She remained resentful, though. She removed brusquely Sonny's arm from her shoulder and walked back to the talent scout. She told him she was withdrawing her application. She returned to Simon, Clara and Sonny, now looking satisfied with herself.

"Now, let me see you give it a try," she said to Sonny.

"Why not? Watch me do it."

He went to the booth and was soon being interviewed. It was a short one, and he left the talent scout, looking disappointed. He was startled when he saw Rod and Andrew watching him.

"Caught you!" Andrew said to Sonny. "So you want to be a big movie star!"

"Come now, you don't have the looks for it," Rod said.

Sonny shrugged his shoulder and said, "I did it just for the heck of it."

"Do you expect us to believe you?" Andrew said. "I never saw you look so serious and determined while you were being interviewed."

"Cut it out, will you?" Sonny said, frowning. "Say, what took you so long? I thought you were never coming."

"I had trouble getting my car started," Andrew said.

"As usual," Rod said.

They joined Simon, Clara and Lorna, who were watching them. Rod and Andrew greeted them a good morning. Simon and Clara nodded in returning their greeting. Lorna smiled in acknowledgment of their greeting.

"How did it go?" she asked Sonny.

"They should have told me they are not looking for a Paul Newman look-alike."

"Paul Newman look-alike, my eye! Crocodile Face is a Paul Newman look-alike!" Lorna exclaimed to the others' laughter.

Sonny ignored Lorna's tart remark and said to Clara, "Mom, can I take a look around here with Rod and Andrew?"

Clara glanced at Simon, who nodded in assent.

"You may go," she said to Sonny, "but be back at noontime."

Sonny scratched his head in protest and said, "That is too soon, Mom. Why not later this afternoon?"

"Why should it take you that long to move around here?"

"Let him go," Simon said.

"All right, if that is what your father says, but don't leave the premises."

"We won't, Mom," Sonny said, now smiling.

"How, about you, sis," he said to Lorna. "Would you like to come with us?"

She shook her head in refusal.

"All right, then, see you later," he said as he walked away with Rod and Andrew.

Simon glanced at Lorna, touched by her looking wistfully at Sonny and his friends.

"Why did you not go with them?" he said to her. "They are fun."

"I will only be out of place with 'The Three Musketeers.' "

He watched Sonny and his friends until they disappeared in the crowd. His son now had company other than his own family, and other interests as well. As he grew older, so will his world. So will Lorna's world.

He laid a hand on Lorna's shoulder in a mute expression of understanding of her. She may have her petty quarrels with Sonny, but he was not her only brother, he was her one true friend. He took Clara's hand and led them away.

By late afternoon, Lorna had nearly filled her bag with giveaways. She had collected penlights, umbrellas, brochures, lighters, ballpoint pens, gift certificates and their family picture. By then, having made the rounds of the convention center twice, they had a good idea of what the fair had to offer. Many of the goods sold there could be found in Los Angeles.

Simon kept it to himself, but he was disappointed with the few shoddy Philippine products sold at the fair: Papier-mâché art. Glass and wooden beads. Woodcarvings. Bolos sheathed in water buffalo horns forged by the same smithies for Bonifacio in the Philippine Revolution nearly a century ago, all of them made, not by machines, but by hand. Philippine industrial progress was not in evidence in the fair because, to begin with, there was virtually nothing of that to speak of. They were a people still stuck in the agricultural age, not too far removed from the stone age, when most of the world was now in the industrial age. The Filipino skill and ingenuity he often heard bragged about were not in evidence at the fair either, because these were mere figments of their vanity and imagination.

It was late afternoon and Simon was tired of window-shopping. He led Clara and Lorna to the area in front of the stage where a big crowd was listening to a choral group singing old songs.

Simon and Clara knew *Oh Susanna,* the song the choral group was singing. They were fond of the oldies, and they listened to it with keen pleasure. The choral group next sang two more Stephen Foster songs, *Beautiful Dreamer* and *My Old Kentucky Home.*

Her eyes bright with wonder, Lorna said, "They are nice, Dad. They must be very old songs."

"Generations of music lovers have enjoyed listening to them," Simon said. "They have been around for a hundred years now."

"I know they came long before Rock n' Roll."

"Your Dad's time is the Boogie and the Slow Drag," Clara said, smiling.

They applauded the choral group. The indefatigable Precy Montes returned to the stage with more choral groups. The massed choral groups, dressed in different costumes, were a colorful sight. They stood facing their conductor, who was waiting for his cue from Precy.

She said, smiling, to the crowd, "And now, ladies and gentlemen, here comes what we have been waiting for—the *Santacruzan!*"

She raised her hand as she was leaving the stage, in a signal for the conductor to take over from her. The conductor then swept up his hands and the massed choral groups began to sing the Maytime hymn to Mary, the mother of Jesus Christ, the Son of God:

> *"Dios te salve Maria, llena eres tu gracia*
> *el senor es contigo, bendita tu eres*
> *entre todas las mujeres y bendito es*
> *el fruto de tu vientre, Jesus."*

Simon watched and listened, his eyes bright from the memory of Maytime, long ago in his hometown in Laguna. What a joyous time it was! He was then a young boy filled with wonder, and the world was a wonderful world! A Santacruzan procession, similar to this one the admiring crowd was watching at the fair, was passing by in the town's main road. Young beautiful women, the *Sagalas,* were passing by with their consorts. Everyone of them regal as a queen, dressed in elegant gowns, with crowns on their heads and scepters in their hands, they were the epitome of beauty and loveliness.

The choral groups sang on as the Maytime Queen herself, the *Reyna Elena,* came more regal than the others. She passed by with her *Constantino,* her boy consort, beneath a wooden arch rich with flowers and leaves. A brilliant crown rested on her head and in her hands was a small wooden cross. She was Queen Helena and her consort was her son, Emperor Constantine, and the cross in her hand symbolized the cross on which Jesus Christ was crucified.

Other memories came bursting forth in his mind. He called them the Milestones of Maytime.

He was on vacation in Ben's hometown in Paete with Bayani, his two best friends in college. They were watching a similar Maytime procession from the church belfry. From there they could see the rest of the town, a small area of light and festivities, and all around them was darkness over the rice paddies of Paete, the waters of Laguna Lake and the hills and mountains of Sierra Madre.

Those were the last days of summer and their last days too as young carefree students. Job and marriage later drew them apart. Since then, they saw less and less of each other. That time was now as far away as Ben, who was living in Guam, and Bayani, who was living in New York. How he wished they could see each other again.

Clara leaned her head lightly on his shoulder, and he held her in the arm. She must have remembered, too. They were married in May and honeymooned in Baguio. Her head nestled on his shoulder, as she did now, they were seated close to each other on a bench in Burnham Park. They watched, happy and content, the fog descending on the pine trees in the park and in the city's verdant hills.

His mind filled with memories, sad and happy, sweet and haunting, that were like shadows hovering over him, he watched the procession of beauties passing by the admiring crowd, while the massed choral groups sang on the Maytime hymn, their voices all over the convention center. He was so touched, his eyes turned misty. How precious, how fleeting were those wonderful moments.

Chapter Nine

Clara stood on the sidewalk of Broadway, a solitary figure watching Simon drive away. It was her first day of work in Super Bargain Store. She had talked about it eagerly back in their car, but now, as she was watching their car until it had turned right at the intersection of Broadway and Eighth Street and disappeared from view, she was nagged by questions about her new job. She had never done a cashier's work before. Could she do it? Will the other employees be friendly and helpful? She will find that out soon enough. She was a fast learner, though. She can do the job. Having reassured herself, she turned, her shoulder set, and walked confidently toward the store.

Its big sign in the building started out at her, friendly and welcoming, and this added to her self-confidence. It was in yellow except the two letter S, which were colored green and drawn like dollar signs. She peered through the accordion iron door, at the staircase and the escalator to the store's glass entrance at the basement. She saw no one. She knocked just the same, hoping someone will hear her and come. No one did, and she pursed her lips in disappointment. Randolph, the store manager who hired her, had told her that today being Monday, a truck day, an advance party of stockers will be there as early as six o'clock in the morning. They should be there now, unloading goods and preparing the store for another day of business.

She was beginning to regret having come so early. It was only seven o'clock. She should have taken the bus and come in just before seven-thirty, her clock-in time. Instead, on Simon's suggestion, she let him drive her to work. He left after dropping her off, so he would be in L&S by his clock-in time, also at seven-thirty.

It was early morning yet and she saw, as she looked around, Broadway deserted except for a handful of people on their way to work. A coffee-and-doughnut shop was the only store open. All the other stores were still closed, their doors and walls defaced by graffiti. The litter in the street was appalling. The sidewalk was strewn with trash, even worn, discarded shoes and clothing. And the smell! It took her a while to get used to the faint smell of mold and urine. Broadway, at that time of the day, looked to her like a failure in municipal services, a place in decline.

A man emerged from the shadow of an alley, a dirty frayed blanket tucked under his arm. He was unshaven, his hair disheveled and his soiled clothes slept in. He looked mean, dispirited and hungry. He was the same panhandler she and Simon saw two weeks ago in Olive Street.

She watched in fear as the man walked toward her. She had heard of stories about women being mugged in the streets of Los Angeles in broad daylight. She considered fleeing, but that might just embolden the man to follow and then attack her in a secluded spot. She did the only thing she could do: she stood her ground and looked about warily. She held her handbag tight in her hand. Any wrong move he made, and she will whack him with it! The panhandler thrust out instead his hand to her.

"Can you spare me a quarter for coffee?" the panhandler said.

The smell of rotten egg and stale beer in the panhandler's

breath was so nauseating, she turned her face away. She won't part even with a penny to this parasite who should work instead of begging. Giving him money will only encourage him to go on begging. She turned him down with a shake of her head. The panhandler stared at her, but she stood firm.

Just then, a car pulled over. Its driver gazed at Clara and the panhandler. Something about him made the panhandler walk away. Clara gazed gratefully at the man in the car, who could be a policeman in plainclothes. She waited until the panhandler was some distance away before thanking the man for coming to her rescue. The man nodded and drove away.

Her nerves were already frayed, and she had not even started work yet. She knocked again, this time more persistently, never mind if she was creating a disturbance there. Finally, someone appeared in the store. It was Randolph. He went up the stairs. She greeted him.

"Good morning to you, too," Randolph said cheerfully. "You are an early bird."

"I thought I should come in early on my first day of work," she said as she passed through the accordion iron door Randolph had opened for her.

The escalator was not yet running at that hour and they took the staircase in going down to the store. Randolph pushed the glass door open and they went inside.

She looked so small, walking beside Randolph; she reached only up to his shoulder. He looked like a muscular black boxer, but he had a friendly face.

The store, as she swept it with her eyes, had a cozy touch about it, an inducement for shoppers to buy there things for the home and the family. Above an aisle was a big sign which read:

Show your love to your mother on Mother's Day
with the perfect gift for her, here in Super Bargain Store.

That will be next month yet, but the store was already spruced-up for a special sale on that day. Signs pointed to the store's various sections: the section for men, women and children; office supplies; kitchen and garden supplies; canned goods and other grocery items; candies and chocolate; books and greeting cards; cosmetics; toys and hardware items; and a general section carrying items on special sale.

She had shopped there once with Simon, her interest then only on its sale items. Now that she was working there, her interest in the store had become intimate and compelling.

"Punch in when you come in," Randolph said as he pointed at a shelf of time cards on a wall.

She followed Randolph's order and punched in her time card on the time clock.

A row of three checkouts stood near the store entrance. Randolph led Clara to the checkout at the left corner.

"You will handle this checkout," Randolph said to her. "Familiarize yourself with it. You will be working directly under Sharon, our customer service manager. She will train you."

Randolph opened the cash register with a key from a bunch of keys he took out from his pocket.

"It looks complicated," he said, "but it is no big deal in operating it. Give it a try."

He gave way to Clara and guided her in operating the cash register.

"See how easy it is to operate?" Randolph said before closing the cash register again.

He pointed at a shelf of magazines, chocolate bars and lighters near the checkout counter and said, "You can also try selling them."

"So, I'll also be making a sales pitch," she said, nodding at her increasing familiarity with her job.

"Consider that as part of your training for a higher position in the future. I don't expect you to stay here a cashier forever."

"In that case," she said as she glanced at the shelves nearby, "I can put here on the counter a table clock over there, some of the watches there, and maybe a box of the men's skin bracer."

"Why should you do that?"

"I can try selling them as the customers pass through here."

"That's a good idea," Randolph said, nodding appreciatively.

"That should be one good reason you hired me."

Randolph looked on while she gathered the items she mentioned from their assigned places and put them on the counter in her checkout.

"I'll soon find out how good I am at selling," she said.

"I have no doubt you will do well. Now, let me show you the

rest of the store."

They went around the store, with Randolph explaining to her what each section carried, how the goods were stocked up, when and why some of the goods were put on special sale, and a host of other things that went in running the store. They came, at the food section, upon a woman on her knees, a box of canned salmon beside her. She was arranging the canned goods in a shelf.

"Hey, Mary," Randolph said to her. "Meet Clara, our new cashier."

Mary looked up and waved a friendly greeting at Clara, who smiled and waved back at her.

Randolph then led Clara to the adjoining toy section.

"They are all kids' stuff, as you can see," Randolph said as he paused before a shelf of toys. "As an employee, you are entitled to a ten percent discount of whatever you buy here."

"I like that," she said, smiling appreciatively.

They next went to the break room. It had a dining table for six persons, a microwave oven, a refrigerator, the faucet in the kitchen sink, a water cooler and a telephone attached to a wall.

Randolph, followed by Clara, walked across the room to the employees' lockers there.

"This will be your locker," Randolph said to her as he opened the locker in a corner of the upper row of two rows of lockers.

"I'll get you a lock," he said as he stepped out of the room.

She inspected her locker while waiting for Randolph. It was big enough for her things. She put her bag on the dining table and took out a piece from a box of tissue paper and wiped with it the dust inside the locker and threw the used tissue paper in a trash can. Then she removed from her bag her purse, her lunch box, the fork and spoon wrapped in tissue paper, and put them inside the locker.

Randolph returned to the break room and gave her the lock and a sealed envelope. She opened the envelope and memorized the lock's numerical combination printed on a card inside the envelope. Then she put the envelope inside her bag, closed her locker and locked it.

"Don't ever forget the lock's numerical combination," Randolph said, "or we'll have to pay a locksmith to open it."

"No, I won't forget it," she said as she looked around at the break room.

"We take our meals here during our lunch break," Randolph said.

"How long is it?"

"It is thirty minutes for lunch, if you are on an eight-hour work schedule, twenty minutes if less than that, and another fifteen minutes for the midafternoon break."

"That is hardly enough time for a quick bite."

"I know, but there is nothing I can do about it. It is the company policy."

They next went to the alley at the back of the store, where two stockers Randolph introduced as Joe and Richard were unloading goods from a trailer.

"This is Clara, our new cashier," Randolph said to the two men.

"Hi, Clara," they said in unison.

"Hi," she likewise said.

"As you can see," Randolph said to her, "Monday, being a truck day, is a busy day for our stockers, including myself. I help them stock up the goods."

"Where do they come from?"

"They come from our main depot in South Bay."

"Will I be doing that, too?"

"No, that is a man's work and I don't want your nail polish ruined."

They went back smiling to Clara's assigned checkout and saw Sharon, the customer service manager. She had her own key to the store. Some of the store employees came in with her. She was powdering her nose inside her glass cubicle, which stood at the other end of the row of checkouts.

"Hey, Sharon," Randolph called out to her. "Meet Clara, our new cashier."

Sharon looked at Clara and Randolph, her face friendly and humorous.

She left her cubicle and walked toward them. She was in a dress tight enough to show her stout, but attractive figure. A yellow ribbon adorned her wire-spring hair waved with curlers. She had an uncanny resemblance to Randolph, although it was unlikely that they were related. Randolph was much taller than Sharon, her complexion much lighter than Randolph's.

"Randolph has told me about you. I'm pleased to meet you," Sharon said, smiling, to Clara, who smiled back at Sharon.

"So, Clara will work directly under me," she said to Randolph.

Randolph nodded and said to Sharon, "I know you and Clara will make a good team. You may introduce Clara to the others. She has already met Mary, Joe and Richard."

He turned to Clara and said, "Don't hesitate to ask Sharon anything you want to know about the store. She knows more about it than anybody else here, myself included."

Sharon smiled, but did not respond to the compliment.

"I'll see you later," Randolph said as he returned to the back of the store.

"Now, let me see," Sharon said to Clara. "Let me introduce you first to our fellow workers."

Sharon told the employees within her sight, "Hey, guys, meet Clara here, our new cashier."

Clara looked on as Sharon introduced the other employees. She smiled and waved a friendly greeting at everyone of them. Rosita was in the middle checkout. A mirror in her hand, she was going over the makeup on her face. Colleen was in the rightmost checkout. She was dusting the cash register and the counter. Divina was rearranging the goods in a shelf in the office supplies section. Salim was farther back, mopping the floor. Mary had moved to the toy section, where she was now rearranging the toys in a shelf. Everyone in the store seemed to be busy, an impression that pleased Clara, for she had no patience with idlers. She followed Sharon to her assigned checkout.

"Have you worked before as a cashier?" Sharon asked her.

"This is my first time."

Sharon said about the cash register, "It's no big deal in operating it, and don't be intimidated by all those keys." .

"I got the same impression from Randolph."

"It's easy to operate once you get the hang of it. You can watch me do it for maybe twenty minutes, then you will take over. But don't worry, I'll be right behind you, and I won't give you a spanking if you make a mistake."

They both laughed.

Clara saw that Sharon was more proficient in operating the cash register than Randolph. Sharon also told her about her other responsibilities as a cashier. Her confidence grew as she became more familiar with her job. It was just one kind of work out of many that Randolph had told her she would have to learn later on, like what Mary was doing. It was the same thing with the recovery work, like what Divina was now doing. She was putting in a cart items the customers had left in the wrong places. It was like good housekeeping done in a big way.

Randolph opened the store at eight o'clock to a number of waiting customers, who then streamed down the stairs and the escalator. The store was now lively with people shopping there. It was a scene Clara knew she will not soon forget. She had anticipated this moment: the start of her work as a cashier. But she must first watch Sharon work on the cash register.

Several customers, led by a middle-aged woman, were done with their shopping and had lined up at her checkout. She stood beside Sharon and watched her pass through the scanner, each item the woman had bought. The cash register then recorded and added up the total amount shown on its monitor. Sharon then took the payment from the woman customer, put it in the cash register and gave the woman her change. She bagged the purchases, which the woman then picked up as she was passing out of the counter. It was a fast simple, but systematic work that Sharon had done. The pace slackened only each time a customer paid with a credit card. It took Sharon a few moments longer to clear it.

At a slack in activity, some twenty minutes later, Sharon said to Clara, "Do you want to give it a try now?"

"Yes," she said eagerly.

Within a short while, an office employee wearing a tie came to her checkout. He put his purchases of a box of biscuits and a bottle of lemonade on the counter, a snack the customer will probably take during his break time.

She worked under Sharon's watchful eyes. An older man followed with his purchases of a picture frame and a can of dog food.

One never knew what people bought in the store. She saw this from what the customers were looking for, or had taken to her checkout. If they were not looking for something in the store shelves, they were examining various items and putting what they liked in the trays they picked up from the store. Others bought just an item or two and were now on their way to her checkout.

Just then, Sharon cleared her throat noisily in an apparent warning over something.

She was about to ask Sharon what it was about, but an old woman customer was already standing in front of her. She said, as she started passing through the scanner the old woman's purchases, "How are you this fine morning, ma'am?"

The old woman ignored her.

She picked up and passed through the scanner, a tin of biscuits. No, she won't be put out by the old woman's ill temper, and she said, smiling, "Mighty fine day to shop."

The old woman stared sternly ahead and made no reply.

She won't allow the old woman's bad disposition to dampen her enthusiasm for her new job. She had a way of dealing with it. She hummed a church hymn while passing through the scanner, the rest of the old woman's purchases. She went on humming the hymn while the cash register added up the total amount of what the old woman had bought, who then paid for them. She was giving the old woman her change and receipt and had put her purchases in a bag when she was pleasantly surprised to see the old woman, now smiling at her.

"I know that hymn," the old woman said. "Do you sing in a church choir?"

"Yes, ma'am, I do. I sing at the choir of St. Stephen Church."

"I know where it is located. I attend Sunday service at the Knox Memorial, not far from there."

"Do you sing in a church choir, too?"

"I used to, but that was a long time ago, before I lost my singing voice. But it's nice to hear a familiar church hymn hummed, of all places, here in your store."

"It is as good as any place to hum a church hymn."

The old woman saw a line of customers had formed in the checkout while she and Clara were comparing notes. She apologized for having kept them waiting.

"You take care now, ma'am, and have a nice day," she said cheerfully to the old woman.

"You, too," the old woman said to her, a broad smile now on her face as she passed out of Clara's checkout.

Sharon was watching them, an amused expression on her face. She said to Clara, once the old woman had passed out of the store's glass door, "You scored a big hit there."

"What big hit?" Clara asked Sharon.

"I'll tell you later."

Time passed unnoticed in the store, busy with shoppers and the employees who served them. Clara realized it was noontime only when Sharon had told her she could now take her lunch while no customers were lined up in her checkout. She locked the cash register and proceeded to the break room. She saw there Salim and Rosita, taking their lunch, seated across each other at the dining table. She glanced at what they were eating.

"Burrito and hamburger," she said, "the two most popular meals in Los Angeles."

Their laughter accompanied her to her locker. She took out from there and put on the dining table, her lunch box and the fork and spoon. She replaced her lunch box's plastic cover with a tissue paper and put it inside the microwave oven. She closed the door, pressed the timer to one minute and then pressed the start button. She watched the lunch box as it began to move in a circle inside the microwave oven. She had one like it in their apartment, but at times she still could not help but marvel at this wonderful kitchen appliance that made cooking and heating food fast and easy. She did not have a microwave oven in Zambales or in Manila.

She was no idler and she was a stickler for neatness. She had time enough while warming her food, and she checked her locker. She remembered having cleaned it before, and she closed it again.

Salim looked on and listened as she and Rosita then engaged in woman talk.

"How do you find it here?" Rosita asked her.

"It's a nice place. I like working here."

"Do you like your pay, too?"

"It is more than what I used to get in my previous job."

"What did you do before?"

"I used to work in a jewelry shop, not far from here."

"Why did you leave it?"

"As I said, I get better paid here."

The microwave oven made a pinging sound, a signal that it was finished heating the food. She took out her lunch box and joined Salim and Rosita at the dining table. She laid her lunch box on the dining table, beside its plastic cover, the fork and the spoon.

Rosita asked her, as she was looking at her lunch box, "Do you always bring your own lunch?"

"Yes. Nothing like eating the food you cooked yourself."

"You should tell that to Salim here. Hamburger is all that he eats, day in, day out. He never gets tired of it."

"I cannot help it," Salim said, his hamburger sandwich held close to his mouth. "I live alone and I don't know how to cook."

"Get married then to a woman who knows how to cook."

"Someone like you, I suppose?"

Rosita said nothing, but she gazed significantly at Salim, who had taken a big bite from his hamburger sandwich. He averted his eyes from her, who was frowning at his cheeks bloated by the hamburger sandwich he was eating with gusto.

Clara saw from the way Salim and Rosita were looking at and talking to each other, that there was something going on between them. It was none of her business, though, and she turned to her lunch box. A delicious smell rose from it the instant she removed its cover of tissue paper.

"You want some?" she asked Rosita and Salim.

"No, thank you," they replied.

Sharon came in just as Clara was about to begin her lunch.

"That looks and smells good," she said, her eyes on Clara's lunch.

She sat down at the table, facing Clara, and removed from a brown paper bag, her lunch of soda and cheese sandwich.

"Do you want some?" she asked Sharon.

Sharon seemed not to hear her, although her eyes were fastened hungrily to her lunch.

She did not wait for Sharon to reply. She put in her lunch box's plastic cover, a portion of her lunch, on top of which she laid the fork.

"Here, take it," she said to Sharon, as she pushed the food-laden plastic cover in front of her.

"You don't have to," Sharon said.

"I have more than enough left. Try it; you will like it."

"All right, if you insist."

The food, placed right in front of Sharon, smelled even more inviting to her. She asked Clara, "What is it called?"

"It is called Adobo. It's a pork-and-chicken stew marinated in garlic, soy sauce and vinegar, then fried on a low fire."

Sharon took a piece and, as she chewed it, she nodded in approval of the food.

"It is good, very delicious," she said. "I have never eaten anything like it before."

"I told you, you will like it."

"Like it? I love it!"

Sharon took another bite, a pleased smile spreading in her face at the food's savory taste.

Suddenly her mouth hung open as, together with Rosita and Salim, she gazed, startled, at Clara, who had bowed her head and made the sign of the cross.

She said grace, ignoring her table companions, who were staring at her. A moment like it was elemental to her. She was thanking God for this blessing of life-sustaining food she was about to receive from the Lord's bounty. She concluded her short prayer with another sign of the cross.

The others at the table regarded her with mingled respect and curiosity as she started to eat her lunch. Her companions at the dining table did not seem like the kind of people who prayed before meals. She said nothing and went on eating.

Sharon finished her Adobo and rice a short while later.

"Thank you, that was really delicious," she said as she was returning to Clara the plastic food cover with the fork on it. "You scored another hit with it, and on your first day of work here."

"What is this 'hit' thing about?" she asked Sharon.

"This delicious food, it's a hit, and then this morning, you made your first hit with the old woman. Do you remember her? She even asked you if you sing in a church choir."

"What about her?" she asked.

"The old woman is a regular costumer," Sharon replied, as she opened her can of soda, removed the wrapper in her cheese sandwich and began to eat her lunch.

"Who? The cranky old woman?" Rosita said. "She spoils my day every time she comes to my checkout. She never runs out of something to complain about."

"She seemed like a nice person," Clara said.

"To you, yes," Sharon said, "but she can be mean to the other cashiers. I've got to hand it to you for working wonders on her."

Clara was tempted to say that people responded according to how one treated them, but she kept silent lest she sounded patronizing to them.

Rosita and Salim had finished their lunch. She cleared the area of the table where she and Salim had eaten and made their food wrappers into a ball, which she then gave to Salim.

"We are going ahead," Rosita said as she stood up at the same time with Salim. She waited as he put the refuse into the trashcan and their empty soda cans in a box. They left the break room together.

"I don't know how you can manage to do any cooking at home and still go to work," Sharon said. "As for me, I cook only on weekends. The rest of the week, my children and I make do with sandwiches. Sometimes we just buy our food. You have children too, I suppose?"

"I've got two children."

"I've got two daughters. Jennifer is fifteen, while Jacklyn is twelve. I want them to pursue a career—Jennifer to be a nurse and Jacklyn, well, she has a nice voice. She can be a singer. I wanted to become one myself. In case you don't know it, I've got a nice voice. People tell me that not only do I sing like Ella Fitzgerald, I even look like her."

She listened politely to Sharon, who was talking incessantly. Was she really like that? She seemed to be aloof to the other employees. Why was she so chummy with her? Perhaps she became friendly when she gave her a portion of her lunch. How quickly she took to her when they first met only that morning.

"I have not told you I'm a single parent, have I?" Sharon said.

"Are you?" she said, surprised. She had never met anyone like her before. "You mean you are divorced?"

"No. I was never married."

"Never?"

"Never. Should I?"

"I guess not," she said, embarrassed, "although I've always thought that people get to have children only when they are married. At least that is how it is done where I came from."

"So, you are married."

"Yes."

"For how long now?"

"For almost twenty years now."

"Twenty years! To the same man?"

"To the same man," she said, smiling in amusement at how incredible it sounded to Sharon.

"How do you do it?" Sharon asked.

She knitted her brow as she searched in her mind for the answer to Sharon's question. She was married to Simon and will stay married to him, till death do them part. It was a vow they made to each other at their church wedding. She said instead, "It takes mutual effort for us to stay that way."

"I've got to hand it to you for doing that. Married to the same man for twenty years! Why, that's incredible!"

"Have you not thought of doing it yourself?"

"No. I cannot imagine myself getting tied up to the same man for the rest of my life. We just don't do it. No commitment. That's how we want it, especially our menfolk. They leave you once they don't feel like livin' with you no more."

"And that is what your man did."

"Exactly."

"Do you still see each other?"

"I don't even know where that good-for-nothing is now. He used to visit us once, twice a month after he left us, but only when he wanted to raise my skirt. He stopped seeing us when Jacklyn was three or four years old. I have not seen him since then."

"How do your children take it?"

"They are used to living without a father. It's better that way considering the kind of a man he is. Still, it's hard to raise them by myself. We are always short in everything, money especially. At least I've got good neighbors in Slauson in South Central where we live. They look after the kids while I'm at work. But I'll just have to wait for a few more years. Jennifer and Jacklyn will be on their own when they turn eighteen."

Clara shook her head. She could never approve of parents shooing their children away once they had reached that age. It was a practice she learned was common among families in America. But she will have nothing of that. Let other people call it clannishness, but she and Simon would rather that Lorna and Sonny will live with them long after they had turned eighteen, even when they are married, and for as long as they want to live with her and Simon.

The rest of the afternoon passed like in the morning, with Clara and the other store employees busy at work. Simon picked her up at five-twenty.

"How was your first day of work?" he asked her the moment she was seated in their car.

"Fine," she said while fastening her seat belt. "I seem to have hit it off with Randolph, our store manager, and Sharon, our customer service manager. They are the two top people there."

"I'm not surprised by that. After all, you have a way with people. What is the store like?"

"It carries all kinds of goods, especially those for the home. There is never a dull moment there. People never stop coming. My feet are sore from standing the whole day. And you should see the people I work with there. They came from all over."

"Something like a mini-United Nations."

"Something like that."

"I hope you work well together."

"We do. We have no choice. We have to work well together."

"Right you are. But tell me about the others."

"Randolph and Sharon are both black; Rosita is a Salvadoran. Colleen is Irish American, I think. Salim, our janitor, is a Pakistani. Kyle, our security man, is black; Joe is an Italian-American, while Richard, I think, originally came from Eastern Europe. Mary was called Maria when she was still in Colombia. Divina is from Mexico. We have one Vietnamese. I'm the only Filipino there."

"Well, then, it's your duty to stand up for your country. Show them how we work," he said with fake seriousness.

"I've already done that. It's easy as pie," she said, smiling.

She looked out of the car, delighted by what she now saw in Broadway. The neon lights at the storefronts and in the movie house were already switched on, the pavement there, clean and tidy. Broadway was now lively with all the lights and the people there. It was so different from how it looked to her, early that morning.

Chapter 10

His arms crossed on his chest, Saul Levy stared at the legal brief lying on his desk. He was tired, his fingers stiff from writing it and not quite sure on how to conclude it.

What he needed was some distraction. He turned around on his swivel chair, stood up and went to the window facing Flower Street. He watched idly the cars and the pedestrians there. A man-made canyon hemmed in by the tall buildings, blocking the light from the late afternoon sun, it was a depressing sight.

He turned his gaze to the other window, at the grand view of Los Angeles. Its vast expanse of homes, buildings and streets was directed toward the distant ocean: a glorious sight of his "little hometown," as he sometimes called Los Angeles.

A January-born, Saul, in keeping with his mountain goat sign of Capricorn, was watching and reflecting on his beloved city, which lay at his feet.

A fill of the grand view stimulated his mind and body, and he sat down, ready to resume work.

His watch told him, though, that it was near quitting time. He had done more than the usual amount of work he usually accomplished in a workday.

He had made consultations with half a dozen prospective clients, held a meeting with his staff, made a court appearance in the morning. On top of these were the calls he made and took, and papers and legal briefs he wrote, edited or studied. This included the brief on a nurse's application for a change in her immigration status.

It lay waiting for him to finish. He read it once more and, satisfied with it, he wrote down its concluding sentence.

It was all mental work he had done that, however, could be just as tiring as operating a jackhammer in a city street. Therese, his beautiful and efficient secretary-receptionist, at least had relieved him of much of the administrative work. And there was Steve, his associate, who attended to some of the clients, including Juan Sindromas. They were not taking his case. Steve should have sent him away by now.

He drew a deep breath at the pleasant distraction of the grand view of Los Angeles and turned his gaze to a knock on the door.

"Yes," he said.

"Have you got a minute?" Steve said as he peered in.

"Sure, come in," he said.

Steve sat down on a chair across his desk. His brow knitted, he seemed to be upset as he said, "We have a problem. Sindromas wants to see you."

"What is there for him to see me about?" Saul said, frowning. "Did you not tell him we are not taking his case?"

"I did, but he insists on seeing you. He said he will not leave until he has talked to you."

He looked away, still frowning. Telling someone to his face that he was unacceptable as a client was a very unpleasant task.

"All right, send him in," he said grudgingly to Steve, "but I want you to stick around."

Steve left, but was back in a short while with Sindromas.

Saul watched them as they advanced toward his desk. An odd-looking pair, Steve was a head taller than Sindromas, who was in a flashy checkered shirt that complemented his tall cowboy boots. He was potbellied. His cheeks were rosy and perfumed with skin bracer. A waxed mustache crowned his mouth. He looked street-wise, a model in self-indulgence. Sindromas swung his hands, and he saw how smooth they were. His nails were even manicured.

Here was, he said to himself, a so-called immigrant agriculturist whose face should have been darkened by long exposure to the sun, and whose hands should have been gnarled from working on the soil, but were not. Sindromas looked more like a nightclub bouncer or a pimp than the agriculturist he claimed to be. The man was a fake, as fake as the vineyard he claimed was sponsoring him for permanent residence. It was, he learned from Steve's research, an unused broken-down barn in Fresno. The vineyard sponsoring Sindromas for permanent residence existed only on paper, the company name and address produced in a printing shop.

He watched Sindromas as he took a seat, facing Steve, who had sat down on the other chair, across his desk.

He said, "There is no point in beating around the bush, is there, Mister Sindromas?"

Sindromas nodded.

"We cannot take your case. Attorney Claremont has already told you that. I'm under the impression that you want to hear it from me, too. So, there it is. We cannot take your case."

"I'm here to ask you to change your decision," Sindromas said.

Sindromas' request took Saul by surprise. He was even more surprised when Sindromas suddenly took out from his pocket, a thick wad of money.

"Here," he said, waving the thick wad of money. "These are all one hundred-dollar bills. I'll pay you double, even triple your fee if you will take my case."

He stared in disbelief at Sindromas' crude attempt to win him over with money.

"I have a lot more of this," Sindromas added. "Just tell me how much you really want."

"I'm sorry," Saul said, "but my answer is still no. Why don't you try another lawyer?"

"I was told to seek only your help."

"Why?"

"Because I was told you are the best immigration lawyer."

He gazed, amused, at Sindromas. Now the man was trying flattery.

"Thank you, Mister Sindromas," he said, "but we are still not taking your case. Good day."

He stood up. So did Steve. Sindromas hesitated, but then he stood up also, put his money back in his pocket and turned to leave.

Suddenly he wheeled around. He raised his clenched fist and shouted, "I've got big people with me! Do not offend me or my backers! It will be bad for your law practice!"

Saul gazed sharply at Sindromas, his jaw tight in anger. Now the brute was trying to intimidate him. Sindromas could bully people where he came from, but not here in America, and not him. He made an effort to remain firm, but calm.

He said, "Please leave now, Mister Sindromas."

"I want you to try throwing me out of here!"

"Come now, Mister Sindromas, enough of that," Steve said as he held Sindromas on the shoulder and, ignoring his protests, took him out of the room.

Saul sat down, so upset by the ugly encounter with Sindromas, it gave him a headache. He took out from a drawer in his desk a bottle of aspirin and took out from it a tablet and swallowed it with a glass of water. His headache was almost gone by the time Steve returned a few minutes later. He sat down on a chair across his desk.

"The guy is unbelievable," Steve said.

"See to it the building security doesn't let him in, in case he decides to come back here."

"Therese has already done that. She overheard what was going on here, she called the building security. Two security officers escorted Sindromas out of the office."

"A good thing I've got a secretary who doesn't have to be told what to do."

"Last case of the day, and it was a bad one. I'm sorry about that, chief. It nearly spoiled our day."

It was Friday, the end of their week of work.

"Let the jury rest for the weekend," he said.

He stood up and took out his briefcase from the cabinet and put it on his desk. Then he gathered the nurse's brief and some folders lying on his desk, put them inside his briefcase and snapped it shut. He had homework to do for the weekend. He sat down again on his swivel chair, his eyes turned to the ceiling and his hands clasped at the back of his head.

His mind, for a change, had turned to something pleasant. He was having a night out with Agnes. They were going to see a movie in Beverley Center, instead of attending a concert in Music Center. She called earlier and told him she was on her way to his office.

He looked sideways at Steve and said, "Are you going anywhere this weekend?"

"We have made no plans, but at the spur of the moment we may pack up our tent, take out from the garage the barbecue grill, the water cooler and so forth, and perhaps go to Big Bear Mountain or Lake Castaic. How about you?"

"We are staying home for the weekend, but tonight we are going to see a movie."

"A movie? I thought you are concert-going people."

"We are, but tonight, we are going to see a movie for a change. We'll have dinner afterwards at Sammy's Steakhouse. From there we are going to Griffith Park."

"Anything special going on there?"

"None, as far as I know. We just want to go there. We have not visited it in ages."

"Vicky and I might as well see a movie, too. We have not seen one on the big screen for a long time."

"So it is with me and Agnes."

"Well, have a nice weekend," Steve then said.

"You, too," he said, smiling and waving in good-bye at Steve.

Now that he was alone, following a habit, Saul rated himself. Overall he had scored well. Three of his clients had passed the interview for permanent residence this morning, a score of one hundred percent. Four new cases were moving forward. He frowned. All that good work was nearly spoiled by that ugly encounter with Sindromas. A good thing he was cautious about him. He was right in refusing to take him as a client; he meant only trouble.

The ugly encounter with Sindromas opened his mind to unpleasant observations he had made but kept to himself about illegal immigrants. They violated the law, demanding special treatment, and getting it, too. How many people like Sindromas were out there? There were so many of them. They were changing the social, political and economic landscape of California and the rest of the United States. The problem had reached grave proportions in Los Angeles because of so many illegal immigrants who have made it their ultimate destination in the United States.

He frowned as he recalled one time he was driving along MacArthur Park. He loved that park. As a young boy, he used to watch movie stars taking a stroll there. People now avoided it ever since vagrants and peddlers of illicit drugs and fake documents had taken over it. One may go to the park at the risk of being mugged or accosted for a quarter by a panhandler, or offered a packet of marijuana for twenty dollars by a drug peddler.

He was driving in Alvarado Street, which bordered the park, when peddlers tried to sell to him fake drivers' licenses and social security cards. Illegal immigrants used them in applying for jobs, food stamps and other welfare benefits. He ignored the peddlers and drove on. As he then turned right on Sixth Street, he saw sidewalk vendors selling merchandise placed on mats spread out on the pavement. Strung up behind them on a sagging wire fence were used clothes also on sale.

It was like being suddenly thrust into a Third World country. More and more areas in Los Angeles were becoming like that. This was one result of illegal immigration, where people like Sindromas manage to get into the country and stay there.

Recalling the ugly encounter with Sindromas upset him, not only because it happened, but also because it will most likely happen again. There were so many of them out there of the likes of Sindromas who might find their way to his law office. At least he had, to counter the likes of Sindromas, Simon Matin and others like him who deserved to be helped. They made his law practice lucrative, too. He could not complain about that. He drew a deep breath. He must stop brooding. It will just spoil his night out with Agnes. A nice movie, followed by a fine dinner at Sammy's Steakhouse, topped by a visit to Griffith Park, will be a perfect way of spending Friday night out with her. He felt good now.

He turned his swivel chair around and looked out through the window at the grand view of Los Angeles. Summer was coming. At five-thirty, the sun was still high. It will be another lovely evening, cool enough for a visit to Griffith Park. He dozed off, filled with satisfaction at the wonderful view.

A knock on the door woke him up. He turned a drowsy eye toward the door. Agnes had arrived.

"So," she said as she came to him, "the world stands still while the Lion of the Legal Profession is taking a nap."

She put her purse on his desk, bent down and kissed him. The feel of her moist lips on his cheek and the trace of perfume in her breast made his heart miss a beat. He raised himself to kiss her back but, unaware of his intention, she had turned his swivel chair around. He dropped back on the chair and sighed in pleasure as she then began massaging with her smooth palms, his neck, chin and shoulder.

"Always the sleepyhead," she said. "You must have had a tiring day."

"You can say that again."

She playfully pinched his jaw and said, "That should wake you up. Ready, darling?"

He, in reply, stretched out his arms and yawned.

They stopped by Therese's desk on their way out of the office. She was clearing it of its clutter of folders, crumpled paper, ballpoint pens and stray paper clips.

"Are you having a night out, too?" Agnes asked her.

"I would love to go out too, but I've got no one to spend it with."

Agnes threw her head back and, regarding Therese skeptically, she said, "A young beautiful woman like you without a date on a Friday night? There is no man in your life right now?"

"None."

"How come?"

"Let us say, because I am choosy."

"So, what kind of a man do you want?"

"Someone like Saul."

Agnes was so taken aback by what Therese said, she shot her and Saul a questioning look. Her eyes were asking if there was something going on between them.

"Look for someone younger and better-looking," he said quickly to Therese, to dispel any wrong ideas Agnes might entertain about him and her.

"And unattached, too," Agnes said sarcastically to Therese. "There are many of them around. I'll even help you find one."

He watched, greatly worried, Agnes and Therese in a verbal fight. He must take Agnes out of there before things really got out of hand between them.

"Take care now and have a nice weekend," he said to Therese.

He turned to Agnes and said to her, "We better get going," as he then held her in the arm and led her out of the office.

Chapter 11

Saul and Agnes left for Beverly Center at the same time that Simon, at the wheel of his car, was approaching Manang Sepa's Restaurant for his dinner appointment there with Jonathan. He was looking forward to a meeting with Jonathan, for he may have found for him a teaching job in Asia Pacific.

He entered the restaurant and joined Jonathan, who was at a dining table, working on his appetite with a glass of beer. He said to the restaurant manager at the counter, "One more beer, please."

The restaurant manager told a waiter to bring to Jonathan's table, beer for Simon.

He asked Jonathan, "How is the food here now?"

"Better than the slop I eat in L and S," Jonathan replied.

"At least it is first-class delicious slop."

They were laughing when the waiter came with a bottle of beer and an empty glass.

"Can I serve you now?" the waiter asked Jonathan while pouring the beer on the glass.

"Ask my friend here first what he wants to eat," Jonathan replied irritably.

"What did you order?" he asked Jonathan.

"I ordered roasted pig's knuckles, their new specialty here, and fish fillet."

"I'll try both of them."

"Double my order then," Jonathan said to the waiter as he resumed watching a slapstick comedy shown on the TV set in the restaurant.

Simon drank his beer and looked around as he waited for the food. The restaurant was empty of patrons except for Jonathan and a couple eating at another table. He had eaten there with Phil and Jonathan twice before. The first time was a few days after its opening several months ago. It was then the talk in their community as a restaurant that served good food at a reasonable price. He wondered why it was almost deserted now. It was late Friday afternoon and Manang Sepa's should be full of patrons enjoying a time for themselves after a week of work.

The waiter came with the food. The servings, he noticed, were now smaller and looked unappetizing. He took a spoonful of the food. It did not taste fresh. He was served food left over from yesterday or even the other day yet. The quality of the food and service at Manang Sepa's was now so bad, people who used to eat there were now avoiding it. That was the reason it was almost deserted on a late Friday afternoon when it should otherwise be full of people.

It reminded him of the many failed Filipino ventures in the restaurant and other forms of business in the United States: here today, gone tomorrow. Manang Sepa's Restaurant will also close down for lack of patronage, if not earlier once the city's sanitation authorities had found out the poor sanitation there and padlocked it. He tried once its restroom and found it filthy. Manang Sepa's was barely hanging on with the patronage of its regular patrons like Jonathan, who could be more forgiving of its increasing deficiencies. But once he had found a better eating-place, it was likely Jonathan will also stop eating there.

He was so disappointed with the restaurant, he did not feel like discussing there the teaching job he was eyeing in Asia Pacific. He will take it up with Jonathan in the Keg Room. He was hungry, though. He took only a light lunch and skipped his afternoon snack in L&S in anticipation of a good filling meal in Manang Sepa's. He continued eating the unappetizing food.

He was seated across Jonathan, his back to the TV set. He could not see the movie, not that he cared to see it, but it could help divert his mind from dismal thoughts about Manang Sepa's and the unappetizing food served there now. He moved to the chair at the left side of Jonathan. He could now eat and drink and see the movie as well.

The scene was also in a restaurant. A man and a waiter were having an argument over a bowl of spaghetti on the table.

"Don't do it!" Jonathan shouted.

He raised his arm, like a policeman stopping vehicular traffic, to no avail, as the waiter then swept the bowl of spaghetti from the table and into the man's lap.

A collective groan rose from everyone in Manang Sepa's. Laughter followed as the man then stood up and chased the waiter out of the restaurant, down the road and into the horizon. The TV screen then went blank and out came the phrase: The End.

Simon continued eating the unappetizing food until he and Jonathan had eaten all of what was on their dining table. They left Manang Sepa's and proceeded to the Keg Room.

The bar was full of a Friday crowd much bigger than in any other day of the week. Two men near the door were watching on the TV set, the Los Angeles Lakers playing against the Phoenix Suns.

"Will you excuse us, please?" Simon said to the men, who then gave him and Jonathan room so they could pass them.

They proceeded to the bar counter full of male patrons, some of them standing behind those who were seated on the bar stools. They were watching the game, drinking glasses in their hands. The Suns were leading the Lakers by a wide margin.

"Hello, there," Lew called out from the corner of the bar counter. Mark was seated beside him.

"I thought you were never coming," Mark said.

"Well, here we are," Jonathan said, smiling, to Lew and Mark.

Suprath, from her customary post at the bar counter, was watching them.

"A busy night," Simon said to her.

Suprath smiled. All those patrons meant money for her bar.

"What is your pleasure?" she asked them. "Beer, wine or liquor?"

"Two beers," Jonathan replied, his fingers raised in a V-sign.

Suprath saw Simon looking at an unoccupied table near the lamp, and she said to him, "Do you want your drinks brought to you there?"

"Yes, please do," he said.

He walked toward the table with Jonathan. He saw, as they sat down there, why no one had taken it. They could not see the basketball game from there. They could hear, though, from the poolroom at the other side of the wooden wall near the table, a game of pocket billiards going on.

"Pocket the seventh ball, and you have won the game," someone said in the poolroom.

"Watch me do it," another man said.

The Keg Room was noisy with bar talk, the basketball game and the game of pocket billiards, punctuated by shouts and laughter. In contrast to the noise there, the Henry Mancini orchestra was playing softly in the jukebox there, the song *Moon River.*

 Simon knew why. Lew was there. He had the song played in the jukebox perhaps as a reminder of an old flame. It was party time at the Keg Room.

A young pretty waitress, a new hire, came to their table with two glasses and two beer bottles.

"Hello, pretty lady," Jonathan said to her. "You brighten this dark corner of the world."

Simon glanced, amused, at Jonathan, who seemed to be charmed by the pretty waitress. He had never seen him take an interest in any woman before.

"What do they call you?" Jonathan asked the pretty waitress.

"I'm called Aspara," she replied, smiling, as she poured the beer on the glasses.

"A name like yours tells me you are from Thailand," Simon said to her.

"Yes, I am from Thailand."

"You are beautiful like your name," Jonathan said. "I will have you in my dreams."

Simon looked away so that Jonathan will not see him smiling in amusement at Jonathan's corny, but apparently sincere expression of infatuation with the pretty Thai waitress. He took out his wallet to pay for their beer, but Jonathan had beaten him to it. He took

Aspara's hand boldly and put into her palm, a ten-dollar bill.

"Keep the change," he said.

He stared at Jonathan, his eyes wide in amazement at Jonathan's crude attempt to impress Aspara with a large tip.

"You are very generous, sir," she said as she pulled her hand gently from Jonathan's grip.

"Call me Jonathan," he said to her.

"Thank you, Jonathan."

Jonathan watched Aspara as she walked back to the bar counter. The men standing there blocked his view of her, and he turned, sighing, to his beer and drank a good measure of it.

"She is some looker," Jonathan said as he put down his glass of beer on the table.

"She is," Simon said with little interest, his thoughts having turned to the teaching job he was eyeing in Asia Pacific. It was time he asked Jonathan about it.

He leaned on his elbows and said to Jonathan, "Have you found an opening in Asia Pacific University for a literature or history teacher?"

"No, not yet," Jonathan replied.

"Have you asked anyone who might know?"

"I already did."

"What did they say?"

"They have no idea when there will be such an opening."

"Perhaps there are people you know who can give you a more definite information."

"I've already done that and they said the same thing."

"I'm sorry if I'm being pushy, but I cannot help but be excited about teaching again."

"Have you applied in other schools?"

"Yes, I have done that. The schools I have written to may have no opening, or my qualifications may not meet their requirements. The others did not even bother to reply. I can understand why. They don't know me from Adam. I'm hoping that with your backing, I stand a better chance of being taken in at Asia Pacific."

Jonathan, his brow creased, said, "I hesitated to tell you this, for I was hoping something might yet turn up in Asia Pacific. I have taken up your application with the person in charge of the teaching assignments. He seemed to be interested at first, but when I told him about your teaching experience, he said he could not take you in, not even if there is an opening for a literature or history teacher. The head of academic affairs told me the same thing."

"Why?"

"I'm sorry to say this, but your teaching experience in the Philippines is not recognized in Asia Pacific. That is what has likely happened to your application in other schools."

His eyes narrowed in anger and disappointment, Simon said, "I can teach history and literature as well as any other teacher, here or anywhere else, but they won't give me the chance! I'm being belittled because of where I came from!"

Jonathan, in a gesture of sympathy, dropped his hand on his shoulder and said, "I'm sorry. I wish I could have done more."

"It's all right. You have done what you could do for me. Thank you."

He shook his head. He will never teach in this country. How naïve he was to think that a work permit will open doors for him, here in America. Not even the backing of Jonathan was of any help. He turned to his beer and drank nearly all of it. He brought the glass down on the table, the frown on his face a sharp contrast to the fun and gaiety in the bar.

"You know," Jonathan said after a while, " if you are a British product of Oxford or Cambridge, a graduate of Heidelberg, a French teacher in Sorbonne, or a graduate in any university here, you will surely be taken in, not only by Asia Pacific University, but even by the topnotch universities here. We have got to face it; we are poorly rated here."

"You, too? You don't strike me as someone who can't make it here. You have a good job. You are living comfortably in your own nice home in a nice neighborhood."

"All that is true, but do you know how I got my job in Asia Pacific?"

"No."

"I gave up my leg for it."

"What?"

"That is how I got my job in Asia Pacific."

"Explain it to me."

"I got it through the preferential treatment Asia Pacific was then giving soldiers wounded in Vietnam War. I fought there. My leg was shattered when my platoon was ambushed in Quang Tri. I nearly lost my life, too. Without that preferential treatment, I may not have landed the job of administrative assistant in Asia Pacific, from which, with hard work and dedication to my job, I rose to my present position. Without that preferential treatment, like you, I may have ended up busing and washing dishes."

"You did not; that is what counts. You have a job someone like me can only dream of. You are a first-class success, and not like me, a first-class failure."

"For saying that, let me treat you to another beer," Jonathan said, smiling.

Simon smiled too, but sourly. What is wrong with him? Instead of complimenting Jonathan, he should be feeling sorry for himself. He was a failure, a first-class failure, but still a failure.

Aspara came back, smiling, to their table. She poured the remaining beer on their glasses. It was a subtle hint for them to order another round of beer. A man at the table nearby called for Aspara. She smiled and nodded at the man in a sign that she will next attend to him.

"Give us two more beers, please," Jonathan said to Aspara.

"Not for me," Simon said. "I'm driving. I'm good for one bottle of beer only."

"Another bottle will hardly make any difference," Jonathan said. "It won't make you drunk since you are drinking on a full stomach."

He pressed on and said, "I'll tell you what, "we'll split your bottle."

"All right, pretty lady," he said to Aspara. "Give us two more beers, please."

She acknowledged Jonathan's order with a nod and a smile. She picked up the two empty beer bottles and went back to the bar counter. It was noisy with an argument going on over the King trial.

A man said to the man seated beside him, "You really think this guy King will win? He might win if he is a Wall Street financier or something like that, but he is not. I'll bet a day's pay he will lose."

"A day's pay it is, then," the other man said.

Aspara came back with the two beer bottles and poured them on the empty glasses of Simon and Jonathan. He gave Aspara another ten-dollar bill in payment for the beer, which she then gave to Suprath. She returned with the change, which Jonathan promptly put back in Aspara's hand. She smiled and thanked Jonathan, who watched her, smiling, as she then served the man at the table nearby.

Simon, on the other hand, was looking sullenly at his glass of beer. His mind had veered back to his failure in getting a teaching job in Asia Pacific University.

"I'll have to accept that certain jobs in this country, like teaching, are closed to someone like me," he said glumly to Jonathan. "We can only go so far in this country. The opportunities open to us here are limited by our national origin."

"That is how they see us," Jonathan said. "Take for example our two friends at the bar counter."

Simon glanced at Lew and Mark. They were conversing, oblivious of the other patrons in the bar counter.

"What about them?" he asked.

"They are good people, very friendly. They will match you glass for glass of wine, bottle for bottle of beer. I have been drinking with them here for years. We have talked about every conceivable subject under the sun. We have had lots of good times here. Would you say then that we are good friends? We are, but our friendship starts and ends here at the bar. I have never been invited to their homes. Not once. I never got to meet their families, and never will. You know why? Because I'm different. To them, I'm still an outsider from some godforsaken country, somewhere in the Pacific Ocean."

He caught Jonathan glancing resentfully at Lew and Mark and, his pride pricked, he said to Jonathan, "So what if they consider you an outsider? Is their company that important to you?"

"Not really. It is just that I don't like being left out."

"You must accept the fact that they limit their friends to their own kind. So does everybody else."

"But we have been keeping good company here for years and years."

"Drinking beer in a place open to everyone is not the same as inviting your friends to your home."

"So, then, people like us who are different will never be really good friends of people like Lew and Mark."

"It will always be like that, although such a difference ideally is meant to be overcome, not to overcome. If, as you said, you are left out because you are different from them, then accept it and be proud of it. I'm different and proud of it even if, because of that, I could not teach here."

"I wonder why you came here, then, considering your grievances against this country."

"I hold no grievances against this country. Despite my disappointment in getting a teaching job here, I remain grateful to this country. It gave me the sanctuary I needed, and this is not to mention the many blessings and opportunities for a better life I and my family are enjoying in this country."

"What did you need a sanctuary for?"

"I was a target of some very bad people. I had to flee our country. Had I not done that, I might have been long dead by now."

"You were a target of assassination?"

"Assassination is a mighty big word applied only to the bigwigs, not to a small fry like me, but yes, you can say I was."

"You don't look like the type. You are too mild-mannered for your strong views and high ideals."

"So were Ninoy Aquino, Abraham Lincoln and John F. Kennedy."

Jonathan laughed at him for taking lightly his serious observation.

He said, "So, you needed a sanctuary. Why did you not choose some other country closer to the Philippines?"

"America came to my mind first because of my rose-tinted view of it. I owe it to my regular diet back in the Philippines of rice, fish and Hollywood."

"So it is with everyone of us, Filipinos."

His face assumed a serious look when Jonathan asked him, "Who, by the way, were gunning after you?"

"You will be surprised, but the threat came from two opposite directions: the dictator Marcos and his goons, and the Communist rebels. I can lump them together with this banditry disguised as Muslim secession in Mindanao, for you cannot tell one from the other for the harm they have caused our country."

"That is a serious stuff you just told me, but why were they after you?"

"It is simple. They did not like me, and I did not like them."

"You are understating it again."

"I can take it lightly, now that I and my family are safe, here in America."

"Anyway, I'm glad you got away," Jonathan said, smiling.

Phil was coming, and Jonathan said, "The Asian Charlie Chaplin is here."

His finger pointed accusingly to them, Phil said, as he was approaching their table, "So, you have started the party without waiting for me!"

"You can catch up with us," Jonathan said.

"I will," Phil said, "but not after I have paid my respects to the lady of the house."

He walked toward the bar counter and said to Suprath, "Here, I am, at your service, ma'am."

Suprath nodded and smiled.

"So, you have a new hire here," he said when he saw Aspara.

Suprath introduced Phil to Aspara, who smiled at Phil.

"Let me introduce myself," he said to Aspara, and with the theatrical flourish of a palace courtier addressing a queen, he bowed, swept his hand toward Aspara and said to her, "I'm Phil, as in philandering philistine."

The men in the bar counter roared with laughter.

"How is the great father?" Lew asked Phil once the laughter in the bar counter had died down.

Phil looked blankly at Lew, as he did not understand Lew's question.

"It means only that," Mark said. "You are a great father, Phil, with your ten children. Are you not happy about that?"

"Am I not? I feel great with all the fun I had in fathering ten children."

The bar counter resounded again to the laughter of the patrons there. It had not died down when Phil turned to Suprath and said to her, "You never looked lovelier than you do tonight."

Suprath smiled and thanked Phil for the compliment. He often said that to her.

"What will you have, Phil?" she asked him.

"Beer, any brand will do for my parched throat."

Suprath put a glass on the bar counter on which she poured Phil's beer. Phil took out from his wallet two one-dollar bills. He gave these to Suprath and told her to keep the change. He picked up the glass and the beer bottle and joined Simon and Jonathan at their table.

He asked, after he had drank a good measure of his beer, "What is on the agenda tonight?"

Jonathan replied, "We were just talking about the doors closed to us in this country."

"An old story," Phil said. "Any new variations?"

"None," Simon said. "I could not get a decent teaching job, while you could not get a decent acting job."

"At least when I die here," Phil said, "I hope to be given a decent burial."

"Don't worry about that," Jonathan said to Phil. "The people here will not throw you to the dogs. They are kind to animals."

Phil laughed so hard at what Jonathan had said about him, tears came out of his eyes.

Suddenly the men in the bar counter shouted in excitement as the Lakers had tied the game with the Suns.

Simon smiled, amused at the TV sportscaster who commented about the game that it could be a finish down the wire, a mixed metaphor.

He stood up, carried away like Phil and Jonathan by the excitement over the game. They went to the bar counter, their eyes on the TV screen. The players and the spectators at the poolroom also came to the bar counter, just as a Lakers player had received a pass and, sidestepping the Suns player guarding him, dunked the ball into the ring. The men shouted for joy, some of them slapping each other's back. Time left was only a few seconds, with the Lakers now ahead by two points. The referee signaled the resumption of play. A Suns player threw a long pass to his teammate, only to have the ball intercepted by a Lakers player, who then held on to it until the buzzer had sounded. The game was over.

The crowd at the bar counter gave thunderous shouts at the Lakers' upset victory over the Suns.

"How is that for a nightcap here?" a patron at the bar counter said.

"I've just become richer by ten dollars," another man said.

"You can share that with your wife, you know," the man seated beside him said.

"Not the money, but I'll have something far more enjoyable to share with my wife when I get home," the man said to the laughter at the bar counter.

Four customers seated on the bar stools thanked Suprath and left on the heels of those returning to the poolroom. The excitement over the Lakers' game had died down, and Simon, Phil and Jonathan returned to their drinks they left on their table. The remaining patrons at the bar counter had turned to talking quietly while drinking beer, wine and liquor. No one seemed to be interested in the post-game analysis, and Suprath switched the TV set to another channel.

"Hold it right there," Lew said to Suprath, at a chorus of voices singing:

> *"Drink! Drink! Drink!*
> *To lips that are red and sweet*
> *As the fruit on the tree . . . ."*

Suprath had by chance switched the TV set to a channel showing the movie, *The Student Prince,* at the scene where the young prince, as he was introduced at the inn to a student fraternity in Heidelberg University, led in singing the drinking song.

Simon, Phil and Jonathan listened to the singing.

"I don't want to miss this," Simon said as he picked up his glass of beer and stood up.

"Neither do we," Phil and Jonathan likewise said.

Their drinks in their hands, they returned to the bar counter. Simon took with Jonathan, two of the vacant bar stools there, but Phil remained standing. His eyes fixed to the movie, he seemed to be moved by the drinking song.

He began to sing it along, tentatively at first. He raised his voice as he gained confidence and caught on with the music and the lyrics. He swung his beer glass as he beat time to the drinking song, to the great danger of spilling its contents. Not a drop, though, was spilled on the floor.

Phil's singing voice surprisingly carried well and strong for an old short man like him. Their shoulders swaying, the others in the bar counter joined in the singing. They sang to Suprath and Aspara, who smiled at them.

At the end of the song, the men raised their glasses to them and shouted, "Let's drink!"

Mark was so impressed with Phil's singing, he said, "You could have joined Domingo, Pavarotti and Careras in their concert."

It was shown on the TV in the bar several nights before.

Lew said, "Had you been here in Los Angeles when they made the movie, your fine singing voice might have landed you the singing part of the student prince."

Phil replied, to laughter in the bar counter, "They would then have to rename the movie, *The Short Student Prince.*"

"You are one real comedian, Phil," Mark said. "You even make fun of yourself."

They fell silent as they watched the following moving scene, where the students, as they were leaving the inn to retire for the night, began to sing a goliardic song in bidding the young prince good night. Lew sang it along with Phil:

> *"Gaudeamus igitur, Juvenes dum sumus.*
> *Gaudeamus igitur, Juvenes dum sumus.*
> *Post jucundum juventutem, Post molestam senectutem.*
> *Nos habebit humus, Nos habebit humus."*

Simon listened, his heart pained by the memory of the beautiful goliardic song. He was a young carefree student the first time he saw the movie in the old Republic Theater in Manila. That was years and years ago, far from where he was now, here in the Keg Room in Los Angeles. He was now like the poet-scholars known as the goliards, on whose verses that and other such songs were based. They wandered in France, England and Germany during the Middle Ages, as he now had wandered, centuries later, here in America.

The beautiful drinking and goliardic songs aside, he watched the rest of the movie with gloomy detachment. Its theme of young love no longer held any connection with him. He was approaching middle age, the youthful zest for life gone out of him. Eventually he and all the rest of them will go the way of the dead king in the movie.

He fought off the depressing thought with the beer glass tipped to his lips. The cold beer coursed down his throat, easing up his depression.

The other bar patrons seemed to be just as affected by the movie. They spoke very little and drank a lot, with Suprath and Aspara replenishing their drinks.

At the movie's final scene, the young prince, now the king, said good-bye to his true love, the barmaid in the Heidelberg inn. The young king then headed off with his professor and counselor to marry a princess to whom he was betrothed.

Inside the carriage, as they were leaving Heidelberg, they heard once again the students retiring for the night, singing the same goliardic song. The professor smiled at the young king and, patting his hand, said, *"Gaudeamus. . . Let us rejoice while we are young."*

For quite a while, Simon gazed downcast at his beer glass, his heart pained by the memory of his lost youth the movie had revived. That time will never come back. He was startled when someone laid a hand on his shoulder.

"Good night, my friend," Lew said, his hand laid on Simon's shoulder.

He looked up at Lew and said, "A pleasant evening to you, too."

"Cheers to all of us for a wonderful time here," Mark, who stood beside Lew, said.

"Cheers!" the others at the bar counter chorused.

"Take care now," Jonathan said.

"Be careful with your driving. You may try crossing the orange light, but not the red light," Phil said, funny even at their parting.

Lew and Mark waved in good-bye at the smiling Suprath and Aspara, and left the bar.

It was only a little past nine in the evening, but Simon, Phil and Jonathan felt they had drunk more than enough. It was time for them to leave, too.

They finished their drinks in a short while and left after thanking Suprath and Aspara for the very nice evening they spent at the bar.

Simon drove out of the Keg Room's parking lot, turned left on Vermont Avenue and drove toward Los Feliz Boulevard. He was taking Jonathan home to Atwater Village and Phil afterwards to his apartment in Sunshine Park.

Jonathan was seated at the front seat. He was, like Simon, listening to Phil, who was at the backseat, humming the movie's goliardic song. It sounded sad as Phil was humming it, not as it was sung by the students in the inn, and not as it was originally intended, as a song in celebration of youth, life, friendship and sensual pleasures.

The song's somber tone affected Simon in like manner. Memories—these were all that he had left now. As for his future, like Jerome Kern's *Ol' Man River*, he will just have to keep on rolling along. At least there were, always with him, Clara, Lorna and Sonny to keep him going.

He had, as well, in the company of these two fellows with him in the car, a balm for loneliness and sad memories. So, he must cast aside all thought about his bleak teaching prospects and memories of his lost youth, revived by the beautiful movie, for the enjoyable evening that overall he had at the Keg Room.

"Cheer up," he said to himself, so that at the end of Phil's humming of the goliardic song, he began to sing the merry drinking song:

"Drink! Drink! Drink!
To eyes that are bright
As stars when they're
Shining on me!"

Phil joined in and pretty soon Jonathan was also singing the drinking song. Onward they sang merrily as the car approached Los Feliz Boulevard.

Simon stopped the car at the intersection's red traffic light. He looked ahead, singing still the drinking song with Phil and Jonathan. He did not recognize in the dark, the driver and the passenger of a car that had turned left from Los Feliz and headed toward Griffith Park. Saul was at the wheel of Agnes' car, with her seated beside him. They did not see Simon either, who had by then turned right on Los Feliz and headed toward Atwater Village.

Chapter 12

The car's headlights pierced the darkness in the winding road in Griffith Park, as Saul drove on toward the observatory high up in the park. A visit there will complete his Friday night out with Agnes.

He glanced at her and caught a sad look in her face. Her mind was still on the movie they just saw. It had so affected her. A father giving away his daughter in marriage was a bit hard to take, more so for the father in the movie who was very fond of his daughter. And yet he could not help but envy the father who had a daughter to give away in marriage. He and Agnes had none. She was happy on their way to the movie and left it depressed. She regained her cheerful self at the dinner they took in Sammy's Steakhouse. Now, on their way to the observatory, she had lapsed once again into a gloomy silence.

The park they saw from their car had the usual Friday crowd of people taking in the night air and the magnificent view of Los Angeles. The observatory came into view with a turn he made toward the parking lot. He circled around until he saw a car moving out and drove his car to the vacated slot.

"It's a lovely evening," he said as he looked around and then held her hand as she was getting out of the car.

She smiled as she looked around too at the observatory and the rest of the park. Her eyes were shining. She was like a person released from the confining thoughts inside the car and into the freedom of the open space around her.

He smiled too, pleased to see her looking cheerful again. After all, Griffith Park was a dear familiar place to them. They had not visited it in years, but nothing had changed there, and this pleased him even more.

He looked up at the sky above Los Angeles. It was dark, but clear. Countless stars, some brighter than the others, glowed in the dark void of the universe, but not as brightly as the new moon in the dark sky. The giant telescope jutting out from the left dome of the observatory was trained to the sky. A peek through it, as he had done countless times, gave a much closer view of objects in outer space.

They proceeded, following their habit, toward the view deck. They stood there for a while, admiring silently the grand view of Los Angeles and the more distant Century City. Visible in the dark to their right was the giant sign of Hollywood. A row of telescopes waited for them, but they did not go there to peek at those living in the homes and apartment buildings far below them.

He laid his arm on her shoulder, her closeness enhancing his enjoyment of the view. The lights in Los Angeles glowed like golden beads. They were strung up in its avenues, buildings and homes. The carpet of lights seemed to start off at the ground not far below their feet, although he knew they were several hundred feet above it. Lights flickered from the airplanes descending in the night sky toward the distant airport. The city of his birth as always was fascinating and dynamic. For quite a while, he looked on at the city, dazzled by its power and splendor.

"We are in luck," she said. "Los Angeles is not shrouded in smog tonight."

"Excellent! We can see the streets down there very clearly."

"Like that one, right below us. Can you tell me the name of that street?"

The street was bound on either side by rows of streetlights that converged in the dark horizon.

He removed his arm from her shoulder and leaned forward on the iron railing, not that a foot closer made any difference, but it helped him focus his eyes and freshen up his memory on the name of the street below them.

"It is Normandie Avenue," he said as he took note of the point where it started at the base of the dark slopes of the park.

"How far does it go?"

"It must be about twenty-five to thirty miles long. It stretches from down there, then across Wilshire Boulevard, then through South Central, and all the way to Rancho Palos Verdes."

"And those two parallel streets? Are they not Vermont and Western?"

"So, you know your geography of Los Angeles."

"Not as well as you do."

They looked over their shoulders when they heard some noisy teenagers approaching the view deck.

He had no intention of having his visit to the park with Agnes spoiled by them, and he led her away.

They walked toward the bust of James Dean, watching over a concrete walk. He seldom missed taking a look at the late movie actor's bust every time he visited the park, and he gazed at it for a moment. He had boundless admiration for James Dean, whose second movie, *Rebel Without a Cause,* he had seen several times. Part of the movie was shot right there in the observatory.

"It is too bad he died so young," he said as he looked on at the bust. "He could have made a lot more great movies."

"I know. You have told me that countless times."

"Have I? Well, I could never have enough of his movies."

"And one other thing as well."

He smiled at what she had alluded to: his zest for sex that had remained undiminished in their twelve years of marriage.

"Perhaps, tonight, I can have enough of it," he said while looking significantly at her.

She smiled, but said nothing.

He would have pressed on had they been alone there. But there were people around. He must then lead her *there*. This was, after all, his intention in taking her to Griffith Park. *There* was a secluded area at the northern side and back of the observatory, a favorite trysting place of lovers visiting the park.

They went up in the stone steps toward the observatory, but as they came near the door, he steered her down toward the trysting place, his eyes lit up in remembrance of the past.

He brought other girls there long before he met Agnes. That was way back in his high school days. He learned from a classmate what a convenient dating place it was. It cost him almost nothing to take his dates there. Best of all, he could claim innocently to his dates and their skeptical parents that it was all for scientific exploration. The scientific exhibits and the moon and the stars they could observe through the telescope will broaden their knowledge of the world and the universe. Who could object to that? Although it got to be tiresome doing that every time he brought a date there, it was only preliminary to the following innocent invitation he would then make for a walk down to the trysting place.

Once he was there with his date, he attempted his own exploration. Not that he always succeeded. He fumbled badly the first time he brought a girl there. The girl, a classmate, laughed to his face at his clumsy effort, called him a fool and left him. That did not stop him, though, from trying again.

He learned fast. Except for one more failure, a mild one at that, the rest went on smoothly and to his expectations.

To be young again! The thought came pleasantly to his mind as he and Agnes then walked on toward the trysting place, the ground between the semicircular wall on the northeast side of the observatory and the stone parapet overlooking Glendale and, farther ahead, a view of downtown Los Angeles.

He glanced at the distant lights of Glendale. Lacking a date,

Therese must be there now in her apartment where she lived alone. She must be curled up in bed, watching TV or reading a book.

They passed by a dark spot, the leafy branches of a tree there obscuring the light in the lamppost. Several couples there were conversing quietly, or were locked in an embrace. They walked on to a marvelous view of the tall buildings of downtown Los Angeles.

It was like in the old days. He brought Agnes there several times during their courtship days. He professed his love for her there. But they stopped coming after they were married. What they could do in complete freedom and privacy at home made a tryst there unnecessary. But they came tonight, and why not, for old times' sake!

It was time to give free rein to his feelings. He laid his arm on her shoulder. She did not respond, as she kept her eyes to the view of downtown Los Angeles. Indiference after a while began to overcome him as well, and he removed his arm from her shoulder.

He said, for lack of anything to say, "Can you tell me where my office is located from among those buildings there?"

"It is hard to tell at night."

"Right, it is too dark."

He was now so annoyed he could have broken out into brutal language as to why she was so unresponsive, so unyielding! He looked elsewhere to distract himself and to keep his temper down. The sight of some couples romancing there sent instead the blood in his arteries rushing up to his head. He could do what the others there were doing, and he laid once again his arm on her shoulder. Then he steered her back to the dark area and halted near the tree.

He looked at her. There was not a sign of acquiescence in her eyes, turned away from him. They were on the distant lights of Glendale. The view was marvelous, a prop useful to his intentions, but damn it! It had also drawn her away from him! No! He was blaming the view for his romantic flair gone rusty from lack of use. He drew a deep breath and let it out. Just do it, he told himself, and he pulled her to him, so roughly her side grazed the stone parapet.

She said, wincing from pain, "What are you doing?"

"I'm sorry."

"Must you do this every time we come here?"

"I've always hugged you here," he replied, now angry and frustrated. "Why do you object to it now? Everyone here is doing it!"

He looked around, suddenly embarrassed by the ugly scene

they were making there.

"Shh," someone in the dark, a man from the sound made by the lips, urged them to be quiet.

"Take it easy, Pop," another man said.

Pop! The word cut deeply into his self-esteem. How silly he must have looked to those young couples romancing there in the dark! Here he was, a respectable lawyer approaching middle age, behaving in a very undignified manner, like a lovesick teenage idiot! He had only cheapened himself and his wife with the impetuous thing he did to her.

He took her hand and said, "Let's get out of here."

They left the trysting place and walked toward the obelisk of the astronomers. It stood in the middle of the park's wide open ground, lively with people taking a stroll there, some of them talking and laughing. Others were basking in the enjoyment of their wonderful time there. A couple were telling their young children not to stray too far from them. The scent of flowers was in the air. It was a moonlit night, but with the electric lights there, one would notice the new moon only if one looked up at the sky.

The frown on his face, as he walked on with her, did not correspond with the gaiety there. He could feel, as they were passing by the obelisk, the seated stone Copernicus gazing down at him in sympathy for his ruined Friday night out with her.

"This would have been a perfect place for our Friday night out," he said to her.

"We can go to other places."

"And see other movies as well. You did not enjoy the movie."

"I did not."

"But it was funny and touching."

"That is why I did not enjoy it. It was so touching, it reminded me of what we'll never have."

"It crossed my mind too," he said, his brow furrowed at the thought that they will never have a child of their own.

A routine medical checkup early in their marriage showed a tumor in her uterus. It was taken out and with it went her capacity of ever conceiving a child.

"Don't you regret having married me then," she said, "for I can never give you a child?"

"Of course not. We have each other. Is that not enough?"

"You will be happier with a woman who can give you a child."

He halted and said, as he looked tenderly at her, "You are not just any woman, nor just any wife. You are my woman; you are my wife; my one and only love."

Her eyes were lit up as he then held her on the shoulder and kissed her lightly on her cheek. He was, by what he had said and what he had done, showing her, his love for her.

The dreary talk and the humiliating incident in the trysting place buried in silence, they proceeded to their car, now smiling in anticipation of what they will do once they were at home.

Chapter 13

Clara thought it odd, as she was scanning a customer's purchases, that the man passing by her checkout was dressed in a drab olive green jacket on a day like it. The temperature outside the store by now must be in the upper eighties. The man was tall and bull-shouldered. He looked around with shifty eyes, and this alarmed her even more. He could be a thief. Simon had warned her that Broadway, which included Super Bargain Store, was infested with thieves and other odd characters, like the panhandler she encountered on her first day of work in the store. The man could easily put on, underneath his jacket, layers of stolen clothing. The man walked on toward the men's section, and she went back to work.

"How would you like to be the proud owner of one of these very nice watches," she said to the woman customer in her checkout, while pointing at a pyramid of watches beside her cash register. "They are a bargain at those prices. They cost double in other stores."

The woman glanced at the watches and shook her head, but she was determined to make a sale.

"If I were you, I'll buy one now," she said. "They will be sold out by the time you come here again."

"Let me see," the woman said, apparently won over by her sales pitch. She picked up a lady's watch and examined it.

"It will look nice on you," she said.

"It looks nice, but is it not expensive at twenty dollars?" the woman said at the price tag.

"Not at all," she said. "It's a quality watch, and it is a bargain at that price. Buy one, at least for yourself."

The woman smiled. She put the watch down on the counter and said, "Okay, I'll take this one."

She scanned the watch's bar code, while the woman took out from her purse two twenty-dollar bills. She gave these to her, who then put the money inside the cash register. She gave the woman her change and bagged her purchases. She complimented the woman for not missing out on a good bargain, as they bade each other a good day. She glanced at the wall clock as the woman was passing out of the store's glass door. It showed the time: two-thirty.

It was the third time she had glanced at the wall clock. Agnes should be arriving any moment now. She called the night before to tell her she was dropping by her store on her way to Saul's office. They had become phone pals. They had been calling each other almost every night for a chat. As she had promised her, she was giving her a stuffed broiled chicken. It was a token of their friendship and an example of her cooking skill that she wanted to show to her and Saul. She smiled when she saw her coming.

"So, this is Super Bargain Store," Agnes said as she looked around at the store.

"Is this your first time to come here?"

"Yes."

"Of course, I should not have asked you that. You do your shopping in Rodeo Drive."

The customers at Clara's checkout looked on, impressed, at Agnes, who smiled, flattered. The rich and famous in Los Angeles do their shopping there. She was in a signature suit of the kind sold in Rodeo Drive. She had just come from City Hall on some errand for her office.

"If you only knew what a bargain hunter I am," she said.

"You have come to the right place then."

"Don't let me keep you from your work."

"I'll be taking a break in a short while. We can talk then."

"I'll look around in the meantime," Agnes said as she walked toward the store's ladies' section.

The line in Clara's checkout had lengthened while she was talking to Agnes. She resumed work and passed through the scanner and bagged a waiting customer's purchases. She took the payment, entered it in the cash register and gave the customer his change.

It was a quick methodical work she concluded with a friendly word of parting with the customer.

The other cashiers had envied and even resented her for her fast efficient work, all because she was new in the store. They thought she was showing off. Eventually they conceded that it was not to make a good impression that she worked fast and efficiently. That simply was how she worked. Typically, then, she rang her cash register oftener than Rosita and Colleen, who were at the other checkouts. By then, the long line in her checkout had shortened to just two customers, a woman and the man in olive green jacket.

"Hey, Clara, can you tell me the price of this bottle of parsley flakes? The barcode is torn," Rosita asked from her checkout.

Clara jogged her memory. She was also conceded to have an uncanny way of remembering the prices of many of the goods sold in the store. She looked over her shoulder and said to Rosita, "It's one dollar and fifty-nine cents."

She turned to the woman customer and said to her, "It is nice to see you again, Missis Whitmore. What a pretty silk dress you are wearing."

"Thank you," Mrs. Whitmore said, her wrinkled face lit up in delight. "My husband gave me this dress as a birthday present. I have not worn it in years."

Clara nodded. The glint of pleasant recollection in Mrs. Whitmore's eyes told her of that time when she showed her dress, then new, to her husband. It was sad, too. Mrs. Whitmore told her once that she was a widow living alone with a cook and housekeeper in Fairfax District. She and her husband once owned a building in Spring Street.

The man in olive green jacket was now near Clara's checkout. She saw from the corner of her eye that the man now looked much bigger in his jacket. It was most likely padded with layers of clothing stolen from the store. The man undoubtedly was a thief. He was so big and intimidating she dreaded facing him once he was right in front of her checkout. To avoid showing fear and anxiety, she turned her attention to Mrs. Whitmore and said to her, "You look fresh like spring in that silk dress, Missis Whitmore."

"Thank you. How nice of you to say that," Mrs. Whitmore said, smiling in keen pleasure.

She took Mrs. Whitmore's payment for what she bought in

the store, put it in the cash register and gave her, her change.

Serving Mrs. Whitmore helped distract her from her fear of the man in olive green jacket, who was now moving closer to her checkout.

Mrs. Whitmore said, as she picked up her bag of purchases from the counter, "Now that you mentioned spring, I would love to show you my garden."

"I would love to go there one of these days," Clara said.

"I'll wait for that day," Mrs. Whitmore said as she passed out of her checkout.

Clara hid with a smile, her anxiety as she then attended to the man who had taken out from his pocket, a dollar bill in payment for what he bought—a small box of cereal worth one dollar.

She put the money inside the cash register and closed it. Then she turned to the microphone hidden at the other side of the cash register and said, "Kyle to number three.'

It was a call for the store security officer to come immediately to her checkout.

The man heard her. He panicked and pushed her aside so violently, she crashed against the cash register and fell on the floor.

The man was rushing out of the store when Kyle came and chased him in the stairs.

Agnes and Sharon saw what happened, and they came rushing to Clara. They helped her stand up. She was unhurt except for a bruise in her arm.

Just then, they saw Randolph running toward the stairs. Clara, with Agnes and Sharon supporting her in the arm, hurried up to the glass door. They watched Randolph and Kyle as they tried to subdue the man at the top of the stairs. A police car came. Two police officers jumped out of the car and helped Kyle and Randolph in subduing the man. He was frisked and handcuffed. The police officers found in his pockets, a calculator, a watch, and a bottle of perfume. They opened his jacket and found there layers of clothing.

Clara's eyes shot wide with fear when a police officer removed a fan knife secreted inside the man's sock. He could have stabbed Kyle and Randolph with it. The police officers took down notes as they interviewed Kyle and Randolph. Then they took the man away.

A crowd in the store saw what Kyle and Randolph had done,

and they commended them for the brave, but dangerous thing they did. Kyle and Randolph said they were just doing their job.

Randolph turned to Clara and said, "You have bruised your arm. Should I call the paramedic?"

"There is no need for that," she replied. "Thank you, but I'm all right."

"Take a break," Randolph said. "In the meantime, I'll take over your checkout."

"We'll take you to the break room," Sharon said.

Clara reluctantly allowed Agnes and Sharon to hold her in the arm as they took her to the break room. She was embarrassed, as it seemed to her everyone in the store was watching her being taken to the break room, like a child being taught how to walk.

Agnes and Sharon's solicitude made her feel good, though. They cared for her. They seemed to be distressed by what the thief had done to her. They set her down on a chair at the dining table in the break room.

Agnes sat down beside her and examined the bruise in her arm while Sharon proceeded to the water cooler and filled a cup there with water. She gave it to Clara, who drank it down.

"Does your arm still hurt?" Agnes asked her.

"Only slightly, the pain will go away in no time at all."

"Do you feel better now?" Sharon asked her.

"Yes. Thank you, both of you, for your help."

It occurred to her then that she had yet to introduce Agnes and Sharon to each other. She did this quickly, and Agnes and Sharon responded by greeting each other. Sharon then turned to her.

"I should have warned you about the thief," she said. "Our store is infested with them. They have been robbing our store blind."

"Is it that bad here?" Agnes asked Sharon.

"It is."

"Where do they come from?"

"They are here all the time in downtown Los Angeles. You won't notice them unless you work here."

"You seem to know them."

"Don't I know them! Many of them come from our branch of the human family tree."

"I cannot understand why anyone would steal bargain items at the risk of being caught and jailed."

"The man must be in need," Clara said. "People steal out of need."

"That is no excuse," Agnes said. "He should look for work instead of stealing."

"How will he find work when he is not looking for it?" Sharon said.

"How can you tell that?" Clara asked Sharon.

"I know, I know. The thief is like some of the men I know. They avoid work. They would rather bum around, maybe beg or even steal rather than work. It is just my luck that some of the men I have met are no good."

"I'm sorry to hear that," Agnes said.

"Thank you," Sharon said. "Perhaps, next time, I'll have better luck with men."

Clara smiled at the subtle shift in their conversation. She listened, amused, to Sharon indulging once again in self-pity. The pain in her arm reminded her that it was she, not Sharon, who should be the object of their sympathy and attention. But here was Sharon having turned to herself again. She had assumed a hurt look and had hogged Agnes' attention as well. The plea for sympathy Sharon made was a refrain she had heard once too often from her. It came from her frank and open nature.

Just then, Mary looked in at the door and said, "Hey, Sharon. You are needed in your booth."

"I've got to go," Sharon said as she stood up from her chair. "I almost forgot some customers who needed my attention."

"Nice meeting you," Agnes said to Sharon.

"Nice meeting you, too," Sharon said to Agnes.

"And stop dwelling on the past," Clara said to Sharon. "Look ahead instead."

"Right on," Sharon said, now smiling. "From now on, I'm gonna have nothin' but fun."

She swung her arms and swayed her hips as she danced across the break room and out at the door.

"Interesting friend you have there," Agnes said to Clara. "She must be fun."

"She is fun, all right, and that is her problem. Men see her as fun, nothing more. No commitment, no responsibility. I'm sorry for her; she has not been lucky with men."

"That reminds me how, on the other hand, I'm so lucky to be married to Saul."

"Proud and happy, too?"

"Yes, proud and happy, too. Seeing him later in his office will make my day."

"Do you often do that?"

"As often as I can."

"Why? To keep tabs on him?" Clara asked, wondering at the same time what had made her pry into the marriage of Agnes and Saul. She was, she decided, simply curious about it.

"Not really," Agnes replied.

"Why, then, do you check on him? Is he that kind of a man, too?"

Agnes seemed to be annoyed by the question and she said, "No, not at all. Why do you ask a question like that?"

"It's just that, well, you know how most men are. They won't pass up the company of women who can give them pleasure."

"Saul is not that kind of a man."

"What if you find out he is not what you think he is? What will you do then?"

Agnes' face suddenly hardened, and she said, "He will be in big trouble!"

Agnes' sharp reply told Clara that Agnes seemed to be dissatisfied with her marriage. It could be in trouble. Race and religion may have come between her and Saul. Love may not be strong enough to bridge this chasm separating them. To make it even harder for her, she and Saul had remained childless. A child could provide the bond that could keep their marriage strong and happy. The lack of a child of their own could have led Agnes to a feeling of inadequacy, and Saul possibly to another woman's arms. She had no doubt that, like her, Agnes looked at marriage as something to be kept for life, but she could be doing it not so much out of enduring love as out of a sense of commitment to Saul.

Agnes rose abruptly from her chair and said, "I need a drink."

She went to the water cooler and filled there a cup with water and drank it down. It seemed to have refreshed her spirit, for then she said as she walked back to her chair, "After what I have heard from Sharon, I still consider myself, in comparison to her, a very lucky woman."

"You are indeed," Clara said, glad to see Agnes no longer so upset. She could only blame herself for having put in Agnes' head doubts about Saul's fidelity. She could also blame Simon's penchant for analysis, which had rubbed off on her. It led her into making those nasty insinuations about Saul.

"You have nothing to worry about Saul," she said penitently. "He is a good man. I saw by the way he looked at you at the fair, how devoted he is to you."

"He is indeed," Agnes, now smiling, said as she held happily, Clara's hands.

"I suppose you can hardly wait to see him," she said.

"Yes, indeed."

She glanced at her watch and said, "I'll have to go. Are you sure you're all right now?"

"Yes, I'm all right now."

"Let us keep in touch. Let us keep on calling each other."

They were at the door when Clara halted and said to Agnes, "Wait, before you go, I brought you something."

She took out from the refrigerator, a paper bag containing a round large object wrapped in plastic and gave it to Agnes.

"What is this?" Agnes asked her.

"It's the broiled stuffed chicken I promised to give you."

"I did not think you were serious about giving me this. But, thanks a lot. Saul and I will have something to feast on."

They hugged each other at the door.

Clara felt good as she watched Agnes walk away. A while ago she was slumped on the floor, hurt and dazed. Agnes and Sharon ministered to her. Randolph was concerned for her, too. Their solicitude made her feel good.

After what she had been through, she was not inclined to go back to work right away. She went back to the dining table, sat down on a chair there and laid her feet on another chair. The break room was windowless and had the smell of food. Sharon's strong fragrance also lingered there. It was apt for a woman like her on the lookout for men. Sharon had enough of long ties with men. Rosita's problem was of a different sort. Unlike Sharon who was only after short casual affairs with men, Rosita was after marriage.

It was a matter brought to her attention by Divina, who asked her if she had noticed that Rosita's belly was growing by the day. She did not notice it, as she was not in the habit of watching other women's bellies. It did not concern her. Divina then said Salim should marry Rosita for the sake of their child.

The child will be a half-breed, she thought smiling. They were a good example of people crossing the racial divide for love. The chasm that should otherwise divide the store's white and black, Hispanic, Asian and Middle Eastern employees had been bridged by this familiarity they developed as they worked in the store and ate and engaged in small talk in the break room. It made them into some kind of a large extended family. For the Salvadoran woman and the Pakistani man, it had grown into something far more intimate.

As for her, it had developed into a friendship with Sharon and the others that now made her feel good for all the shock and injury she had sustained a while ago. It was something she felt she must share with Simon. She went to the telephone to tell him what happened in the store.

Chapter 14

"You have a call," Sonia said to Simon as he was cleaning up a dining table.

He left it, thanked Sonia and picked up the phone. His back turned to her and his hand cupped over the phone to keep out the noise in the restaurant, he listened as Clara told him about the shoplifting incident in the store, the injury she sustained and the help she got from Agnes and Sharon.

"Are you sure you are all right?" he said, his voice kept low.

"I'm glad to hear that," he continued after hearing Clara's reply. "I'll pick you up at around five-twenty, as usual. Wait for me by the store entrance. Take care."

He put the phone back to its cradle and resumed cleaning the dining table, his mind on the shoplifting incident in Clara's store. They seemed to be hounded by all sorts of trouble wherever they went. But, then, who was not? The thing to do was to ride through whatever storm was upon them, no matter how serious or even life-threatening it was.

Three customers, food trays in their hands, were approaching the dining table. He gave it several quick sweeps with the cloth in his hand and nodded at the men that the table was ready for them.

He was done with this task in the dining area, and he went back to his post in the kitchen sink and washed the dishes he had taken from the dining tables there. It took him a while to do this. Then he washed the pots and pans and the kitchen utensils Josefino had put there beside the kitchen sink.

He was returning them clean and dry to the kitchen when he noticed the floor there was wet and might be slippery. He asked the cooks if mopping it will interfere with their work there.

"No. Go ahead," Naty replied.

They stepped aside as he mopped the kitchen floor clean and dry.

It was past three in the afternoon. For the first time since that morning, L&S was empty of patrons. The three men who had taken a late lunch had left. He cleared the dining table and washed the used dishes and utensils.

He was midway in the next task he undertook of cleaning the floor in the restroom when Leonard called out to him to come to the dining area.

"I'll be there in a minute," he replied.

He mopped the restroom floor quickly, returned the mop to the utility closet and washed his hands. He joined Leonard and Sonia at a dining table in the dining area, wondering why Leonard had called for him. The inscrutable expression in Leonard's face told him nothing.

"We have been watching you work these past few months," Leonard said to him. "Sonia and I are very much satisfied with the good work you are doing for us."

He nodded, pleased, but otherwise showed no emotion. He was not a bit surprised by what Leonard had said about him. He worked hard and was polite to the restaurant patrons and helpful to the other workers. It occurred to him then that Leonard might give him a raise.

"We are opening a branch in Eagle Rock," Leonard said. "We want you to manage it for us."

He gazed, wide-eyed in surprise, at Leonard. He could not believe what he heard from him. Leonard wanted him, the busboy, dishwasher and janitor in L&S, to be its branch manager in Eagle Rock?

"Well!" he said.

"Well, what?" Leonard said. "Are you accepting it?"

"I don't know what to say. I've never managed a restaurant before."

"There is always the first time," Leonard said. "We have asked around and learned good things about you. You are an educated man, honest and efficient. You will make good as our branch manager. But you still have not given us your answer. Can you do it? Are you accepting it?"

He remained quiet. Of course, he could do it! He had been watching how Leonard and Sonia ran L&S. All he had to do was to run the branch restaurant, the way they ran the main restaurant. As for accepting it, he had other plans. He still wanted to teach. That could be just a pipe dream, though, unlike the manager's job in L&S. It was there for him to take. He had to consider too what it would mean for his family. With a better pay coming, they will have more money set aside for the children's education and his planned move to Glendale. They might even be able to come up within a few years with a down payment for a home of their own.

"I can give it a try," he said at length.

"That is not good enough for us," Leonard said.

"Why can't you be more decisive?" Sonia said.

"All right," he said, feeling challenged. "I can do it, and I will do it."

"That is more like it," Leonard said.

"Tell me more about the job," he said.

He listened, as in the next few minutes Leonard and Sonia filled him in on his new job. They told him a host of things that went in running a restaurant. He nodded, pleased, when Leonard mentioned his new salary. It will be more than double his pay as a busboy, dishwasher and janitor. He will also have health insurance. To top it all, he will have the calling card of a restaurant manager. His head swelled with pride and gladness. He was no longer a busboy, dishwasher and janitor, but a restaurant manager.

Leonard interrupted him from his thoughts when he said, "You must see the place first thing tomorrow morning."

"Where is it located?" he asked.

"It's in a mall at the corner of Lincoln and Gooseberry," Sonia replied. "The present tenant, a delicatessen, will leave at the end of the month. We have two weeks to have it ready."

"I'll have to prepare myself for it," he said.

"You will do that," Leonard said. "Today is the last day you'll be busing and washing dishes. We are getting another man who will take over your job. For the next two weeks then, you will watch me and Sonia run the restaurant. We'll fill you in the rest of the way."

Leonard and Sonia cut their meeting short when they saw four men had come in. They stood up and left the dining table. Leonard went back to his post behind the counter, while Sonia returned to her post at the cash register. He had nothing else to do just then, but he could not just sit idly at the dining table.

He stood up also and went to his corner near the kitchen sink. He sat down on a stool there and savored the good fortune that had come his way. To be a restaurant manager was the next best thing to a school teacher. His mind remained fixed to it. Too bad he came from an economic and cultural laggard of a country. While he had sufficient academic credentials—a master's degree in history and literature, and years of experience teaching the two subjects, they were recognized and accepted only in the Philippines.

He shook his head in disappointment over his failed attempts to land a teaching job in America. His failure to get a teaching job in Asia Pacific was particularly painful. But he was not giving up; he was not a quitter. Then he remembered something.

"What is impossible one way maybe possible another way," his philosophy professor once said to him over what seemed to him was a difficult philosophical problem.

He nodded. So could he find a way to achieve his dream of teaching again. He will get a master's degree in history and literature in an American university, if that was what he needed to teach in America.

Simon glanced at Clara as she sat down in their car and fastened her seat belt. She looked none the worse for all that she had been through earlier in her store.

"So," he said to her, "you had your first brush with a thief in Broadway."

"It was nothing. I got a little scare and a small bruise on the arm, but I'm all right. You should have seen how our manager and our security guy tackled the thief in the stairs. It was like watching a cop-and-robber movie."

"So, we have been through a lot today."

"You, too?"

"Yes. Guess what happened in L and S this afternoon?"

He stopped the car at the red light in the intersection of Broadway and Eighth Street.

"Tell me what happened there," she said. "Don't keep me in suspense."

"L and S is opening a branch in Eagle Rock, and I will be its manager."

"Really! That is great! I'm so happy for you. You deserve it," she said, as she then smiled and kissed him on the cheek.

He was so pleased by her kiss and was about to kiss her back, but then the traffic light had turned to green. He had the car moving again and turning toward Eighth Street.

"When," she asked, "will you start on your new job?"

"In about two weeks. In the meantime, Leonard and Sonia will train me."

"It should be easy as pie for you."

"I like to think so."

"It would be nice if we could find an apartment in Glendale, not far from the restaurant."

"We can start looking around this Sunday. I hope we can find one that, with my new job, won't require a credit check. Better still if we can find one as inexpensive as our apartment in Avery Avenue."

"That will be a minor miracle. The rent for an apartment in a nice place like Glendale can be quite high. It may eat up all of our additional earnings. There might then be very little left for Lorna and Sonny's college education. How, then, can we send them to college?"

"We can find a way. With their high grades in school, Lorna and Sonny can qualify for a grant or financial aid. Whatever we have saved will then go to their books and other school expenses."

"I hope they will qualify for that. Without it, they cannot go on to college, and I won't settle for anything less than college degrees for Lorna and Sonny. A college education is that important to their future."

"It is. Without it, they may end up a busboy and dishwasher like me."

"Come now, dear, stop degrading yourself. I admire you for taking that job in L and S to feed your family, but you can now put that behind you. You are now a restaurant manager."

"Lorna and Sonny can do much more with college degrees from Cal Tech and USC."

He glanced at Clara and saw in the sparkle in her eyes, perhaps the thought of Sonny an aerospace engineer and Lorna a doctor. He and Clara could not do half as much as what their children could do. With their inborn abilities and their American education, they could achieve whatever they will set out to do in this country. And then to live in Glendale! That will be the fulfillment of his American Dream. How he loved to live there, a place with the ambience of a small American town and the amenities and sophistication of a big city like Los Angeles. It will be like the Norman Rockwell illustrations on the cover of *Saturday Evening Post* come to life.

He could see himself there now, taking a walk with Clara, Lorna and Sonny on its quiet pleasant streets, or window-shopping in Brand Avenue's tidy little shops. Glendale Galleria, the city library and the Holy Family Church were near each other, and he could easily cover them on foot. He drove on at a moderate speed toward First Street, his mind dwelling with pleasure at thoughts about Glendale and his children's college education.

"Things are certainly looking up for us, are not they?" Clara said, smiling. "This calls for a celebration. I'll cook something special after I get back from my choir practice. But first I must do some shopping in Central Market."

"Why not at Tom's?"

"We are almost there and the prices there are lower than at Tom's."

Central Market was only a few blocks away, and they arrived there within a few minutes. He parked their car in an unoccupied metered parking space. He dropped a quarter on the parking meter. With the time left by its previous occupant, they could park there for nearly half an hour yet.

The market was still open for shoppers, many of whom had dropped by after work from the offices nearby. He picked up a shopping tray and went straight with Clara to the seafood section.

"What will it be, lady?" the fish vendor asked her.

Clara replied with a smile. She was looking at the trays of seafood inside the glass counter in front of her.

It was near closing time and some of the stalls were already closed. The fish vendor looked tired, his work apron dirty with fish scales and fish blood. He waited patiently for Clara.

She gazed, undecided, at a tray of fillet of pinkish Pacific Red Snapper.

"Are they still fresh?" she asked the vendor.

"Look, lady," the vendor replied irritably, "they were taken from San Pedro and brought straight here just this morning."

"All right, if that is what you say," she said, similarly irritated. "Give me two pounds of that."

She inspected the other seafood items while the vendor took out several pieces of the Pacific Red Snapper and weighed them.

"It's a bit more than two pounds," the vendor said to her, who nodded in approval.

"Give me also a pound of shrimp, the ones with the heads on," she said, "and a pound of squid."

The vendor took her orders quickly.

"How about that?" Simon said at a tray of salmon heads.

"They will make for a tasty sour soup mix," she replied.

She turned to the vendor and said, "Can you also give me two of the salmon heads?"

She was done with her shopping in a few minutes, an unusual thing for her to do, who usually took her time in shopping. Many of the stalls had closed by the time she decided at the last minute to visit the produce section. She bought mangoes there, her favorite fruit. Their sweet and inviting smell greeted them, some twenty minutes later, when Simon opened the door to their apartment.

"Hi, Mom, Dad," Sonny said when he saw them coming in.

He rose from the floor, took Clara's hand and, in a gesture of respect, pressed it to his forehead. He did the same to Simon's outstretched hand and took from him the bags of fruit and seafood and brought them to the kitchen.

Rod and Andrew were seated, cross-legged, on the carpet, open books on their laps. They greeted Simon and Clara a good afternoon, which they returned with a similar greeting.

Simon swept the floor with his eyes. It was littered with books, notebooks, calculators, ballpoint pens and soda cans. Sonny and his friends were reviewing for the school examinations.

His head swelled with pride. They maybe mere apartment

dwellers living in a bad neighborhood, and Rod and Andrew may live in nice homes in nice neighborhoods, but here they were, reviewing with Sonny on whom they pinned their hope of getting good grades in school.

"Where is Lorna?" Clara asked Sonny as he was returning from the kitchen.

"She is in your room, Mom, probably watching TV."

Clara put her handbag on top of the cabinet. Then she went to the closet near the master bedroom door. She removed there her shoes and replaced them with her slippers.

Simon looked around as he waited for his turn in the closet. The sweet inviting smell of mango that greeted him, when he opened the door to their apartment, came from a platter of sliced mangoes on the dining table.

"Do I have any mail?" Clara asked him as he was going over the mail in their letter tray.

"Here is one for you," he said as he gave it to her.

He smiled when he saw there an envelope addressed to him. It was from the credit card company. He opened it and nodded. Inside was his secured credit card. He removed it from the envelope, read it, pleased with himself. A simple purchase with this credit card of anything in any store will establish for him a credit record required in renting an apartment in Glendale.

"Take a look at this," he said to Clara as he showed her his secured credit card.

"We have been waiting for that," she said. "We now have what we need to move to a better place like Glendale."

He took his turn in the closet and replaced his shoes and socks with his slippers. He could barely make out a news report in the TV set in the master bedroom with Sonny and his friends having a noisy spirited discussion on world history.

"Excuse me, Dad," Sonny said. "Perhaps you can help us with this question."

"What is it about?"

"It's about the European world explorations in the fifteenth and sixteenth centuries, what our teacher called the Age of Discovery. Can you tell us, Dad, what brought them about?"

"It's a good question," he said as he walked toward Sonny and his friends. "The answer is, in three words, gold, silk and spices."

Sonny and his friends looked at each other, a puzzled look in their faces.

"I don't see the connection, sir," Andrew said.

"You won't unless you dig deep into the question and the answer I gave you."

As he spoke, his eyes lit up as he remembered the time when, as a history teacher in Laguna, he tackled a question like that.

"It is a smart question," he continued. "It makes you think. It tells you that history is not just names and dates and events taking place seemingly at random. History is essentially cause and effect. It's a theory I developed in the course of teaching the subject.

"I'll explain it. Europe, for centuries, imported, among other products, silk from China and gold from India. It depended on the Indies, chiefly the spice islands of Ternate and Tidore in present-day Indonesia for its supply of spices. Without spices like cinnamon, pepper, nutmeg and cloves, you can imagine how tasteless food is. That is how important they were to the European households. Those products were brought by overland trade routes to Europe. Venice and Genoa controlled the trade from the thirteenth to the fifteenth century, but they charged exorbitant fees. This forced Spain and Portugal, the two maritime powers at that time, to seek a sea route to China, India and the Indies, and thus put an end to the two cities' monopoly of the trade in gold, silk, spices and other products."

"I still don't get it, sir," Rod said.

He looked down patiently at Rod. He had students in Laguna who were just like him, slow but sharp.

"Can't you see what it means?" Sonny said to Rod. "In looking for those alternative sea routes to China, India and the Indies, the Europeans were, in effect, exploring the world."

"Exactly," Simon said. "It marked the start of the great European explorations of the world. Vasco da Gama discovered a sea route from Europe along West Africa to India. Columbus, in seeking a westward sea route to India, discovered instead the New World, America. Cortez conquered Mexico, while Pizarro got Peru. Magellan's expedition, which sailed from the Atlantic to the Pacific, arrived in the Philippines in 1521. On its return to Spain, it was the first to circumnavigate the world. It proved that, contrary to popular belief then, the world is round.

"Other European countries like England, France and the

Netherlands were not far behind. They also crossed the seas and covered lands in search of trade. They established trading posts and naval and military stations to protect and enhance their commercial interests in lands, near and far. While some of those lands had bigger populations, they were way behind the economically, militarily and technologically advanced European countries. Eventually they conquered and colonized those lands. Onward they went, carving out empires from much of the world. Some of them lasted until the first half of this century, when those empires were finally put to an end by the rise of nationalism in those lands. So, you see, it was historical cause and effect all the way."

Simon paused, pleased to see in the faces of Sonny, Rod and Andrew complete absorption of his impromptu lecture on world history.

"Does that answer your question?" he asked them.

"Yes, sir," Andrew said. "I never saw history in a better light as I do now."

"So do I," Rod said.

"Thank you for your help, Dad," Sonny said.

Simon smiled, pleased with himself.

"That should settle one subject you are reviewing," he said. "I can see from the books and calculators lying on the carpet that you are also reviewing on algebra. How are you getting along there?"

"We'll tackle that, too, Dad. We have to review also on English and sociology."

"You are doing all of that in one seating?" Simon said.

"If you had started earlier, you would not be cramming now," Clara, who had been listening while reading her letter, said irritably.

"I'm not cramming, Mom," Sonny said patiently. "I've already reviewed for the exams. I'm just going over them, one more time with Rod and Andrew."

"That is exactly right, ma'am," Rod said to Clara. "Sonny is helping us prepare for the exams."

"As they say," Andrew said, "two heads are better than one."

"But there are three of us," Rod said.

"That is right," Andrew said. "You and I are each half a head compared to Sonny's head."

They laughed and playfully shoved each other, while Simon and Clara watched them, smiling.

"That does not come as a surprise to me," Clara said to Rod and Andrew. "After all, here is Sonny's father from whom he got his brains."

Simon smiled, pleased by the compliment from Clara. He followed her when she then proceeded to their bedroom. Lorna was in the bed, watching TV. She left it when she saw them.

"Have you prepared anything for our dinner?" Clara asked her as she was taking Clara's hand and pressing it to her forehead. She did the same gesture of respect to Simon.

"I took out what were left in the freezer," Lorna said, "the big milkfish, which I fried, and a side of beef, which I made into a stew. There were also some vegetables left over from last night, which I made into a salad. Do you want me to prepare dinner now?"

"Yes, while I'm taking a quick shower," Clara said.

She said to Simon when Lorna had left the bedroom, "Will you unzip my dress, please?"

As he did so, he ran his fingers on her smooth cream-complexioned back.

It tickled her and she moved away from him and said, "What do you think you are doing?"

"Nothing. I just could not help doing it."

"Whatever you are getting at, this is not the time for it," she said as she went to the closet.

She returned to their bedroom, dressed in her bathrobe, a loose shirt and a pair of slacks draped over her arm for a quick shower in the bathroom. A few minutes later, she returned to their bedroom as the TV announcer was reporting on the acquittal in the King trial of the four accused police officers.

"What," she asked Simon, "was the videotape for, then?"

"Apparently it did not do much."

The TV set showed a small crowd of white people at the steps and the grounds of the courthouse in Simi Valley where the trial was held. The crowd there stood quietly as if nothing of far-reaching consequence had taken place inside the courthouse.

The way the trial ended, no protest placards waved, no shouting in the courthouse steps and grounds, seemed like a letdown to Simon after a year of following it and all the fear and anxiety the media had generated over it. If what he was seeing on TV was any indication, the trial could be a forgotten issue in a day or two.

"It may not have ended the way I thought it would end," Clara said, "but at least it is over."

"Yes, it looks like it is over," he said as he waited, seated on the bed, for a report on the reaction of the black residents of Los Angeles to the verdict.

She said, as she was leaving the bedroom, "Come on, dear, let us take our dinner."

Simon left the bed, switched off the TV set and followed Clara to the dining table. Lorna was already seated there, waiting for them. A big milkfish steaming hot on its platter was laid on the dining table, beside a bowl of rice. A bowl of salad and a platter of beef stew were laid beside them. Also at the dining table was the platter of sweet and luscious mangoes.

Simon sat down at the dining table and asked Sonny, Rod and Andrew to join them at dinner.

"Thank you, sir," Andrew replied, "but we are still full from the sandwiches Lorna gave us."

"How about you, Sonny?" Clara asked him.

"Mom!" Sonny groaned as he rubbed his stomach. "I can't take anymore after those huge ham-and-egg sandwiches Lorna gave us. But we'll later help ourselves to the mangoes."

They said grace and proceeded with their dinner. They ate with zest, Simon especially. The food on the table confirmed what the love of his life, seated to his right, had said about things looking good for them. Here they were in the middle of the week, enjoying something of the good life in America. Later tonight, after he had brought Clara to her choir practice in St. Stephen Church, he will have his own time with his friends in the Keg Room. It will be a nice way of spending another fine evening in Los Angeles.

Chapter 15

Simon watched a car ahead as his car was entering the wide parking lot of St. Stephen Church. He slowed down until it had stopped in front of the church's lower wall. He drove his car beside it, its driver he could now recognize was Marian, a choir member. She and Clara, who was seated beside him, greeted each other a good evening.

"I'm going now, dear. Drive safely," Clara said to Simon.

She left the car and walked with Marian toward the elevated church courtyard, where they met and greeted the other choir members.

An assortment of races bound by a common love for church music, the choir members he was watching from the car were mostly Italian-Americans and Irish-Americans, with a sprinkling of Filipinos and Latinos. They were waiting for Reilly, their Irish-American choirmaster, who had the key to the side door of the church.

It was safe enough to leave Clara. He was about to back his car when he saw another car coming. He waited until it had rattled to a stop beside his car. Reilly stepped out of the car and walked hurriedly toward the choir members waiting for him in the courtyard.

He glanced at Reilly's car, which seemed to him was about to fall apart. Sonny could make it run like a new car again. He must tell Clara to suggest this to Reilly. Pleased with this thought, he drove his car out of the church parking lot. He was going to the Keg Room.

The bar was empty except for Suprath, who was at her usual post behind the bar counter, Jonathan, who was hunched over his glass of beer, and two other male patrons.

He smiled and nodded in greeting Suprath, who nodded in return. She did not seem to be her usual cheerful self tonight.

"What's up?" he said as he sat down beside Jonathan.

Jonathan shrugged his shoulder in reply.

He glanced at Jonathan and Suprath, puzzled by their cold reception. They seemed to be grouchy tonight.

"I'll have the usual," he said to Suprath.

He took out from his wallet two one-dollar bills and put them on the counter. As he waited for his beer, he looked around at the empty bar and the dark poolroom.

"It looks like a slow night," he said to Suprath.

A moody expression on her face, Suprath made no reply as she poured on a glass, half of the contents of the beer he ordered.

He noticed the pretty waitress was not around, and he asked Suprath, "Is Aspara on her night off?"

"She has left us," Suprath replied.

"Gone with the wind," Jonathan said, frowning, "to Las Vegas for a quickie wedding."

Simon's eyes turned wide in surprise. Aspara got married? He was about to ask Jonathan about it, but decided not to when he saw him staring morosely at the wine and liquor bottles behind Suprath. He was sorry for Jonathan. He liked Aspara. He could even be in love with her.

"I was taken by surprise when she told me yesterday she was getting married," Suprath said.

He asked Suprath, "Do I know the man she married?" A bar patron there might have won her love.

"I don't think you would," Suprath replied. "I don't know the man either. All she told me was that she met the man in McClellan's."

It was a department store where Aspara worked part-time as a stocker.

He asked Suprath, "Was she not in a hurry to get married?"

"She was. Her visa was about to expire and marrying an American citizen was the only way she could stay here legally."

He leaned on his elbows and looked down at his glass of beer. Aspara's surprise marriage pained him, too. Behind that friendly smile of hers was a mind worrying about her future in this country. Jonathan could have courted and married her. That would have solved her immigration problem, but he had done nothing more than flirt with her. Something must have stopped him from seriously pursuing the girl. What it was he did not care to know now.

He glanced at Suprath, who likewise looked depressed. She will have to look for another barmaid, although he was doubtful if she could find soon enough, someone as nice and pretty as Aspara. She was one extraordinary girl.

They come and go, he thought about the girls who had worked in the Keg Room. They were Suprath's compatriots who left Thailand for the proverbial greener pastures in America. But work as a barmaid in the Keg Room was not a career job, only a steppingstone to more stable better-paying jobs elsewhere. Working there provided them a chance, though, to meet eligible bachelors like Jonathan.

He asked Suprath if Aspara was coming back, but she had turned her gaze to Phil, who was rushing in.

"Turn the TV on," he said.

"Why?" Suprath asked.

"Don't you people know?" Phil said. "Riots have broken out in South Central!"

Everyone in the bar counter met the startling news with doubt and shock. To confirm what Phil said, they turned their gaze to the TV set, which Suprath had switched on. It came to life, showing an aerial view of a section of Los Angeles burning.

Above the TV set, the wall clock told the time: 6:40. It was early evening of April 29, 1992, not too long after the jury had handed its verdict in the King trial.

Everyone in the bar counter watched, wide-eyed and open-mouthed from shock, as the TV screen showed a reporter in a helicopter looking down at a section of Los Angeles burning.

"It looks like a war zone here in South Central," he said. "The last time I saw something like that was in the Tet offensive in Vietnam in 1968."

"Is it that bad?" the anchorman, shown in a corner of the TV screen, asked.

"Yes, it is that bad."

"Where are you now?"

"We are over the area where the riots started."

The TV camera was panned to a street closed to vehicular traffic.

"Can you identify that street?" the anchorman asked the reporter.

"It is Normandie Avenue."

"What is that burning there?"

"It's a building, the second one set on fire there."

The reporter said, as the helicopter then circled the area, "You won't believe how quickly the riots have spread from the beating incident that took place down there this afternoon."

"That is right," the anchorman said. "That is where it all started, late this afternoon."

The TV screen showed a close-up of the anchorman's face. He told the reporter he was taking over as he then said, "For the benefit of our late viewers, we will show again the beating incident that triggered the riots in South Central."

His hand wrapped around the cold beer glass, Simon watched a crowd jeering, raising their fists and making the dirty-finger sign at passing motorists at the intersection of Normandie Avenue and Florence Boulevard. A truck came by on Normandie and stopped at the turn of the traffic light to red.

Suddenly three dark young men dashed toward the truck and pulled the driver out, a blond-haired man with a long blond beard. They dragged him down into the pavement and, as the crowd cheered them on, they punched and kicked the man repeatedly in the face, chest and groin.

Suprath staggered from shock at the blows dealt to the man.

"Take it easy," Simon said as he sprung up from his stool and held Suprath in the arm to help her keep her balance

Phil sprinted around the counter and held Suprath in the other arm. They helped her sit down on a stool there.

"Are you all right?" Phil asked Suprath, who nodded in reply.

She looked shaken, though, and Phil filled a glass with water from the faucet there and gave it to her. She drank down its contents. She was now fully recovered from shock, and she thanked Phil and Simon for their help. Phil patted her in the arm and went back to his stool at the other side of Jonathan. They resumed watching TV.

"There you have it," the anchorman said, "the spark that set Los Angeles on fire. We'll turn you now to one of our ground units. Where are you now, John?"

The TV screen showed John holding a microphone.

"I'm here in Crenshaw near Manchester," John replied. "There is looting going on at the supermarket behind me."

The bar counter was quiet, but for the noise in the TV set.

Simon watched with growing anger and disgust people going emptyhanded inside the supermarket and people coming out with loot. They ignored the two police officers, one of them a woman, who were standing by helplessly near the entrance to the supermarket.

Law and order had broken down in South Central.

The TV camera then showed a middle-aged woman leaving the supermarket, the cart she was pushing full of loot.

"What is going on here, ma'am?" John asked the woman, the microphone thrust to her face.

The woman looked distrustfully at John while wiping with her palm, the sweat in her dark brow.

"I'm speakin' for them others here," the woman said, "but nothin' like this would have happened if they didn't let those cops go free. It ain't right; it ain't right at all."

"And you want to make it right with what you and the others are doing here," John said.

The woman looked sharply at John and pushed her cart away.

A man at the bar counter said, "Why are they taking it out on the supermarket? It has got nothing to do with the trial! The same thing with the truck driver!"

The others at the bar counter met the man's outburst with silence.

"There is something going on at the other side of the street," John said.

The TV screen then showed a crowd watching a row of stores there. The TV camera was zoomed in on three men attempting to force open with a crowbar, the accordion iron door of a delicatessen. A few feet away from them, a couple of men were trying to break down with a wooden pole, a laundry shop's door lock, its sign—Kim Cleaners—conveying distress. The men working with the crowbar broke through first. They surged inside the delicatessen, followed by those who broke off from the crowd. The men with the wooden pole increased their pace of pounding until finally the laundry shop's door lock broke. They rushed in, followed by the rest of the crowd.

Simon was so overwhelmed by the violence he was seeing in the TV screen and, his palm pressed to his brow, he shut his eyes. It sent his mind reeling instead to a violent student protest rally in Manila twenty years ago. The students were in Mendiola Street, marching toward Malacanang Palace, shouting, *"Makibaka! Huwag matakot kay Marcos"*— "Fight on! Don't be afraid of Marcos!" Police and army troops in the meantime were waiting for them at the palace gates.

When he opened his eyes, he saw smoke now rising from the rooftops of the stores beside the delicatessen and the laundry shop. Smoke rose too in the night sky above Mendiola Street when the police and army troops started firing their guns and throwing tear gas canisters at the student protesters.

He was not supposed to be there. He was on his way home from a school in the area, but was caught up in the students' protest rally. He was running away from there when a tear gas canister hit him in the head, sending him down on the pavement, like the poor truck driver in Normandie Avenue. His throat seemed to burst from the tear gas' acrid smoke, and he lifted his beer glass to his lips, the cold beer dousing the burning feeling in his throat. Luckily for him, another student helped him get up on his feet. Blood was streaming down from the cut the tear gas canister had made on his head. He was dizzy and his eyes and nose were also hurting from the smoke, but he was fleet-footed enough to escape from the violence in Mendiola Street, where several students lost their lives.

Suddenly, as he was watching the crowd in the TV screen, fear cold as ice shot up in his spine. The young men he was seeing in the TV screen were just like Sonny, eager and daring. What if Sonny had gone out of their apartment with Rod and Andrew to watch the fires? He stood up from his stool. He must check on his children.

"Will you excuse me, please? I must make a phone call," he said to the others at the bar counter.

He went to the public phone booth nearby on Vermont Avenue. A man was using it. He waited, worrying over Sonny and Lorna. Almost a minute had passed before the man left the phone booth. He called the apartment, and was relieved to hear Lorna's voice.

He asked her, "Do you have the TV turned on?"

"Yes, Dad. It's unbelievable!"

"Where is Sonny?"

"He is in the carport with Rod and Andrew."

"What are they doing there?"

"Sonny is fixing Andrew's car. What can you expect from that junk? They asked Einstein Junior to fix it. I heard them talking about giving the car a road test after Sonny had fixed it. You know that, Dad. They always turn to Sonny for such things."

"Tell Sonny when he gets back, not to leave the apartment. I'll be home soon with your mother."

"All right, Dad, I'll tell him that, and be careful, Dad."

He left the phone booth, relieved to know his children were safe at home. He glanced at his watch: seven-forty, more than an hour yet left of Clara's choir practice. He must drive to the church and tell Reilly to cut short their choir practice. The riots were spreading fast and might reach it by then.

He walked back to the bar and saw Mark and Lew seated at the corner of the bar counter. Their faces were tight with anger and contempt as they watched the mob shown on the TV screen. They were leaving the store and the laundry shop, exulting over their loot. Cradled in the arms of some of them were bundles of clothes. The others were carrying boxes of groceries.

He said to Mark and Lew, "It is bad, is it not?"

"It's terrible," Lew said.

"The stores have been set on fire," John said in the TV screen.

The camera showed the arsonists darting out of the burning stores, to the cheers of the crowd. They danced around, raised their arms and gave each each other a high-five for what they had done there.

"This is one time I regret having left Montana," Mark said. "That will never happen there."

"Why?" Jonathan asked Mark.

"We don't have people like them in Montana."

"Too bad we are in the wrong place in America," Phil said. "But it will pass."

"The fires are spreading fast," the anchorman said. "The firemen could not stop the fires with so many of them sprouting from one place to another. We have just received a report that a shopping mall on Ninth Street has been set on fire."

Simon was so stunned by what he heard, he finished drinking his beer quickly and stood up. Ninth Street was near St. Stephen Church. He must take Clara out of there.

"I've got to go," he said.

"It's not quitting time yet," Phil said.

"What's the hurry?" Jonathan said.

"I've got to pick up my wife."

"Don't worry about these two guys," Mark said about Phil and Jonathan. "We'll take them home."

He nodded and smiled at Mark and Lew, waved in good-bye at everyone there, and left the bar.

As he drove south, he saw far ahead in the gloomy sky, helicopters with their searchlights trained to the ground. They were either police helicopters assisting units on the ground, or news helicopters reporting to the rest of the world on the looting and the burning of Los Angeles.

After the violence and destruction he saw on TV in the Keg Room, the peaceful contrast in St. Stephen Church was so startling, it seemed unreal to him. And yet, as he also knew, the church was like that at night, a spot of peaceful solitude in its neighborhood of office and apartment buildings.

He stood beside his car, savoring the peace and quiet there, and looked around. The statue of Michael Archangel stood in a corner of the parking lot. A sword in his hand, the angel of God was poised to smite the devil lying at his feet. The figure of Virgin Mary, Mother of the Lord Jesus, stood at the other corner, her arms extended to those in need of her motherly help and comfort.

The parking lot was shrouded in darkness. It was empty but for the choir members' cars parked in a row facing the church's lower wall. In the buildings across Wilshire Boulevard, lights shone in offices where people on night shift were at work. It was quiet and peaceful there but, he feared, not for long. Not far from there, a shopping mall in Ninth Street was already burning.

He walked toward the side door of the church. He must tell Reilly to cut short his choir practice. The kind of person that he was, oblivious to everything else but his church music, the choirmaster could be unaware of the riots going on, not far from there.

The choir began to sing a beautiful church hymn as he was about to open the glass door. He looked up at the choir loft and listened, entranced by the beautiful church hymn the choir was singing like a heavenly host. It gave him such a heavenly feeling of being way above all worldly pain and conflict, his fear of the riots vanished.

The church, with its massive frame and stone parapet, seemed to him now, was like an impregnable medieval fortress. Evil could not prevail there. No one will dare attack the church. And he was not deluding himself. He had seen in living in Los Angeles the real strength of this country. It lay in freedom and opportunity that went hand in hand with justice, law and order. The forces of the law will soon stop the violence and disorder in the city. There was nothing to fear.

He entered the church once the choir had finished singing the church hymn. He saw Clara, Reilly and the rest of the choir looking down at him. He was early, too early. He waved at them as he proceeded toward a pew and sat down there. He had changed his mind about telling Reilly to cut short their choir practice. They could take all the time they needed. There was no need to take Clara out of there, now that he had assured himself of her and the rest of the choir's safety from the riots going on in the city.

It was so quiet inside the church, he could hear a slight

coughing by someone in the choir loft. The church was in partial darkness, the light there coming from the electric lamps in the ceiling above the choir loft behind him at the back of the church nave, and from the glow of votive candles on an iron stand set against a wall. The figure of Jesus Christ, nailed to a huge cross hanging by wire above the communion table, seemed to gaze down at him, suffering and yet forgiving.

Reilly's voice broke the silence in the church with a word of advice for the choir to avoid singing in vibrato. The choir had resumed its practice.

"Now!" Reilly said as the tenors, the baritones and the basses, the sopranos, the mezzo-sopranos and the altos then alternated in singing a musical passage.

There was no continuity in what Simon was hearing from the choir loft, and he relegated the choir singing to the back of his consciousness. He had fallen into musing as he gazed at the crucifix in the altar, his palm pressed to the rosary in his pocket. He prayed with it, not as an amulet, not out of some hazy notion about some magical power that it possessed, but for the feeling it gave him, as his fingers worked on its beads, of communing with the heavenly hosts.

The choir had stopped singing. As the church fell silent again, he dwelt deeper into his thoughts. His Christian faith was unshakeable, for it was anchored on human reason and divine revelation and intervention. He was born and raised a Catholic, but as a history teacher, he had studied other religions as well. He found them all, except his Christian faith with its Jewish roots, to be man-conceived, the only two religions based on divinity and not on myth.

His studies confirmed what he had been taught from childhood about his Christian faith. Unlike the founders of other religions, Jesus Christ was not a mere prophet or religious teacher and reformer. He was the Son of God, a fact supported by his birth, not by a human father, but by the Holy Spirit, by the miracles he performed, by his power over nature and death, by him having been sent to the world by God the Father in heaven to redeem mankind from sin. Jesus' birth, ministry, death, resurrection and ascension into heaven were the five singular events in human history, witnessed by scores of people. No human being had ever made and could ever make a similar claim of divinity and support it with the power over evil, nature and death, as shown by Jesus Christ.

He kept his gaze to the crucifix. It gave him no small amount of assurance that he was a believer in the one true faith in Jesus Christ, the Son of God, who was categorical in saying, "I am the way, the light, and the truth. No one goes to the Father except through me." There was no other way to salvation in heaven except through Jesus Christ.

At Reilly's command, the choir resumed singing a hymn, distracting him from his thoughts.

He turned around and watched Clara and the other choir members, who were now singing with such exalted voices, with Reilly accompanying them, a hand playing on the organ, while his other hand kept beat to their singing.

Reilly said, at the end of the hymn they had sung with such exalted voices, "That was very good, but we can still do better. We will sing the hymn again, and this time I want you to sing it as if the Lord's angels are singing it with you."

Chapter 16

"What do you think?" Andrew asked Sonny as he was driving his car in Hancock Park.

Sonny was listening to the steady hum of the car engine, and he replied, "It sounds okay now after I adjusted the timing."

Rod was at the backseat. He leaned forward and said, "Try putting it on higher gear."

"Why should I do that?" Andrew asked Rod.

"Try it," Rod repeated. "Let us see how it will run."

Andrew shifted gears and stepped on the gas. The engine snarled in protest.

The car running behind them dropped back as their car gained speed, the speedometer needle turned to forty-five miles an hour. They were running way beyond the speed limit there of thirty miles per hour. They were in the old-money district of Hancock Park, a place patrolled regularly by police cars to protect the rich people living there. A police car might suddenly appear behind them, its lights flashing in a signal for them to pull over.

"All right," Sonny said to Andrew, "slow down before you get pulled over for speeding. We are not in a freeway. Now, put the car back on third gear."

Andrew slowed the car down and then shifted gears. The engine purred contentedly.

"That does it," Sonny said. "Your car is now running well, considering it is as old as your dad."

"It is only seventeen years old," Andrew said.

"All right, it's only seventeen years old," Sonny conceded. "Now, let's go back."

"C'mon," Rod said, "it's too early to go back to your apartment. Let us see what is going on in South Central. There is no thrill in watching the fires on TV."

Andrew ignored Rod and drove on toward Avery Avenue.

Rod's suggestion had piqued Sonny's interest, though. He found no thrill either in watching the fires on TV. There was nothing like being right in front of a building burning and feel the heat on his face and smell the wood burning and hear it crackling in the fire.

Just then, he saw in his mind's eye, the flames being swept aside by Lorna. Her finger pointed at him, she was motioning for him to go home that very moment. He frowned. She will never stop running his life.

"What do you think?" Andrew asked him. "Do we watch a fire, or do we go back to your apartment?"

"Drive to where we can watch a fire."

"That is more like it," Rod said, delighted.

"All right, driver," he said to Andrew, "let us go to La Brea. There might be something interesting going on there."

Andrew turned his car around and headed toward La Brea Avenue. The street, like inside the car, was peaceful and quiet. There was nothing going on there.

Rod broke the silence inside the car when he said, "I cannot understand why those people broke out into riots in South Central."

"They are against the verdict, that is why," Sonny said.

Andrew was angry, and he said, "That is no excuse for what they are doing. It is shameful and barbaric. They are burning homes, shops and buildings and hurting a lot of people who had nothing to do with the trial. The violent destructive things they are doing are so disproportionate to the beating the cops gave the black motorist."

"A similar riot," Sonny said, "happened there before, in 1965."

"Is that so? I did not know that," Rod said.

"How would you know that?" Andrew said. "You were not born yet in 1965."

"So were you," Rod said.

"So were all of us," Sonny said to their laughter.

"Where," Andrew asked Sonny, "did you pick up that story on the riots there in 1965?"

"From my dad. He told me one time."

"What brought it about?"

"You won't believe it. It was over a driving violation."

"You must be kidding."

"No, I'm not kidding. A cop arrested a motorist for drunk driving."

"Just that?"

"No, it was not just that. It led to a heated argument. The bystanders joined in. More cops came. Riots broke out then for several days in Watts in South Central, where scores of people were killed, hundreds were injured and homes and buildings were looted and burned to the ground."

"That's terrible," Andrew said. "If they did that then virtually over nothing, they are doing that now virtually over nothing as well."

"It is not exactly over nothing, then and now," Sonny said. "My dad said there is this resentment that some blacks continue to harbor against white people. It boiled over as a result of the verdict in the King trial."

"I'm sorry about that," Andrew said, "but no one gains from those riots."

"No one," Sonny said, "except the looters."

Andrew drove on in La Brea, the shops there closed early in the night. Fear had made them do it.

Sonny sighed as he recalled what his father had told him about the violence in the student protest rallies in Manila some twenty years ago. The shops and the stores there were closed early each time a student protest rally was announced on the radio and in the papers. Like the riots he saw on TV a while ago, they often ended in violence, with students throwing stones and gasoline bombs at the police and the soldiers, who in turn fired live and rubber bullets and threw tear gas canisters at the student protesters. The student protest rallies in Manila were hardly any different from the ongoing riots in Los Angeles in the fear, violence and destruction they brought about.

His father himself was injured in the head in a student protest rally, all because he happened to be in the vicinity where it took place. His father once told him that people everywhere were the same in their capacity for violence, and that they differed only in the manner and purpose of inflicting it. What his father said was confirmed by the violent student protest rallies in Manila and the riots now going on in Los Angeles.

"There is nothing going on here," Rod said. "Why don't we try Olympic Boulevard?"

Andrew glanced tolerantly at Rod from the car's rear view mirror and drove on. After a while, though, he turned the wheel toward Olympic Boulevard, the heart of Koreatown.

It was like being abroad, somewhere in Seoul, the neon signs in Korean characters competing with those in English. Most of the shops and stores there were closed for a good reason: Koreatown was near the South Central and the riots.

They were crossing Western Avenue when Sonny saw to his right, above the rooftops in the distance, the glow of a fire.

"Turn the car around," he said quickly to Andrew. "I just saw a fire on Western."

"I saw it, too," Rod said.

"Let us take a look," Andrew said.

He turned the car around at the next intersection, drove on, and turned left on Western. The fire loomed large as they approached it.

Andrew drove his car to a side street and parked it there. They were now only two blocks away from the fire.

"We'll have to go on foot the rest of the way," Andrew said as they were getting out of the car.

"So you don't have to worry about your car," Sonny said to Andrew.

"He has to take care of it. It is his only treasure," Rod said, laughing, to Sonny.

Andrew ignored, smiling, Rod and Sonny making fun of his car. He continued to check its doors and tires while Rod and Sonny watched and waited.

"C'mon, Andrew, we don't have the whole night," Sonny finally said. "We'll go ahead."

He walked with Rod toward the fire while Andrew checked

his car quickly. Then he followed them and caught up with them soon enough. They were now only a block away where the fire was raging, deep inside the black community of South Central.

They were swept along by people rushing toward the fire. They crossed a street and joined a crowd watching in a parking lot, some of the stores there that were already burning.

Sonny's throat went dry from awe and fear as he watched the burning stores. This must be how hell looked like! A paint store was the only one left untouched by the fire. The liquor store beside it was already burning. In a short while, tongues of fire from the liquor store had begun to lick at the paint store. Flames then appeared under the paint store door and began licking at its storefront. Other tongues of fire then moved in various directions in the paint store until they joined up in a wall of fire at the storefront. An explosion suddenly rocked the paint store. It shattered the glass display window as fumes from burning paint then shot out from the paint store.

"Let's move back!" Rod shouted.

They were moving away with the crowd when Andrew, who was tall, caught a whiff of the fumes. It sent him into a coughing fit. Sonny laid his arm on Andrew's shoulder and, together with Rod, helped him move farther away from the fire. They halted once they were far enough from it. Andrew then stooped down and, his hands pressed to his knees, he coughed and sneezed out the fumes from his nose and throat, as tears blurred his eyes.

"Are you all right?" Sonny asked Andrew while rubbing his back.

Andrew nodded. He stood straight up and took out a handkerchief from his pocket. He wiped with it the tears in his eyes and blew his nose on it.

"You look like you have inhaled a lungful of fumes," Sonny said to Andrew.

"I'm all right now," Andrew said.

Andrew's red watery eyes and his cracked voice told Sonny otherwise. He began to worry they might get seriously hurt the longer they stayed there.

"Okay, guys, let us get moving," he said to Rod and Andrew.

They did not seem to hear him, as their eyes were now turned toward the paint store, the flames eating it up. Its roof and skeletal frame were all that remained of it. In just a short while, even those were now being eaten up by the flames.

"Look! It is going down!" Rod shouted as the paint store then crashed down in one fiery burst.

His face flushed from the heat, Sonny shook his head in regret at the destruction of the paint store. It was a total waste. He no longer found thrill in watching the fire.

Unlike him, though, he could see how the fire had mesmerized Rod and Andrew. They were watching it, their eyes wide and their mouths hanging open in wonder and excitement.

Just then they heard shouting from the other side of the parking lot.

"Let us see what is going on there," Rod said.

Sonny hesitated, but Andrew had thrown his arm on his shoulder, and he allowed himself to be led on.

They joined an unruly crowd there being kept back by some Asian shopkeepers who were standing guard at the shops and stores behind them.

Suddenly a tough-looking dark-faced young man stepped forward. He was holding a wine bottle filled with gasoline, a tongue of cloth hanging down from its mouth.

"Get out of there before we burn down your damned stores," the toughie said to the shopkeepers, who stood their ground.

For a moment the toughie and the shopkeepers glared at each other, with neither of them backing down.

Sonny watched the standoff with dread. It might, he feared, turn violent.

Someone in the crowd shouted, "Go ahead and be done with it!"

Another man yelled, "Burn down those damned stores!"

The toughie, egged on by the crowd, lit up his gasoline bomb. He was about to throw it toward the shopkeepers when suddenly they whipped out their guns hidden at the back of their waists.

One of them shouted, his gun pointed at the toughie, "Throw that bomb, and you are dead!"

The toughie froze, the gasoline bomb in his raised hand held motionless.

Sonny sighed in relief when the toughie lowered his arm and blew out the flame from his gasoline bomb. He retreated through the crowd, his head bowed in defeat.

He turned around when he reached the street. Emboldened by the crowd now shielding him from the shopkeepers' guns, the toughie lit up his gasoline bomb again.

He shouted, as he threw his gasoline bomb toward the shopkeepers, "Damn you, slit-eyed bloodsuckers! That will blow you all to hell!"

The bomb flew above the crowd and landed in a fiery burst, a few feet in front of the shopkeepers. The shopkeeper nearest the explosion was hit in the face and stomach by pieces of glass. He keeled over, his hands pressed to his face and stomach.

In an instant the other shopkeepers were firing their guns wildly while the crowd broke into a stampede.

"Let's get out of here!" Rod shouted at Sonny and Andrew.

They were running away from the shooting when suddenly Sonny pitched forward. A bullet had pierced his head.

Chapter 17

Steve glanced at Ophie as he was putting down a tray of sushi on the buffet table. His wife Vicky's fellow teacher in the University of Southern California, Ophie was surveying the food laid out there.

Around them in the garden, guests like her were eating, drinking and conversing, often to the accompaniment of laughter.

He smiled, pleased by the festive atmosphere in his wife's birthday party, and he said to Ophie, "They are all good, but you can try this sushi for a start."

"I know, they are very good," Ophie said as she was putting in her plate, two pieces of sushi. "I can say that of those I have eaten, like these egg rolls, and not because Vicky herself had cooked them."

He pointed at a tray of shish kebab, the diced meat in bamboo skewers a tantalizing golden brown.

"It may have come originally from a country far away," he said, "but it will go well with your sushi. Why don't you get some?"

"I'll do exactly as you told me."

Steve looked on appreciatively as Ophie took two sticks of shish kebab and two fried chicken drumsticks.

"I'll move on now," she said. "It's a great party you're holding for Vicky."

"Do come back for more."

She smiled as she then joined her dinner companions at a table in the garden, festive with people having a grand time there, with music adding to the gaiety there.

Patti Page was singing *Mockingbird Hill* in the stereo system in the garden. The song she was singing was a reminder to the guests that while their host may now be a lawyer practicing in Los Angeles, his heart and soul will always belong to the potato fields of Idaho, where he was born and raised.

He surveyed again the well-laden buffet table. The big birthday cake with its twenty-five tiny pink candles representing Vicky's age stood in the middle of the table. At either side of the cake stood two fruit-stands with their pyramids of sweet and juicy Washington apples, around which were pears, plums, green and black grapes, oranges and persimmons. Arrayed on the table were Southern fried chicken, baked Alaska salmon, British roast beef, Italian lasagna, the egg rolls, called Filipino lumpia, Turkish shish kebab, Japanese sushi, Chinese chow mein, and a big bowl of Caesar salad.

He and Vicky had agreed on the international food motif for her birthday party to show to their guests her cosmopolitan taste and skill in cooking.

Just about everyone they knew came to the party. Steve's boss, Saul Levy, was there along with Therese, his pretty blonde secretary-receptionist, and Nola and Susan, the other employees of the Levy law office. Agnes, Saul Levy's wife, would have come too had she not been asked to work overtime in her office. Some of Vicky's friends from her college days were there. So were some of their neighbors. Mitchell and Grace, Steve's parents living in Idaho, timed their visit to Vicky's birthday. Her parents Anthony and Joan, who lived in Rancho Palos Verdes, and their friend Austin, were there. So were some of Vicky's fellow teachers in USC. She will fondly remember her birthday party long after it was over.

Austin glanced at the pine tree near the picket fence as he was coming to the buffet table. Glowing in the tree was a spiral of tiny golden lights Steve strung up there the day before.

"Christmas in April—that's the idea behind it," he said to Austin.

"All you need is snow, which we seldom have in these parts," Austin said while nodding in approval of the lighted tree.

He took a plate from a tower of paper plates on the table. He seemed undecided on what to get there, but then he settled for the baked Alaska salmon. He scooped a piece into his plate, which he topped with spoonfuls of lasagna and several pieces of lumpia.

"Why don't you try the rest?" Steve suggested.

"I will, later on. Thanks just the same," Austin said.

He joined an elderly couple, Steve's neighbors, seated at a table a few feet away from there.

Therese came to the buffet table. She seemed undecided between the chow mein and the lasagna.

"The Chinese say chow mein is for long life," Steve said.

"Who will argue with that? Not me," she said, smiling.

She scooped chow mein into her plate. She was having her second helping.

"Try also the lumpia, it is good," he said.

"Not that. I've already eaten a lot of it."

She turned her gaze to Saul, who was refilling his wineglass at the bar in a corner in the garden. He took a sip and then came to her and Steve.

"Our boss is happily tippling on," she said, smiling, to Saul. "That must be your fourth or fifth refill."

"Only my third," he replied. "Do I look like I've had more than my fill of this liquid diet?"

Therese and Steve smiled, but did not reply.

"It must be this wine," he said, "which I think is a Napa Valley Merlot."

"You are right, chief," Steve said. "It's a Napa Valley Merlot."

He peered down at the dark wine and said, "It tastes pretty stiff. It must be from a high degree of fermentation."

He glanced at Therese, but she had turned her back to him as she faced George, Vicky's fellow teacher in USC, who had come to the buffet table. On his plate was a mound of salad.

"What do you think of the lumpia?" he asked Therese.

"They are good, like the rest. Try a few pieces."

"I will if they are not filled with meat. I am a vegetarian."

"They have got a little shrimp," Steve said. "Vicky cooked them herself. In case you don't know it, my wife is an accomplished cook."

"Really? Then, I should try them. I guess a little shrimp will do me no harm," George said as he put several pieces of lumpia on his plate. "You know, we must be careful with what we eat. Most people do not know it, but some foods we eat don't agree with or may even be harmful to our digestive systems."

"I can't agree with you more," Therese said.

"Then, you can tell me more about this lumpia and the rest of the food on the table," George said to Therese.

"I'm not much of a cook myself, but I know a little about food in general."

"There is a table over there," George said. "We can talk and try this food. Is that okay with you?"

Therese hesitated, but then she said, "Well, all right."

Saul took another sip from his wineglass. Its tangy taste still on his tongue, he nodded when Therese asked to be excused and left with George.

He watched them walk away, feeling oddly resentful of the teacher for taking Therese away from him. Some men have a way with women; he had to admit that about George. The teacher was only a casual acquaintance, and yet he had pulled away from him his own secretary-receptionist. He took another sip of his wine and found himself slipping into lethargy. It was from the effect of the wine, but he remained clearheaded enough to admit to himself that whoever Therese went with was none of his business.

"Enjoying yourself, chief?" Steve asked him cheerfully.

"Yes, very much so, thank you," he replied, his eyelids beginning to drop from the effect of the wine.

Steve saw his droopy eyes, and he said, as he picked up a plate and gave it to him, "Here, everything on the table will go well with your wine."

He smiled at Steve's subtle suggestion to take food to neutralize the effect of the wine on him.

"Thanks, but I don't need that," he said as he waved aside the offered plate. "I'll just pick, here and there."

He inspected the table and took a piece of sushi. He took a bite and, liking its taste, he swallowed it whole. He ate another piece of sushi. He moved on and picked up a lumpia. He dipped it in a saucer of sweet-and-sour sauce and ate it with gusto. He ate several pieces of it. He tried the other dishes. His attention in the next few minutes was on the food on the table. The food he was taking was beginning to neutralize the drowsy effect of the wine on him.

After a while, when he had eaten enough food, he washed it down with his glass of wine and looked around, smiling.

His casual manners at the buffet table blended perfectly with the occasion. Steve had told him that Vicky's birthday party would be a festive informal affair. He complied by leaving his coat and tie in his car. He hitched a ride with Therese in her new American car. It was a sporty type, and she showed it off by driving it at eighty to ninety miles per hour on the Harbor Freeway. She slowed down only when he warned her about driving too fast and getting pulled over by a Highway Patrol car. He will have to tell her again to go easy on the gas pedal at the drive back to their office after the party. From there, he will drive home in his car he left in the underground building garage. It was a perfect arrangement he had made with Therese, as perfect as the wine he was drinking.

A helicopter appeared in the dark sky, its searchlight inquisitive. It circled the area, several hundred feet above them. The noise from its rotor blades competed with the music in the stereo system. Everyone there looked up as its searchlight checked the neighborhood.

"It could be another car chase," Steve said.

"Or a thief the police are trying to catch," he said to Steve. "Do you often have that sort of thing going on here?"

"Much too often," Steve replied, his cheeks flushed in embarrassment.

"I guess the same thing happens elsewhere in this town," he said out of sympathy to Steve.

He pursed his lips, discomposed by the lie he said. Never in the thirty years he had been living in Santa Monica did he see a helicopter flying above his neighborhood in search of the bad guys.

He watched Steve, feeling sorry for him, as he tried to ignore the embarrassing presence of the police helicopter by tidying up further the tidy buffet table. Steve was born and raised in a quiet rustic town in Idaho, so different from where he was living now. But he had nothing to be embarrassed about. There was nothing he could do about a bad neighborhood except to leave it. Finding a good neighborhood was also largely a matter of luck, although there were some places that had certain reputations, good or bad. Steve and

Vicky chose to live there for its proximity to the University of Southern California, where she was teaching sociology.

He could also symphatize with Steve over what the newspapers had been reporting about the incidence of crime having gone up in Los Angeles. Steve should therefore feel protected, not embarrassed, that a police helicopter was circling above them. It was an angel in the sky watching over them, although just then, the helicopter was flying away.

Mitchell was coming. He said to Steve, "Vicky needs you in the kitchen, son."

"It must be for the roast beef that needs to be sliced."

He asked to be excused and left. Mitchell stayed on, prompting Saul to strike a conversation with him. It was the polite thing to do.

"How do you find your stay here?" he asked Mitchell.

Mitchell shrugged his shoulder and said, "Los Angeles is not like Idaho. I mean, the hurried pace, the noise, the excitement, like the police helicopter searching for the bad guys."

"I know. I will also have to get used to waking up to the cock's crow, which I understand is your morning wake-up call in Idaho."

"That is better than waking up to the sound of gunfire. I know you have plenty of shooting here."

"Yes, in the Hollywood movies."

"Shall we say both in the movies and in real life?"

He nodded, conceding the point to Mitchell, who then said, "Why is there so much violence here?"

He looked sharply at Mitchell. He won't stand for anyone making unfounded sweeping accusations against Los Angeles. But the old man, strong-jawed like his son, seemed more mystified than critical. They did not have this happening in Idaho.

"There is bound to be some friction with so many people living close to each other, as what we have here in Los Angeles," he said. "It is far different in Idaho, where you have all the living space you need."

"You can say that again, but people different from you and me living here compound the problem. You are an immigration lawyer, my son's boss. Tell me, is it not about time that we closed our borders?"

"If we do that, other countries will protest."

"Let them protest as much as they want to, but we should put our country's interest first."

"It is in our country's interest to keep its doors open to the rest of the world, for as long as those who come here, are coming here legally."

"That will be the end of America as I know and love it."

He knitted his brow at Mitchell's show of racial prejudice, but he kept quiet. He would rather not give a reply that he might only regret later on. Mitchell's face was weather-beaten, his back slightly stooped from years of laboring in the potato fields of Idaho. Mitchell was like the rest of them who lived relatively isolated by their notion of an exclusively white America.

A sip from his wineglass loosened up his mind. If Mitchell and his kind could help it, they would have America reverted to its early days. Except for the native American tribes, it was then an all-white country, mostly of British stock. Now, with wave after wave of immigrants, many of them of color, coming to America, they felt so beleaguered, they do not distinguish anymore between legal and illegal immigrants. It was a subject he did not want to discuss with Mitchell. It might just lead to a heated argument, and he did not want this to happen. He did not want to antagonize Mitchell, his associate's father. He did not want his evening spoiled, too.

"Will you excuse me, please?" he said as he turned to leave, but Mitchell was blocking his way.

"I must say this," Mitchell said, wagging his finger for emphasis, "every responsible citizen of this country should think seriously about this flood of people coming here from Mexico and every godforsaken country in Asia, Africa, the Middle East and South and Central America. It will only lead to America's undoing. Look at what is happening now, centuries after we made the mistake of taking in these other people. We became a country divided by race. We should have closed our borders to the rest of the world a long time ago."

Mitchell advanced his radical views so vehemently, he had to catch his breath. As he waited for him to reply, he could feel Mitchell was expecting his response to be in support of his low opinion of "these other people."

It was getting too much for him to take in silence. He was

getting upset and yet he still remained hesitant to pursue the subject.

He took a large measure of wine from his wineglass to calm himself. It coursed down his throat, warm and strong, making him feel buoyant.

He smiled at Mitchell and said, "If we will do that, Steve and I will both be out of jobs, since by then we won't have any clients left. You don't want that to happen, do you?"

Mitchell was not be swayed, and he said, "Of course, I don't. I was referring only to the immigration of people different from you and me."

He was so upset now, and he said, "If this country had been so restrictive, I may not be here today. My parents would not have made it here. In case you don't know it, I am Jewish."

Mitchell shot him a surprised and confused look.

"I'm sorry, I did not know that," he said, his hands raised in apology.

"That is all right," he said, now more amused than annoyed. "You did not mean what you said."

"Not by any means. I was not referring to Jews at all, and not to you in particular. We are both white, after all."

"Maybe so, but not to Hitler and his kind. To them, Jews are not white enough."

"I mean, you know," Mitchell stammered.

He turned his eyes toward Vicky, who was coming from the house.

"There you are," she said. "Agnes is on the phone."

"Will you excuse me, please?" he said to Mitchell.

He went inside the house with Vicky. She led him to the master bedroom where she showed the phone on the night table. Then she left and shut the door. He laid his wineglass on the night table and, as he lifted the phone to his ear, he heard voices picked up by the extension phone in the kitchen. He waited until it had clicked shut.

"What's up, honey?" he said to Agnes. "You should have come. Vicky is having a grand party."

"That is nice to hear, dear. Please tell Vicky and Steve how sorry I am for missing out on their party. Did you tell them I was working overtime?"

"I told them that. Where are you now?"

"I just got home."

"Why did you call?"

"You have not heard it then."

"Heard what?"

"The riots! The looting! There are fires all over Los Angeles! Violence has broken out over the acquittal of the policemen in the King trial! Hell has broken loose in South Central, not far from where you are! You can see everything on TV. It's in all the channels. It's bad, very bad!"

"I'll take a look right now."

"And, darling, take care, will you? And don't be home late."

"No, I won't. Thanks for calling and take care of yourself, too. Lock the doors and leave the lights open at the front and back of the house."

He returned the phone to its cradle. A TV set stood in a corner of the bedroom and he switched it on. The screen came to life, orange-hued from a fire raging in a building.

"The fire there is the fifteenth I've counted so far," the announcer said gravely. "More fires are coming because the firemen have been prevented from leaving their fire stations by snipers shooting at them. Some of them have been shot and wounded as they were responding to calls for help."

The TV screen then showed an aerial view of Los Angeles dotted with fires. Its dark sky was coated with a grayish haze from the smoke rising from the numerous fires on the ground. It was a surreal vision of hell descended upon his beloved city.

Shocked but caught by what he was seeing on the TV screen, he sat down on the edge of the bed and looked on. His worst fears about the outbreak of violence and destruction in Los Angeles that will follow the acquittal of the police officers in the King trial were now being realized right in front of his eyes.

He turned to an open window in the bedroom when he heard a country singer breaking into song in the stereo system in the garden. *Home on the Range,* the song being sung, sounded more to him like a dirge for Los Angeles. Its lyrics of bright blue skies and of deer and antelope playing were arresting in contrast to the burning and destruction of Los Angeles, as shown in the TV set.

Someone was knocking at the door.

"Yes?" he said. "Come in."

"There you are," Therese said as she opened the door.

"Everyone is looking for you."

"Is that so?" he said, having recovered by then from shock. "And why is your friend, the finicky eater, not with you?"

She looked behind her and, seeing no one there, she said, "Too bad, he is just as finicky with people. He is not my type. I excused myself and left him to look for you."

He nodded, pleased by what Therese said. Satisfied by the way it turned out for her and the teacher, he turned his gaze back to the TV screen.

"This is not the time nor the place to watch TV," she said. "What are you watching anyway?"

Her eyes turned wide from shock by what she then saw in the TV screen.

"My goodness!" she exclaimed. "What is going on there? Fires are all over there!"

"You are now seeing the violent destructive aftermath of the King trial. Los Angeles is burning."

Steve appeared at the door.

"What are you two doing here?" he asked. "This is not the time to watch TV. Let's go to the garden. Vicky is about to blow the candles in her birthday cake."

He turned to leave, but was stopped by what the TV announcer then said about another shopping mall in South Central starting to burn.

"What fire? What shopping mall?" he asked as he stepped close to the TV set. "My gosh!" he said. "What's going on there?"

For quite a while, they stared mutely at the TV screen, as the announcer did a recap of the trial and how the violence started.

Their absence in the garden had been noticed. Mitchell came looking for them. Other guests had strayed into the bedroom. They were instantly hooked to the fiery spectacle shown in the TV screen. Word about the riots and the fires spread quickly in the house and in the garden. The bedroom was soon full of people. Other guests then proceeded to the adjacent family room where they watched the fires in the TV set there. The guests had set aside Vicky's birthday party.

Saul asked himself, as he watched the TV screen now showing a supermarket and the stores beside it beginning to burn, what those who looted and then set them on fire had gained from it. A few cans of tomato sauce? A bag of chicken leg quarters?

He expected the looting. There were unscrupulous people who would take advantage of a bad situation. What upset him most was why they had to burn down as well the stores and the supermarket. The losers there were not only the owners and their workers, but the very people who looted and burned them down. They shopped there. Those were their stores and their supermarket.

He looked on in disgust at the TV screen. The riots now going on in South Central were the same orgy of self-inflicted injury as the Watts riots that happened there in 1965. This time, though, not only was it much bigger, it was destroying a lot more property and affecting badly a lot of people who had nothing to do with the King trial. The city's black residents had turned once again to their ancient ways. It was if they were not in Los Angeles, but were instead back in Africa, their violent reaction to the trial verdict, a throwback to their savage tribal wars there.

"We'll turn you now to our news chopper. Come in, Miles," the anchorman said.

He faded out of the screen, replaced by Miles, a TV reporter, who was looking on at an aerial view of Los Angeles burning.

"I can see from here that fires have spread beyond South Central," Miles said. "I can see, north of me, fires in Koreatown. A number of stores down below me have also been set on fire. Nearby is the campus of the University of Southern California."

"That is not far from here," Anthony, Vicky's father, said.

A helicopter passed above the house, so low the whirr of its rotor blades drowned out the TV reporter's voice.

By now, Saul felt suffocated by the muggy air in the bedroom full of people. He stood up and left it for a breath of fresh air in the garden. Steve and Therese followed. They saw Vicky seated all alone in the garden. She was staring sadly at the lighted tree and the buffet table. The guests had abandoned her birthday party.

Steve sat down beside her. Saul and Therese, not wanting to intrude on them, stood back.

"It's all right, dear," Steve said as he laid a comforting arm on Vicky's shoulder. "I'm making this promise, here and now, in the presence of my boss, that this won't be the last birthday party I'm holding for you. You will have another one next year. It will be bigger, we will invite more people and we will hold it in a hotel."

Vicky said, "Thank you, dear, that is consoling."

Saul gazed admiringly at how smoothly Steve had eased up the disappointment Vicky must have felt over her ruined birthday party.

A helicopter appeared in the sky. It circled the area nearby, its searchlight panning the ground. Saul watched it anxiously. It appeared to him no longer as an angel in the sky watching over them, but as a messenger of ill tidings. Fearful thoughts ran through in his mind. They were not far from the riots and the fires. They were not safe there. There was no time to lose. They must leave right away.

"I think you should seriously consider leaving," he said to Steve.

"Is it that bad?" Steve said.

"It is, and it will only get worse."

By then, some of the guests had returned to the garden. They watched Saul and Steve, who had stood up and faced Saul.

Steve said, frowning, "I hate to break up my wife's birthday party and flee from my own home, all because of some very nasty people out there who are on a looting and burning spree!"

"I know how you feel," Saul said, "but you cannot stay here. You will only be putting yourself and your family in danger if you'll stay here. Your safety is more important than protecting your home."

"Saul is right, son," Anthony said. "Let the police deal with those people. That is their job."

Saul watched Steve as his eyes darted from him to Anthony. Steve was considering what to do.

"I guess you are right," he said. "The safety of my family comes first."

"You can stay with us for the night, or until this blows over," Anthony said to Steve.

"We'll be glad to have you stay with us, too. There is enough room in the house," Joan said to Grace and Mitchell.

They smiled and nodded in appreciation of Joan's offer.

"Thanks, Mom, Dad," Steve said to them.

His equanimity now restored, Steve said to everyone there, "Let us get cracking. The food first. Vicky and I will take as a compliment to her cooking, if you'll take home all the food on the table and in the kitchen."

They burst into laughter. They helped themselves to the food, which they put in paper plates and plastic bags. Then they helped

Steve in clearing the buffet table and in returning it along with the stereo system, the bar, the tables and the chairs inside the house and the garage.

It was time to leave. The guests were gathered in the garden. One after the other they said good night to Steve and Vicky, their child Little John cradled in her arm.

"I'm sorry it turned out this way," Ophie said to Steve and Vicky.

"It's all right," Steve said. "We will have another one on Vicky's birthday next year. By then, we will make sure not to time it with another riot."

They laughed at Steve's most welcome sense of humor.

"Well, we are off. We had a grand time here. Good night," Ophie said as she left with George.

The other guests followed suit.

"Good night. We had a wonderful time; thank you."

"Take care now and head straight for the Harbor Freeway."

"Good night. I hope you enjoyed the party."

"We did, tremendously."

"We will go ahead. We have to prepare yet the guest and other rooms in the house," Anthony said to Steve and Vicky as he was leaving with Joan and Austin.

Saul watched them leave. With everyone there gone or going and with the wine, food and music gone as well, the garden now looked gloomy and deserted.

"Anyone passing by won't imagine that, a while ago, it was full of people eating, drinking and having fun," Therese said.

"It certainly looks different with everyone gone or going," Saul said.

He felt low, and that he could imagine, was how Steve must also feel at their forced and hurried departure from his house.

"Would you like me to drive, son?" Mitchell said to Steve. "You must be fagged out by now from all the work you have been doing here since yesterday. You can give me directions to Rancho Palos Verdes."

"I'm okay, Dad. I'll drive," Steve said. "Okay, everyone to the car while I'm closing the lights in the house and in the garden."

Mitchell, Grace and Vicky, her sleeping child cradled in her arm, filed into Steve's car in the garage.

Saul said to Steve, "It might be a good idea to leave some lights open, so your house won't look deserted."

Steve nodded and entered the house. He switched the lights off in the garden and in some of the rooms in the house, but kept the lights open in the living and dining rooms. Then he came out and shut the door.

They said good night to each other and parted, with Steve walking toward the garage, and Saul and Therese going to her car parked in the street.

Therese's car was in metallic green and it gleamed from the streetlight above. She took out the car key from her purse and opened the car door. She slid inside and opened the other car door for Saul.

He put on his safety belt once he was inside the car, as he settled himself comfortably for their ride back to their office.

Therese said, as she turned the ignition on, "I'm sorry for Vicky and Steve at her ruined birthday party."

"So am I," he replied as he glanced at Steve's car moving out into the street.

He watched Therese once Steve's car was out of sight. She had turned on the air-conditioner and she was breathing in the cool air and the pleasant smell of pine from the air vent.

"Is it too cold or just right?" she asked.

"It is just right," he said at the bracing effect of the cool air on his face.

Therese then drove out of the curb.

"One good thing about Vicky's birthday party was the food," she said. "Everything in the buffet table was delicious. The food was so good I overate. Tomorrow, I'll be back to my lunch of carrot and apple."

"You better watch out. You might find yourself growing white fur like a rabbit if you will not stop eating that kind of food."

Therese laughed heartily and drove on. The street looked unfamiliar to Saul. Therese had taken another route to Harbor Freeway. She could have followed Steve's car, but then, Steve was going south to Rancho Palos Verdes, while they were going north to their office in downtown Los Angeles.

He glanced at her as she drove on in the quiet street. She stopped at an intersection, turned left and drove on.

His eyes, blurry a while ago from the effect of the wine, had since then cleared from the food he took, the shock of what he saw on TV, the frantic activity at their hurried departure from Steve's house and, quite pleasantly, the cool air from the air-conditioner.

He looked at the street they were now passing by. He could not recall them having passed that way earlier on their way to Steve's house.

He asked her, "Did you drink anything hard at the party?"

"No, I did not. Why do you ask?"

"Well, if I were the one driving, with so much wine that I have drunk, I might lose my sense of direction."

"Are you trying to tell me something?"

"Yes. I don't think we passed this way to Steve's house. Are we on the right track to the freeway?"

"I think so, although it looks different at night."

Suddenly she stopped the car and asked, "Should we turn back?"

He frowned as it then occurred to him that they might be lost. She could have followed Steve's car to Harbor Freeway. But blaming her now will only make matters worse for them. It was his fault too for not telling her to do that. Now they were in South Central, the very place they must avoid.

He said, "Can you find your way back to Steve's house? From there we can trace the route to Harbor Freeway."

"I'm not sure if I can."

"Drive on, then, while I look for a street sign to the freeway."

As she drove on, he became more apprehensive when he saw no street sign to the freeway. They might only be going deeper into the riots in South Central. The street they were passing by now was lined with old unkempt houses and tenement buildings splattered with graffiti, the sidewalks there littered with trash. It was a place mired deep in resentment and desperation. A fire loomed ahead—a sign of danger.

"Slow down," he said. "Now, turn the car around."

Suddenly, as she was turning the car, they heard loud explosions from behind them. They looked back and saw flames shooting up in the sky. She pressed out of panic her foot to the gas pedal, sending the car zooming away. She swerved the car right so abruptly in the next intersection, the tires screeched on the asphalt surface of the street.

"Easy now," he said, his hand pressed to the dashboard to keep himself from being flung forward and hitting his head on the windshield.

"I'm sorry," she said.

"It's all right, but please slow down."

He must take over the wheel. She was in no condition to drive. Still, he hesitated to tell her that to spare her feelings. She drove on, at a moderate speed this time, and turned right at another intersection. A short while later, they saw another fire ahead in the street. A big unruly crowd was watching it.

"Pull over," he said quickly.

She stopped the car, her hands holding tight the steering wheel. She seemed petrified with fear of the unruly crowd that was shouting obscenities as the fire they were watching raged on.

"Now, turn the car around," he said in a firm, but calm tone of voice.

She made no move. She did not seem to hear him.

A shiver of fear ran up in his spine when he saw some of the men at the edge of the crowd now moving toward them. They were a mere one hundred yards or so away from them.

He said to her, "Let's get out of here."

He moved quickly when he saw no reaction from her. He removed her seat belt, wrenched her hands from the steering wheel and pulled her to his side. He tried to move over to the driver's side, but found the space too narrow, with the steering wheel blocking him. There was only one thing to do. He pulled open the lock in the driver's side door. Then he swung his door open, hurried out and locked it.

The men were now running toward the car. He dashed around the car, jumped inside, and locked the door. He put the car gear to "drive," turned the steering wheel quickly, and pressed his foot to the gas pedal. In his haste he miscalculated the turn he made with the steering wheel. The street was narrow and the car jumped into the sidewalk, sideswiping a trashcan and sending it rolling down the street.

The men had the car surrounded before he could back it up. They were shouting, their mouths filthy with obscenities, as they kicked the doors and pounced on the roof, the windows, the hood, and the back of the car with their fists and the stones in their hands.

The sight of Therese, a blonde beauty for the taking, sent them into frenzy. The man near her grabbed the door handle and tried to pull the car door open. He was grinning at her, saliva dribbling down from his mouth, his eyes wild with lust.

Therese screamed from fright and she covered her face with her hands.

They were trapped—the thought shot through Saul's mind. He saw himself beaten up and left dead on the sidewalk. As for Therese, those animals will drag her out into the sidewalk and there take turns at her. He clenched his teeth at this evil thing waiting for them.

"No!" he shouted at the men.

He turned the car toward the street and pressed his foot to the gas pedal. The car screamed forward, past the men. He sped on, disregarding the stones pelting the car. He glanced at the rear-view mirror and saw the men shaking their fists at him. He slowed down as they receded in the distance. He and Therese were now out of danger. They had narrowly escaped from harm, even death.

He stopped the car at an intersection and then turned left to what looked like a quiet street. He glanced at Therese and saw her still shaking from fright. The terrible thing she went through! He stopped the car and out of pity hugged her.

"It's all right," he said as he brushed her hair with his palm. "We are out of danger now."

Suddenly she broke out a cry of pain.

"It's all right, it's all right," he said softly to her.

He kept on brushing her hair with his palm until her cry had subsided into muffled sobs.

"Take me home, please," she said, her voice weak and tired.

"I'll take you home right now," he said as he wiped with his fingers the tears in her eyes.

Then he set her gently to her seat and put on her seat belt. He did the same with his seat belt. He glanced at her and, satisfied that she was all right now, he had the car running at a moderate speed.

He stopped at each intersection and read the street names until he saw to his relief, Vernon Avenue and its sign to Harbor Freeway. He entered the avenue and drove on until he saw the freeway. He entered its northbound ramp and put the car on cruise control once it was running on the freeway.

He saw, as he drove on in the elevated freeway, fires in South

Central and beyond. They were trapped somewhere there earlier with those animals pounding on the car. They could loot and burn down the entire South Central for all he cared. He and Therese were safe now. That was the only thing that mattered to him. He glanced at her and saw her staring blankly at the car floor. She was still in a daze.

"Come on, snap out of it," he said as he shook her knee. "There is nothing to fear. We are out of danger now."

"I'm so glad," she said as she removed her seat belt and turned to him.

He saw what she wanted to do and he raised his right arm, allowing her to nestle her head on his shoulder. He drove on. The air-conditioner's cool air and the steady hum of the car engine soon lulled her soon to sleep.

Downtown Los Angeles loomed ahead, its tall well-lit buildings and the absence of fire there a reassuring sight to him. Traffic on the freeway was light.

He had settled down into a complete calm. She was asleep. Her breathing, deep and rhythmic, and the softness of her body stirred in him a strange new feeling for her, tender and affectionate. He savored the feeling, but then fought it off with an effort of reason. He never considered then, and must not consider now, anything more than the fact that he was her boss, and that she was nothing more to him than as his secretary and receptionist. He must focus his eyes and mind on the freeway. The last thing he wanted there was to be involved in a vehicular accident.

The car passed downtown Los Angeles. He turned from Harbor Freeway to Golden State Freeway. From there he took the Glendale Freeway. After a few more minutes of driving, he took the exit in Colorado Avenue and stopped the car at the red traffic light there.

"We are almost there," he said as he woke her up with a few light taps on her arm.

He lifted his arm from her shoulder when she turned and sat straight on her seat.

"I think I know this place," she said, smiling, as she watched the cars passing by in Colorado Avenue.

The traffic light changed to green, and he drove the car left to Colorado Avenue. From there, he turned right to Glendale Boulevard and left again to Woodruff Avenue. He drove past office and apartment buildings, shops and restaurants, and crossed Brand Boulevard. They were now in the heart of Glendale. He drove on and crossed Central Boulevard. They were now in her neighborhood in Woodruff Avenue, a lovely tree-shaded street. He had brought her there a few times to her apartment before she got her own car.

He had the car moving at a crawl when it entered the driveway and stopped at its slot in the carport at the back of the apartment building.

"What do you know? We made it safely," he said as he turned the ignition off.

"Thank you, Saul," she said. "You are my hero."

Suddenly she kissed him on the cheek and said, smiling, "There is more of where it came from."

He did not expect the kiss from her and he was not quick enough to kiss her back. He regretted immediately his lack of response when he saw her looking away in disappointment. He shook his head. His mind was still on their narrow escape from harm, even death, in South Central.

"That is a big dent, there in the hood," he said to divert her attention.

She followed as he then stepped out of the car. She said, when she saw the damage done to it, "What did they do to my car?"

The bumper, the right fender, the doors and the left rear light were smashed. The side windows were cracked like spider webs. The roof and the hood were badly dented. They were lucky they got away safely.

"It took the blows meant for us," he said to her. "But don't worry about it. I'll drive it back to the office and have it towed to a body shop tomorrow."

"Thank you for all the trouble you're taking for me."

"It is no trouble at all."

They walked on toward the apartment building, with her holding on to his arm. He was going to see her right to the door of her apartment at the second floor of the apartment building. They walked past the iron railing of the open side to their left of the corridor. It faced another apartment building. The play of orange light in its frosted glass windows showed its residents there were watching on TV the fires in South Central.

He pulled the screen door open the moment they reached her

apartment. He waited while she searched for the door key in her purse. She seemed tense as it took her a while before she found it and opened the main door.

He said, once she was inside her apartment, "Well, then, good night, sleep tight."

"Won't you come in first for a cup of coffee? You need it for your long drive yet to the office and your home."

He nodded. It was a reasonable suggestion. A cup of hot coffee will help keep him alert on the road. It will also mean a short stay in her apartment, and he won't mind that either.

"I guess you are right. I do need coffee to buck me up," he said as he stepped inside the apartment.

She was closing the door when she brushed herself against him. He was even more surprised when she then turned and faced him.

She looked so desirable. That and the softness of her body when she brushed against him, and her fragrance, sweet and tempting in the airless apartment, sent his head spinning. He took her in his arms and kissed her.

She said, as he released her, "I've long dreamed of this moment—the two of us in each other's arms."

The lovely phrase she said delighted him even more at her confession of love unrequited until now. He had long nursed the thought that she had such a feeling for him, but had done nothing about it until now.

She yielded with a sigh when he kissed her again. Her head then laid on his shoulder, he led her to her bedroom, the coffee forgotten.

A shaft of light from the lamppost in the street lay across the bedroom carpet. Quietly, in the partial darkness, they released each other. She turned her back to him as she removed her dress. It fell dully on the carpet. He removed his shoes and clothes, fumbling in his haste with the shirt buttons. He was overcome with wild impulses when she then turned and faced him. He took her in his arms and they were soon joined together on the bed.

They dozed off, spent by the fury of such a quick one. A paramedic truck speeding by on Woodruff Avenue, its siren blaring, woke them up.

"Happy, dear?" she said in a tired, but cheerful tone of voice.

"Very happy."

"You will even be happier with what I will tell you."

"What is it?"

"I have just made you a father!"

"What?" he said as he stared, unbelieving, at her. "Tell me that again."

She raised her head and, smiling down at him, she said, "Well, you are now a father!"

"How can you tell that?"

"I know, I know. A woman knows."

He turned his gaze to the ceiling. A love child. He had long given up ever having his own child. Not by Agnes anyway. But now, here was Therese. It was possible.

She seemed hurt by his coldness as she then turned and likewise gazed at the ceiling.

"You don't seem to be happy about it," she said. "Don't you want me to bear your child? I know you have always wanted to have one of your own."

"It is not that. It's just that I've stopped thinking about it until now. Let us not talk about it."

They lay quietly, with him wondering what had made him suddenly turn cold and distant to her. He glanced at her and was glad to see her smiling at him.

"Anyway, whatever will happen next," she said, "our night here together means only one thing."

"And what is that?"

"That you and I are meant for each other."

He smiled. He had not thought of anything more than their moment together. Perhaps she was right. So be it. She moaned with pleasure when he came to her again, and with great passion that lasted far longer than the first one. Now completely spent, but happy, she fell into a deep sleep.

He stayed awake. So, she will give him a child. Better if a son. But a son by her who was not his wife? It will complicate matters and might ruin his marriage. He turned his eyes away from her to put the disconcerting thought out of his mind.

The window curtain was swaying slightly from the push of air into the room. Chilled by the air, he tucked his feet under the bedsheet and pulled it up to their shoulders.

He glanced at the clothes scattered on the carpet. The rush to sex. It was amazing how he had done it in quick succession. Where did he get the stamina for it? From the novelty of doing it with her and the complete abandon by which she gave herself to him. He frowned as he recalled how, on the other hand, sex had become dull and joyless to Agnes, who seemed to do it now only as an obligation she must meet as his wife. Her inability to conceive had made sex unfulfilling for her. It had become for him at most a frenzied act of lust, and with the thrusting of the buttocks, a pure animal act.

Now here was Therese having given sex a new thrill and meaning for him with her startling news that she had made him a father. Perhaps she was only kidding him. Conception did not always follow the sex act. But child or no child, from now on he would have more of her, who was now sleeping, happy and content. She was right, of course. They were meant for each other. What they had was more than a one-night fling, but the beginning of something wonderful and lasting.

The bedsheet rose and fell to her rhythmic breathing. Only a while ago she gasped and moaned and uttered sweet demanding words as her soft young and beautiful body took the blows he gave her with his love.

It fed his vanity to think that, a charmer that he was, he could have taken her long before. The opportunities were there, when they were alone in the office, in the lawyers' conventions out of town, and in the few times he had brought her here in her apartment. He took her only now, prompted by their harrowing experience in the riots in South Central. It was a case of danger shared transformed into love shared.

A faint sound of voices made him turn his gaze toward the window. They were coming from a doorstep in the ground floor of the apartment building. A man and a woman, probably after an embrace, were bidding each other good night. A car door slammed shut, the car engine started, hummed and faded away. Everything was quiet again. It was time for him to leave, too. He moved out of the bed slowly and carefully so as not to wake her up by any abrupt movement on the bed.

He looked around as he stood up. The bedroom floor was littered with their clothes and shoes. He was putting on his pants when he saw a reflection of himself in the dresser mirror. His stooped shoulder and his potbelly gave the lie to all his cherished notions of himself as still a strong and youthful charmer. Shamed by his appearance, he kept his eyes averted from the mirror and continued to dress up. Afterwards, he picked up her clothes and put them on a chair, her shoes at the foot of the bed.

For a moment before leaving, he gazed tenderly at her. He had a wonderful time with her. He bent down and kissed her lightly on the forehead. He left the bedroom and closed the door slowly. His throat was parched and, before leaving the apartment, he drank in the kitchen a glass of water. He locked the door as he stepped out of the apartment. His hands thrust deep inside his pockets, he walked on in the silent corridor, his shoulder humped by the cool night air.

He was approaching the staircase when he saw a vision of Agnes staring down at him, a hurt and angry look in her face. He shook his head free of the vision and the guilty feeling it gave him, ascribing it to his imagination playing tricks on him, and he walked down quickly on the staircase.

Upon arriving home, Agnes will ask him about Vicky's birthday party. He will tell her as much as he could. He will tell her about his narrow escape with Therese from harm in South Central. He will tell her that he brought Therese home. That will be all. One thing he will never tell Agnes was that, tonight, he found in Therese a new love in his life.

Chapter 18

Simon thought it unusual that Avery Avenue was deserted at this time of the night when it was only a little past nine o'clock. At this hour, the street should be busy with the drug peddlers doing brisk business with motorists pulling over for a packet or two of cocaine or marijuana.

He drove on, his eyes turned like Clara's to the empty street. They were headed home from her choir practice in St. Stephen Church.

"It looks like our good neighbors have retired early," she said.

"They must have gone somewhere, most likely to watch the fires and loot in South Central."

"I don't like this place, I never did," she said, frowning, as she looked on at the street. "This is not a good place to raise our children.

We should move out of here."

"Let us not argue over it. After all, we have agreed to look for an apartment in Glendale."

He turned their car toward its parking space in the carport, switched the ignition off and stepped out of the car with Clara. They passed through the gate and stepped up to their apartment. The moment he opened the door, they were struck by a building on fire shown in the TV screen.

Lorna was on the couch, watching the fire. She stood up and came to them. She took Simon's hand and pressed it to her forehead. She did the same gesture of respect to Clara, who was looking on at the TV screen.

"It looks bad, doesn't it, Mom?" she said to Clara.

"It looks much worse than what I imagined it to be. How long has it been going on?"

"Four or five hours now."

"Where is Sonny?" Simon asked as he was looking around at the living room.

"He is not home yet, Dad," Lorna replied, frowning.

"Why, where did he go? Did you not tell him not to leave the apartment?"

"I did, but he said he and his friends will be gone for just a short while. They went out to give Andrew's car a road test."

"I remember you told me that."

"It looks like they cut their studies short. They left their things here," Clara said at their books and notebooks placed beside the TV set.

"A car, never mind if it's a junk, seems to be more important to them than their studies. How long have they been gone?"

"More than an hour now."

Clara glanced anxiously at Simon.

"They will be back before you know it. They could be at Tony's, eating hamburger," Simon said in reassuring Clara about Sonny.

"But, Dad, you did not see the huge sandwiches I made for them."

"You know how growing boys are. No sooner have they finished eating when they are at it again."

"Just the same, talk to your son when he gets home. Driving

out with his friends at this time of the night and with the riots going on! If he were younger, I will give him a spanking he won't soon forget."

Clara was frowning as she went inside the master bedroom. Simon was tired of watching the same scene of violence and destruction repeated in many places in the city. He sat down on his easy chair and removed his shoes there. Lorna picked them up and brought them to the closet. She came back with his slippers.

"Thank you," he said to Lorna as he was putting on his slippers. "Are you after something?"

"No, Dad," Lorna said as she stood up. "Are you and Mom hungry enough for a snack?"

"Good idea. Prepare some for us and also for Sonny and his friends. I'm sure they won't mind eating again when they see food on the table."

Lorna left for the kitchen to prepare their snacks.

As he waited for the food, Simon, for lack of anything to do, looked out at Myrtle's garden. It was dark, but there was light in her house. The phone rang. He stood up to take the call, but Lorna, who was nearer, had already picked it up.

"Oh, it's you," she said. "Where are you now? What? Oh, no!"

"What's the matter?" he asked.

She did not answer, as she appeared numb from shock.

He realized immediately that something serious had happened. He took the phone from Lorna and asked, "Who is this?"

"It's Andrew, sir."

"Yes, Andrew. Why did you call?"

"It's about Sonny, sir. He has been shot in the head."

"What! How . . . how is he?"

"We don't know yet, sir. He is still in the operating room, here in St. Luke's Hospital."

"How did it happen?"

Simon listened, his heart pounding, as Andrew told him what happened. It was insane! His son was shot merely for watching a fire? He made an effort to stay calm so as not to worry Lorna any further.

He asked Andrew, "How was he when you brought him there?"

"He is hanging on, sir."

The electrifying thought shot across Simon's mind. His son was hanging on. That was the important thing.

He asked, "Is he conscious?"

"I could not tell, sir. His eyes were closed, but yes, he was conscious. He touched my hand as he was being wheeled into the operating room."

He nodded, encouraged by what he heard from Andrew. He tapped Lorna on the shoulder to reassure her that Sonny was all right.

"Hello, sir? Are you still there, sir?" Andrew asked.

"I'm still here. Will you wait for us? We are going there right now."

"We'll do that, sir."

He was putting the phone back to its cradle when he was startled to see Clara coming out of their bedroom.

"Who called?" she asked.

"It was Andrew who called."

"What did he call about?"

Clara's eyes were fastened to him. She was waiting for an answer, and he said, "He called to tell us that Sonny has been injured."

"Sonny is injured? Where?"

"I did not quite get what Andrew said," he said evasively. "The line had turned bad. The telephone connection must have gone haywire from so many fires breaking out in Los Angeles."

He saw how his evasiveness had only made Clara shocked and dizzy with fear for Sonny, she had to hold on to the cabinet to keep her balance. He held her in the arm and, together with Lorna, he set her down on a chair at the dining table.

"Tell me what happened, please. I must know," Clara pleaded. "How badly hurt is he?"

"I don't know," he finally said, "but he has this wound in the head."

He avoided saying it was a gunshot wound. Clara reacted nonetheless with a piercing cry. Lorna was swept along. She dropped down to her knees and threw her arms around Clara. They wept, their tears streaming down their faces.

"He will pull through. I'm sure he will," he said in reassuring them about Sonny.

Simon asked the receptionist about Sonny the moment he arrived in the hospital with Clara and Lorna. They were directed to the waiting area. Its bare walls and clean floor, while suggestive of the hospital's cold efficiency, was hardly a cheerful sight to them.

A young couple were seated on a couch. The man, his arm on the woman's shoulder, was staring ahead. Rod and Andrew were seated on the chairs there. They were the only people in the waiting area. They stood up and said good evening to them when they saw them coming. Simon and Clara nodded in response to their greeting, but the stern look in Lorna's face showed her putting the blame on them for Sonny's injury.

"Where is Sonny?" Simon asked them.

"He is in there, sir," Andrew said as he pointed at the door to the operating rooms. It had a small glass window, which allowed a peek inside.

They followed when Simon went to the door with Clara and Lorna.

He peered inside. The door led to a corridor between two operating rooms. Two sides of them were walled in glass. At the operating room on the left, two nurses were dressing up an old man. The operation was finished and the rest of the surgical team had left.

He turned his gaze to the operating room to the right and saw Sonny lying face down on the operating table. Five masked figures in green surgical gowns were performing the delicate operation of removing the bullet lodged in his head.

Fear for Sonny's life brought forth a lump in Simon's throat. His son was covered up to his shoulder with a white sheet. Gloved hands holding surgical instruments were working on his wound—a patch of red at the back of his head. Sonny's life was hanging in the balance. He looked on anxiously, by turns silently urging Sonny to hang on and praying for God to keep him alive.

"How . . . how is Sonny?" Clara asked anxiously.

It took him a moment to reply. He must be careful with what he said.

"He is hanging on," he said calmly. "The doctors are still working on his wound."

She gripped his arm at the word about Sonny's wound. He patted her hand in reassuring her that everything that could be done was being done for Sonny.

He looked again at the operating room. It was bright with light coming from the electric lamps overhead. A monitor, its green line moving up and down, showed the steady rise and fall of Sonny's heartbeat. Sonny was hanging on.

He looked away from the window, reassured about Sonny's condition.

"Sonny's heart is working fine," he said to Clara, who seemed relieved by what he said.

He turned to Rod and Andrew and asked them, "How long has he been there?"

"About an hour now, sir," Andrew replied.

"A priest gave Sonny the last rite before he was operated on," Rod said.

"Just in case," Andrew said.

Simon stared at Rod and Andrew, stunned by what they said. The last rite. He was relieved, but at the same time frightened by what it meant. Extreme Unction was given only to those on the verge of death. But it was given to Sonny, so he would be ready to meet God. Just in case.

"We are sorry, sir, about what happened," Andrew said.

"It happened so fast," Rod said. "We were running away from the shooting when it happened."

"It is not your fault," Simon said.

Lorna moved toward the window. He stopped her with a wave of his hand. It would be heartbreaking for her to watch her brother fighting for his life.

The door suddenly opened. They stepped aside as a hospital orderly wheeled out the old patient, a nurse walking beside him. The couple stood up from the couch and approached the patient.

"You have nothing to worry about," the nurse said to them. "The old man is doing fine. He will be under sedation for a while, though."

The worried look in the woman's face disappeared in a smile of relief, and she said, "Thank God."

Simon gazed wistfully at the old patient being moved away in the corridor. How he wished Sonny's operation will turn out just as well.

As he looked on, his heart suddenly turned cold with resentment. The old man was out of danger and was now safe and sound, while his son's life still hung in the balance. More than the old man who had lived his life, his son deserved to live. Sonny was young and he had a whole life ahead of him. But why should he question the old man's good fate? He should pray instead for his son's life to be spared.

He thought of looking again at the window, now that the door had closed again, but the fear and anxiety of watching Sonny fighting for his life had become too much for him to bear. He took Clara's hand and, together with Lorna, they walked toward the couch. He sat down there, between them, while Rod and Andrew returned to their chairs.

A few minutes passed. Clara took out a rosary from her dress pocket and began to pray silently.

His rosary left in his pocket, Simon prayed along with Clara. It was the best thing they could do for Sonny. She stopped praying, her thumb on the bead in the Second Glorious Mystery, the Ascension of Jesus Christ into heaven, when the surgeon, still clad in a green surgical gown, came out of the door.

Simon stood up and gazed anxiously at the tired wan look in the doctor's face.

"Good evening," the doctor said to him and Clara. "Are you the patient's parents?"

His heart was racing, and he barely nodded in reply.

"I'm sorry," the doctor said sadly."We did everything we could, but it was beyond us."

He stared, unbelieving, at the doctor, the thought swirling in his mind that it could not be true! His son could not be dead!

His mind thrashing about in anger and bewilderment, he asked why fate decreed that the old man should live while his son should die!

He dropped down on the couch, but in the same instant, he held Clara and Lorna on their shoulders, for they had flung themselves at him and began to cry.

Generous tears broke out of his eyes as he wept silently. His eyes blurred by tears, the doctor was now an indistinct figure standing before them. The doctor was saying once more how sorry he was.

Clara and Lorna wept on, their cries, now shrill and protesting, resounded in the waiting area, their mournful cries sweeping the doctor back to the operating rooms.

Her body shaking from grief, Clara wept on when suddenly she sat straight and said, "I want to see my son."

Simon helped her rise up from the couch. Their heads bowed by grief, they walked slowly with Lorna toward the operating rooms.

Sonny was laid in a gurney, a white sheet covering him. An orderly about to push it in the corridor stepped back when he saw them coming.

Clara knelt down before the gurney, tears streaming down her face as she removed the white sheet over Sonny's face, who seemed to be merely asleep. She caressed his face and hair.

Lorna knelt down too and tearfully embraced Sonny.

Simon looked down with mournful eyes at his son. Perhaps by some miracle or force of will, he could make him open his eyes and smile at them as if nothing had happened to him.

But nothing happened. Sonny lay still, dead on the gurney. Sonny's death then struck him so hard, he was swept along by Clara and Lorna's mournful cries now piercing the dead silence in the corridor.

Chapter 19

Simon woke up with a hangover made even more disagreeable to him by the noise in Avery Avenue. He had downed nearly a bottle of brandy the night before in an attempt to drown out all thought and feeling over the death of his son. He crawled into bed, drunk, beside Clara, but found no relief in sleep either. Sonny came to him in a dream, giving off the odor of a burning candle as he pleaded not to be taken away. He had grasped his hand, but then a force stronger than his own had pulled him away.

He gazed drowsily at the smoke-shrouded sky through the open louvered glass window. As in his dream, he thought he saw Sonny up there. It pained his heart, and he turned his gaze to Clara.

The sedative he gave her had thankfully sent her to sleep. Tears had dried up in her face wracked with pain and sorrow. How Sonny's death must have crushed her! The pain and grief she bore at the death of their son were much more than he could ever feel or fathom. She bore their son and raised him to manhood only to have him so suddenly and for no reason taken away from her.

There was no letup in the noise in the street. He turned slowly on the bed so as not to disturb Clara in her sleep. He stood up and, parting wide enough the curtain that ran across the bedroom window, he peered out.

He saw no one in the porch of the old man's house across the yard, but he could see in Avery Avenue, people passing by in both directions. Those coming from Third Street were carrying bags and boxes of merchandise, or were pushing carts full of goods looted, perhaps from Tom's Supermarket and the stores and shops there. Those going toward Third Street seemed in a hurry not to be left out of the looting going on there. Farther away, in the direction of Third Street, smoke darkened the sky. Tom's Supermarket and the shops and stores there not only had been looted, some if not all of them had been set on fire by the very same people who looted them. The fires, the riots and the looting had reached his neighborhood.

Some of those in the street, he recognized, were his neighbors from the other apartment buildings. A group of them on their way to Third Street were greeting a man pushing a cart. He watched them, angry and disgusted, as they inspected and gloated over the loot in the cart. It was from the violence of a riot and looting like that, that his son died.

He closed the window and shut out the noise in the street, thankful that the noise there did not disturb Clara in her sleep. He left for the bathroom to wash away his hangover.

A short while later, he gazed at the picture window as he was leaving the bathroom. The windowsill, the couch and the vine-topped, chain-link fence were splashed with sunlight. Myrtle's home and garden were cast, though, in the shadow of the trees there. The rest of the apartment was also dark and so tomblike, he could almost feel there the cold presence of death. He looked again at the picture window. It now appeared to him as like the opening of an elevated concrete grave.

The couch next claimed his attention at the many times he had talked about a host of subjects with Sonny seated there, while he was seated on his easy chair. He walked toward it and as he sat down there, he was filled with regret. Sonny died without even knowing that his father had moved up a bit with his new restaurant manager job, and that with his credit card, they could now move to Glendale, without him. The thought dimmed his eyes, and he wept, the tears falling on his hands and on the carpet. How he missed his son.

He was startled when, suddenly, he felt warm air brushing his hair. It must be Sonny's life force now residing in his soul, touching those he loved and held in his life—his books laid beside Rod and Andrew's things, his repair kit peeking out from underneath the couch, and himself, his father. Sonny was now a disembodied being called the soul. It was there in their apartment, a place dear to him, until its departure for its just reward.

Just then, he heard shouts and laughter coming from the street. The looters and the arsonists! His eyes narrowed in anger, he rose from the couch and looked out from the picture window.

The men in their apartment building were watching from behind the closed iron gate, people passing by in the street. The bulge in their waists showed they were armed, ready to shoot those out there in the street who would threaten them, their families and their homes in their apartment building.

"Give it to them!" he said between his clenched teeth. A hail of bullets! Those looters and arsonists out there in the street deserved nothing less than that!

Watching them had put him in such a bad temper, to calm himself, he left for the kitchen to make coffee. He was much calmer now as, seated at the dining table while waiting for the water to boil, he went over his tasks for the day. He must attend to Sonny's cremation. He must tell Leonard about Sonny's death and that he won't be coming to work for the next few days. He had an appointment with Saul that he must keep despite the second thought he was now having about their application for political asylum.

The kettle announced with shrill whistling that the water was boiling. He turned off the electric stove and poured the boiling water into his cup with its spoonful of sugar and instant coffee and stirred it with a teaspoon. He returned to his chair, the coffee cup in his hand.

He had taken only a few sips when he brought the cup down on the table, his gaze turned to Clara, who had appeared from the bedroom. The noise in the street must have wakened her up. She sat down on the chair at the head of the table. Her face, haggard from sorrow, and her eyes, red from weeping, spoke of her grief over the death of their son. He made a small gesture of easing it up by offering her the cup of coffee. She complied with a sip of the coffee.

"Thank you," she said, her voice hoarse, as she gave the coffee cup back to him.

"Did you sleep well?"

"Well enough with the sedative you gave me."

He nodded, satisfied, and said, "I have an appointment with Attorney Levy this morning. From there I'll go to the mortuary."

"Do you want me to go with you?"

"No. Stay home with Lorna. You two need to rest."

"I'll call our friends and relatives so they can attend Sonny's interment. When are we going to hold it?"

"There will be no interment for Sonny. I'm thinking of having him cremated."

She shot him a questioning look and said, "Why should we have Sonny cremated?"

She said, before he could reply, "No! I will not allow it!"

"Why are you so against it?"

"You are asking me why?" she said, the tone of her voice now angry and accusing. "Were you not against it yourself? I knew nothing about what cremation meant until you told me that it is short-circuiting nature, and that burning a human being's body is like burning its soul in the fires of hell or purgatory! Why will you do it now to our own son?"

"It is the practical thing to do for Sonny."

"The practical thing to do for him?"

"Yes, so we can take his ashes with us when we leave this country."

"Leave this country? Why should we do that?"

"After what happened to our son, I don't want to live here anymore."

"Why do you blame the entire country for what happened to our son?"

He blinked his eyes, surprised by what she said. Of course, the country was to blame! Mainstream American society laid the condition that led to the riots where his son fell a victim. But in his heart of hearts, he knew he was only using his son's death as an excuse for leaving America. Every time he faced something fearful or dreadful, his first instinct was to flee. He did this in Zambales and in Manila. But fleeing his homeland, where both Marcos' military agents and the Communist rebels had hounded him, was not the same as leaving America. He was under no similar threat here. He was leaving America because he was disillusioned with it over the death of his son. Clara was right. He should not blame the entire country for the death of their son. Sonny died, an accidental victim of a senseless mob violence. That was all there was to it.

Tears had gathered in Clara's eyes as she said firmly, "I want my son given a proper church burial. I want him to face the Lord as he was when he left us, not as a pile of ashes."

He listened, contrite. He had erred. Anger and bitterness had clouded his judgment. He was against cremation on religious grounds and should not condemn outright those who were cremated. It was not their own doing. It was a decision made for them by the living unless, when they were still alive, they had made known their wish to be cremated. Others could also be given allowance for their cremation, if this were done according to their religious belief.

He looked down at his coffee cup, grateful to Clara for remaining levelheaded in the face of this tragedy in their family, while he had been unhinged by it. He shook his head at the perversity that made him decide on Sonny's cremation. Clara was against it. Lorna would be too, if she were asked. There was no reason either for them to change their plans. If a way could be found for Sonny to speak to them, he will tell them to go ahead and move to Glendale, even without him. Clara was right. Sonny should be given a proper church burial. Let nature take its course. Let the nematodes have their triumph. In time, Sonny's mortal remains will be reduced to dust: to nothing. From nothing to nothing, it was thus ordained from above. But Sonny had a soul. It was destined for eternal life, and that too was ordained from above.

He raised his head, his heart pained when he saw Clara now crying softly. He went to her, filled with remorse. He bent down and laid a comforting arm on her shoulder and caressed her hair. Her body shook as she wept on.

Suddenly they turned to someone knocking on the apartment door. He went there, wondering who could be calling on them at such an early hour.

"Who is it?" he asked.

"It's me, Agnes."

He opened the door and saw her looking so angry and so deeply agitated.

"I'm sorry for barging in on you like this," she said. "But I need to talk to someone. I've left Saul. I'm through with him!"

Chapter 20

Saul watched wearily in his office, a news helicopter flying south in the smoke-shrouded sky over Los Angeles. It was reporting on the burning and the looting still going on in the city. It was in turmoil, so was he. Agnes had left him. She found him out, all because he was so careless. Therese's lipstick marks on his cheek and mouth gave him away. He should have looked himself over before leaving her apartment last night. Had he done that, he would have seen the lipstick marks and removed them. Agnes saw them when he arrived home and questioned him about them. He could only mumble an answer that far from satisfied her. Even worse, he confirmed rather than allay her suspicion with the awkward and hesitant way by which he parried her questions. Some lawyer he was, unable to fend off his own wife interrogating him like a court prosecutor on his arrival home last night.

He sighed. Agnes was bound to know anyway. There will be other mistakes, and he could not keep it a secret if Therese had indeed become pregnant.

How he wished he could keep them both! But what could he do, but look on helplessly, like what the news helicopter was doing. He was caught in a dilemma. He won't throw away his marriage for this love affair. On the other hand, he had in this love affair a wonderful thing that filled a void in his marriage. But how could he keep them both? It was a problem whose solution called for the wisdom of Solomon, and he was not like Solomon. Agnes, sadly, had made the decision for him by leaving him. He sighed again as he recalled the note she left on the coffee table. Their marriage was over.

Wearied by this tangle of thoughts in his mind, he turned his swivel chair away from the dreadful sight of Los Angeles still burning. But now, he could also feel his empty stomach grumbling for food. He missed those full breakfasts Agnes cooked for him every morning. His back and legs were aching, too. Agnes locked him out of their bedroom, and he slept on the couch, cold and miserable.

Someone was knocking at the door. It opened with Therese holding the doorknob. A vibrant smile was on her face. In her other hand was a saucer on which lay a cup of steaming hot coffee.

She closed the door and said, "Did you have a good night sleep, dear?"

"I can't complain."

"I was in the bathroom when you came in. I made coffee for you when Nola told me you're already here."

He gazed keenly at her as she was approaching his desk. Underneath her dress was her soft beautiful body he touched and entered last night. Her fragrance and the nearness of her had so aroused him, he was seized with a desire to take her in his arms.

He was about to rise up, but was stopped by the sight of the door behind her. It was not locked. Someone might suddenly come in and see them locked in an embrace. He could not allow that to happen, and he sat back, frustrated, on his swivel chair.

She had noticed nothing odd about his behavior as she was putting on his desk, the cup of coffee on a saucer.

"Thank you for the coffee," he said, the casual tone of his voice betraying nothing of his keen desire to take her in his arms. He turned his attention to the cup of coffee, the better to take hold of himself, and he drank a good measure of it. It coursed down his throat, hot and strong.

His composure now restored, he looked up at her and said, "You look your usual vibrant cheerful self this morning."

"I feel more than that. I feel wonderfully in love."

He smiled, feeling likewise in love, and he held her hand tightly. That much he allowed himself. She smiled and likewise gripped his hand.

He jerked his head in surprise when suddenly she turned her gaze to the building across the street. Someone in the building there was watching them. He released her hand, and she in turn went through the motion of clearing his desk.

"Steve called a while ago," she said, the tone of her voice now businesslike. "He said he will not be coming to work today."

"Why? What happened?"

"His house was looted after we left it. He is there now with Vicky, cleaning it up. At least the looters did not burn down their house."

"A good thing they fled last night and escaped from harm."

"Yes, a good thing they did that. This is a terrible thing happening in Los Angeles, is it not? And no end in sight yet.

"It won't last long. A day or two more of that and it will be over. You can tell Steve, if he calls again, to take as much time as he needs to fix up his place. In the meantime, I'll handle his caseload. How many appointments do I have this morning?"

"You have three, with Simon Matin first on the list. He is outside, waiting to be called."

"Very well. Send him in."

Therese moved toward the door. She looked back when he said to her, "By the way, the towing truck is coming at around ten o'clock. Don't worry about your car. I'll have it fixed."

"Thank you, you are very kind. Anything else?"

"Yes. Let me take you home until your car is fixed."

"Nothing will please me more," she said, her eyes shining in delight.

She left, but came back a moment later with Simon. In her hand was a folder, Simon's file, which she put down on his desk. She left the room as he was reaching out to shake Simon's hand.

"So, how are things with you and Clara?" he said to Simon, while motioning him to a chair.

"So, so," Simon replied quietly.

The dark bags under Simon's eyes told him that Simon did not have a good night sleep, too. Trouble with the wife, too? It was none of his business, though. He went directly to the business at hand. He told Simon his application for their political asylum was moving along. He added that his office was sending as part of his application for political asylum, some more papers and documents. Then he opened the folder, glanced at its contents, and pulled out a brief and handed it to Simon.

"I would like you to read this," he said to Simon. "Our office prepared it in support of your application for political asylum. It is based largely on what you told me when you and Clara came here. If you agree with what it says, then we will send it, along with the other documents, to INS."

He looked out idly at the wide view of Los Angeles while Simon was reading the brief. It was the same dreary sight of the sky over Los Angeles, grayish with smoke from numerous fires on the ground. There were as many fires now as last night, but he was confident that, with the Marines and the National Guard coming to the city, together with the police, they could finally put an end to this insanity going on in the city. A newspaper reported that it was the worst civil disturbance in the history of the United States.

At the spur of the moment, he lifted the phone and called Steve to check on how he and Vicky were doing. The line was dead. The looters stole the phones in the house.

Simon had finished reading the brief. He took it back and waited for his comment.

"It is clear and concise," Simon said. "Thank you for showing us up as good prospective citizens of this country." His face turned sad when he then said, "But you will have to remove any mention of Sonny's name."

"Why?"

"He died last night."

"What? How did it happen?"

Simon told him briefly how Sonny died.

He shook his head and said, "That is terrible! Your son was killed merely for watching a fire? I'm sorry to hear that. Is there anything I can do for you?"

"You can pray for him."

He gazed keenly at Simon. He understood fully how, at such a time, the best thing one could do and must do, and which Simon must be doing, was to turn to God. He was not much of a praying person, but he said with all sincerity, "Yes, I'll pray for your son."

"Thank you very much," Simon said.

There was something else he felt he could do for Simon.

"One more thing," he said. "Allow me to cut my professional fee by one-half. I wish I could set everything aside, but we have office expenses."

He watched Simon, whose eyes were wide in surprise at his generous offer.

"You don't have to do that," he said, "but thank you."

They fell silent and, feeling awkward about it, he said to Simon, "It must be hard to lose a son."

"No words can express the feeling."

He cast about in his mind for what could further console Simon, but found nothing that could help. He looked around, his eyes settling on the Cézanne still life painting hanging on the wall. It was a reproduction, a good one Agnes gave him on his birthday a few years ago, now a sad memento of their failed marriage. The loss of a son and the loss of a wife were the same in the sadness that came in their wake. Telling Simon he was not alone in his sorrow could help him.

It will also help him unburden himself.

"I have also lost someone dear to me," he said to Simon. "You will learn about it sooner or later, I might as well tell you now that Agnes left me this morning."

"I know."

"You do?"

"Agnes came to our apartment early this morning. I left her there with Clara. She is staying with us until she has decided what to do next."

"Can you do me the favor of encouraging her to come back to me?"

"Clara is already doing that," Simon said, his voice now more involved, the pallor in his face gone, too. "I will do my bit too when I get home. Agnes is hurt. Let her wound heal. Clara and I will do whatever we can do to help preserve your marriage."

He was so touched by Simon's concern for him and Agnes, he said, "I'm deeply grateful for what you and Clara are doing for me and Agnes."

Simon had set aside his own grief over the death of his son to help him out. Only a kind person, a true friend, will do that. It was now in this light that he regarded Simon.

Chapter 21

Simon watched from his car, the churchgoers in the parking lot walking in the mild morning air toward St. Stephen Church. It was Sunday, a day of worship, a day of blessing. The church belfry and the tall office buildings across Wilshire Boulevard were pointed to the sky. It was a clear light blue with patches of white clouds. It bore no trace of the fires that had raged in Los Angeles until two days ago.

He looked on at the parking lot, the pleasure in the lovely day mixed with the grief and anger still clutched in his heart over the death of his son. Clara and Lorna were getting off from their car.

He shut the car door and met them in front of the car. Their eyes, clouded by mourning, were averted from the lovely day. They reflected his own eyes in his sad embittered face he saw earlier in the bathroom mirror in their apartment. Clara held on to his arm as they walked toward the church courtyard. Her choir gown draped over her other arm, she was holding in her hand, a binder of sheet music.

Her handbag in her hand, its strap slung on her shoulder, Lorna was walking ahead of them, like she used to do with Sonny. She was not her cheerful self as she was in other Sundays in St. Stephen Church. The pain and sadness over Sonny's death troubled Simon's heart, too. They were attending Mass in St. Stephen Church with Sonny no longer with them.

Some of the churchgoers at the elevated courtyard were taking advantage of the few minutes left before the start of the Mass to talk and smoke in the open air. Their cheerful voices and their laughter spoke of their relief and deliverance from the recent riots.

He ascended the stone steps to the courtyard with Clara and Lorna, his feelings opposed to the cheerfulness of the throng there. They did not lose a son as he did. He walked past them with Clara and Lorna toward the open church door. They walked on to the vestibule, then to the staircase of the choir loft. He waited with Lorna until Clara had ascended it. Then he walked back with Lorna to the vestibule and proceeded to the interior of the church.

The church nave was quiet. Some of the pews were still empty, but he knew from experience they will be full of people just before the readings of the Holy Bible. He looked around for a suitable pew as he and Lorna were walking on the carpeted side aisle. They took a middle pew and sat down at the other end along the middle aisle. They were near enough to the altar of the sanctuary from all the troubles that hounded him.

The church was bathed with light from the small spotlights in the ceiling, the glow of burning votive candles on an iron stand by a wall, and the stained glass windows bright with sunlight. The Fourteen Stations of the Cross—the Passion of Jesus Christ—were rendered in stone on the church walls. Right before him and Lorna was the large wooden crucifix hanging by wire from the ceiling, above the communion table. They gave him no small amount of comfort in the Son of God present in his life to help and guide him in whatever he did and faced.

A patch of the blue sky he could see through the glass side door was clear of smoke and fire. Los Angeles had finally prevailed over evil that had struck it for three terrible days. The city had returned to normal. Life must go on. He must move on, too. There was his new managerial job in L&S. He must prepare himself for it.

He was going back to school, when time permitted it, never mind if he will be an overage student, if what he needed to land a teaching job was a master's degree from an American university. There was the book about his homeland he had long wanted to write. He will have to find the time for that, too. As for Clara, she will go on working at Super Bargain Store, while keeping an eye on a better job elsewhere. As for Lorna, she will pursue medicine in USC. He hoped to find an apartment in Glendale by next week. That will bring him closer to the Keg Room for the friendly sessions there with Phil and Jonathan, Lew and Mark.

He was glad he and Clara had persuaded Agnes to give Saul a chance to rebuild their marriage. That will take some doing, though, for there was Therese for them to consider. He was hopeful, though, that they could somehow work it out.

The choir led by Clara began to sing a beautiful church hymn, and he stood up together with Lorna and the rest of the congregation. The Mass was about to begin. All worldly thoughts cast aside from his mind, he watched the Eucharistic procession coming in from the vestibule, while the choir sang on the beautiful church hymn.

The solemn Eucharistic procession proceeded in the middle aisle, led by a server in white vestments, the wooden cross in his hands raised high. Another server followed. Behind him was the woman lector with the Holy Bible in her hands raised high. Father Finley brought up the rear. He was now and then nodding at familiar faces he met along the aisle.

The procession passed his pew to the choir singing on the church hymn. Father Finley stepped up into the altar. Then he turned, kissed the edge of the communion table, made the sign of the cross and, together with the congregation, said the opening prayer:

"We bow to you, Lord, your humble servants. We give you thanks, we give you praise as we ask for your forgiveness of our sins."

Their eyes turned to the missals in their hands, he and Lorna joined the congregation in reciting a litany of prayers. The lector then walked up to the podium for the first reading of the Holy Bible, on the suffering Moses and the Israelites went through in the desert of Shur, shortly after they left Egypt.

He listened, struck by the coincidence of what Moses and the Israelites had suffered with his own suffering. They went through days without food and water, as he would now go through life without his son. Only yesterday his son was laid there in front of the altar at the necrological service Father Finley held for him. Only yesterday his son was laid to rest in Hillcrest Memorial Park.

Oh, how sad it was for a father to bury his own son! His heart had bled then, as it was still bleeding now, over the death of his son. He was jolted when he found himself addressed in a biblical passage the lector was reading:

"I am the Lord, the one who heals you."

The words came like a balm to his sad embittered heart. He had been in a daze since his son died, bone-tired and weary, grieving, bitter and forsaken. These were all swept away as he shut his eyes and he drifted into a state between sleep and wakefulness. His spirit had entered the place beyond the universe where the dead, upon leaving the world, passed on their way to judgment.

A host of the departed, the blessed and the damned, was moving on. They were parted before an angel of God in white vestments, a sword in his hand. Amid the lowing of the wind, the damned were cast away into a dark abyss, while the blessed, his son among them, walked on in a path of light, to a heavenly host singing with the choir, another beautiful church hymn.

He was startled and he sat upright when he felt Lorna tugging at his coat sleeve.

"Wake up, Dad," she whispered into his ear. "You have dozed off."

He smiled. He did not doze off. His spirit had gone to where Sonny had gone for his just reward. He remained half-awake as he listened to the next reading of the Holy Bible, but was fully awake when Father Finley read a passage from the Gospel of Saint John about Jesus Christ, the light and savior of the world.

The homily Father Finley then delivered on the light of goodness shining once again in Los Angeles flowed like a sparkling stream into his consciousness, and on to the affirmation of his Christian faith in the Nicene Creed and the hymn singing that followed it.

They were now at the Liturgy of the Eucharist, at the Offertory, the Presentation of Gifts. An elderly couple coming from the middle aisle were approaching the altar, bearing vessels of wine and water and the chalice of the Sacred Host. They gave the symbolic gifts to Father Finley, who passed them on to the two servers by his side, and took with him to the communion table, the chalice of the Sacred Host.

He knelt down when Father Finley then prayed for God's blessing upon the faithful as he consecrated the Sacred Host at the reenactment of the Last Supper Jesus Christ took with his twelve apostles.

Father Finley then raised the Sacred Host and said:

"Take this, all of you, and eat it: this is my body, which will be given up for you."

Father Finley then held the chalice, raised it and said:

"Take this, all of you, and drink from it: this is the cup of my blood, the blood of the new and everlasting covenant. It will be shed for you and for all so that sins maybe forgiven. Do this in memory of me."

He heard those words said in every Mass he had attended, but this time he felt as if they were addressed to him. Jesus Christ died for the forgiveness of sins, including his own. He was forgiven, so he must also forgive. He must remove from his heart all the anger and the bitterness over the death of his son. If he wanted it redressed, so will it be redressed, here on earth and in heaven, and not by him.

The blood of the Savior had doused the anger, the pain and the bitterness that had burned in his heart. He had found peace, and he dwelt in this feeling as he prayed along with the rest of the congregation, the Lord's Prayer.

He turned his eyes, pleased and surprised, to the choir loft when Clara began to sing there, Schubert's sacred church hymn, the *Mille cherubini in coro*:

"Dormi, dormi
sogna, piccolo amor mio.
Dormi, sogna,
posa il capo sul mio cor."

He listened, his head bowed and his eyes shut. Clara had sung the beautiful church hymn countless times, back in their home country. It had never deeply affected him as it did now, for never did Clara sing it before as she did now, like a lullaby, like a farewell hymn to their departed son.

The choir joined in and the beautiful church hymn now sounded to him as if the Lord's angels were singing it with her:

"Mille cherubini in coro
ti sorridono dal ciel.
Una dolce canzone
t'accareza il crin.
Una man ti guida lieve
fra le nuvole d'or,
sognando e vegliando
su te, mio tesor,
proteggendo il tuo cammin.

"Dormi, dormi,
Chiudi gli occhi,
ascolta gli angioletti,
dormi, dormi,
sogna, piccolo amor."

He was startled, and he opened his eyes and sat upright when Lorna tugged again at his coat sleeve. He saw her turn her head toward the usher, who was waiting for them in the middle aisle. It was time for the Holy Communion. He stood up with Lorna and joined the line of communicants in the middle aisle, while listening to Clara and the choir singing on the beautiful church hymn.

"Body of Christ," Father Finley said as he was putting the Sacred Host in his palm. He dipped it in a vessel of wine in the server's hands and put it in his tongue. He made the sign of the cross and followed Lorna back to their pew and knelt down there.

The Sacred Host tasted for what it was, a piece of unleavened bread, dipped in wine, melting in his tongue, but which, having been consecrated in the Holy Eucharist, was now transubstantiated into the body and blood of Jesus Christ.

He had taken part in the feast of the body and blood of the Son of God. He should be what he had received and be Christ-like, loving and forgiving.

He felt, toward the end of the Mass, his heart lifted at the intimations, in the worship of God the Father, of Jesus Christ and the Holy Spirit, of eternal life in heaven. He had transcended anger and sorrow at the death of his son, satisfied in knowing that Sonny was there now in their ultimate sanctuary.

There, in the presence of God the Father, Jesus Christ and the Holy Spirit, with Mother Mary, the angels and the saints, his son now stood, beyond the reach of all worldly pain and conflict.

The joy in the morning was etched in Father Finley's smiling face as he stood by the door to the vestibule. The Mass had ended and he was greeting Simon and Lorna as they were passing out, along with the rest of the congregation, from the church nave. They smiled as they approached the priest.

"I'll pray for the soul of Sonny," Father Finley said to them.

He thanked the priest for his kind words and walked on with Lorna toward the big door leading to the courtyard.

Their faces bright with anticipation, the people around them seemed to be looking forward to the rest of the day to be spent in simple pleasures. A walk on the beaches of Los Angeles for a breath of sea air. An hour or two in any of the city's shopping malls. Or best of all, a family gathering at home, in a restaurant, or in a picnic in Griffith Park, perfect that lovely day. Sunday for them was spent in the enjoyment of the blessings of the day.

A shadow passed across Simon's face as he remembered how, only last Sunday, Sonny was with them, here in the church. They will later return to their apartment, now forever empty of Sonny's presence.

The choir singing from the choir loft above the vestibule made him pause. The lyrics, which spoke of the comfort in the Lord's saving grace, had a soothing effect on him, and the bitterness that for a while pained his heart, then passed away.

He walked on with Lorna toward the courtyard. It was shaded yet from the midmorning sun by the tall belfry and the massive wall of the church. They waited for Clara, who came out of the church in a short while.

"You did not tell me you were going to sing Schubert's beautiful church hymn," Simon said to Clara. "But I am glad you did."

"It was so beautiful, Mom," Lorna said. "You sang it for Sonny, did you not, Mom?"

Clara smiled, the sadness in her eyes an hour ago replaced by a look of gladness now in her face. The sacred hymn she sang like a lullaby for Sonny had lifted her spirit at the thought of Sonny, now in heaven and watching over them.

She held Simon's arm and, together with Lorna, they walked toward their car parked in the wide church parking lot, washed by the sunlight of a lovely Sunday morning in Los Angeles.

It was a lovely day, a day as lovely as God had made it.

They were going to Hillcrest Memorial Park, and there they will spend, beside the flowers in Sonny's grave, the rest of the lovely day.

Made in the USA
San Bernardino, CA
07 March 2020